P9-BYQ-396

# Don't miss any of the acclaimed Kinsey Millhone mysteries in this bestselling series!

### "G" IS FOR GUMSHOE

### "H" IS FOR HOMICIDE

### "I" IS FOR INNOCENT

### "J" IS FOR JUDGMENT

### "K" IS FOR KILLER

When Kinsey Millhone agrees to do a favor for Henry Pitts, her lovable octogenarian landlord, she literally gets taken for the ride of her life. The family of a recently deceased WWII veteran wants her to find out why the military has no record of his service. All Kinsey has to do, she thinks, is cut through some government red tape. But when the dead man's house is ransacked and his old army buddy is beaten up, she quickly realizes he was not all he seemed. Before long Kinsey is trailing crooks halfway across the country, impersonating a hotel maid, tangling with a baseball-bat-wielding grandmother, and running from one very dangerous character. With her money almost gone and her nerves frayed, Kinsey's got to solve a decades-old crime and make it back home in time for Henry's wedding . . . if she can make it back at all. . . .

*Please turn the page for more reviews. . . .*

# "FANS WILL BE JOYFUL."
## —*St. Louis Post-Dispatch*

# "L"
# IS
# FOR
# LAWLESS

## Sue Grafton

FAWCETT CREST • NEW YORK

A Fawcett Crest Book
Published by Ballantine Books
Copyright © 1995 by Sue Grafton

http://www.randomhouse.com

Library of Congress Catalog Card Number: 96-96368

ISBN 0-449-22149-0

This edition published by arrangement with Henry Holt and Company.

Manufactured in the United States of America

First International Ballantine Books Edition: May 1996
First Domestic Ballantine Books Edition: September 1996

10 9 8 7 6 5 4 3 2 1

*For dear friends ...*
*Sally and Gregory Giloth*
*and*
*Connie, Marshall, and Laura Swain*
*with love.*

# Acknowledgments

The author wishes to acknowledge the invaluable assistance of the following people: Steven Humphrey; Eric S. H. Ching; Louis Skiera, Veterans Services representative; B. J. Seebol, J.D.; Carter Hicks; Carl Eckhart; Ray Connors; Captain Edward A. Aasted, Lieutenant Charlene French, and Jack Cogan, Santa Barbara Police Department; Merrill Hoffman, Santa Barbara Locksmiths; Vaughan Armstrong; Kim Oser, Hyatt Dallas/Fort Worth; Sheila Burr, California Automobile Association; A. LaMott Smith; Charles de L'Arbre, Janet Van Velsor, and Cathy Peterson, Santa Barbara Travel; and John Hunt, CompuVision, who retrieved chapter 14 from the Inky Void.

# 1

I DON'T MEAN to bitch, but in the future I intend to hesitate before I do a favor for the friend of a friend. Never have I taken on such a load of grief. At the outset, it all seemed so *innocent*. I swear there's no way I could have guessed what was coming down. I came *this* close to death and, perhaps worse (for my fellow dental phobics), within a hairbreadth of having my two front teeth knocked out. Currently I'm sporting a knot on my head that's the size of my fist. And all this for a job for which I didn't even get paid!

The matter came to my attention through my landlord, Henry Pitts, whom everybody knows I've been half in love with for years. The fact that he's eighty-five (a mere fifty years my senior) has never seemed to alter the basic impact of his appeal. He's a sweetheart and he seldom asks me for anything, so how could I refuse? Especially when his request seemed so harmless on the face of it, without the faintest suggestion of the troubles to come.

It was Thursday, November twenty-first, the week

1

before Thanksgiving, and wedding festivities were just getting under way. Henry's older brother William was to marry my friend Rosie, who runs the tacky little tavern in my neighborhood. Rosie's restaurant was traditionally closed on Thanksgiving Day, and she was feeling smug that she and William could get hitched without her losing any business. With the ceremony and reception being held at the restaurant, she'd managed to eliminate the necessity for a church. She'd lined up a judge to perform the nuptials, and she apparently considered that his services were free. Henry had encouraged her to offer the judge a modest honorarium, but she'd given him a blank look, pretending she didn't speak English that well. She's Hungarian by birth and has momentary lapses when it suits her purposes.

She and William had been engaged for the better part of a year, and it was time to get on with the big event. I've never been certain of Rosie's actual age, but she has to be close to seventy. With William pushing eighty-eight, the phrase "until death do us part" was statistically more significant for them than for most.

Before I delineate the nature of the business I took on, I suppose I should fill in a few quick personal facts. My name is Kinsey Millhone. I'm a licensed investigator, female, twice divorced, without children or any other pesky dependents. For six years I'd had an informal arrangement with California Fidelity Insurance, doing arson and wrongful death claims in exchange for office space. For almost a year now, since the termination of that agreement, I'd been leasing an office from Kingman and Ives, a firm of attorneys here in Santa Teresa. Because of the wedding I was taking a week off, looking forward to rest and recreation when I wasn't helping Henry with wedding preparations. Henry, long retired from his work as a commercial baker, was making the wedding cake and would also be catering the reception.

There were eight of us in the wedding party. Rosie's sister, Klotilde, who was wheelchair bound, would be serving as the maid of honor. Henry was to be the best man, with his older brothers, Lewis and Charlie, serving as the ushers. The four of them—Henry, William, Lewis, and Charlie (also known collectively as "the boys" or "the kids")—ranged in age from Henry's eighty-five to Charlie's ninety-three. Their only sister, Nell, still vigorous at ninety-five, was one of two bridesmaids, the other being me. For the ceremony Rosie had elected to wear an off-white organza muu-muu with a crown of baby's breath encircling her strangely dyed red hair. She'd found a bolt of lavish floral polished cotton on sale . . . pink and mauve cabbage roses on a background of bright green. The fabric had been shipped off to Flint, Michigan, where Nell had "run up" matching muumuus for the three of us in attendance. I couldn't wait to try mine on. I was certain that, once assembled, the three of us would resemble nothing so much as a set of ambulatory bedroom drapes. At thirty-five, I'd actually hoped to serve as the oldest living flower girl on record, but Rosie had decided to dispense with the role. This was going to be the wedding of the decade, one I wouldn't miss for all the money in the world. Which brings us back to the "precipitating events," as we refer to them in the crime trade.

I ran into Henry at nine that Thursday morning as I was leaving my apartment. I live in a converted single-car garage that's attached to Henry's house by means of an enclosed breezeway. I was heading to the supermarket, where I intended to stock up on junk food for the days ahead. When I opened my door, Henry was standing on my front step with a piece of scratch paper and a tape dispenser. Instead of his usual shorts, T-shirt, and flip-flops, he was wearing long pants and a blue dress shirt with the sleeves rolled up.

I said, "Well, don't you look terrific." His hair is stark white and he wears it brushed softly to one side. Today it was slicked down with water, and I could still smell the warm citrus of his aftershave. His blue eyes seem ablaze in his lean, tanned face. He's tall and slender, good-natured, smart, his manner a perfect blend of courtliness and nonchalance. If he wasn't old enough to be my granddaddy, I'd snap him up in a trice.

Henry smiled when he saw me. "There you are. Perfect. I was just leaving you a note. I didn't think you were home or I'd have knocked on the door instead. I'm on my way to the airport to pick up Nell and the boys, but I have a favor to ask. Do you have a minute?"

"Of course. I was on my way to the market, but that can wait," I said. "What's up?"

"Do you remember old Mr. Lee? They called him Johnny here in the neighborhood. He's the gentleman who used to live around the corner on Bay. Little white stucco house with the overgrown yard. To be accurate, Johnny lived in the garage apartment. His grandson, Bucky, and his wife have been living in the house."

The bungalow in question, which I passed in the course of my daily jog, was a run-down residence that looked as if it was buried in a field of wild grass. These were not classy folk, unless a car up on blocks is your notion of a yard ornament. Neighbors had complained for years, for all the good it did. "I know the house, but the name doesn't mean much."

"You've probably seen 'em up at Rosie's. Bucky seems to be a nice kid, though his wife is odd. Her name is Babe. She's short and plump, doesn't make a lot of eye contact. Johnny always looked like he was homeless, but he did all right."

I was beginning to remember the trio he described: old guy in a shabby jacket, the couple playing grab-ass, looking too young for marriage. I cupped a hand to my ear. "You've been using past tense. Is the old man dead?"

"I'm afraid so. Poor fellow had a heart attack and died four or five months back. I think it was sometime in July. Not that there was anything odd about it," Henry hastened to add. "He was only in his seventies, but his health had never been that good. At any rate, I ran into Bucky a little while ago and he has a problem he was asking me about. It's not urgent. It's just irksome and I thought maybe you could help."

I pictured an unmarked key to a safe-deposit box, missing heirs, missing assets, an ambiguity in the will, one of those unresolved issues that the living inherit from the newly departed. "Sure. What's the deal?"

"You want the long version or the short?"

"Make it long, but talk fast. It may save me questions."

I could see Henry warm to his subject with a quick glance at his watch. "I don't want to miss the flight, but here's the situation in a nutshell. The old guy didn't want a funeral, but he did ask to be cremated, which was done right away. Bucky was thinking about taking the ashes back to Columbus, Ohio, where his dad lives, but it occurred to him his grandfather was entitled to a military burial. I guess Johnny was a fighter pilot during World War Two, part of the American Volunteer Group under Claire Chennault. He didn't talk much about it, but now and then he'd reminisce about Burma, the air battles over Rangoon, stuff like that. Anyway, Bucky thought it'd be nicer: white marble with his name engraved, and that kind of thing. He talked to his dad about it, and Chester thought it sounded pretty good, so Bucky went out to the local Veterans Administration office and filled out a claim form. He didn't have all the information, but he did what he could. Three months went by and he didn't hear a thing. He was just getting antsy when the claim came back, marked "Cannot Identify." With a name like John Lee, that wasn't too surprising. Bucky called the VA and the guy sent him another form to complete, this one a request for military records. This time it was only three weeks and the damn thing came back with the same rubber stamp. Bucky isn't dumb, but he's probably all of twenty-three years old and doesn't have much experience with bureaucracy. He called his dad and told him what was going on. Chester got right on the horn, calling Randolph Air Force Base in Texas, which is where the Air Force keeps personnel files. I don't know how many people he must have talked to, but the upshot is the Air Force has no record of John Lee, or if they do, they won't talk. Chester is convinced he's being stonewalled, but what can he do? So that's where it stands. Bucky's frustrated and his dad's madder than a wet hen. They're absolutely determined to see Johnny get what he deserves. I told 'em you might have an idea about what to try next."

"They're sure he was really in the service?"

"As far as I know."

I felt an expression of skepticism cross my face. "I can talk to Bucky if you want, but it's not really an area I know anything about. If I'm hearing you right, the Air Force isn't really saying that he wasn't *there*. All they're saying is they can't identify him from the information Bucky's sent."

"Well, that's true," Henry said. "But until they locate

his records, there isn't any way they can process the claim."

I was already beginning to pick at the problem as if it were a knot in a piece of twine. "Wasn't it called the Army Air Force back in those days?"

"What difference would that make?"

"His service records could be kept somewhere else. Maybe the army has them."

"You'd have to ask Bucky about that. I'm assuming he's already tried that line of pursuit."

"It could be something simple . . . the wrong middle initial, or the wrong date of birth."

"I said the same thing, but you know how it is. You look at something so long and you don't even really see it. It probably won't take more than fifteen or twenty minutes of your time, but I know they'd be glad to have the input. Chester's out here from Ohio, wrapping up some details on his father's probate. I didn't mean to volunteer your services, but it seems like a worthy cause."

"Well, I'll do what I can. You want me to pop over there right now? I've got the time if you think Bucky's home."

"He should be. At least he was an hour ago. I appreciate this, Kinsey. It's not like Johnny was a close friend, but he's been in the neighborhood as long as I have and I'd like to see him treated right."

"I'll give it a try, but this is not my bailiwick."

"I understand, and if it turns out to be a pain, you can dump the whole thing."

I shrugged. "I guess that's one of the advantages in not being paid. You can quit any time you want."

"Absolutely," he said.

I locked my front door while Henry headed toward the garage, and then I waited by the drive while he backed the car out. On special occasions he drives a five-window coupe, a 1932 Chevrolet with the original bright yellow paint. Today, he was taking the station wagon to the airport since he'd be returning with three passengers and countless pieces of luggage. "The sibs," as he called them, would be in town for two weeks and tended to pack for every conceivable emergency. He eased to a stop and rolled down the window. "Don't forget you're joining us for dinner."

"I didn't forget. This is Lewis's birthday, right? I even bought him a present."

"Well, you're sweet, but you didn't have to do that."

"Oh, right. Lewis always tells people not to buy a present, but if you don't, he pouts. What time's the celebration?"

"Rosie's coming over at five forty-five. You can come anytime you want. You know William. If we don't eat promptly, he gets hypoglycemic."

"He's not going with you to the airport?"

"He's being fitted for his tux. Lewis, Charlie, and I get fitted for ours this afternoon."

"Very fancy," I said. "I'll see you later."

I waved as Henry disappeared down the street and then let myself out the gate. The walk to the Lees' took approximately thirty seconds—six doors down, turn the corner, and there it was. The style of the house was hard to classify, a vintage California cottage with a flaking stucco exterior and a faded red-tile roof. A two-car garage with dilapidated wooden doors was visible at the end of the narrow concrete drive. The scruffy backyard was now the home of a half-dismantled Ford Fairlane with a rusted-out frame. The facade of the house was barely visible, hidden behind unruly clusters of shoulder-high grass. The front walk had been obscured by two mounds of what looked like wild oats, brushy tops tilting toward each other across the path. I had to hold my arms aloft, wading through the weeds, just to reach the porch.

I rang the bell and then spent an idle moment picking burrs from my socks. I pictured microscopic pollens swarming down my gullet like a cloud of gnats, and I could feel a primitive sneeze forming at the base of my brain. I tried to think about something else. Without even entering the front door, I could have predicted small rooms with rough stucco arches between, offset perhaps by ineffectual attempts to "modernize" the place. This was going to be pointless, but I rang the bell again anyway.

The door was opened moments later by a kid I recognized. Bucky was in his early twenties. He was three or four inches taller than I am, which would have put him at five nine or five ten. He wasn't overweight, but he was as doughy as a beer pretzel. His hair was red gold, parted crookedly in the center and worn long. Most of it was pulled back and secured in some scraggly fashion at the nape of his neck. He was blue eyed, his ruddy complexion looking blotchy under a four-day growth of auburn beard. He wore blue jeans and a dark blue long-sleeved corduroy shirt with the tail hanging out. Hard to guess what he did for a living, if anything. He might have been a rock star with a six-figure bank account, but I doubted it.

"Are you Bucky?"

"Yeah."

I held my hand out. "I'm Kinsey Millhone. I'm a friend of Henry Pitts's. He says you're having problems with a VA claim."

He shook my hand, but the way he was looking at me made me want to knock on his head and ask if anyone was home. I plowed on. "He thought maybe I could help. Mind if I come in?"

"Oh, sorry. I got it now. You're the private detective. At first, I thought you were someone from the VA. What's your name again?"

"Kinsey Millhone. Henry's tenant. You've probably seen me up at Rosie's. I'm there three or four nights a week."

Recognition finally flickered. "You're the one sits in that back booth."

"I'm the one."

"Sure. I remember. Come on in." He stepped back and I moved into a small entrance hall with a hardwood floor that hadn't been buffed for years. I caught a glimpse of the kitchen at the rear of the house. "My dad's not home right now, and I think Babe's in the shower. I should let her know you're here. Hey, *Babe*?"

No reply.

He tilted his head, listening. *"Hey, Babe!"*

I've never been a big fan of yelling from room to room. "You want to find her? I can wait."

"Let me do that. I'll be right back. Have a seat," he said. He moved down the hall, his hard-soled shoes clumping. He opened a door on the right and stuck his head in. There was a muffled shriek of pipes in the wall, the plumbing shuddering and thumping as the shower was turned off.

I went down a step into the living room, which was slightly bigger than the nine-by-twelve rug. At one end of the room there was a shallow brick fireplace, painted white, with a wooden mantelpiece that seemed to be littered with knickknacks. On either side of the fireplace there were built-in bookcases piled high with papers and magazines. I settled gingerly on a lumpy couch covered with a brown-and-yellow afghan. I could smell house mold or wet dog. The coffee table was littered with empty fast-food containers, and all the seating was angled to face an ancient television set in an oversize console.

Bucky returned. "She says go ahead. We gotta be somewhere shortly and she's just now getting dressed. My dad'll be back in a little while. He went down to Perdido to look at lighting fixtures. We're trying to get Pappy's apartment fixed up to rent." He paused in the doorway, apparently seeing the room as I did. "Looks like a dump, but Pappy was real tight with a buck."

"How long have you lived here?"

"Coming up on two years, ever since Babe and me got married," he said. "I thought the old bird'd give us a break on the rent, but he made a science out of being cheap."

Being cheap myself, I was naturally curious. Maybe I could pick up some pointers, I thought. "Like what?"

Bucky's mouth pulled down. "I don't know. He didn't like to pay for trash pickup, so he'd go out early on trash days and put his garbage in the neighbors' cans. And, you know, like somebody told him once when you pay utility bills? All you have to do is use a one-cent stamp, leave off the return address, and drop it in a remote mailbox. The post office will deliver it because the city wants their money, so you can save on postage."

I said, "Hey, what a deal. What do you figure, ten bucks a year? That'd be hard to resist. He must have been quite a character."

"You never met him?"

"I used to see him up at Rosie's, but I don't think we ever met."

Bucky nodded at the fireplace. "That's him over there. One on the right."

I followed his gaze, expecting to see a photograph sitting on the mantelpiece. All I saw were three urns and a medium-size metal box. Bucky said, "That greeny marble urn is my grammaw, and right beside her is my uncle Duane. He's my daddy's only brother, killed when he's a kid. He was eight, I think. Playing on the tracks and got run over by a train. My aunt Maple's in the black urn."

For the life of me, I couldn't think of a polite response. The family fortunes must have dwindled as the years went by because it looked like less and less money had been spent with each successive death until the last one, John Lee, had been left in the box provided by the crematorium. The mantel was getting crowded. Whoever "went" next would have to be transported in a shoe box and dumped out the car window on the way home from the mortuary.

He waved the subject aside. "Anyway, forget that. I know you didn't stop by to make small talk. I got the paperwork right here." He moved over to the bookshelf and began to sort through the magazines, which were apparently interspersed with unpaid bills and other critical documents. "All we're talking is a three-hundred-dollar claim for Pappy's burial," he remarked. "Babe and me paid to have him cremated and we'd like to get reimbursed. I guess the government pays another hundred and fifty for interment. It doesn't sound like much, but we don't have a lot to spare. I don't know what Henry told you, but we can't afford to pay for your services."

"I gathered as much. I don't think there's much I can do anyway. At this point, you probably know more about VA claims than I do."

He pulled out a sheaf of papers and glanced through them briefly before he passed them over to me. I removed the paper clip and scrutinized the copy of John Lee's death certificate, the mortuary release, his birth certificate, Social Security card, and copies of the two Veterans Administration forms. The first form was the application for burial benefits, the second a request for military records. On the latter, the branch of service had been filled in, but the service number, grade, rank, and the dates the old man had served were all missing. No wonder the VA was having trouble verifying the claim. "Looks like you're missing a lot of information. I take it you don't know his serial number or the unit he served in?"

"Well, no. That's the basic problem," he said, reading over my shoulder. "It gets stupid. We can't get the records because we don't have enough information, but if we had the information we wouldn't need to make the request."

"That's called good government. Think of all the money they're saving on the unpaid claims."

"We don't want anything he's not entitled to, but what's fair is fair. Pappy served his country, and it doesn't seem like such a lot to ask. Three hundred damn dollars. The government wastes billions."

I flipped the form over and read the instructions on the back. Under "Eligibility for Basic Burial Allowance," requirements indicated that the deceased veteran must have been "discharged or released from service under conditions other than dishonorable and must have been in receipt of pension or had an original or reopened claim for pension," blah, blah, blah. "Well, here's a possibility. Was he receiving a military pension?"

"If he did, he never told us."

I looked up at Bucky. "What was he living on?"

"He had his Social Security checks, and I guess Dad pitched in. Babe and me paid rent for this place, which was six hundred bucks a month. He owned the property free and clear, so I guess he used the rent money to pay for food, utilities, property taxes, and like that."

"And he lived out back?"

"That's right. Above the garage. It's just a couple little rooms, but it's real nice. We got a guy who wants to move in once the place is ready. Old friend of Pappy's. He says he'd be willing to haul out the junk if we give him a little break on the first month's rent. Most stuff is trash, but we didn't want to toss stuff until we know what's important. Right now half Pappy's things have been packed in cardboard boxes and the rest is piled up every which way."

I reread the request for military records. "What about the year his discharge certificate was issued? There's a blank here."

"Let's see." He tilted his head, reading the box where I was holding my thumb. "Oh. I must have forgot to mark that. Dad says it would've been August seventeenth of 1944 because he remembers Pappy coming home in time for his birthday party the day he turned four. He was gone two years, so he must have left sometime in 1942."

"Could he have been dishonorably discharged? From what this says, he'd be disqualified if that were the case."

"No, ma'am," Bucky said emphatically.

"Just asking." I flipped the form over, scanning the small print on the back. The request for military records showed various address lists for custodians for each branch of the service, definitions, abbreviations, codes, and dates. I tried another tack. "What about medical? If he was a wartime veteran, he was probably eligible for free medical care. Maybe the local VA clinic has a file number for him somewhere."

Bucky shook his head again. "I tried that. They checked and didn't find one. Dad doesn't think he ever applied for medical benefits."

"What'd he do when he got sick?"

"He mostly doctored himself."

"Well. I'm about out of ideas," I said. I returned the papers to him. "What about his personal effects? Did he keep any letters from his Air Force days? Even an old photograph might help you figure out what fighter group he was with."

"We didn't find anything like that so far. I never even thought about pitchers. You want to take a look?"

I hesitated, trying to disguise my lack of interest. "Sure, I could do that, but frankly, if it's just a matter of three hundred dollars, you might be better off letting the whole thing drop."

"Actually, it's four hundred and fifty dollars with interment," he said.

"Even so. Do a cost/benefit analysis and you'd probably find you're already in the hole."

Bucky was nonresponsive, apparently unpersuaded by my faint-hearted counsel. The suggestion may have been intended more for me than for him. As it turned out, I should have taken my own advice. Instead I found myself dutifully trotting after Bucky as he moved through the house. What a dunce. I'm talking about me, not him.

# 2

I FOLLOWED BUCKY out the back door and down the porch steps. "Any chance your grandfather might have had a safe-deposit box?"

"Nah, it's not his style. Pappy didn't like banks and he didn't trust bankers. He had a checking account for his bills, but he didn't have stock certificates or jewelry or anything like that. He kept his savings—maybe a hundred bucks all told—in this old coffee can at the back of the refrigerator."

"Just a thought."

We crossed the patched cement parking pad to the detached garage and climbed the steep, unpainted wooden stairs to a small second-story landing just large enough to accommodate the door to Johnny Lee's apartment and a narrow sash window that looked out onto the stairs. While Bucky picked through his keys, I cupped a hand to the glass and peered into the furnished space. Didn't look like much: two rooms with a ceiling slanting down from a ridge beam. Between the two rooms there was a door frame with the door removed.

16

There was a closet on one wall with a curtain strung across the opening.

Bucky unlocked the door and left it standing open behind him while he went in. A wall of heat seemed to block the doorway like an unseen barrier. Even in November, the sun beating down on the poorly insulated roof had heated the interior to a stuffy eighty-five degrees. I paused on the threshold, taking in the scent like an animal. The air felt close, smelling of dry wood and old wallpaper paste. Even after five months I could detect cigarette smoke and fried food. Given another minute, I probably could have determined what the old man cooked for his last meal. Bucky crossed to one of the windows and threw the sash up. The air didn't seem to move. The floor was creaking and uneven, covered with an ancient layer of cracked linoleum. The walls were papered with a pattern of tiny blue cornflowers on a cream background, the paper itself so old it looked scorched along the edges. The windows, two on the front wall and two on the rear, had yellowing shades half pulled against the flat November sunlight.

The main room had a single bed with an iron bedstead painted white. A wooden bureau was pushed against the back wall while a suite of old wicker porch furniture served as a seating area. A small wooden desk and a matching chair were tucked into one corner. There were ten to twelve cardboard boxes in a variety of sizes strewn across the floor. Some of the boxes had been packed and set aside, the flaps folded together to secure the contents. Two bookshelves had been emptied, and half the remaining books had toppled sideways.

I picked my way through the maze of boxes to the other room, which held an apartment-size stove and refrigerator, with a small microwave oven on the counter between them. A kitchen sink top had been set into a dark-stained wooden cabinet with cheap-looking hinges and pulls. The cabinet doors looked as though they'd stick when you tried to open them. Beyond the kitchen there was a small bathroom with a sink, a toilet, and a small claw-foot tub. All of the porcelain fixtures were streaked with stains. I caught sight of myself in the mirror above the sink and I could see my mouth was pulled down with distaste. Bucky had said the apartment was nice, but I'd rather shoot myself than end up in such a place.

I glanced out one of the windows. Bucky's wife, Babe, was standing at the back door across the way. She had a round face with big brown eyes and an upturned nose. Her hair was dark and straight, anchored unbecomingly behind her ears. She was wearing flip-flops, tight black pedal pushers, and a black sleeveless cotton top, stretched over drooping breasts. Her upper arms were plump and her thighs looked like they would chafe against one another when she walked. Everything about her looked unpleasantly damp. "I think your wife's calling you."

Babe's voice drifted up to us belatedly. "Bucky?"

He went to the landing. "Be right there," he yelled to her, and then in modulated tones to me: "You going to be okay if I just leave you here?" I watched him twist the apartment key from his key ring.

"I'm fine. It really sounds like you've done everything you could."

"I thought so, too. My dad's the one who's really got a bug up his butt. By the way, his name is Chester if he gets back before we do." He handed me the key. "Lock up when you're done and drop the key through the mail slot in the front door. If you find anything that looks important, you can let us know. We'll be back around one. You have a business card?"

"Sure." I took a card from my bag and handed it to him.

He tucked the card in his pocket. "Good enough."

I listened to him clatter down the outside stairs. I stood there, wondering how long I could decently wait before I locked up and fled. I could feel my stomach squeeze in the same curious twist of anxiety and excitement I experience when I've entered someone's premises illegally. My presence here was legitimate, but I felt I was engaging in an illicit act somehow. Below, I heard Babe and Bucky chatting as they locked the house and opened the garage door beneath me. I moved to the window and peered down, watching as the car emerged, seemingly from beneath my feet. The car looked like a Buick, 1955 or so, green with a big chrome grille across the front. Bucky was peering back over his shoulder as he reversed down the driveway, Babe talking at him nonstop, her hand on his knee.

I should have left as soon as the car turned out of the drive, but I thought about Henry and felt honor-bound to make at least a *pretense* of searching for something relevant. I don't mean to sound coldhearted, but Johnny Lee meant absolutely nothing to me, and the notion of mucking through his possessions was giving me the creeps. The place was depressing, airless and hot. Even the silence had a sticky feel to it.

I spent a few minutes wandering from one room to the next. The bathroom and the kitchen contained nothing of significance. I returned to the main room and scouted the periphery. I pushed aside the curtain covering the closet opening. Johnny's few clothes were hanging in a dispirited row. His shirts were soft from frequent washings, threadbare along the collar, with an occasional button missing. I checked all the pockets, peered into the shoe boxes lined up on the shelf. Not surprisingly, the shoe boxes contained old shoes.

The chest of drawers was full of underwear and socks, T-shirts, fraying handkerchiefs; nothing of interest hidden between the stacks. I sat down at his small desk and began to open drawers systematically. The contents were innocuous. Bucky had apparently removed the bulk of the old man's files: bills, receipts, canceled checks, bank statements, old income tax returns. I got up and checked some of the packed cardboard boxes, pulling back the flaps so I could poke through the contents. I found most of the relevant financial detritus in the second box I opened. A quick examination showed nothing startling. There were no personal files at all and no convenient manila envelopes filled with documents that pertained to past military service. Then again, why would he keep war-related memorabilia for forty-some-odd years? If he changed his mind about applying for VA benefits, all he had to do was supply them with the information he probably carried in his head.

The third box I looked into contained countless books about World War II, which suggested a lingering interest in the subject. Whatever his own contribution to the war, he seemed to enjoy reading other people's accounts. The titles were monotonous, except for the few punctuated with exclamation points. *Fighter! Bombs Away! Aces High! Kamikaze!* Everything was "Strategic." *Strategic Command. Strategic Air Power over Europe. Strategic Air Bombardment. Strategic Fighter Tactics.* I dragged the desk chair closer to the box and sat down, pulling out book after book, holding each by the spine while I riffled through the pages. I'm always doing silly shit like this. What did I imagine, his discharge certificate was going to drop in my lap? The truth is, most investigators have been trained to investigate. That's what we do best, even when we don't feel enthusiastic about the task at hand. Give us a room and ten minutes alone and we can't help but snoop, poking automatically into other people's business. Minding one's own business isn't half the fun. My notion of heaven is being accidentally locked in the Hall of Records overnight.

I scanned several pages of some fighter pilot's memoirs, reading about dogfights, bailouts, flames spurting from tailguns, Mustangs, P-40s, Nakajima fighters, and V formations. This war stuff was full of drama, and I could see why men got hooked on the process. I'm a bit of an adrenaline junkie myself, having picked up my "habit" during two years on the police force.

I lifted my head, hearing the chink of footsteps on the outside stairs. I checked my watch: it was only 10:35. Surely it wasn't Bucky. I rose and crossed to the doorway, peering out. A man, in his sixties, had just reached the landing.

"Can I help you?" I asked.

"Is Bucky up here?" He was balding, the white hair around his pate clipped close. Mild hazel eyes, a big nose, dimple in his chin, his face lined with soft creases.

"No, he's out at the moment. Are you Chester?"

He murmured, "No, ma'am." His manner suggested that if he'd worn a cap, he would have doffed it at that point. He smiled shyly, exposing a slight gap between his two front teeth. "My name's Ray Rawson. I'm an old friend of Johnny's ... uh, before he passed away." He wore chinos, a clean white T-shirt, and tennis shoes with white socks.

"Kinsey Millhone," I said, introducing myself. We

shook hands. "I'm a neighbor from down that way." My gesture was vague but conveyed the general direction.

Ray's gaze moved past me into the apartment. "Any idea when Bucky's due back?"

"Around one, he said."

"Are you looking to rent?"

"Oh heavens, no. Are you?"

"Well, I hope to," he said. "If I can talk Bucky into it. I put down a deposit, but he's dragging his feet on the rental agreement. I don't know what the problem is, but I'm worried he'll rent it out from under me. For a minute, when I saw all those boxes, I thought you were moving in." The guy had a southern accent I couldn't quite place. Maybe Texas or Arkansas.

"I think Bucky's trying to get the place cleared. Were you the one who offered to haul all the stuff out for a break in the rent?"

"Well, yeah, and I thought he was going to take me up on it, but now that his dad's in town, the two keep coming up with new schemes. First, Bucky and his wife decided they'd take this place and rent out the house instead. Then his dad said he wanted it for the times he comes out to visit. I don't mean to be pushy, but I was hoping to move in sometime this week. I've been staying in a hotel . . . nothing fancy, but it adds up."

"I wish I could help, but you'll have to take it up with him."

"Oh, I know it's not your problem. I was just trying to explain. Maybe I'll stop by again when he gets back. I didn't mean to interrupt."

"Not at all. Come on in, if you like. I'm just going through some boxes," I said. I moved back to my seat. I picked up a book and riffled through the pages.

Ray Rawson entered the room with all the caution of a cat. I pegged him at five ten, probably 180 pounds, with a hefty chest and biceps for a guy his age. On one arm he sported a tattoo that said "Marla"; on the other, a dragon on its hind legs with its tongue sticking out. He looked around with interest, taking in the arrangement of the furniture. "Good to see it again. Not as big as I remember. The mind plays tricks, doesn't it? I pictured ... I don't know what ... more wall space or something." He leaned against the bedstead and watched me work. "You looking for something?"

"More or less. Bucky's hoping to turn up some information about Johnny's military service. I'm the search-and-seizure team. Were you in the Air Force with him, by any chance?"

"Nope. We met on the job. We both worked in the shipyards in the old days—Jeffersonville Boat Works outside of Louisville, Kentucky. This was way back, just after the war started. We were building LST landing craft. I was twenty. He was ten years older and like a dad in some ways. Those were boom times. During the Depression—back in 1932—most guys weren't even pulling in a grand a year. Steelworkers made half that, less than waitresses. By the time I started working things were really looking up. Of course, everything's relative, so what did we know? Johnny did all kinds of things. He was a smart guy and taught me a lot. Can I lend you a hand?"

I shook my head. "I'm almost done," I said. "I hope you don't mind if I keep at it. I'd like to finish before I head out." I picked up the next book, leafing through the pages before I stacked it with the others. If Johnny was opposed to banks, he might have taken to hiding money between the pages.

"Any luck?"

"Nope," I said. "I'm about to tell Bucky to forget it. All he needs to know is his granddad's fighter unit. I'm a private investigator. This is my pro bono work, and it doesn't feel that productive, to tell you the truth. How well did you know Johnny?"

"Well enough, I guess. We kept in touch . . . maybe once or twice a year. I knew he had family out here, but I never met them until now."

I had a rhythm going. Pick a book up by the spine, flip the pages, set it down. Pick a book up by the spine, flip, set. I pulled the last book from the box. "I've been trying to place your accent. You mentioned Kentucky. Is that where you're from?" I stood up, tucking my fists in the small of my back to get the kinks out. I bent down and started returning books to the box.

Ray hunkered nearby and began to help. "That's right. I'm from Louisville originally, though I haven't been back for years. I've been living in Ashland, but Johnny always said if I came out to California I should look him up. What the heck. I had some time, so I hit the road. I knew the address and he told me he was living in the garage apartment out back, so I came up here first. When I didn't get an answer, I went over and knocked on Bucky's door. I had no idea Johnny'd passed on."

"Must have been a shock."

"It was. I felt awful. I didn't even call first. He'd written me a note a couple months before, so I was all set to surprise him. Joke's on me, I guess. If I'd known, I could have saved myself a trip. Even driving, it's not cheap."

"How long have you been here?"

"Little over a week. I didn't plan to stay, but I drove over two thousand miles to get here and didn't have the heart to turn around and drive back. I didn't think I'd like California, but it's nice." Ray finished packing one box and tucked the top flaps together, setting that box aside while I started work on the next.

"Lot of people feel it takes some getting used to."

"Not for me. I hope Bucky doesn't think I'm ghoulish because I want to move in. I hate to take advantage of someone else's misfortune, but what the heck," he said. "Might as well have *some* good come out of it. Seems like a nice area, and I like being near the beach. I don't think Johnny'd mind. Here, let me get these out of your way." Ray lifted one box and stacked it on top of another, pushing both to one side.

"Where are you now?"

"Couple blocks over. At the Lexington. Right near the beach and room doesn't even have a view. Up here, I notice you can see a little slice of ocean if you look through those trees."

I looked around the room with care but didn't see anything else worth examining. Johnny hadn't had that much, and what he owned was unrevealing. "Well, I think I'll give up." I dusted my jeans off, feeling grubby and hot. I went into the kitchen and washed my hands at the sink. The plumbing shrieked and the water was full of rust. "You want to check anything while you're here? Water pressure, plumbing? You could measure for cafe curtains before I lock up," I said.

He smiled. "I better wait until I sign some kind of rental agreement. I don't want to take the move for granted, the way Bucky's been acting. You want my opinion, the kid's not all that bright."

I agreed, but it seemed politic to keep my mouth shut for once. I returned to the main room, found my shoulder bag, and slung the strap across my shoulder, then dug the key from my jeans pocket. Ray moved out of the apartment just ahead of me, pausing on the stair below me while I locked up. Once the place was secured

I followed him down the stairs and we walked down the driveway together toward the street. I made a quick detour, moving up onto the front porch, where I tucked the key into the mail slot in the middle of the front door. I rejoined him, and when we reached the street, he began to move in the opposite direction.

"Thanks for the help. I hope you and Bucky manage to work something out."

"Me too. See you." He gave a quick wave and moved off.

When I reached home, Henry's kitchen door was open and I could hear the babble of voices, which meant that Nell, Charlie, and Lewis were in. Before the day was over, they'd be into Scrabble and pinochle, Chinese checkers, and slapjack, squabbling like kids over the Parcheesi board.

By the time I unlocked my front door, it was almost eleven. The message light was blinking on my answering machine. I pressed the playback button. "Kinsey? This is your cousin Tasha, up in Lompoc. Could you give me a call?" She left a phone number, which I duly noted. The call had come through five minutes before.

This was not good, I thought.

At the age of eighteen, my mother had been estranged from her well-to-do family when she rebelled against my grandmother's wishes and ran off with a mailman. She and my father were married by a Santa Teresa judge with my aunt Gin in attendance, the only one of her sisters who dared to side with her. Both my mother and Aunt Gin had been banned from the family, an exile that continued until I was born some fifteen years later. My parents had given up any hope of offspring, but with my arrival tentative contact was made with the remaining sisters, who kept the renewed conversations a secret. When my grandparents left on a cruise to celebrate their anniversary, my parents drove up to Lompoc to visit. I was four at the time and remember nothing of the occasion. A year later, while we were driving north to another furtive reunion, a boulder rolled down the mountain and crashed through the car windshield, killing my father on impact. The car went off the road and my mother was critically injured. She died a short time later while the paramedics were still working to extract us from the wreckage.

After that, I was brought up by Aunt Gin, and to my knowledge, there was no further communication with the family. Aunt Gin had never married, and I was raised in accordance with her peculiar notions of what a girl-child should be. As a consequence, I turned out to be a somewhat odd human being, though not nearly as "bent" as some people might think. Since my aunt's death some ten years ago, I'd made my peace with my solitary state.

I'd learned about my "long-lost" relatives in the course of an investigation the year before, and so far, I'd managed to keep them at arm's length. Just because *they* wanted a relationship didn't obligate *me*. I'll admit I might have been a little crabby on the subject, but I couldn't help myself. I'm thirty-five years old and my orphanhood suits me. Besides, when you're "adopted" at my age, how do you know they won't become disillusioned and reject you again?

I picked up the phone and dialed Tasha's number before I had time to work myself into a snit. She answered and I identified myself.

"Thanks for calling so promptly. How are you?" she said.

"I'm fine," I said, desperately trying to figure out what she wanted from me. I'd never met her, but during our previous phone conversation, she'd told me she was an estate attorney, handling wills and probate. Did she need a private detective? Was she hoping to advise me about living trusts?

"Listen, dear. The reason I'm calling is we're hoping we can talk you into driving up to Lompoc to have Thanksgiving with us. The whole family's going to be here and we thought it'd be a nice time to get acquainted."

I felt my heart sink. I had zero interest in the family gathering, but I decided to be polite. I injected my voice with a phony touch of regret. "Oh, gee, thanks, Tasha, but I'm tied up. Some good friends are getting married that day and I'm a bridesmaid."

"On *Thanksgiving*? Well, that seems peculiar."

"It was the only time they could work out," I said, thinking ha ha tee hee.

"What about Friday or Saturday of that weekend?" she said.

"Ah." My mind went blank. "Mmm . . . I think I'm busy, but I could check," I said. I'm an excellent liar in professional matters. On the personal side I'm as lame as everybody else. I reached for my calendar, knowing it was blank. For a split second I toyed with the possibility of saying "yes," but a primitive howl of protest welled up from my gut. "Oh, gee. Nope, I'm tied up."

"Kinsey, I can sense your reluctance, and I have to tell you how sorry we all are. Whatever the quarrel between your mother and Grand had nothing to do with you. We're hoping to make up for it, if you'll let us."

I felt my eyes roll upward. Much as I'd hoped to avoid it, I was going to have to take this on. "Tasha, that's sweet and I appreciate your saying that, but this is not going to work. I don't know what else to tell you. I'm very uncomfortable with the idea of coming up there, especially on a holiday."

"Oh, really? Why is that?"

"I don't know why. I have no experience with family, so it's not anything I miss. That's just the way it is."

"Don't you want to meet the other cousins?"

"Uh, Tasha, I hope this doesn't sound rude, but we've done all right without each other so far."

"How do you know you wouldn't like us?"

"I probably would," I said. "That isn't the issue."

"Then what is?"

"For one thing, I'm not into groups and I'm not all that crazy about being pushed," I said.

There was a silence. "Does this have something to do with Aunt Gin?" she asked.

"Aunt Gin? Not at all. What makes you ask?"

"We've heard she was eccentric. I guess I'm assuming she turned you against us in some way."

"How could she do that? She never even *mentioned* you."

"Don't you think that was odd?"

"Of course it's odd. Look, Aunt Gin was big on theory, but she didn't seem to favor a lot of human contact. This is not a complaint. She taught me a lot, and many lessons I valued, but I'm not like other people. Frankly, at this point, I prefer my independence."

"That's bullshit. I don't believe you. We'd all like to think we're independent, but no one lives in isolation. This is family. You can't repudiate kinship. It's a fact of life. You're one of us whether you like it or not."

"Tasha, let's just put it out there as long as we're at it. There aren't going to be any warm, gooey family scenes. It's not in the cards. We're not going to gather around the piano for any old-fashioned sing-alongs."

"That's not what we're like. We don't do things that way."

"I'm not talking about you. I'm trying to tell you about me."

"Don't you want anything from us?"

"Like what?"

"I gather you're angry."

"Ambivalent," I corrected. "The anger's down a couple of layers. I haven't gotten to that yet."

She was silent for a moment. "All right. I accept that. I understand your reaction, but why take it out on us? If Aunt Gin was inadequate, you should have squared that with her."

I felt my defenses rise. "She wasn't 'inadequate.' That's not what I said. She had eccentric notions about child rearing, but she did what she could."

"I'm sure she loved you. I didn't mean to imply she was deficient."

"I'll tell you one thing. Whatever her failings, she did more than Grand ever did. In fact, she probably passed along the same kind of mothering she got herself."

"So it's *Grand* you're really mad at."

"Of course! I told you *that* from the beginning," I said. "Look, I don't feel like a victim. What's done is done. It came down the way it came down, and I can live with that. It's folly to think we can go back and make it come out any different."

"Of course we can't change the past, but we can change what happens next," Tasha said. She shifted gears. "Never mind. Forget that. I'm not trying to provoke you."

"I don't want to get into a tangle any more than you do," I said.

"I'm not trying to defend Grand. I know what she did was wrong. She should have made contact. She could have done that, but she didn't, okay? It's old business. Past tense. It didn't involve any of us, so why carry it down another generation? I love her. She's a dear. She's also a bad-tempered, penny-pinching old lady, but she's not a monster."

"I never said she was a monster."

"Then why can't you just let it go and move on? You were treated unfairly. It's created some problems, but it's over and done with."

"Except that I've been marked for life and I've got two dead marriages to prove it. I'm willing to accept that. What I'm not willing to do is smooth it all over just to make her feel good."

"Kinsey, I'm uncomfortable with this ... *grudge* you've been carrying. It's not healthy."

"Oh, come off it. Why don't you let me worry about the *grudge*?" I said. "You know what I've finally learned? I don't have to be perfect. I can feel what I feel and be who I am, and if that makes you uncomfortable, then maybe *you're* the one with the problem, not me."

"You're determined to take offense, aren't you?"

"Hey, babe, I didn't call you. You called *me*," I said. "The point is, it's too late."

"You sound so *bitter*."

"I'm not bitter. I'm realistic."

I could sense her debate with herself about where to go next. The attorney in her nature was probably inclined to go after me like a hostile witness. "Well, I can see there's no point in pursuing this."

"Right."

"Under the circumstances, there doesn't seem to be any reason for having lunch, either."

"Probably not."

She blew out a big breath. "Well. If there's ever anything I can do for you, I hope you'll call," she said.

"I appreciate that. I can't think what it'd be, but I'll keep that in mind."

I hung up the phone, the small of my back feeling damp from tension. I let out a bark and shook myself from head to toe. Then I fled the premises, worried Tasha would turn around and call back. I hit the supermarket, where I picked up the essentials: milk, bread, and toilet paper. I stopped by the bank and deposited a check, withdrew fifty bucks in cash, filled my VW with gas, and then came home again. I was just in the process of putting groceries away when the phone rang. I lifted the receiver with trepidation. The voice that greeted me was Bucky's.

"Hey, Kinsey? This is Bucky. I think you better get over here. Somebody broke into Pap's apartment and you might want to take a look."

# 3

I KNOCKED AT Bucky's front door for the second time that day. The early afternoon sun was beginning to bake the grass, and the herbal scent of dried weeds permeated the November air. To my right, through a stucco arch-way opening onto a short length of porch, I could see the scalloped edge of the old red-tile roof. In Santa Teresa the roof tiles used to be handmade, the C-curve shaped by laying the clay across the tile worker's thigh. Now the tiles are all S shaped, made by machine, and the old roofs are sold at a premium. The one I was looking at was probably worth ten to fifteen grand. The break-in artists should have had a go at that instead of the old man's apartment with its cracked linoleum.

Babe opened the door. She had changed clothes, dis-carding her black T-shirt and black pedal pushers in favor of a shapeless cotton shift. Her eyes were enor-mous, the color of milk chocolate, her cheeks sprinkled with freckles. Her excess weight was evenly distributed, as if she'd zipped herself into an insulated rubber wet suit.

"Hi. I'm Kinsey. Bucky called and asked if I'd stop by."

"Oh, yeah. Nice to meet you. Sorry I missed you earlier."

"I figured we'd meet eventually. Is Bucky out back?"

She ducked her head, breaking off eye contact. "Him and his dad. Chester's been screaming ever since we got home. What a butt," she murmured. "He's all the time hollering. I can't hardly stand that. I mean, we didn't make the mess, so why's he yelling at us?"

"Did they call the police?"

"Uhn-hun, and they're on their way. Supposably," she added with disdain. Maybe in her experience the cops never showed up when they said. Her voice was breathy and soft. She was a bit of a mumbler, managing to speak without moving her lips. Maybe she was practicing to be a ventriloquist. She stepped back to let me enter, and then I followed her through the hallway as I had earlier with Bucky. Her rubber flip-flops made sucking noises on the hardwood floor.

"I take it you just got home," I said. I found myself talking to the back of her head, watching the bunch and release of her calves as she moved. Mentally, I put her on a weight program . . . something really, really strict.

"Uhn-hun. Little while ago. We went out to Colgate to visit my mom. Chester got home first. He bought this ceiling light he was fixing to put in? When he went upstairs, he could see where the window was broke, all this glass laying on the steps. Somebody really tore the place up."

"Did they take anything?"

"That's what they're trying to figure out. Chester told Bucky he shouldn't have left you alone."

"Me? Well, that's dumb. Why would I tear the place apart? I'd never work that way."

"That's what Bucky said, but Chester never listens to him. By the time we got here, he was having a conniption fit. I can't wait 'til he goes back to Ohio. I'm a nervous wreck. My daddy never yelled, so I'm not used to it. My mom'd knock his block off if he ever talked to her that way. I told Bucky he better tell Chester to quit swearing at me. I don't appreciate his attitude."

"Why don't you tell him?"

"Well, I tried more'n once, but it never does any good. He's been married four times and I bet I can guess why they divorce him. Lately, his girlfriends are all twenty-four years old and even *they* get sick of him once he buys 'em a bunch of clothes."

We trooped up the steps to the garage apartment, where the door was standing open. The narrow window next to it had an irregular starburst of glass missing. The method of entry wasn't complicated. There was only one door into the place, and all the other windows were twenty feet off the ground. Most burglars aren't going to risk a ladder against the side of a building in broad daylight. It was obvious the intruder had simply come up the stairs, punched out the glass, reached around the frame, and unlocked the deadbolt from the inside. It hadn't been necessary to use a pry bar or any other tools.

Chester must have heard us because he came out to the landing, barely looking at Babe, who eased back against the wooden porch railing, trying to make herself as inconspicuous as possible. Her father-in-law had apparently dismissed her as a target . . . for the moment, at any rate.

It was easy to see where Bucky got his looks. His father was big and beefy, with wavy blond hair long enough to touch his shoulders. Was that a dye job? I tried not to stare, but I could have sworn I'd seen that color in a Clairol ad. He had small blue eyes, blond lashes, and graying sideburns. His face was big and his complexion was ruddy. He wore his shirttail out, probably to disguise the extra thirty pounds he carried. He looked like a fellow who'd played in a rock-and-roll band in his youth, writing his own excruciatingly amateurish tunes. The earring surprised me: a dangling cross of gold. I also caught a glimpse of some sort of religious medal on a gold chain that disappeared under his V-neck T-shirt. His chest hair was gray. Looking at him was like seeing previews of Bucky's coming attractions.

Might as well be direct. I held my hand out. "Kinsey Millhone, Mr. Lee. I understand you're upset."

His handshake was perfunctory. "You can knock off the 'Mr. Lee' shit and call me Chester. Might as well be on a first-name basis while I chew your ass out. You better believe I'm upset. I don't know what Bucky asked you to do, but it sure wasn't this."

I bit back a tart reply and looked past him into the apartment. The place was a shambles: boxes overturned, books flung here and there, the mattress rolled back, the sheets and pillows on the floor. Half of Johnny's clothes had been pulled from the closet and piled in a heap. In the kitchen, through the doorway, I could see cabinet doors standing open, pots and pans strewn across the floor. While the disorder was extensive, nothing appeared to be damaged or destroyed. There was no sign that anyone had taken a blade to the bedding. No graffiti, no food emptied out of canisters or pipes torn from the walls. Vandals will often festoon the walls with their own fecal paint, but there was nothing like that here. It looked more like the methods big-city cops might employ at the scene of a drug bust. But what was the object of the exercise? Fleetingly, I entertained the notion

that I was being set up, called in as a witness to a
phony crime scene so that Bucky and his father could
claim something valuable had been taken.

Bucky appeared from the kitchen and caught sight of
me. In one split second we exchanged curiously guilty
looks, like co-conspirators. There's something about being accused of criminal behavior that makes you feel
like you did it even if you're innocent. Bucky turned to
his dad. "Toilet tank's cracked. Might have been like
that before, but I never noticed."

Chester pointed a finger. "You're paying for it if it
has to be replaced. Bringing her into it was your bright
idea." He turned to me, jerking a thumb over his shoulder toward the bathroom. "You ought to see in there.
Medicine cabinet's pulled all the way out the wall. . . ."

He droned on, pouring out the details, which seemed
to give him satisfaction. He probably liked to bitch, reciting his grievances in order to justify his ill treatment
of other people. His irritation was contagious, and I
could feel my temper climb.

I cut into his monologue. "Hey, I didn't do this,
Chester. You can rant and rave all you want, but the
place was fine when I left. I locked up and put the key
back through the mail slot like Bucky suggested. Ray
Rawson was here. If you don't believe me, you can ask
him."

"Everybody's innocent. Nobody did nothing. Everybody's got some kind of bullshit excuse," Chester
groused.

"Dad, she didn't do it."

"You let me take care of this." He turned and looked
at me narrowly. "You trying to say Ray Rawson did
this?"

"Of course not. Why would he do this when he's

hoping to move in?" My voice was rising in response to his, and I worked to get control.

Chester's attitude became grudging. "Well, you better have a talk with him and find out what he knows."

"Why would he know anything? He left the same time I did."

Bucky interceded, trying to introduce a note of reason. "Pappy didn't have a pot to piss in, so there's nothing here to take. Besides, he died in July. If burglars thought there was anything of value, why wait until now?"

"Maybe it was kids," I said.

"We don't have kids in this neighborhood as far as I know."

"True enough," I said. Ours was primarily a community of retirees. It was always possible, of course, that a roving band of thugs had targeted the apartment. Maybe they figured that any place this crummy looking had to be a cover for something good.

"Nuts!" Chester said with disgust. "I'm going down and wait for the police. Soon as you two crime experts finish your analysis, you can get the place cleaned up."

I gave him a look. "I'm not going to *clean* the damn place."

"I wasn't talking to you," he said. "Bucky, you and Babe get busy."

"You better wait for the cops," I said.

He swung around and stared at me. "Why is that?"

"Because this is a crime scene. The cops might want to dust for prints."

Chester's face seemed to darken. "This is bullshit. There's something not right about this." He made a motion in my direction. "You can come on down with me."

I glanced back at Bucky. "I wouldn't touch anything

if I were you. You don't want to screw around with evidence."

"I hear you," he said.

Chester gestured impatiently for me to pick up the pace.

On the way down the steps, I glanced at my watch. It was 1:15 and already I was tired of taking crap from this guy. I'll take crap when I'm paid for it, but I don't like doing it without compensation.

Chester clumped into the kitchen and went straight to the refrigerator, where he jerked open the door. He took out a jar of mayonnaise, mustard, bottled hot sauce, a packet of bologna, and a loaf of Wonder white bread. Had he ordered me to come down here so I could supervise his lunch?

"I apologize if I was rough, but I don't like what's going on," he said gruffly. He wasn't looking at me, and I was tempted to do a double take to see if there was someone else in the room. He'd dropped the imperious attitude and was talking in a normal tone of voice.

"You have a theory?"

"I'll get to that in a bit. Grab a chair."

At least he had my attention. I took a seat at the kitchen table and watched in fascination as he started his preparations. Somehow in my profession I seem to spend a lot of time in kitchens looking on while men make sandwiches, and I can state categorically, they do it better than women. Men are fearless. They have no interest in nutrition and seldom study the list of chemicals provided on the package. I've never seen a man cut the crusts off the bread or worry about the aesthetics of the "presentation." Forget the sprig of parsley and the radish rosette. With men, it's strictly a grunt-and-munch operation.

Chester banged a cast-iron skillet on the burner,

flipped the gas on, and tossed in a knuckle of butter, which began to sizzle within seconds. "I sent Bucky out to live with his granddad, which turned out to be a mistake. I figured the two of them could look after each other. Next thing I know, Bucky's hooked up with that gal. I got nothing against Babe . . . she's a dimwit, but so's he . . . I just think the two of 'em got no business being married."

"Johnny didn't warn you?"

"Hell, he probably encouraged it. Anything to make trouble. He was a sneaky old coot."

I let that one pass, leaving him to tell the story his way. There was an interval of quiet while he tended to his cooking. The bologna was pale pink, the size of a bread-and-butter plate, a perfect circle of compacted piggy by-products. Chester tossed in the meat without even pausing to remove the rim of plastic casing. While the bologna was frying, he slathered mayonnaise on one slice of bread and mustard on the other. He shook hot sauce across the yellow mustard in perfect red polka dots.

As a child I was raised with the same kind of white bread, which had the following amazing properties: If you mashed it, it instantly reverted to its unbaked state. A loaf of this bread, inadvertently squished at the bottom of a grocery bag, was permanently injured and made very strange-shaped sandwiches. On the plus side, you could roll it into little pellets and flick them across the table at your aunt when she wasn't looking. If one of these bread boogers landed in her hair, she would slap at it, irritated, thinking it was a fly. I can still remember the first time I ate a piece of the neighbor's homemade white bread, which seemed as coarse and dry as a cellulose sponge. It smelled like empty beer bottles, and if you gripped it, you couldn't even see the dents your fingers made in the crust.

The air in the kitchen was now scented with browning bologna, which was curling up around the edges to form a little bowl with butter puddled in the center. I could feel myself getting dizzy from the sensory overload. I said, "I'll pay you four hundred dollars if you fix me one of those."

Chester glanced at me sharply, and for the first time, he smiled. "You want toasted?"

"You're the chef. It's your choice," I said.

While we chowed down, I decided to satisfy my curiosity as well. "What sort of work do you do back in Columbus?"

He snapped back the last of his sandwich like a starving dog, wiping his mouth on a paper napkin before he responded. "Own a little print shop in Bexley. Offset and letterpress. Cold and hot type. Brochures, flyers, business cards, custom stationery. I can collate, fold, bind, and staple. You name it. I just hired a guy looks after the place when I'm gone. He does good I'll let him buy me out. Time I did something else. I'm too young to retire, but I'm tired of working for a living."

"What would you do, come out here to live?"

Chester fired up a cigarette, a Camel, unfiltered, that smelled like burning hay. "Don't know yet. I grew up in this town, but I left as soon as I turned eighteen. Pappy came out here in 1945, which is when he bought this place. He always said he'd be in this house until the sheriff or the undertaker hauled him out by his feet. Him and me never could get along. He's rough as a cob, and talk about *child abuse*. You never heard about that in the old days. I know a lot of guys got knocked around back then. That's just what dads did. They came home from the factory, sucked down a few beers, and grabbed the first kid came handy. I been punched and kicked, flung against the wall, and called every name in the book. If I got in trouble, he'd make me pace until I dropped, and if I uttered one word of protest, he'd douse my tongue with Tabasco sauce. I hated it, hated my old man for doing it, but I just thought that's the way life was. Now all you have to do is pop a kid across the face in public, you're up on charges, buddy, looking at jail time. Foster home for the kid and the whole community up in arms."

"I guess some things change for the better," I remarked.

"You got that right. I vowed I'd never treat my kids that way, and that's a promise I kept. I never once raised a hand to 'em."

I looked at him, waiting for some rueful acknowledgment of his own abusiveness, but he didn't seem to make the connection. I moved the subject over slightly. "Your father died of a heart attack?"

Chester took a drag of his cigarette, removing a piece of tobacco from his tongue. "Keeled over in the yard. Doctor told him he better lay off the fat. He sat down one Saturday to a big plate of bacon and eggs, fried sausages, and hashed browns, four cups of coffee, and a cigarette. He pushed his chair back, said he wasn't feeling so hot, and headed out to his place. Never even reached the stairs. 'Coronary occlusion' is the term they used. Autopsy showed an opening in his artery no bigger than a thread."

"I take it you don't think his death is related to the break-in."

"I don't think he was murdered, if that's what you're getting at, but there might be some connection. Indirectly," he said. He studied the ember on the end of his cigarette. "You have to understand something about my old man. He was paranoid. He liked passwords and se-cret knocks, all this double-o-seven rigmarole. There were things he didn't like to talk about, the war being foremost. Once in a while, if he was tanked up on whis-key, he'd rattle off at the mouth, but you ask him a question and he'd clam right up."

"What do you think it was?"

"Well, I'm getting to that, but let me point this out first. You see, it strikes me as odd, this whole sequence of events. Old guy dies and that should have been the end of it. Except Bucky gets the bright idea of applying for these benefits, and that's what tips 'em off."

"Tips who?"

"The government."

"The government," I said.

He leaned forward, lowering his voice. "I think my old man was hiding from the feds."

I stared at him. "Why?"

"Well, I'll tell you. All the years since the war? He never once applied for benefits: no disability, no medi-cal, no GI Bill. Now why is that?"

"I give up."

He smiled slightly, unperturbed by the fact that I wasn't buying in. "Clown around if you like, but take a look at the facts. We fill out a claim form . . . all the in-formation's correct . . . but, first, they say they have no record of him, which is bullshit. Fabrication, pure and simple. What do you mean, they don't have a record of him? This is nonsense. Of course they do. Will they ad-mit it? No ma'am. You following? So I get on the phone to Randolph—that's the Air Force base where all the files are kept—and I go through the whole routine again. And I get stonewalled, but good. So I call the National Personnel Records Center in St. Louis. No deal. Never heard of him. Then I call Washington,

D.C. . . . we're talking the *Pentagon* here. Nothing. No record. Well, I'm being dense. I'm not getting it myself. All I know to do is raise six kinds of hell. I make it clear we're serious about this. A lousy three hundred dollars, but I don't give a good goddamn. I'm not going to let it drop. The man served his country and he's entitled to a decent burial. What do I get? Same deal. They don't know nothin' from nothin'. Then we have this." He jerked a thumb toward the garage apartment. "See what I'm saying?"

"No."

"Well, think about it."

I waited. I didn't have the faintest idea what he was getting at.

He took a deep drag from his cigarette. "You want to know what I think?" He paused, creating drama, maximizing the effect. "I think it took 'em this long to get some boys out here to find out how much we knew."

This sentence was so loaded, I couldn't figure out which part to parse first. I tried not to sound exasperated. "About *what*?"

"About what he did during the war," he said, as though to a nitwit. "I think the old man was military intelligence."

"A lot of guys worked in military intelligence. So what?"

"That's right. But he never *admitted* it, never said a word. And you know why? I think he was a double agent."

"Oh, stop this. A spy?"

"In some capacity, yes. Information gathering. I think that's why his records are sealed."

"You think his records are sealed. And that's why you can't get verification from the VA," I said, restating his point.

"Bull's-eye." He pointed a finger at me and gave me a wink, as though I'd finally picked up the requisite IQ points.

I looked at him blankly. This was beginning to feel like one of those discussions with a UFO fanatic, where the absence of documentation is taken for proof of government suppression. "Are you saying he worked for the Germans, or spied on them for our side?"

"Not the Germans. The Japanese. I think he might have worked for 'em, but I can't be sure. He was over in Burma. He admitted that much."

"Why would that be such a big deal all these years later?"

"You tell me."

"Well, how would I know? Honestly, Chester, I can't speculate about this stuff. I never even knew your father. I have no way of guessing what he was up to. If anything."

"I'm not asking you to speculate. I'm asking you to be objective. Why else would they say he wasn't in the Air Force? Give me one good reason."

"So far you don't have any proof that he was."

"Why would he lie? The man wouldn't lie about a thing like that. You're missing the point."

"No, I'm not. The *point* is, they're not really saying he wasn't there," I said. "They're saying they can't identify him from the information you submitted. There must be a hundred John Lees. Probably more."

"With his exact date of birth and his Social Security number? Come on. You think this stuff isn't on computer? All they have to do is type it in. Press Enter. Boom, they got him. So why would they deny it?"

"What makes you think they have all this data on computer?" I said, just to be perverse. This was hardly the issue, but I was feeling argumentative.

"What makes you think they don't?"

I barely suppressed a groan. I was hating this conversation, but I couldn't find any way to get out of it. "Come on, Chester. Let's don't do this, okay?"

"You asked the question. I'm just answering."

"Oh, forget it. Have it your way. Let's say he *was* a spy, just for the sake of argument. That was forty-some-odd years ago. The man is *dead* now, so why does anybody give a shit?"

"Maybe they don't care about *him*. Maybe they care about something he has. Maybe he took something that belongs to them. Now they want it back."

"You are making me crazy. What *it*?"

"How do I know? Files. Documents. This is just a hunch."

I wanted to lay my little head on the table and weep from frustration. "Chester, this makes no sense."

"Why not?"

"Because if that's the case, why call attention to it? Why not just pay you the three hundred bucks? Then they can come out at their leisure and look for this *thing* . . . this whatever you think he has. If he's been in hiding all these years . . . if they've *really* been looking and now they know his whereabouts, why arouse your suspicions by refusing to pay some dinky little three-hundred-dollar claim?"

"Four hundred and fifty with interment thrown in," he said.

I conceded the arithmetic. "Four fifty, then," I said. "The same question applies. Why cock around?"

"Hey, I can't explain why the government does what it does. If these guys were so bright, they'd have tracked him down years ago. The VA application was the tip-off, that's all I'm saying."

I took a deep breath. "You're jumping to conclusions."

He stubbed out his cigarette. "Of course I'm jumping. The question is, am I right? The way I see it, the boys finally got a lock on him, and that's the result." He tipped his head in the direction of the garage apartment. "Here's the only question I got . . . Did they find what they came for or is it still hidden somewhere? I'll tell you something else. This Rawson fellow could be part of it."

This time I groaned and put my head in my hands. This was making my neck tense, and I massaged my trapezius. "Well, look. It's an interesting hypothesis and I wish you a lot of luck. All I offered was to see if I could locate a set of dog tags or a photograph. You want to turn this into some kind of spy ring, it's not my line of work. Thanks for the sandwich. You're a genius with bologna."

Chester's gaze suddenly shifted to a spot just behind me. There was a sharp rap at the back door, and I felt myself jump.

Chester got up. "Police," he said under his breath. "Just act normal."

He moved toward the door to let the guy in while I turned and squinted at him. Act *normal*. Why wouldn't I act normal? I *am* normal.

On the back step, I could hear the uniformed police officer's murmured introduction. Chester ushered him into the kitchen. "I appreciate your coming out. This is my neighbor, Kinsey Millhone. Officer Wettig," he said, using this phony Mr. Good Citizen tone of voice.

I glanced at the officer's name tag. P. Wettig. Paul, Peter, Phillip. This was not anyone I knew from my dealings with the department. Gutierrez and Pettigrew had always handled this beat. Despite my skepticism,

Chester's conspiracy theory was apparently having an effect, because I was already wondering if his 911 call had been intercepted and an imposter sent instead. Wettig was probably in his late forties, looking more like a lounge singer than a uniformed patrolman. He wore his blond hair long, pulled into a little pigtail in back; brown eyes, short blunt nose, round chin. I pegged him at six three, weighing in at 210. The uniform looked authentic, but wasn't he a little *old* to be a beat cop?

"Hi. How are you?" I said, shaking hands. "I expected to see Gerald Pettigrew and Maria Gutierrez."

Wettig's look was neutral, his tone of voice bland. "They split up. Pettigrew's on Traffic now, and Maria moved over to the county sheriff's department."

"Really. I hadn't heard that." I glanced at Chester. "You want me to stay? I can hang around if you like."

"Don't worry about it. I can call you later." He glanced at Officer Wettig. "I guess I better show you the apartment."

I watched as Chester and the officer walked down the back steps and across the concrete drive.

As soon as they were out of sight, I moved down the hallway and peered out the front. A black-and-white patrol car was parked at the curb. I found the telephone, which was located in what looked like a little prayer niche in the hall. I pulled out the telephone directory and dialed the regular phone line for the Santa Teresa Police Department. Someone in Records answered.

I said, "Oh, hi. Can you tell me if Officer Wettig is working this shift?"

"Just a second and I'll check." She clicked off, putting me on hold. Moments later she clicked back in again. "He's on until three this afternoon. You want to leave a message?"

"No, thanks. I'll try again later," I said, and hung up. Belatedly I blushed, feeling slightly sheepish. Of course there was an Officer Wettig. What was wrong with me?

# 4

AFTER I LEFT Bucky's, I came home and took a brief but refreshing nap, which I suspected, even then, was going to be one of the highlights of my vacation. At 4:57 I ran a brush through my hair and trotted down the spiral stairs.

The lowering cloud cover was generating an aura of early twilight, and the streetlights winked on as I locked my apartment. Even with the late afternoon drop in temperature, Henry's back door was open. Raucous laughter spilled through the screen door, along with a tantalizing array of cooking smells. Henry was playing some kind of honky-tonk piano in the living room. I crossed the flagstone patio and knocked on the screen. Preparations for Lewis's birthday dinner were already under way. For his birthday, I'd bought a sterling-silver shaving set with a mug and a brush that I'd found in an antique store. It was more "collectible" than antique, but I thought it would be something he could either use or admire.

Lewis was polishing silverware, but he let me in.

He'd taken off his suit coat, but he still wore dress pants, a vest, and a crisp white shirt with the sleeves rolled up. Charlie had one of Henry's aprons tied around his waist, and he was in the process of putting the finishing touches on Lewis's birthday cake. Henry had told me Charlie was becoming self-conscious because his hearing had deteriorated so much. He'd had his hearing officially tested about five years before. At that point, the audiologist had recommended hearing aids, for which Charlie had been fitted. He'd worn them for a week or so and then put them in a drawer. He said the ones he tried felt like someone had a thumb in each ear. Every time he flushed the toilet, it sounded like Niagara Falls. Combing his hair sounded like someone walking on gravel. He didn't see what was wrong with people talking loud enough for him to hear. Most of the time, he had a hand cupped to his right ear. He said "What?" quite a lot. The others tended to ignore him.

The cake he was working on had listed to one side, and he was using an extra inch of white frosting to prop it up. He glanced up at me. "We don't let the birthday person bake his own birthday cake," he said. "Nell does the layers, unless it's her birthday, of course, and I do boiled frosting, which she never seems to get right."

"Everything smells great." I lifted the lid to a covered casserole. Inside, there was a mass of something lumpy and white with what looked like pimento, hard-boiled egg, and clumps of pickle relish. "What's this?"

"Say again?"

Lewis spoke up. "That started out as potato salad, but Charlie set the timer and never heard it ring, so the potatoes cooked down to mush. We decided to add all the regular ingredients and call it Charlie Pitt's Famous Mashed Potato Salad. We're also having fried chicken, baked beans, coleslaw, deviled eggs, and sliced cucumbers and tomatoes with vinegar. I've had this same meal every birthday for the last eighty-six years, since I was two," he said. "We each have something special, and the rule in our family is that the siblings cook. Some are better than others, as it turns out," he added with a glance at Charlie.

I turned to Charlie. "What do you have for your birthday?"

"What's that?"

I raised my voice and repeated my question.

"Oh. Hot dogs, chili, dill pickles, and potato chips. Mother used to fuss because I refused to have a proper vegetable, but I insisted on potato chips and she finally gave in. Instead of birthday cake, I always ask for a pan of Henry's brownies, which he usually has to send halfway across the country."

"What about Henry?"

Charlie cupped a hand to his ear, and Lewis answered for him. "Country ham, biscuits with red-eye gravy, collard greens, black-eyed peas, and cheese grits. Nell, now she insists on meat loaf, mashed potatoes, green beans, and apple pie with a big wedge of cheddar cheese on top. Never varies."

William came into the kitchen in time to catch Lewis's last remark. "What doesn't?"

"I was telling Kinsey about our birthday dinners."

I smiled at William. "What's yours?"

Lewis cut in again. "William always begs for a New England boiled dinner, but we vote him down."

"Well, I like it," he said staunchly.

"Oh, you do not. Nobody could like a New England boiled dinner. You just say that because you know the rest of us would be forced to eat it as well."

"So what does he end up with?"

"Anything we feel like cooking," Lewis said with satisfaction.

We heard a tap at the back door. I turned and saw that Rosie had arrived. The minute she and William saw each other, their faces lighted up. There were seldom any public displays of affection between them, but there was no doubt about their devotion. He was undismayed by her crankiness, and she took his hypochondria in stride. As a consequence, he complained less about imaginary ailments and her sour moods had diminished.

Tonight she was decked out in a dark red muumuu with a purple-and-navy paisley shawl, the rich colors adding a note of drama to her vibrantly dyed red hair. She seemed relaxed. I'd always thought of her as someone abysmally shy, ill at ease with strangers, overbearing with friends. She tended to be quite flirtatious with men, barely tolerant of women, and oblivious of kids. At the same time, she tyrannized the restaurant staff, paying them the lowest wages she could get away with. William and I were forever trying to persuade her to loosen up the purse strings. As for me, she'd bullied me unmercifully since the day I'd moved into the neighborhood. She wasn't mean, but she was opinionated, and she never seemed to hesitate in making her views known. Since I'd begun eating most of my dinners at the restaurant, she'd routinely told me what to order, ignoring any tastes or requirements of mine. Though I like to think of myself as hard-assed, I'd never had the nerve to stand up to her. My only defense in the face of her dictatorship was passive resistance. So far, I'd refused to get a husband or a dog, two (apparently) interchangeable elements she considered essential for my safety.

Now that she was poised on the brink of matrimony, she seemed at peace with herself: playful, full of smiles.

William's siblings had accepted her without a moment's hesitation ... except for Henry, of course, who was dumbfounded when the two connected. I began to see the wedding not so much as a union between her and William, but as an official ceremony by which she'd be initiated into the tribe.

From the other room, Henry began to pound out his rendition of "Happy Birthday" to Lewis, which he belted out at top volume. We joined him in a sing-along that continued for an hour before we ate. After dinner, Henry drew me aside. "What's the story on the break-in?"

"I'm not really sure. Chester seems to think there's some nefarious plot afoot, but I have trouble buying it. Somebody broke in ... there's no doubt about that. I'm just not sure it has anything to do with his dad."

"Chester thinks there's a link?"

"He thinks it's *all* connected. I think the guy's seen too many bad movies. He suspects Johnny was a double agent during World War Two and somehow has this stash of stolen documents in his possession. He feels the VA claim was what alerted the government, and that's who broke in."

Henry's look was confused. "Who did?"

"The CIA, I guess. Somebody who finally figured out where the old man was hiding. Anyway, that's his theory, and as they say, he's stickin' to it."

"I'm sorry I got you into it. Chester sounds like a nut."

"Don't worry about it. It's not like he actually hired me, so what difference does it make?"

"Well, it sounds like you did what you could, and I appreciate that. I owe you one."

"Oh, you do not," I said with a wave of my hand. In

the years of our friendship, Henry had done so much for me, I never would catch up.

At ten, when they hauled out the Monopoly board and the popcorn paraphernalia, I excused myself and went home. I knew the game would continue until midnight or one, and I wasn't up to it. Not old enough, I guess.

I slept like a stone until 6:14 A.M., when I caught the alarm mere seconds before it was set to ring. I rolled out of bed and pulled on my sweats in preparation for my run. Through the spring and summer months, I run at six, but in winter the sun doesn't rise until nearly seven. By then I like to be out on the path. I've been jogging since I was twenty-five ... three miles a day, usually six days a week, barring illness, injury, or an attack of laziness, which doesn't happen often. My eating patterns are erratic and my diet is appalling, so the run is my way of atoning for my sins. While I'm not crazy about the pain, I'm a sucker for the exhilaration. And I do love the air at that hour of the day. It's chilly and moist. It smells of ocean and pine and eucalyptus and mown grass. By the time I cool down, walking back to my place, the sun has streaked across the lawns, unrolling all the shadows behind the trees, turning dew to mist. There's no moment so satisfying as the last moment of a run: chest heaving, heart pounding, sweat pouring down my face. I bend from the waist and bark out a note of pure bliss, relieved of tension, stress, and the residual effects of all the Quarter Pounders with Cheese.

I finished my run and did a cool-down walking home. I let myself into the apartment, took a shower, and got dressed. I was just spooning down the last of my cold cereal when the telephone rang. I glanced at the clock. It was 7:41, not an hour at which I would ordinarily expect the world to intrude. I grabbed the phone on the second ring. "Hello?"

"Hey, it's me. Chester. Hope I'm not bothering you," he said.

"This is fine. What are you doing at this hour?"

"Was that you I seen running along Cabana a little while ago?"

"Yeeees," I said cautiously. "Is that what you called to ask, or was there something else?"

"No, no, not at all. I just wondered," he said. "I got something I want to show you. We came across it last night."

"What kind of 'it'?"

"Just come over and take a look. It's something Bucky discovered when he was cleaning out Pappy's place. I wouldn't let anyone touch nothing 'til you saw for yourself. You might have to eat crow." He sounded nearly gleeful.

"Give me five minutes."

I rinsed my dish and my spoon, put the cereal and the milk away, and ran a damp sponge across the kitchen counter. One of the joys of living alone is the only mess you clean up is the one you just made. I tucked my keys in my jacket pocket, pulled the door shut, and took off. In the time since I'd run, the neighborhood was coming alive. I spotted Lewis halfway down the block, taking his morning constitutional. Moza Lowenstein was sweeping off her front porch, and a fellow with a parrot on his shoulder was out walking his dog.

This was one of those perfect November days with cool air, high sun, and the lingering smell of wood fires from the night before. Along our block, the palm trees and evergreens provide constants in a landscape that seems to shift subtly with the passing seasons. Even in California we experience a rendition of autumn, a sporadic mix of colors provided by the ginkgo, the sweet gum, the red oak, and white birch. An occasional maple tree might punctuate the foothills with an exclamation point of vibrant red, but the brightest hues are supplied by the blaze of forest fires that sweep through annually. This year the arsonists had struck four times across the state, leaving thousands of acres an ashen gray, as eerie and as barren as the moon.

When I got to Bucky's, I circled the main house and walked up the drive. The crudely patched concrete parking pad was littered with assorted cardboard boxes, and I assumed that progress was being made with Johnny's personal effects. I headed up the wooden stairs to the apartment above. The door was standing open, and I could hear the murmur of voices. I stepped through the doorway and paused in the entrance. Without the maze of bulky boxes, the space looked smaller and dingier. The furniture remained, but the rooms seemed almost imperceptibly diminished.

Bucky and Chester were standing near the closet, which had been emptied of the remaining clothes. Both men were wearing versions of the same short-sleeved nylon Hawaiian shirt: Bucky's in neon green, Chester's in hot blue. Nearby, Babe was folding and packing the garments into an old steamer trunk. Coat hangers were piled up to the right of her as each piece of clothing was removed. She was wearing her usual flip-flops, along with shorts and a tank top. I had to admire the comfort with which she occupied her overblown body. I'd have been cold in that outfit, but it didn't seem to bother her.

Chester smiled when he saw me. "Hey, there you are. We were just talking about you. Come over here and take a look at this. See what you think." Mr. Friendly, I thought.

Bucky stepped back, showing me a panel he'd swung

away from the back wall of the closet. A small residential safe had been tucked into the space, encased in what appeared to be a block of poured concrete. The safe door was approximately sixteen inches wide and fourteen inches tall. The panel itself appeared to be carefully constructed, a flush-mounted plywood partition with insert hinges. The magnetic latch looked to be spring-loaded and probably released at a touch.

"Impressive. How'd you find that?" I asked.

Bucky smiled sheepishly, clearly pleased with himself. "We'd emptied the closet and I was sweeping it out when I bumped my broom handle up against the back wall. Sounded funny to me, so I got a flashlight and started looking at it real close, you know, knocking across the wall. Seemed like there was something goofy about this one section, so I give it a push and this panel popped open."

I hunkered down in front of the opening, peering into the cavity that had been hidden in the "found" space between the joists. The front face of the safe was imposing, but that might have been deceptive. Most home safes are not built to withstand a professional burglar with the proper tools and sufficient time to force his way in. The safe I was looking at was more likely a fire safe, in which what appears to be a solid steel wall is only a thin metal outer shell filled with insulating material. The function of such a safe is protection from a home fire of fairly short duration. Insulation in an old safe might be something as basic as natural cement. A more modern safe might rely on vermiculite mica or diatomaceous earth, particles of which can often be traced back from a burglary suspect's tools and clothing to the specific safe manufacturer.

On closer inspection, I could see the safe wasn't ac-

tually embedded in concrete. The concrete formed a
sort of housing into which the safe had been shoved.

"We got a locksmith on his way," Chester said. "I
couldn't stand the wait, so I called an emergency
number and told 'em to send somebody out. We could
have all the answers right behind this dial." He was
probably picturing maps and ciphers, a small wireless
radio, a Luger, and transmission schedules written in in-
visible ink.

"Have you looked for the combination? It's possible
he wrote it down and tucked it someplace close. Most
people don't trust their memories, and if he'd needed to
get into it, he wouldn't want to waste time searching."

"We thought of that, but we looked every place we
could think of. What about you? You searched pretty
good yourself. You come across anything might be the
combination to that?"

I shrugged. "I never came across any numbers, unless
he was using his birthdate or Social Security."

"Can they do that?" Bucky asked. "Make up a combination to suit any set of numbers you give?"

I shrugged. "As far as I know. I'm not an expert, but
I always assumed you could do that."

"What do you think, should we pull that thing out?"
Chester asked.

"Couldn't hurt. The locksmith will probably have to
do it anyway once he gets here," I said.

I rose to my feet and stepped out of the closet, allowing Bucky and Chester sufficient room to maneuver the
safe from its resting place. It took a fair amount of huffing and puffing before they managed to set it down on
the floor in the middle of the room. Once they'd eased
the safe out of its concrete housing, we could take a
better look. The three of us inspected the exterior surfaces as if this were some mysterious object that had

appeared from outer space. The safe was maybe sixteen inches deep, with a two-tone beige-and-gray finish and rubber mounting feet. It didn't look old. The dial was calibrated with numbers from one to a hundred, which meant you could generate close to a million combinations. There wasn't any point in trying to guess the right one.

Babe had abandoned her packing and was watching the whole procedure. "Maybe it's open," she said to no one in particular.

We turned in unison and looked at her.

"Well, it *could* be," she said.

"It's worth a try," I said. I reached down and pulled the handle without success. I turned the dial a few numbers in one direction and then the other, still pulling the handle, thinking the dial might have been left close to the last digit in the combination. No such luck.

"What do we do now?" Bucky asked.

"I guess we wait," I said.

Within the hour, the safe technician arrived with a big red metal toolbox. He introduced himself as Bergan Jones from Santa Teresa Locksmiths, shaking hands first with Chester, then with Bucky and me. Babe had gone back to folding clothes, but she nodded at him shyly when he was introduced to her. Jones was tall and bony looking, sandy haired, stoop shouldered, with a high shiny forehead, sandy brows, and big glasses with tortoise-shell frames. I placed him in his middle fifties, but I could have been off five years in either direction.

"Hope you can help us out here," Chester said, waving at the safe, which Jones had already spotted.

"No problem. I probably open thirty safes a month. I know this model. Shouldn't take me long."

The four of us stood and watched in fascination as Jones opened his toolbox. There was something in his manner of an old-fashioned doctor on a house call. He'd made his initial diagnosis, the condition wasn't fatal, and we all felt relief. Now it was just a matter of the proper treatment. He took out a cone-shaped device that he attached to the dial, screwing it down tightly. Within minutes he'd popped the dial off and set it aside, then removed the two screws holding the dial ring in place, slipped off the ring and set it with the dial. Next he took out an electric drill and began to bore a hole through the metal in the area that had been covered by the dial and ring.

"You just drill right through?" Babe said. She sounded disappointed, perhaps hoping for dynamite caps or nitroglycerin.

Jones smiled. "I wouldn't put it quite like that. This is a residential fire safe. If this were a burglary safe, we'd run into hardplate: barrier material just behind this steel plating. I got a pressure bar for that, but it'd still take me thirty minutes to drill a quarter-inch hole. Lot of them have auxiliary spring-loaded relocking devices. You hit the wrong spot and you can fire the relockers. If this happens, it gets a lot worse before it gets better again. This is easy."

We were quiet while he drilled, the low-pitched whine of metal making conversation awkward. The hair on the backs of his hands was a fine gold, his fingers long, wrists narrow. He was smiling to himself, as if he knew something the rest of us hadn't considered yet. Or maybe he was just a man who enjoyed his work. As soon as a hole had been drilled, he took out another device.

"What's that?" I asked.

"Ophthalmoscope," he said. "Gadget your doctor uses to peer in your eyes. This shines light on the combination wheels so I can see what we got going." He began to peer into the newly drilled hole, moving closer while flicking an outer dial on the scope to adjust the focal length. While squinting through his ophthalmoscope, he carefully rotated the protruding spindle stub to the left. "This turns the drive wheel, which in turn picks up the third combination wheel. The third wheel moves the second wheel, which then turns the first wheel," he said. "It takes four rotations to get the first wheel moving. That's the one closest to the front of the safe. Here it comes. Perfect. The gate's exactly under the fence. Now we'll just keep reversing the direction of our rotation and lessening the number of turns. Soon as I get all three wheels lined up, the fence will be in position to drop when the lever nose hits the gate in the drive wheel. We keep turning and the lever pulls back the lock bolt and it's all over."

With that, he gave the handle a pull and the safe door opened. Chester, Bucky, and I gave out a simultaneous "Ooo" like we were watching fireworks.

Babe said, "Heck, it's empty."

"They must have got it already. God*damn*," Chester said.

"Got what?" Babe said, but he ignored the question, shooting her a cross look.

While Bergan Jones wrote down the combination and put his tools away, Bucky peered into the safe, then got down on his back like an auto mechanic and shone a light into the interior. "Something taped up here, Dad."

I leaned over and peered with him. An item had been secured to the top of the safe: a lumpy-looking ten-inch-by-ten-inch square of beige tape.

Chester stepped over Bucky's legs and crouched by the safe, squinting at the patch. "What *is* that? Peel it off and give it here. Let me take a look at that thing."

Gingerly Bucky loosened one corner, then pulled it

away like a Band-Aid from a wound. A big iron key adhered to the tape. It appeared to be an old-fashioned iron skeleton key with simple cuts in the end. He held it up. "Anybody reconnize this?"

"Beats me," I said, and then turned to Chester. "You know what it is?"

"Nope, but Pappy used to fool around with locks now I think of it. He got a kick out of it. He liked to take a lock out of a door and file a key to fit."

"I never saw him do that," Bucky said.

"This is when I was a kid. He worked for a locksmith during the Depression. I remember him telling me what a hoot it was. He had this collection of old locks—probably close to a hundred of them—but I haven't seen them for years."

I turned the key over in my hand. The design was ornate, the handle scalloped, with a hole in the other end like a skate key. Viewed straight on, the bit was shaped almost like a question mark. "The lock and keyhole would be odd looking, to say the least. You don't remember anything like it around here?"

Chester's mouth pulled down. "Not me. What about you guys? You know the place better than I do at this point."

Bucky shook his head, and Babe gave a little shrug. I held the key out to Bergan Jones. "Any ideas?"

Jones smiled slightly, snapping down the locks on his toolbox. "Looks like a gate key. One of those big old iron jobs like they have on estates." He turned to Chester. "You want me to bill you on this?"

"I'll write you a check. Come on down to the kitchen and we'll take care of it. You probably gathered by now my pappy died a few months back. We're still trying to get his affairs sorted out. The safe came as a surprise. People ought to leave instructions. What the hell this is and who's supposed to get that. Anyways, we do appreciate your help."

"That's what I'm in business to do."

The two men departed, leaving Bucky, Babe, and me to contemplate the key. Bucky said, "Now what?"

"I have a friend who knows a lot about locks," I said. "He might have a suggestion about what kind of lock this might fit."

"Might as well. Won't do us any good otherwise."

Babe took the key and inspected it, frowning. "Maybe Pappy kept it because he liked the way it looked," she said. "It's neat. It's old-timey." She handed it to Bucky, who passed it back to me.

"Yeah, but why bother to keep it in a fireproof safe? He could have stuck it in a drawer. He could have wore it on a chain around his neck," he said.

"If you don't object, I'll see what my local expert has to say."

"Fine with me," Bucky said.

I slipped the key in my jeans pocket without mentioning the fact that my local expert was the burglar who'd also given me the set of key picks I carry in my handbag.

Walking back to my place, I found myself reviewing the entire sequence of events. I have to confess the past twenty-four hours had piqued my curiosity. It wasn't necessarily Chester's spy theory, which still seemed farfetched. What bothered me were the vague, unanswered questions surfacing in the old man's life. I like order and tidiness; no clutter and no dust bunnies hidden under the bed.

As soon as I got home, I sat down at my desk, pulled out a pack of index cards, and started making notes. It was amazing how many details I could actually recall once I began committing them to paper. When I'd exhausted the subject, I pinned the cards up on the cork-board that hangs above my desk. I put my feet up on the desk and leaned back in my swivel chair with my hands locked behind my head and studied the whole collection. Something wasn't right, but I couldn't figure out what it was. I shifted some cards around and pinned them up in a new configuration. It was something I'd read. Burma. Something about Chennault and the American Volunteer Group. For the moment the truth eluded me, but I knew it was there. I thought about nailing down the unit he'd served in. Was that really the issue here, or was there something else at stake? In scanning Johnny's books, I'd seen several AVG fighter pilots mentioned by name. One or more of those guys had to be alive today. Couldn't they provide a way to pinpoint Johnny's fighter group? It'd be a pain in the ass, and *I* sure wasn't going to do it, but I could at least steer Chester in the right direction. I'd have to check back through the books and see if I could find the reference, but what the hell, I wasn't doing anything else. Besides, once I start worrying a knot, I can't let go of it

I put in a call to my burglar friend, whose number had been disconnected. Rats. Later in the morning I'd try the Santa Teresa Police Department. Detective Halpern in Major Crimes would probably know where he was.

# 5

BY TEN A.M. I found myself back at Bucky's. I knocked
on the door, but after several minutes went by and nobody answered, I headed down the driveway toward the
back. The miscellaneous collection of cardboard boxes
had been shoved to one side to make the driveway pass-
able. The garage door on the left was standing open and
the Buick was missing. Maybe the three of them had
gone out to breakfast. The other half of the two-car garage was piled high with junk, an impenetrable mountain of boxes, old furniture, appliances, and lawn care
equipment.

The cardboard box full of World War II books was
right on top. I dragged it over to the stairs and made
myself comfortable while I sorted through the contents.
I finally found what I was looking for at the bottom of
the box in a book called *Fighter! The Story of Air Combat 1936–45* by Robert Jackson.

On 4 July 1942 the American Volunteer Group officially ceased to be an independent fighting unit and

became part of the newly-activated China Air Task Force, under command of the Tenth Air Force. Command of the CATF devolved on Claire Chennault, who exchanged his Chinese uniform for an American one and was given the rank of brigadier-general.

The AVG pilots, who had held the fort in Burma for so long against impossible odds, scattered far and wide. Few of them elected to remain in China. Those who did formed the nucleus of the new 23rd Fighter Group, still flying war-weary P-40s.

A few names followed: Charles Older, "Tex" Hill, Ed Rector, and Gil Bright. What interested me was the fact that the AVG pilots were recruited by the Central Aircraft Manufacturing Company between April and July 1941. All of them were serving U.S. military personnel, bound to CAMCO by a one-year contract. But Bucky had told me Chester remembered his father arriving home after two years overseas in time for his fourth birthday party, August 17, 1944. Because he was so specific, the date had stuck in my mind and I'd jotted it down on an index card. The problem was, the AVG had already been out of business for two years at that point. So where did the truth lie? Had Johnny actually served with the AVG? More important, had he served at all? Chester would see the discrepancy in dates as confirmation of his theory. I could just imagine his response. *"Hell, the AVG was just a cover story. I could have told you that."* Chester probably envisioned his father parachuting behind enemy lines, perhaps even feigning capture so he could confer with the Japanese high command.

On the other hand, if he'd never *been* in the service, then maybe he'd only acquired the books so he could bullshit about the subject. And that might explain why he was unwilling to talk about the war. It was always going to be risky because he might well run into someone who'd been in the very unit he was claiming to have served. By creating the impression of government secrecy, he could account for his reluctance to discuss the details that might give him away.

I scanned the backyard, staring at the Ford Fairlane, sitting up on concrete blocks. Why did I care one way or the other? The old guy was dead. If it comforted his son and his grandson to believe he was a war hero (or, more grandiose yet, a spy whose cover had gone undetected now for more than forty years), what difference did it make to me? I wasn't being paid to shoot holes in Johnny's story. I wasn't being paid to do anything. So why not let it drop?

Because it's contrary to my nature, said she to herself. I'm like a little terrier when it comes to the truth. I have to stick my nose down the hole and dig until I find out what's in there. Sometimes I get bitten, but that's the chance I'm usually willing to take. In some ways, I didn't care so much about the nature of the truth as knowing what it consisted of.

I became aware of the big six-inch key digging into my hip. I stretched my leg out and slid my hand into my jeans pocket. I pulled out the key and held it in my palm, hefting the weight. I rubbed my thumb along the darkened surface. I squinted at the tarnished metal just as Babe had done. The name of the lock company seemed to be faintly stamped on the shaft, but I couldn't figure out what it said in this light. It didn't appear to be any of the lock companies I knew: Schlage, Weslock, Weiser, or Yale. The safe had been an Amsec, strictly a combination lock, so I didn't think the key was in any way connected with that.

I hauled myself to my feet and slid the key back in

my pocket. I was restless, trying to figure out what to do until Chester got home. It was always possible his memory was faulty. I'd only heard the story from Bucky, and he might have gotten the dates wrong. Ray Rawson had told me he worked with Johnny in the boatyards just after the war started, which had to be sometime in 1942. It struck me as odd that someone who'd known Johnny in the "olden" days had suddenly shown up on the old man's doorstep. Despite the off-hand explanation, I wondered if there was something else going on.

The Lexington Hotel was located on a side street a block off lower State Street near the beach. The structure was a chunky five-story box of weary-looking yellow brick, spanning an arcade that ran across the ground floor. On one side of the building, a jagged crack, like a lightning bolt, staggered through the brick from the roof to the foundation, suggesting earthquake damage that probably dated back to 1925. The letters of the word *Lexington* descended vertically on a sign affixed to one corner of the building, a buzzing yellow band of neon with dead bugs in the loops. The marquee boasted •DAILY MAID •PHONE •COLOR TV IN EVERY ROOM. The entrance was flanked by a Mexican restaurant on one side and by a bar on the other. A blaring jukebox in each establishment competed for air space, a jarring juxtaposition of Linda Ronstadt and Helen Reddy.

I moved into a lobby that was sparsely furnished and smelled of bleach. Two rows of potted fan palms were arranged on either side of a length of trampled-looking red carpet that heralded the path to the front desk. The desk clerk was not in evidence. I picked up the house phone and asked the operator to connect me with Ray

Rawson's room. He answered after two rings and I identified myself. We spoke briefly and he directed me to his fourth-floor digs. "Take the stairs. The elevator takes forever," he said as he hung up.

I took the stairs two at a time just to test my lung capacity. By the second-floor landing, I was winded and had to slow down. I clung to the stair railing while I climbed the last flight. Being fit in one sport seems to have no bearing on any other. I know joggers who wouldn't last twenty minutes on a stationary bike and swimmers who couldn't jog more than a mile without collapsing.

I composed myself slightly before I knocked at 407. Ray opened the door with a buzzing portable electric shaver in his hand. He was barefoot, in chinos and a white T-shirt, his balding head still damp from the shower. The already closely clipped fringe of gray had been trimmed since yesterday. His smile was embarrassed, and the gap between his two front teeth gave him an air of innocence. He motioned me in. "You're too quick. I was trying to get this done before you got all the way up here. Be right back."

He moved into the bathroom, the buzzing sound of the shaver fading as he closed the door.

His room was spacious and plain: white walls, white bedspread, rough white cotton curtains pulled back on fat wooden rods. There were only two windows, but both were double wide, looking out onto the backside of the building across the alleyway. The carpet was gray and seemed relatively clean. The glimpse I had of the bathroom showed glossy white ceramic tile walls and a floor of one-inch black and white hexagonals. Ray returned, smelling strongly of aftershave.

"This is not bad," I said, turning halfway around.

"Fifty bucks a night. I asked about weekly rates, just

until I get a place of my own. I don't suppose Bucky's said anything about the rental."

"Not to me," I said. "Did you hear they had a break-in?"

"Who did? You mean, Bucky and them? When was this?"

I gave him the *Reader's Digest* condensed version of the story, watching as his smile was extinguished by disbelief and then concern.

"Jeez. That's terrible," he said, and then he caught my expression. "Wait a minute. Why look at me? I hope you don't think I had anything to do with it."

"It just seems odd there wasn't any problem until you showed up. Johnny died four months ago. You blow in last week and now Chester's suddenly got problems."

"Come on. Hey. I was sitting in the bar last night, watching big-screen TV. You can ask anyone."

"Mind if I sit?"

"Sure, go ahead. Take the good one. I'll take this."

There was one hard wooden chair and one uphol-stered chair. Ray steered me toward the latter and took the wood chair for himself. He placed his hands on his knees, rubbing the fabric as if his palms were sweating. "I'm probably the oldest and best friend Johnny ever had. I'd never do anything to mess with his son or his grandson or anything like that. You have to believe me."

"I'm not accusing you, Ray."

"Sure sounds like that to me."

"If I thought you'd broken in, I probably wouldn't have come up here. I'd have gone to the cops and had 'em dust for prints."

"They didn't do that?"

"Chester can't be sure anything was taken, which means it wasn't even a burglary as far as the cops are concerned. The techs here only lift prints at the scene of a major crime. Felonies, not misdemeanors. Malicious mischief wouldn't qualify unless thousands of dollars' worth of damage had been done, which wasn't true in this case." What I didn't bother to say was the procedure is lengthy and the department is perpetually backed up. Three weeks is standard. In a rush situation, prints could be lifted, photographed, and traced, with the resultant tracings being faxed to CAL ID in Sacramento. The turnaround time could be a day or two. In this case, we didn't even have a suspect. Except maybe him, I thought. I watched him, acutely aware of the key in my pocket. I didn't want him to know about that just yet. He seemed like a man who had something on his mind, and I wanted to hear his tale before I told him mine. "What's in Ashland?" I asked.

There was a millisecond's pause. "I got family back there."

"Was Johnny really in the service?"

"I have no idea. I already told you, I lost track of him for years."

"How'd you connect up again?"

"Johnny got in touch."

"How'd he know where to find you?"

Impatience flashed across his face as if his picture were being taken. "Because he had my address. What *is* this? I don't have to answer this stuff. It's none of your damn business."

"I'm just trying to get to the bottom of this."

"Well, try somewhere else."

"Chester thinks Johnny was a spy during World War Two, some kind of double agent for the Japanese."

Ray rolled his eyes briefly and then gave his head a quick shake. "Where'd he get that?"

"It's too complicated to explain. He says the old man was very paranoid. He thinks that's part of it."

Ray said, "The old guy *was* paranoid, but it didn't have anything to do with the Japs."

"What, then?"

"Why should I tell you? I have no reason to trust you any more than you trust me."

"And here I thought we were such pals," I said.

"Well, we're not," he said mildly.

I eased the key out of my pocket and held it up to the light. "You know anything about this?"

His gaze flicked to the key. "Where'd you get that?"

"It was in a safe Bucky found in Johnny's apartment. Have you ever seen it before?"

"No."

"What about the safe? Did you know about that?"

He shook his head slowly. This was like pulling teeth.

"I don't understand what the deal is," I said.

"There's no deal. It's nothing."

"If it's nothing, why not tell? It can't do any harm."

"Look, I might know who busted in. If it's who I think, then some guy might have followed me out here. That's all it is, and I could be wrong about that."

"What was he after?"

"Jeez. Don't you ever give up?"

"You must have *some* idea."

"Well, I don't."

"Of course you do," I said. "Why else would you drive all the way out here from Ashland?"

Agitated, he got up and crossed to the window, shoving his hands in his pockets. "Hey, come on. Enough. I'm getting tired of this. You can't force me to answer, so you might as well lay off."

I got up and followed him to the window, leaning

against the wall so I could watch his face. "Here's the way my mind works. This sounds like something criminal." I tapped my temple. "I'm thinking to myself, What if Johnny never went into the Air Force? I keep having trouble with that piece of it. If he wasn't in the service, then the whole picture shifts. Because then you have to wonder where he was all that time."

Ray's gaze met mine. He started to say something, but he seemed to think better of it.

"Want to hear my theory? I just came up with this," I said. "He might have been in prison. Maybe this business about the Air Force—this AVG bullshit—was just a polite explanation for his absence. The war had started by then. It sounds a lot more patriotic to say your husband's gone overseas than he's been sent up." I waited a moment, but Ray made no response. I cupped a hand behind my ear. "Care to comment?"

He shook his head. "It's your theory. You can think anything you want."

"You're not going to help me out?"

"Not a bit," he said.

I pushed away from the wall. "Well. Maybe you'll change your mind. I live around the corner from Johnny's, five doors down on Albanil. You can stop by and chat when you're ready." I moved toward the door.

"I don't get this," he said. "I mean, what's it to you?"

I looked back at him. "I have a hunch, and I'd like to find out if I'm right. In my line of work, it's good practice."

For lunch, I treated myself to a Quarter Pounder with Cheese and then spent the afternoon curled up with the new Elmore Leonard novel. I'd been telling myself how much fun it was having nothing to do, but I noticed that I was faintly disconcerted by the idleness. Generally, I don't think of myself as compulsive, but I don't like wasting time. I tidied my apartment and cleaned out some drawers, went back to my book, and tried to concentrate. Late in the afternoon, I shrugged into my blazer and walked up to the corner for a bite to eat. I was thinking about an early movie if I could figure out what to see.

The neighborhood was quiet, half the front porches picked out in light. There was a chill in the air, and the dark seemed to be coming down earlier and earlier. I could smell somebody's supper cooking, and the images were cozy. Once in a while I find myself at loose ends, and that's when I feel the lack of a relationship. There's something about love that brings a sense of focus to life. I wouldn't complain about the sex, either, if I could remember how it went. I'd have to get out the instructor's manual if I ever managed to get laid again.

Rosie's was nearly empty, but shortly after I sat down, I spotted Babe and Bucky coming through the door. I waved and the two of them approached my back booth, walking hip to hip, their arms wound around each other's waists.

I said, "Where's your dad, Bucky? I've been hoping to run into him. We need to talk."

"He took a load over to the dump, but he should be back shortly," Bucky said. "You want to join us? We thought we'd sit at the bar and watch the six o'clock news until Dad gets here." In the half-light of the tavern, he was looking nearly handsome. Babe was in boots, a long jeans skirt, and a blue jeans jacket.

"Thanks, but I may try to eat quick and catch an early movie."

"Well, we'll be over there if you should change your mind." They sauntered off to the bar.

Meanwhile, Rosie appeared from the kitchen and I

watched her draw two beers before she came over to me. She had already pulled out her pencil and order pad and was scribbling away. "I got perfect dish for you," she said as she snatched my dinner menu. "Is slices pork liver with sausage and garlic pickles, cook with bacon. Also, I'm making you apple-and-savoy-cabbage salad with crackling biscuits."

"Sounds inspired," I said. I didn't say by what.

"You gonna have this with beer. Is better than wine, which don't mix good with garlic pickles."

"I should say not."

I ate, I must say, with a hearty appetite, though I'd probably have indigestion later. The place was beginning to fill up with the Happy Hour crowd people from the neighborhood and singles getting off work. Rosie's had become a favorite hangout among the local sporting set, thus ruining it for those of us in search of peace and quiet. If it weren't for my fondness for Rosie and the close proximity to my apartment, I might have moved on to some new eatery. I saw Bucky and Babe move over to a table. Chester came in moments later, and the three conferred before ordering supper. By then the place was so noisy that it didn't seem tactful to join them and launch into talk about Johnny's past history.

At 6:35 I paid my check and headed out the front door. I was already losing interest in the movie, but there was always a chance I could generate enthusiasm from "the sibs."

When I got home, I crossed the back patio and knocked at the frame. I heard a muffled "Yoo-hoo!" I peered in through the screen and spotted Nell sitting in a wooden kitchen chair pulled up close to the stove. She was peering in my direction, and when she saw me she motioned me in.

I opened the door and stuck my head in. "Hi, Nell.

How are you?" The stove had been dismantled—the oven door open, oven racks removed—apparently in preparation for a thorough cleaning. The counter was lined with newspaper on which the oven racks were laid, still seething with oven cleaner.

"Fine and dandy. Come on in, Kinsey. It's good to see you." Ordinarily she wore her thick silver hair pulled back in an elaborate arrangement of tortoise-shell combs, but today she'd tied her hair into the folds of a scarf, which made her look like an ancient Cinderella.

"You're industrious," I said. "You just got here and already you're hard at work."

"Well, I'm not happy until I can take a stove apart and really clean in there good. Henry's extremely able when it comes to household chores, but a stove is the sort of thing needs a woman's touch. I know that sounds sexist, but it's the truth," she said.

"You need help?"

"I could sure use the company." Nell was wearing a pinafore-style apron over her cotton housedress, her long sleeves protected by cuffs of paper toweling that she'd secured with rubber bands. She was a big woman, probably close to six feet tall in her prime. Wide shouldered, heavy breasted, she had good-size feet and hands, though her knuckles were now as knotted as ropes beneath the skin. Her face was long and bony, nearly sexless in its character, sparse white brows, electric blue eyes, her skin vertically draped with seams and folds.

All the shelves had been emptied from the refrigerator, the countertops crowded with leftovers in covered bowls, olive and pickle jars, condiments, raw vegetables. The storage drawers had been removed and one was sitting in a sink full of soapy water. She'd tossed a number of items in the kitchen wastebasket, and I could see that she'd dumped something gloppy in the disposal.

"Don't look at that. I think it's still alive," she said. She was wringing out the cloth she was using to wipe down the shelves. "Once I finish this, I intend to take a bubble bath and then I'll get into my robe and slippers. I have some reading to catch up on. I keep thinking any day now my eyes are going out on me and I want to get in as much as possible." She had unscrewed a jar lid and was peering in. She sniffed, unable to identify the contents. "What in heaven's name is this?" She held it up to the light. The liquid was bright red and syrupy.

"I think it's the glaze for the cherry tart Henry makes. You know he cleaned the refrigerator just two days ago."

She screwed the lid back on and put the jar on the counter. "That's what he said. As it happens, cleaning refrigerators is one of my specialties. I taught Henry how to do it back in 1912. His problem is he isn't sufficiently rigorous. Most of us aren't when it comes to our own trash. As long as I'm here I might as well get everything shipshape."

"Was that your lot in life, teaching all the boys how to do things around the house?"

"More or less. I helped Mother raise and educate all ten of us at home. After Father died, I felt obliged to stay on until she recovered her spirits, which took close to thirty years. She was heartsick when she lost him, though as I recollect, the two of them never got along that well. My, my. How she did grieve for the man. It occurred to me later she was putting on a bit just to keep me underfoot."

"Ten kids? I thought there were only five. You, Charlie, Lewis, William, and Henry."

She shook her head. "We were the five *surviving*

children. We took after the Tilmanns, on our mother's side. In our family, there was a distinct division among the children she bore. Half took after her side of the family and the other half took after the Pitts on Father's side. Line us up for a photograph and you could see it plain as day. Now this is a fact. All Father's people up and died. It was a pitiful genetic line when you stop and calculate. They were small people with tiny heads, so they didn't have the brains our side of the family did and they had no physical stamina whatsoever. Our father's mother was a 'Mauritz' by birth. The name translates as 'Moorish,' which suggests a bunch of blackamoors somewhere up the line. They were swarthy, all of them, and just as feeble as could be. Our grandmother Mauritz died of the influenza, and so did two brothers above me. It was a mess. She went and he went and the other one went. Our sister, Alice, was another one we lost. Dark skinned, tiny head, she died of the influenza within a day of taking sick. Four cousins, an aunt. Sometimes two would go on the same day and we'd have a double funeral. That entire line was wiped out in a five-month period between November and March. Those of us who took after Mother are the only ones left, and we expect to go on for years. Mother lived to be a hundred and three. Right about the time she turned ninety, she got so crabby we threatened to withhold her sour mash whiskey if she didn't straighten up. She only required six tablespoons a day, but she believed it was absolutely essential to life. We put the bottle right up on the shelf where she could see it but couldn't reach. That settled her right down, and she went on for another thirteen years just as gentle as a lamb."

She closed the refrigerator door temporarily and returned to the sink, where the dishwater was now cool enough to allow her to wash the meat bin. She opened the cabinet under the sink, and I saw a frown cross her face.

"What's the matter?"

"Henry's out of the oven cleaner I like to use on these racks." She peered in the cabinet again. "Well, I'll just have to use a little elbow grease."

"You want me to make a quick run to the market? I can pick some up. It won't take ten minutes."

"No, that's all right. I can always use a scrub pad. It'll clean up in a jiffy. You have other things to do."

"I don't mind a bit. I was thinking about a movie, but I've lost interest, to tell the truth."

"Are you sure you don't mind?"

"Scout's honor," I said.

"I'd surely appreciate it. We're low on milk, too. Once the kids have their milk and cookies tonight, there won't be enough for breakfast. This is really awfully sweet."

"Don't even think about it. I'll be back shortly. What kind of milk? Low fat?"

"Half a gallon of skim. I'm trying to wean the kids off fat where I can."

I searched through my handbag for the car keys and then eased the strap across my shoulder as I headed out the door. My car was parked about two doors down. I fired up the ignition and pulled away from the curb. At the corner of Albanil and Bay, I turned right, passing Bucky's place, which had become my new reference point in the neighborhood. I'd probably never pass the house again without turning to look. I peered down the drive toward the garage apartment. Lights were on upstairs, and I saw a shadow move across the front windows.

I slowed to a stop, peering up at the apartment. I

didn't think any of the Lees were home. The last I'd seen, the three of them were still up at Rosie's having supper. The lights went out and I saw someone emerge onto the darkened landing. Well, this was interesting. I spotted a parking place and pulled in at the curb. I turned the engine off and doused my headlights. I adjusted the rearview mirror so that it was angled on the drive, and then slid down in the seat.

A man moved out of the driveway with a hefty-looking duffel bag in his right hand. He was walking in my direction, his head down, his shoulders hunched. From the dim glow of the street lamp, I could see it wasn't Bucky, Chester, or Ray. This guy had a full head of dark, curly hair. His clothing was dark, and he must have been wearing rubber-soled shoes because his footsteps made hardly any sound on the pavement as he passed. He set off across the street. I kept him in sight, watching with curiosity as he approached a white Ford Taurus parked at the far curb, facing the opposite direction. He shifted the duffel to his left hand while he took out his car keys and unlocked the door on the driver's side. Puzzled, I glanced back toward Bucky's, but the premises were still dark and there were no signs of life.

The man opened the door and shoved the duffel toward the passenger seat, slid in behind the wheel, and slammed the car door shut. I watched as he checked his reflection in the rearview mirror, smoothed his hair back, and settled a Stetson on his head. I eased out of sight while he started his ignition, flipped the lights on, and took off, his headlights raking my windshield. As soon as he turned the corner, I started my car and pulled away from the curb. I did a quick U-turn, yanked on my headlights, and took the corner maybe six seconds after he had. I caught a glimpse of his taillights as he turned right on Castle. I had to floor it to maintain visual

contact. Within minutes he'd turned onto the northbound freeway on-ramp, heading toward Colgate. I
eased into the line of traffic two cars behind him and
kept my foot firmly pressed to the accelerator.

# 6

A ONE-CAR SURVEILLANCE is usually a waste of time, especially at night, where a second set of headlights becomes conspicuous in a subject's rearview mirror. In this case, whatever this guy was up to, I didn't think he had any idea I was following. Coming out of Johnny's garage apartment, he'd seemed neither watchful nor cautious, and I had to believe a tail was the last thing he expected. I hadn't expected it myself, so I was at least as surprised as he was. He did nothing on the freeway—no tricky lane changes, no sudden exits—to indicate that he was aware of my presence. The Stetson, in silhouette, gave me a nice visual cue against the wash of approaching headlights. He took the off-ramp at upper State Street, and I slid into the lane behind him. While I steered with my left hand, I scrounged around in my handbag for a scrap of paper and a pen. At least I could take his license plate number while I had him in range. The nature of the plate number indicated that the car was a rental, a further clue being the Penny-Car-Rental on the license plate rim. Big duh. I made a note of the number on the back of an old grocery list. Later, I'd find someone to check the rental car records.

It was 7:17 by the time the white Taurus pulled into the gravel courtyard of the Capri, a ten-unit "motor hotel" off the frontage road. The perimeter of the parking area was delineated by a drooping strand of Christmas tree lights that had been strung from pole to pole. The motel itself was made up of two rows of small frame and clapboard cottages, each with a carport affixed to one side. The darkness had draped the exteriors in sufficient shadow to conceal the flaking paint, warping window screens, and poor construction. Most of the cottages appeared to be empty: windows unlighted, no vehicles in the carports. A pint-size U-Haul truck was parked in front of one unit. The first two cottages on the left were occupied, along with the second unit on the right, which was where the Taurus was now parked.

The driver locked his vehicle and moved up to the cottage's small concrete porch, with its light offering forty watts' worth of illumination. I waited until he'd unlocked the cottage and entered before I eased my VW along the gravel parking lot to a darkened unit across the way. I backed into the carport, doused my headlights, and rolled the window down. The stillness was punctuated by the ticking of my engine as the metal cooled. Also, by a failing green Christmas tree bulb that flickered and buzzed somewhere above my head like a jolly green bee. I sat in the dark, pondering how long I'd be willing to wait before I headed for home. Poor Nell must be wondering how far away the supermarket was. I'd promised her a quick trip—fifteen minutes max. I'd now been gone twice that long. I had a squirrelly feeling in the pit of my stomach, a strange emotional concoction of anxiety and excitement. What was in the duffel the guy had taken off the premises? Could

be burglars' tools. I was operating on the assumption
that this was the same guy who'd tossed the place before, though I couldn't imagine what was worth coming
back for. Ray Rawson had some suspicions about who
the break-in artist might have been, but he'd given no
indication why anyone would bother. I wished now I'd
pressed him for the information. Meanwhile, it was
worth a short wait. If I ran out of patience, I'd make a
note of the motel address and use a phone ruse in the
morning to find out who was staying there.

I checked my watch again. It was now 7:32. The fellow had been in there fifteen minutes or so. Was he in
for the night? I really couldn't sit here indefinitely, and
I didn't think it made sense to go prowling around the
cottage, trying to peer in the windows. The guy might
be traveling with a bad-tempered mutt that would set up
a stink. This was the kind of place that would *have* to
accommodate kids and weird pets. How else would they
get business except by accident?

Just about the time I was ready to pack it in, I saw
some movement on the cottage porch. The man
emerged accompanied by a woman, who now carried
the duffel bag. He still wore his hat and he was toting
a suitcase, which he stowed in the trunk. She handed
him the duffel and he tucked it in with the suitcase. He
opened the car door, giving her an assist as she got into
the seat on the passenger side. I noticed they didn't
bother with any checkout procedure. Either they were
only leaving for a short time or they were decamping
without paying. He went around to the driver's side. I
started my engine at the same time he started his, using
his noise as a cover for mine. His taillights came on, the
two bright red spots overlaid with the white of his
backup lights.

I left my headlights off, waiting until the Taurus

backed out and made a right turn into the street. The Taurus took off toward the highway, and I followed at a discreet distance. I wasn't happy with the arrangement. There wasn't much other traffic on the road, and if I had to tail the guy for long, I was going to get burned. Fortunately he headed for the northbound freeway on-ramp, and by the time I eased in behind him, there were sufficient cars on the road to camouflage my presence.

The driver of the Taurus stayed in the right lane and proceeded for two off-ramps before he finally took the exit designated for the airport and the university. With two bags in the trunk, I didn't think they were on their way to a UCST night class. The ramp curved up and around to the left, widening into six lanes. A Yellow Cab merged with us from an access road, and I eased back on the accelerator, allowing the taxi to slip in between us. The Taurus stayed in the right lane and turned off at Rockpit, turning right again at the stop sign. I stayed in the slipstream as first the Taurus and then the taxi turned in at the airport.

I watched as the Taurus moved into the left lane and slowed at the ticket meter for the short-term parking lot. The ticket arm went up like an automated salute. Meanwhile, the taxi kept to the right, pulling up at the curb in the passenger loading zone, where two passengers got out with their luggage. I waited until the Taurus drove into the short-term lot before I eased the VW forward. The ticket dispenser buzzed and a parking ticket emerged from the slot like a tongue. I snagged it and rolled forward into the lot.

The Taurus had turned into the first aisle on the left and was now parked in the front row, close to the road. I caught a quick glimpse of the couple as they crossed toward the terminal. He carried both the suitcase and the duffel. She was wearing a raincoat pulled around her for warmth. I scanned the spaces available and pulled into the first empty spot. I parked, locked up, and dogtrotted after them. The two were engaged in conversation, and neither seemed aware of my company.

It was fully dark by now, the terminal building lighted up like one of those miniature cottages you put under the Christmas tree. There were two skycaps at the curb, putting tags on the suitcases of the two travelers the taxi had disgorged. The couple went into the terminal. I noticed they were bypassing the car rental offices. Were they skipping? I doubled my pace, my shoulder bag banging against one hip as I jogged down the short walk to the entrance. The terminal at the Santa Teresa Airport has only six working gates.

In the left wing, Gates 1, 2, and 3 serviced commuter airlines: the puddle-jumpers doing short runs to and from Los Angeles, San Francisco, San Jose, Fresno, Sacramento, and other points within about a four-hundred-mile radius. In the main lobby, United Airlines was sharing counter space with American. I did a quick visual survey, checking out the passengers seated in various groupings of linked upholstered chairs. The Stetson should have made the guy fairly easy to spot, but there was no sign of the pair.

Most departing passengers were processed through Gate 5, which was plainly visible across the small lobby. At this hour of the night, air traffic wasn't heavy and a check of the departures monitor indicated only two outbound flights. One was a United prop jet to Los Angeles, the other an American Airlines flight to Palm Beach with an intervening stop at Dallas/Fort Worth. Dead ahead was Gate 4, which was used as the arrival gate for United's incoming flights. Arched windows looked out onto a small grassy area, defined by outdoor lights and surrounded by a stucco wall topped with a three-foot rim of protective window glass. I could hear the high-pitched drone of a small plane approaching along the runway. I moved to the double doors and checked the courtyard. There were maybe six or eight people scattered across the area: a woman with a toddler, three college students, an older couple with a dog on a leash. No sign of the couple I was looking for.

As I passed through the main lobby toward the commuter wing, I spotted the Stetson, black felt with a broad brim and a high soft crown. The guy was in the gift shop, paying for a couple of magazines. I was catching him in profile, but the light was excellent. As if obliging me, he took off his hat and ruffled his hair before he readjusted the angle of the hat on his head. I studied him with care so that I could identify him again if it ever came to that. I put him in his late fifties, with small dark eyes in a lean, hawkish face. He had a bushy salt-and-pepper mustache. What by streetlight had appeared to be dark, curly hair I could now see was heavily interwoven with strands of silver. He wore cowboy boots, jeans, and a heavy dark wool jacket. I pegged him at six feet, though the boots might have added inches, maybe 160 to 175 pounds. He tucked the magazines under his arm and crammed the change in his pocket. I backed away from the door as he turned in my direction.

Behind me was a bank of public telephones. In part as cover and in part out of desperation, I turned to the first phone and hauled up the phone book that was chained to the metal shelf below. I busied myself looking up Bucky's number while the guy came out of the gift shop behind me. Obliquely, I watched as he crossed the lobby, joining the woman, who was now standing at the ticket counter with her back to me, the duffel at her

feet. Where had she come from? Probably the ladies'
room. The line she was standing in was designated for
the purchasing of tickets. She'd taken off her raincoat,
which was now folded across one arm. The passenger
in front of her finished his business and she moved to
the counter, placing a big soft-sided suitcase on the
weighing apparatus. She reached back with one foot,
shifting the duffel forward until it rested against the
counter beside her.

The ticket agent greeted her, and the two exchanged
a few words. While the agent tapped on her computer
keyboard, the woman reached over and picked up a
cardboard identification strip from a container on the
counter. She filled in the details and then gave the tag
to the ticket agent, who was just in the process of assembling the ticket. The woman laid out a sheaf of bills,
which the ticket agent counted and then put away. She
secured the woman's identification to the suitcase, along
with a claim tag, and then placed the suitcase on the
conveyor belt. The moving bag was spirited through a
small opening like a coffin on its way to the flames.
The two finished their transaction, and the agent
passed the woman's ticket envelope across the counter
to her.

When the woman turned to her companion, I could
see that she was six or seven months pregnant. Was this
his daughter? She was much younger than the fellow
who accompanied her: early to mid-thirties, gaudy auburn hair piled in a tangled knot on top. Her complexion had the pasty look of too much foundation, overlaid
with a shade of powder that made her face seem faintly
dirty. Her maternity outfit was one of those oversize
pale blue denim dresses with short sleeves and a
dropped waist, against which her belly bulged. Under
the dress she wore an oversize white T-shirt with long

sleeves. She also wore red-and-white-striped tights and high-topped red tennis shoes. The dress itself I'd seen in a gardening catalog, a style favored by former hippies who'd given up dope and communal sex for organic vegetables and all-natural fiber clothes.

The guy picked up the duffel and the two moved aside as the next passenger in line moved up to the counter. He put the duffel down again and they stood to one side, engaged in desultory conversation. These people were about to get on a plane, and what was I supposed to do? A citizen's arrest seemed like dicey business at best. I couldn't even swear that a crime had been committed. On the other hand, what else was this guy doing up in Johnny Lee's apartment? I'd been a cop just long enough to have a nose for these things. To all appearances, the duffel bag was about to be transported out of state. I had no idea if the pair intended to return to Santa Teresa or were engaged in unlawful flight.

I turned back to the phone book and flipped through the pages with agitation, talking to myself. Come on, come on. Lawrence. Laymon. I ran a finger down the columns. Leason. Leatherman. Leber. Ah. Fifteen listings under Lee, but only one on Bay. Bucyrus Lee. Bucky's name was Bucyrus? I found a quarter in my blazer pocket, dropped it in the slot, and dialed the number. The receiver was picked up on the second ring. "Hello, Bucky?"

"This is Chester. Who's this?"

"Kinsey . . ."

"Shit. You better get over here. All hell's broken loose."

"What's going on?"

"We came home from Rosie's to find Ray Rawson crawling down the drive. Face all bloody, hand swoll up the size of a baseball mitt. He's got two fingers snapped sideways and God knows what else. Somebody busted in again and ripped into the space under the kitchen cabinet . . ."

Over the intercom system, an announcement was being made about an American Airlines flight. "Hang on a second," I said. I put my hand across the mouthpiece. I'd missed the specifics, but it had to be the boarding call for the flight to Palm Beach. Out of the corner of my eye, I saw the guy pick up the duffel, and together he and the pregnant woman moved out of the terminal, turning left toward the American Airlines departure gate. I could feel my heart pound. I turned my attention back to Chester. "Is Rawson okay?"

"Hey, we got cop cars all over and an ambulance on the way. He don't look so good. What's all that racket? I can hardly hear you."

"That's why I called. I'm at the airport," I said. "I saw a guy coming out of the apartment with a duffel. It looks like he and some woman are about to get on a plane. I tailed him this far, but once we lose track of that bag, it's only my word against his."

"Hang on. I'll grab Bucky and head out. Just don't let go of him until we get there."

"Chester, the plane's *boarding*. Do you know what he took?"

"I have no idea. I can't even get in until the place clears out. What about airport security? Can't they give you a hand?"

"What airport security? There's not an officer in sight. I'm here by myself."

"Well, for God's sake, do *something*."

I flashed through the possibilities. "Authorize a ticket and I'll follow him," I said.

"To where?"

"The plane's on its way to Palm Beach with a stop in Dallas. Make up your mind because two minutes more and he's out of here."

"Do it. We'll settle later. Call me when you can."

I banged the receiver down and checked the departures monitor again in passing. Beside the posted departure time for American flight 508, the word *boarding* was blinking merrily. The terminal had emptied of waiting passengers, who were apparently assembling at the gate. I trotted across the lobby to the American Airlines ticket counter. One of the two agents was busy with a passenger, but the other caught my eye. "I can help you over here."

I moved to her station. "Are there any seats available on the flight to Palm Beach?" I had no idea if the couple were on their way to Dallas or Palm Beach, but I had to assume the latter if I intended to stick with them.

"Let me see what we have. I know the flight's not full." She began to type rapidly on the computer keyboard in front of her, pausing while her eye took in the data appearing on the screen in front of her. "We have seventeen seats . . . twelve in coach and five in first class."

"What's coach fare?"

"Four hundred and eighty-seven dollars."

That wasn't bad. "And that's round trip?"

"One way."

"Four hundred and eighty-seven dollars one way?" My voice squeaked like I had just that minute reached puberty.

"Yes, ma'am."

"I'll take it," I said. "You better leave the return open-ended. I'm not sure how long I'll be staying." The truth was, I had no idea where the couple was headed. Their real destination could be Mexico, South America, or just about anywhere. I hadn't seen any sign of passports changing hands, but I couldn't rule out the possibility. Since this wasn't the same agent who'd dealt with the pregnant woman, there wasn't any point in quizzing her. I pulled out my wallet and took out a credit card, which I placed on the counter. She didn't seem to question the wisdom of the impulse. Oh, man. Chester had better pay up or I was sunk.

"Would you prefer an aisle seat or window?"

"Aisle. Near the front." For all I knew the couple would be first off the plane, and I wanted to be ready to cut and run when they did.

She typed another entry, tapping away in a leisurely manner. "You have bags to check?"

"Just carry-on," I said. I wanted to scream at her to hurry, but there wasn't any point. The ticket machine began to rattle and hum, generating my ticket, the boarding pass, and the credit card voucher, which I signed where specified. I could feel my eyes cross slightly when I saw what I'd paid. The round-trip coach fare without benefit of upgrade certificates or advance purchase discounts had cost me $974. I did some quick arithmetic. The limit on this credit card was $2,500, and I was still paying off some purchases I'd made over the summer. By my calculations, I had about four hundred bucks left. Oh, well. It wasn't like I didn't have money in my savings account. I just couldn't get to it at this hour of the night.

I took my ticket envelope, thanked the agent, and scurried out the front of the terminal and around to Gate 6, where I placed my handbag on the conveyor moving through the X-ray machine. I removed Johnny's key from my jeans pocket and tucked it in my handbag. I walked through the metal detector without incident and reclaimed my handbag on the other side. First-class

passengers and parents with small children had already
passed through the gate and had left the terminal. I
could see them straggling across the tarmac toward the
waiting plane. General boarding was now under way,
and I took my place at the rear of the slow-moving line.
The man in the Stetson was clearly visible.

About six passengers ahead of me, the couple stood
together, saying little or nothing. She now carried the
magazines, and he toted the duffel. Their behavior with
each other seemed strained, their faces devoid of anima-
tion. I saw no evidence of affection except for the belly,
which suggested at least one round of intimacy six or
seven months back. Maybe they'd been forced to get
married because of the baby. Whatever the explanation,
the emotional dynamic between them seemed dead.

When they reached the gate, the guy handed her the
duffel and said something. She murmured her response
without looking at him. She seemed withdrawn, decid-
edly chilly in her reaction to him. He put an arm around
her shoulder and gave her cheek a kiss. He stepped
back then and tucked his hands in his pockets, looking
on while she handed her boarding pass to the gate agent
and walked out with the duffel in her hand. Uh-oh, now
what? He waited by the gate until she'd moved out of
sight. I hesitated, considering my options. I could always follow him, but the duffel was the point, at least
until I found out what was in it. Once the booty was
gone, how was anyone going to trace it back to the
source?

The guy turned in my direction, heading for the exit.
He caught my eye briefly before I could avert my gaze.
I flicked another look at him and snapped a mental photograph of his grizzled face, the scar on his chin, a
deeply indented line of white that began with his lower

lip and continued down along his neck. He'd either gone through a window or had his face slashed.

The gate agent took my proffered ticket, handing back the torn stub from my boarding pass. If I was going to bail out, now was the time to do it. Ahead of me, across the poorly lighted expanse of asphalt, I saw the pregnant woman reach the top of the portable staircase and pass through the door of the plane. I took a deep breath and walked out onto the tarmac, where I crossed the open space to the stairs. The air was brisk and the perpetual wind that seems to whip along the runway cut through the fabric of my tweed blazer. I climbed the portable stairs, shoes *tink*ing on the metal treads as I ascended.

I was happier once I'd crossed the threshold of the 737 into the lighted warmth of the interior. I glanced at the three first-class passengers, but the pregnant woman wasn't among them. I checked the seat number on the stub of my boarding pass: 10D, probably over the wing on the left side of the plane. While I waited for the passengers ahead of me to stow carry-on bags and settle in their seats, I managed to skim my gaze across the first few rows of coach. She was sitting eight rows back in a window seat on the right. She'd taken out a compact and was peering into the mirror. She took out a bottle of makeup, opened it, and dotted beige across her cheeks, blending it in.

At eye level, most of the luggage bins above the seats were standing open. I moved forward, waiting for the college student ahead of me to shove a canvas bag the size of an ottoman in the overhead compartment. As I passed row eight, I saw the duffel, half concealed by the pregnant woman's folded raincoat, both items shoved in between a bulging canvas garment bag, a briefcase, and a luggage cart—the very items destined to tumble out and bonk you on the head on landing. If I'd had the nerve, I'd have simply picked up the duffel and toted it with me, shoving it under my seat until I had a moment to search the contents. The pregnant woman glanced in my direction. I turned away from her casually.

I took my seat and tucked my shoulder bag under the seat in front of me. The two seats next to me were empty, and I sent up small airline-type prayers that I'd have the row to myself. In a pinch, I could flip the arms up and stretch out for a nap. The pregnant woman got up just then and stepped out into the aisle, where she reached up into the overhead bin. She pushed the garment bag aside and wrestled a hardback book from an outer pocket of the duffel. The girl stewardperson moved down the aisle behind her, snapping the overhead bins shut with a series of small bangs.

Shortly after the doors closed, the girl stewardperson stood up in front of the assembled company and gave detailed instructions, with a practical demonstration, on how to fasten and unfasten our seat belts. I wondered if there was anybody present still befuddled by this. She also explained what to do if we were on the verge of being smashed, crushed, and burned by hurtling at high velocity from our flying altitude of twenty-six thousand feet straight down through the earth's crust. To me, the little hang-down oxygen bag seemed irrelevant, but it apparently made her feel better to pass along tips about the application of this device. To distract us from the possibility of death en route, she promised us a drink cart and a snack once we were airborne.

The plane rolled away from the terminal and taxied out onto the runway. There was a pause, and then the plane began to surge forward, picking up speed with much earnest intent. We rumbled and bumbled like the little engine that could. The plane lifted off into the night sky, the lighted buildings below becoming rapidly smaller until only a hapless grid of lights remained.

# 7

I CHECKED THE seat pocket in front of me: barf bag, laminated card with cartoon safety procedures, boring airline magazine, and a gift catalog in case I wanted to do my midair Christmas shopping. This was going to be a long trip, and me without my trusty Leonard novel. I felt my gaze return to the pregnant woman, who was seated across the aisle and two rows forward. At this remove, I could only see a portion of her face. The tangle of auburn hair made me long to have at her with a brush.

I still couldn't believe I was doing this. I decided I'd better do a quick inventory to assess my situation. I had the clothes on my back, which consisted of my Reeboks and socks, underwear, jeans, turtleneck, and blazer. I put my hands in my blazer pockets and came up with last week's movie receipt, two quarters, and a ballpoint pen, plus a paper clip. I felt my right-hand jeans pocket, which was empty. In the other pocket I had a wadded-up tissue, which I pulled out and used to blow my nose. One by one, I removed the items from my handbag and laid them on the seat beside me. I had my wallet with my California driver's license and my PI license; two major credit cards, one of which was good for $2,500 (less the current balance, of course), the other of which I now noticed had expired. Well, damn. I had $46.52 in cash, my telephone charge card, and an ATM card, which would be useless outside California. Where was my checkbook? Ah, sitting at home on my desk, where I'd been paying bills. Virtue is pointless in a crunch, as it turns out. If I'd neglected my debts, I'd have my checkbook with me, extending my tangible assets by three or four hundred bucks. Tucked in the inner compartment of my wallet, I had my key picks, always a handy item for the impromptu jet-setter.

Additionally, I had the toothbrush and toothpaste and the clean pair of underpants I always carry with me. I also had my Swiss Army knife, my sunglasses, a comb, a lipstick, a corkscrew, the key from Johnny's safe, two pens, the used grocery list on which I'd made a note of the Taurus's license plate number, a small bottle of aspirin, and my birth control pills. Whatever else happened, I wasn't going to get pregnant, so why fret? I was, after all, on vacation, and I had no other pressing responsibilities.

I didn't have the faintest idea what I'd do once we'd landed. Obviously, I'd wait and see what course of action my traveling companion elected. If she was leaving the country, there was nothing I could do about it, as the one thing I didn't have in my possession was my passport. I could probably travel into Mexico using my driver's license, but I didn't like to do that. I'd heard too many stories about Mexican jails. On the plus side, my return ticket was paid for, so I could always get straight back on a plane and come home. In the meantime, the

worst that could happen was I'd make a fool of myself
. . . not exactly unprecedented in my experience.

As soon as the seat belt sign went off, I unbuckled
myself and searched through the overhead bin for a pillow and a blanket. I moved to the back of the plane and
utilized the in-flight plumbing, washed my hands,
checked my reflection in the lavatory mirror, and picked
up a copy of *Time* magazine as I returned to my seat.
The pilot came on the intercom and said some piloty
things in a reassuring tone. He told us about our flying
altitude, the weather, and the flight course, along with
our estimated time of arrival.

The drink cart came by and I treated myself to three
bucks' worth of bad wine. I could hardly wait to eat my
four-hundred-and-eighty-seven-dollar snack, which
turned out to be a cherry tomato, a sprig of parsley, and
a "deli" bun the size of a paperweight. Dessert was a
foil-wrapped chocolate wafer. Once we'd been fed, the
cabin lights went down. Half the passengers opted for
sleep while the other half flipped on their reading lights
and either read or did paperwork. Forty-five minutes
passed and I noticed the pregnant woman walking past
my seat.

I turned and watched with interest as she headed toward the two lavatories at the rear of the plane. I
scanned the other passengers in the immediate vicinity.
Most were asleep. No one seemed to be paying any attention to me. The minute the woman closed herself
into the toilet, I eased out of my seat and moved two
rows forward, where I sat down in the aisle seat two
over from hers. I made a brief display of checking the
seat pocket, as if searching out some pertinent item
therein. I wasn't going to have the time (or the audac-
ity) to take down the duffel. The woman had apparently
taken her handbag with her—not very trusting of

her—so I couldn't rifle the contents. I checked her seat pocket. Nothing of interest in there. All she'd left behind was the hardback Danielle Steel novel, closed now and lying in the middle seat. I checked the inside cover, but there was no name written in the book. I noticed she was using her boarding pass as a bookmark. I plucked it out, slid the stub in my blazer pocket, and returned to my seat. No one shrieked or pointed or denounced me on sight.

Moments later, the pregnant woman passed me again, returning to her seat. I saw her pick up her book. She rose halfway and checked the seat cushion under her, then leaned down and searched in the area around her seat for the missing boarding pass. I could almost see the question mark appear, cloudlike, in the air above her head. She seemed to shrug. She got up again and took a pillow and weensy blanket from the overhead bin, flipped the light out, and settled down in her seat with the blanket across her chest.

I eased the stub of her boarding pass from my blazer pocket and took in the minimal information printed on it. Her name was Laura Huckaby, her destination Palm Beach.

Dallas/Fort Worth was in the central time zone, two hours ahead of us. After three plus hours in the air, it was 1:45 in the morning by the time we finally landed. A few minutes prior to our arrival, the stewardperson came on the intercom with the gate numbers for various connecting flights. She also advised us that the plane would be on the ground for approximately one hour and ten minutes before the continuation of flight 508 to Palm Beach. If we intended to deplane, we'd need to have our boarding passes with us for reboarding purposes. Poor Laura Huckaby was now minus her boarding pass, thanks to my chicanery. I watched her with guilt, expecting her to engage in an anxious conversation with the girl stewardperson or else remain, unhappily, in her seat until the flight took off again.

Instead, once we were parked at the gate and the seat belt sign was turned off, she got up, retrieved her raincoat and the duffel, tucked the book in the outer pocket, and joined the slowly moving line of departing passengers. I didn't know what to make of this, but I was compelled to follow. We stumped along the jetway in haphazard fashion, an irregular assortment of exhausted late-night travelers. The few passengers with carry-on bags gravitated toward the exits, but most people headed toward the baggage claim area. I kept Laura Huckaby well within my sights. Her auburn hair had been flattened in sleep, and the back of her jumper was pleated with horizontal wrinkles. She still had the raincoat draped over one arm, but she had to pause twice to switch the duffel from hand to hand. Where was she going? Did she think this was Palm Beach?

The Dallas/Fort Worth Airport was done in neutrals and beiges, the floor tiles clay colored. The corridors were wide and quiet at that hour of the morning. A group of Asian businessmen was driven past us in a whirring electric cart, a repetitious tone beeping to warn unwary pedestrians. The overhead lighting made us all look jaundiced. Most concession kiosks were gated and dark. We passed a restaurant and a combination news and gift shop selling hard- and paperback books, glossy magazines, newspapers, Texas barbecue sauces, Tex-Mex cookbooks, and T-shirts with Texas logos. The baggage claim area for flight 508 appeared ahead of us beyond a revolving door. Laura Huckaby pushed through ahead of me and then hesitated on the far side, as if to get her bearings. I thought at first she might be looking for someone, but that didn't seem to be the case.

I moved past her and crossed to the carousel where the bags would be coming in. I couldn't figure out what was going on. Had she always intended to deplane at this point? Was her suitcase checked all the way through to Palm Beach or only as far as Dallas/Fort Worth? A row of linked chrome-and-faux-leather chairs was arranged to the left. A television set had been mounted up on the wall in one corner, and most of the heads were tilted in that direction. Pictured, in garish color, was the wreckage of a recent plane crash, black smoke still rising from the charred fuselage in a harshly lighted landscape. The reporter spoke directly to the camera. She wore a camel-hair overcoat, snow billowing around her. The wind whipped her hair and stung her cheeks with hot pink. The sound was barely audible, but none of us had any doubts about the subject matter. I crossed to the water fountain and took a long, noisy drink.

Out of the corner of my eye I saw Laura Huckaby approach the wall-mounted directory, where she studied a set of printed instructions about how to call the shuttle service for the numerous hotels in the vicinity. She picked up the phone receiver and punched in four numbers. A brief conversation followed. I waited until she'd hung up again and then I intersected her path, falling in behind her as she approached the escalator. We descended to street level, where we proceeded through a set of plate-glass doors.

Outside, the night air was surprisingly cold. Despite the artificial lighting, a pervasive gloom blanketed the pickup area. Landscaping had been tucked in between the sidewalk and the building. Along the buff-colored facade, the grass was planted in tufts at distinctly placed intervals like the plugs on a hair transplant. I proceeded to the area marked "Courtesy Shuttles," where I turned and waited, peering patiently along the roadway. Laura Huckaby and I made no eye contact. She seemed tired and preoccupied, exhibiting no interest in her fellow travelers. At one point she winced, pressing a fist into the small of her back. Two others joined us: a portly gentleman in a business suit, toting a briefcase and a garment bag, and a young girl in a ski parka with a bulging backpack. A few cars passed at speeds sufficient to create an exhaust-laden breeze that swirled around our feet. At this hour of the morning, air traffic had diminished, but I could still hear the dull rumble of jets taking off from time to time.

Several courtesy shuttles passed us in succession. She made no move to flag them down, nor did the other two waiting with us. Finally, a red bus swung around the curve into view. On the side, in flowing gold script, *The Desert Castle* was written with a symbolic castle depicted in silhouette. Laura Huckaby raised a hand, signaling the bus. The driver spotted the gesture and pulled over to the curb. He stepped out of the bus and helped the businessman with his luggage while she and I got on the bus, the businessman following. The young woman with the backpack remained where she was, her gaze still focused anxiously on approaching vehicles. I found a seat near the rear of the darkened bus. Laura Huckaby ended up near the front, her cheek propped wearily against the palm of her hand. Most of her hair was straggling out of her topknot.

The driver returned to his seat and closed the door, then picked up a clipboard and turned halfway toward us to confirm the names on his list. "Wheeler?"

"Here." The man in the business suit identified himself.

"Hudson?"

To my surprise, Laura Huckaby raised her hand. Hudson? Where did that come from? Interesting development. Not only had she deplaned in a city that was not her intended destination, but she'd apparently made hotel reservations in another name. What was she trying to pull?

"I'm meeting someone," I said, speaking up in response to his inquiring look.

The driver nodded, set the clipboard aside, put the bus in gear, and took off. We followed a complicated course of crisscrossing lanes around the terminal and finally sped through the open countryside. The land was flat and very, very dark. An occasional lighted building shot up out of the blackness like a shimmering mirage. We passed what must have been restaurant row: steak house after steak house as gaudily lighted as one of the main streets in Las Vegas. A big commercial hotel finally loomed into view, one of those tasteless facilities with the room price—$69.95 single occupancy—posted right below the name. The red neon letters of the Desert Castle appeared to empty of color and then fill up again. In subscript the sign read WHERE YOU'RE GUARANTEED A GOOD KNIGHT'S SLEEP. Oh, please. The logo consisted of the outline of two green neon palms, flanking a red neon tower with crenellated battlements.

We passed an oasis of tall palms that surrounded a mock-up of the tower depicted on the building, a structure of faux stone complete with an empty moat and drawbridge. When the shuttle pulled into the hotel's passenger loading area, I hung back until Laura Huckaby (aka Hudson) had been assisted to the curb. There didn't seem to be any bellhumans on duty. The man in the business suit picked up his briefcase and his garment bag. The three of us moved into the lobby through revolving doors, with me bringing up the rear. Aside from the duffel, Laura Huckaby was without luggage.

Inside, the "merrie aulde England" motif had been given full play. Everything was crimson and gold, heavy velvet drapes, crenellated moldings, and tapestries hung from metal pikes sticking out of the "castle" walls. Just beyond the elevators, an arrow pointed the way to the rest rooms, which were marked Lords and Damsels. At the reception desk, I made sure I was third in line, reluctant to attract Laura Huckaby's attention. Given the hotel rates, I could afford maybe two nights' stay, but I'd have to be careful about additional charges. I had no idea how long Laura Huckaby would be here. She completed the check-in procedure and crossed to the elevators with the duffel in tow. By craning my neck slightly, I could see that the bank of elevators had a vertical strip of lights, indicating the floor each elevator was on at any given moment of operation. She entered the first elevator, and once the doors closed, I murmured, "I'll be right back," to no one in particular and sped in that direction. The red light advanced systematically from floor to floor and stopped on twelve.

I returned to the counter just as the man ahead of me finished checking in and crossed to the elevators. I moved up to the desk. Given the decor, I expected the clerk to be wearing a wimple or a corselet at the very least. Instead, she wore a regulation hotel management ensemble: white shirt, navy blazer, and a plain navy skirt. Her name tag read Vikki Biggs, Night Clerk. She was in her twenties, probably new to the staff and therefore relegated to the graveyard shift. She gave me a form to fill out. I jotted down my name and address and then watched while she ran off a credit card voucher.

She glanced at the address as she stapled the voucher to the registration form. "My goodness. Everybody's coming in from California tonight," she said. "That other woman was flying in from Santa Teresa, too."

"I know. We're together. She's my sister-in-law. Is there any way you could put me on the same floor with her?"

"We'll sure try," she said. She tapped a few lines on the ubiquitous keyboard, watching the monitor, her expression studious. Sometimes I want to lean across the desk and take a look myself. From Vikki's perspective, the news wasn't that good. "I'm sorry, but that floor's booked. I have a room on eight."

"That's fine," I said. And then as an afterthought, "What room is she in?" As if Vikki Biggs had just mentioned it and it had slipped my mind.

Ms. Biggs was no dummy. I'd apparently just crossed over into hotel management no-no land. She screwed her mouth sideways in a look of regret. "I'm not allowed to give out room numbers. I'll tell you what, though. You can give her a call as soon as you get to your room and the hotel operator will be happy to connect you."

"Oh, sure. No problem. I can always check with her later. I know she's as tired as I am. Flying the red-eye is a drag."

"I'll bet. You here for business or pleasure?"

"Little bit of both."

Ms. Biggs put my room key in a folder and slid it across the counter toward me. "Enjoy your stay."

Going up in the elevator, I was treated to symphonic music while I stared at myself in the smoky-glass mirror. "You look disgusting," I said to my reflection. Once on the eighth floor, the lighting was dim and it was dead quiet. Thieflike, I padded down the wide carpeted corridor and unlocked my door. The medieval affectations hadn't extended this far. I found myself transported from fourteenth-century England to the wild and woolly West, decor left over from some previous ownership. The room was done up in burnt orange and browns, the wallpaper textured like wood paneling. The bedspread was patterned in cactus and saddles, with a variety of cattle brands stitched across the surface. I did a quick roundup survey, circling the room to appraise the accommodations.

To the right of the door was a double closet containing four wooden hangers, an iron, and an ironing boardlet two feet long with short metal feet. Across from the closet was a dressing area with a mirrored vanity and sink, with a hair dryer affixed to the wall on the right. On the counter was a four-cup coffee maker with packets of sugar and nondairy creamer. A basket held small bottles of shampoo, conditioner, and lotion, plus a little mending kit and a shower cap in a box. In the bathroom, there was a fiberglass tub with a shower nozzle extending from the wall at about neck level. The plastic shower curtain was patterned with horseshoes and bucking broncos. There was a toilet, three bath towels, a bathmat, and one of those rubber tub mats designed to reduce the chances of a nasty spill and an even nastier lawsuit.

There was no minibar, but there was a jar of cellophane-wrapped hard candies in four gaudy flavors. Well, hey. What a treat. I'd also been blessed with a telephone, a television set, and a clock radio. In the morning, I'd call Henry and get an update on the situation in Santa Teresa. In the meantime, I closed the drapes and peeled off my clothes, which I hung neatly on my meager allotment of hangers. In the interest of sanitation, I laundered my underpants while I had the chance, using a dollop of hotel shampoo. In a pinch, I could use the hair dryer and the iron to dry them before I put them on again. A quick call to American Airlines showed no flights of any kind out of Dallas to Palm Beach until later that day, which meant Laura should be in for the night.

It was close to three-thirty A.M. when I put out the Do Not Disturb sign and slipped between the sheets buck naked. I fell almost instantly into a deep, untroubled sleep. If Laura Huckaby pulled a fast one and checked out any time within the next eight hours, then forget it. I'd put myself on a plane and head home.

I woke at noon and used my travel toothbrush to get the fur out of my mouth. I showered, shampooed my hair, and got back into yesterday's clothes, using my spare underpants since my newly laundered panties were still damp to the touch. I then enjoyed a wholesome meal of hot coffee with two packets each of sugar and whitener and four hard candies, two orange and two cherry. When I finally opened the drapes, I staggered back from the harsh Texas sun. Outside, I could see dry, flat land all the way out to the horizon, with scarcely a tree or a shrub in sight. Light blasted off the only other building in view: an office complex with a mirrored exterior on the far side of the cul-de-sac. To the right, a four-lane highway disappeared in two directions with no clear indication of the destination either way. The hotel seemed to be built in the middle of a commercial/industrial park with only one other tenant. As I watched, a group of runners appeared on my left. They looked to be kids, maybe middle-school age, that stage of adolescence where body sizes and types are all over the place. Tall, short, squat, and thin as rails, knobby kneed they ran, with the slower ones bringing up the

rear. They were dressed in shorts and green satin sin-
glets, but they were too far away for me to read the
school name on their uniforms.

I pulled the drapes shut and went over to the bed,
where I stretched out, propping pillows behind me
while I put in a call to Henry. As soon as he answered,
I said, "Guess where I am."

"Jail."

I laughed. "I'm in Dallas."

"That doesn't surprise me. I talked to Chester this
morning and he said you were off on some kind of wild-
goose chase."

"What's the latest from Bucky's? Has anybody figured out what was stolen last night?"

"Not as far as I know. Chester did tell me the kickplate at the bottom of the kitchen cabinet was pried off.
It looks like the old man constructed some kind of hidden compartment when he put the sink in. The space
might have been empty to begin with, but more likely
somebody walked off with whatever was in there."

"A secret compartment in addition to the safe? That's
interesting. Wonder what he had to hide."

"Chester thinks it was war documents."

"He told me about that. I can't believe it, but I intend
to find out. The fellow I saw passed the duffel over to
his wife or girlfriend, and she carried it with her on the
plane last night. The guy wasn't on the flight, but he
probably intends to join her. She was booked through to
Palm Beach, but she got off in Dallas, so naturally I
did, too."

"Oh, naturally. Why not?"

I smiled at his tone. "At any rate, you might have the
police check the Capri Motel. I didn't have a chance to
tell Chester about that. I'm not sure about the number,

but it was the second unit on the right. Her pal might still be there if he hasn't taken off by now."

"I'm making notes," Henry said. "I'll pass this along to the police, if you like."

"What about Ray? Do they think he was in on it?"

"Well, he must have had *some* connection. Police tried to question him, but he clammed right up. If he knew anything about it, he wouldn't say."

"Sounds like somebody pounded on him for the information about the kickplate."

"That'd be my guess. One of the officers took him over to the emergency room at St. Terry's, but as soon as the doctor finished treating him, he disappeared and nobody's heard from him since."

"Do me a favor. Go over to the Lexington Hotel and and see if he's there. Room 407. Don't call first. He may not be answering his phone—"

Henry cut in. "Too late. He's already gone, and I don't think there's much chance of his turning up. Bucky went over there this morning and his room's been cleaned out. Not surprisingly, the police are interested in him as a material witness. What about you? You want me to tell the detective what you saw?"

"You can, but I'm not sure how much good it will do. As soon as I figure out what's going on, I'll call the Santa Teresa cops myself. The police here won't have jurisdiction, and at this point I'm not even sure what kind of crime we're discussing."

"Assault, for one thing."

"Yeah, but what if Ray Rawson doesn't show up again? Even if he surfaces, he might not know the identity of his assailant or he might refuse to press charges. As for the alleged burglary, we don't even know what was stolen, let alone who did it."

"I thought you saw the guy."

"Sure, I saw him come out of Johnny's place. I can't swear he stole anything."

"What about this gal with the duffel?"

"She might not even know the significance of the bag she's toting. She certainly wasn't involved in the assault."

"Wouldn't she be guilty of receiving stolen goods?"

"We can't even swear there was a theft," I said. "Besides, she might not have the slightest idea anything's amiss. Husband comes home. She's going off on a trip. He says, Do me a favor and take this with you when you go."

"What do you intend to do?"

"I'm not sure. I'd love to get my hands on that duffel. It might give us a feeling for what the deal is here."

"Kinsey . . . ," Henry warned.

"Henry, don't *worry*. I'm not going to take any risks."

"I hate when you say that. I know what you're like. Where are you staying? I want the telephone number."

I gave him the telephone number printed on the telephone pad. "It's a hotel called the Desert Castle, near the airport in Dallas. Room 815. The woman's up on twelve."

"What's the plan?"

"Beats me," I said. "I'm just going to have to wait and see what she does. She's ticketed on through to Palm Beach, so if she gets back on a plane, I guess I'll get on, too."

He was silent for a moment. "What about money? Do you need additional funds?"

"I've got about forty bucks in cash and a plane ticket home. As long as I'm careful with my credit card, I'll do great. I hope you'll impress Chester with my professionalism. I'm really not interested in getting stiffed for expenses."

"I don't like it."

"I'm not crazy about the situation myself. I just wanted you to know where I was."

"Try not to commit a felony."

"If I knew the Texas statutes, it would help," I said.

# 8

I WENT DOWN to the lobby. I cruised the area, trying to get a feel for the place. By day, the red velvet and gilt had all the drab ambiance of an empty movie theater. A white guy in a red uniform pushed a whining vacuum cleaner back and forth across the carpeting. The night clerk was gone and the reception desk was personed by a corps of wholesome-looking navy-suited youths. No one on duty was going to give me any help. Any odd request would be referred to the shift supervisor, the assistant manager, or the manager, all of whom would regard me with the sort of skepticism I deserved. In my quest for information, I was going to have to use ingenuity, which is to say the usual lies and deceit.

Most hotel guests tend to see a facility in terms of their own needs: the concierge's desk, restaurants, the gift shop, rest rooms, public telephones, the bell stand, conference halls, and meeting rooms. In my initial foray, I was looking for the executive offices. I skirted the perimeter and finally pushed through a glass door into a lushly carpeted corridor defined by pale wood paneling and indirect lighting. The offices of various department heads were identified in gleaming brass letters.

In this part of the hotel, there was no attempt to carry out either the medieval or the buckaroo conceit. Since this was a Saturday, the glass-fronted offices of the sales manager and the director of security were dark and the doors locked. Hours of operation were neatly lettered in gold, making it clear I would have free rein until Monday morning at nine. I assumed there were security guards on duty twenty-four hours a day, but I hadn't seen one yet. The sales manager's name was Jillian Brace. The director of security was Burnham J. Pauley. I made a note to myself and continued my swing through the administrative quarters and out a door at the far end of the empty hallway.

I returned to the front desk and waited until one of the desk clerks was free. The kid who approached me was in his mid-twenties: clean-shaven, clear complected, blue eyed, and slightly overweight. According to his name tag, he was Todd Luckenbill. Mr. and Mrs. Luckenbill had made sure his teeth were straight, his manners were impeccable, and his posture was good. No earrings, no jewels in his nose, and no visible tattoos. He said, "Yes, ma'am. May I help you?"

"Well, I hope so, Todd," I said. "I'm passing through Dallas briefly on a family matter, but it happens my boss has been looking for a hotel where we can book a big sales conference next spring. I thought I might recommend this place, but I wasn't sure what sort of group package you offered. I wonder if you could direct me to the sales manager. Is he here today?"

Todd smiled, his tone slightly chiding. "Actually, it's not a 'he.' Jillian Brace is our sales manager, but she doesn't work on weekends. You might try her Monday morning. She's usually here by nine and I'm sure she'd be happy to talk to you."

"Gee, I'd love to do that, but I have a flight out at six. Do you think you could get me her business card? I can always give her a call when I get back to Chicago."

"Sure. If you can wait just a minute, I'll bring you one."

"Thanks. Oh, and one more thing while I'm thinking about it. My boss is concerned about conference security. We had a little problem with one of the big hotels last year, and I know he's reluctant to schedule anything until he's confident about security procedures."

"What kind of business are you in?"

"Investment banking. Very high level stuff."

"You have to talk to Mr. Pauley about that. He's the director of security. You want me to get you his card, too?"

"Sure, that'd be great. I'd really appreciate it, if it's not too much trouble."

"No problem."

While he was off on his mission, I picked up a couple of postcards from a counter display. The glossy photograph on the front showed the claret red lobby with two heralds in livery tooting on horns much longer than their arms. I checked, but they didn't seem to be on the premises this morning. Todd returned moments later with a fistful of the promised business cards. I thanked him and crossed the lobby to an alcove furnished with a mahogany table and two velvet-covered banquettes.

I found some hotel stationery in the drawer and made a few notes. Then I took a deep breath, picked up one of the house phones, and asked the hotel operator to connect me with Laura Huckaby. There was a pause, and then the operator said, "I'm sorry, but I don't show a registration for anyone by that name."

"You don't? Well, that's odd. Oh, yeah. Wait a minute. Try Hudson."

The operator made no response, but she was apparently putting me through to a guest by that name. I hoped it was the right one. I made a note of the name and circled it so I wouldn't forget.

A woman answered after one ring, sounding anxious and out of sorts. "Farley?"

Farley? What kind of name was that? I wondered if he was the guy she'd left at the airport back in Santa Teresa.

"Ms. Hudson? This is Sara Fullerton, Jillian Brace's assistant down in Sales and Marketing? How are you today?" I used that false, warm tone all telephone solicitors are taught in telephone soliciting school.

"Fine," Laura said cautiously, waiting for the punch line.

"Well, that's good. I'm glad to hear that. Ms. Hudson, we're conducting a confidential survey of certain select guests, and I wonder if I might ask you a few questions. I promise this won't take more than two minutes of your time. Can you spare us that?"

Laura didn't seem interested, but she didn't want to be rude about it. "All right, but please be quick. I'm waiting for a call, and I don't want the line tied up."

My heart began to pound. If this was not the right guest, the truth would soon surface. "I understand, and we appreciate your help. Now, according to our supplemental registration records, we show that you arrived last night from Santa Teresa, California, on American Airlines flight 508, is that correct?"

There was a silence.

"Excuse me, Ms. Hudson. Is that correct?"

Her tone was wary. "Yes."

"And your arrival time was approximately one forty-five A.M.?"

"That's right."

"Did you have any difficulty reaching the hotel shuttle service when you called from baggage claim?"

"No. I just picked up the phone and dialed."

"Was the shuttle service prompt?"

"I guess. It took about fifteen minutes, but that seemed okay."

"I see. Was the driver courteous and helpful?"

"He was fine."

"How would you rate the check-in procedure? Excellent, very good, adequate, or poor?"

"I'd say excellent. I mean, I didn't have any problems or anything." She was really getting into this now, trying to be objective but fair in her response.

"We're glad to hear that. And what is the anticipated length of your stay?"

"I don't know yet. I'll be here at least one more night, but I don't know much beyond that. You want me to notify you as soon as I find out?"

"That won't be necessary. We're happy to have you with us for as long as it suits. Now if I could just ask you to confirm your room number, that's all we'll need."

"I'm in 1236."

"Perfect—1236 corresponds with our records. And that completes the survey. We appreciate your patience, Ms. Hudson, and we hope you enjoy your stay. If we can be of any further service, please don't hesitate to get in touch."

Now all I needed was a way to get into her room.

I did a second tour of the lobby, this time looking for access to the back side of the hotel. I was interested in

the freight elevators, service stairs, any unmarked door,
or any door labeled Staff. I found one that said Employ-
ees Only. I pushed my way in and descended a short
flight of concrete stairs to a door marked No Admit-
tance. They must not have been serious because the
door was unlocked and I walked right in.

Every hotel has its public face: clean, carpeted, upholstered, glossy, paneled, and polished. The actual run
ning of a hotel is done on much less glamorous terms.
The corridor I stepped into had plain concrete walls and
a floor of brown vinyl tile. The air here was much
warmer and smelled like machinery, cooked food, and
old mops. The ceilings were high and lined with pipes,
thick cables, and heating ducts. I could hear the clatter
of dishes, but the acoustics made it difficult to determine the source.

I checked in both directions. To my left, wide metal
doors had been rolled up and I could see the loading
zone. Big trucks were backed up against the loading
docks and security cameras were mounted in the corners, mechanical eyes observing anyone who passed
within range. I didn't want my presence noted, so I
turned around and walked the other way.

I moved on down the corridor and turned a corner
into the first of several kitchens that opened off one another like a maze. Six ice machines were lined up along
the wall in front of me. I counted twenty rolling metal
food carts with racks for trays. The floors were freshly
washed, glistening with water and smelling of disinfec-
tant. I walked with care, passing big stainless-steel
mixing bowls, soup vats, and industrial dishwashers billowing steam. Occasionally, a food service worker, in a
white apron and a hairnet, would glance up at me with
interest, but no one seemed to question my presence
down there. A black woman was chopping green

peppers. A white man was encasing one of the rolling carts with plastic sheeting to protect the food. There were big room-size ovens and stainless-steel refrigerators larger than the morgue at St. Terry's Hospital. More workers in white aprons, hairnets, and plastic gloves were washing salad greens, arranging them on plates that had been laid out on the stainless-steel counter.

I stuck my head into a big storage room the size of a National Guard armory, where there were cartons of ketchup bottles; cases of mustard, olives, pickles; shelves filled with packaged bread; racks of croissants, homemade tarts, cheesecakes, pies, rolls. Plastic bins were filled with fresh produce. The air was saturated with strong smells: cut onions, simmering tomato sauce, cabbage, celery, citrus, yeast; layer upon layer of cooking and cleaning odors. There was something unpleasant about the suffusion of scents, and I was keenly aware of my olfactory nerves conducting a confused array of data to ancient parts of my brain. It was a relief to come out on the far side of the complex. The temperature in the air dropped, and the scents were suddenly as clean as a forest's. I found the main corridor and took a right.

Ahead of me, a regular choo-choo train of linen carts was lined up against the wall. The canvas sides were yellow and bulged with the mountains of soiled sheets and towels. I set off, walking with great purpose, glancing into every room I passed. I paused in the door to the hotel laundry: a vast room filled with wall-mounted washing machines, most of which were much taller than I. A moving track was suspended from the ceiling and enormous mesh bags of linens swung around the curve on a series of hooks. Somewhere I could hear massive dryers at work. The air was dense with the smell of damp cotton and detergent. Two women in uniform were working in tandem with a machine whose function seemed to be the pressing and folding of hotel sheets. The women's motions were repetitious, taking sheets out as the machine finished its two-fold process. Each packet was refolded and stacked to one side, with no margin for error as the machine pushed the next newly pressed sheet into range.

I continued down the corridor, slowing my pace. This time I passed a little half door with a narrow shelf that formed a small counter. The sign above the door said Employee Linens. Well, well, well. I paused, looking in on what must have been the laundry facility for employee uniforms. As in a dry cleaning establishment, several hundred matching cotton uniforms had been cleaned and pressed and hung on a mechanical conveyor awaiting pickup by the staff. I leaned across the Dutch door, peering through a thick forest of cleaners' bags. There didn't appear to be anyone in attendance.

"Hello?"

No answer.

I turned the knob and opened the half door, easing in. I sorted through uniforms in rapid succession. Each uniform seemed to consist of a short red cotton skirt with a red tunic worn over it. Impossible to guess what sizes they were. A paper pinned to each hanger gave the first name of the wearer: Lucy, Guadalupe, Historia, Juanita, Lateesha, Mary, Gloria, Nettie. On and on the names went. I selected three at random and eased out again, closing the door behind me.

"Can I help you?"

I jumped, nearly bumping into the hefty white woman in a red uniform who was standing right behind me in the corridor. My mind went completely blank.

The woman's nostrils flared like she could smell deception. "What are you doing with those uniforms?" I could practically see up her nose, and it was not a pretty picture. Her name tag read Mrs. Spitz, Linen Service Supervisor.

"Ah. Good question, Mrs. Spitz. I was just looking for you. I'm Jillian Brace's assistant up in Sales and Marketing." With my free hand, I reached in my blazer pocket and pulled out a business card, which I flashed at her.

She snatched the card and studied it, squinting. "This says Burnham J. Pauley. What's going on here?" She had a big face, and every feature on it seemed to quiver with suspicion.

"Well," I said. "Gosh. I'm glad you asked. Because. As a matter of fact, Corporate is considering new uniforms. For security reasons. And Mr. Pauley told Ms. Brace to show him a sample of what we had on hand."

"That's the most ridiculous thing I ever heard," she snapped. "We just got those uniforms, as *Corporate* well knows. Besides, that's not proper procedure, and I'm sick of it. I told Mr. Tompkins at our last department meeting, this is *my* operation and I mean to keep it that way. You wait right here. I'm going to call him this minute. I will not have anyone from Corporate interfering in my business." Even her breath smelled indignant. Her eyes swung back to mine. "What's your name?"

"Vikki Biggs."

"Where's your name tag?"

"Upstairs."

She pointed a finger at me. "Don't you move. I intend to get to the bottom of this. Corporate has a nerve sending anyone down here like this. What's Miss Brace's extension?"

"It's 202," I said automatically. Now you see? This is the beauty of keeping up those skills. In a crisis situation, I had only to open my mouth and a fib flopped out. An unpracticed liar can't always rise to the occasion like I can.

She let herself in through the Dutch door, moving with surprising speed. The door snapped shut behind her. I folded the hangers across my left arm and walked on with apparent purpose, heart thumping. I rounded the corner and broke into a trot. I found the stairwell and headed up the stairs two at a time. I didn't dare risk the hotel elevators. I pictured Mrs. Spitz notifying Security, guards swarming the exits in search of me. By the third floor I was winded, but I kept right on climbing. I passed the sixth floor, gasping, thighs burning, knees feeling like my kneecaps were about to pop off. I finally staggered through the door at the landing marked "8" and found myself back on familiar turf, one bend of the corridor away from my room.

I let myself into 815. I flung the contraband uniforms across the back of a chair and collapsed on the bed, which was now neatly made. I had to laugh while I lay there, trying to catch my breath. Mrs. Spitz better have her hormone levels checked or her medication adjusted. She was going to get herself fired if she continued to mouth off at Corporate. I half expected someone to come pounding at my door with demands and accusations, an itemized accounting of the lies I'd told.

I got up and crossed to the door, where I slipped on the security chain. I spent the next few minutes trying on stolen uniforms. The first was the best fit. I looked at myself in the full-length mirror. The skirt was big in the waist, but it didn't seem to matter much with the tunic pulled over it. Pinned to each tunic was a ruffle of white, which formed a sort of collar once it was buttoned into place. The tunic itself had a little puff to the sleeve. Color wasn't bad. Worn with bare legs and my running shoes, I looked like I could clean a bathroom in nothing flat. I changed back into my jeans and hung my uniform in the closet. I wasn't sure what to do with the two remaining uniforms, so I folded them together and stuck them in the desk drawer. Before I left the hotel, I'd find a place to put them.

I ate a room service lunch, fearful of venturing out into the hotel so soon. At two o'clock, I went out into the corridor on a prospecting expedition, checking the general layout of the floor. I located the fire extinguisher, two fire exits, and the ice machine. A house phone sat on a console table across from the elevators. In the utility alcove at the end of the hall, I could see two linen carts angled into the space. I walked down there and spent a few minutes acquainting myself with available equipment. Extra irons and ironing boards, two vacuum cleaners. Beyond the alcove was a big linen closet, lined with shelves stacked nearly to the ceiling with clean sheets and towels. I could see cases of toilet paper and short towers of plastic pallets containing the miniature toiletries. Nice. I was liking this. An armload of towels usually provides good cover for getting into a room. I found a plastic door placard reading Maid in Room, which I snagged while I was at it.

Having exhausted the possibilities, I went down to the gift shop and bought a book to read. I was forced to choose among fifteen torrid romance titles, which was all the hotel stocked. I paid for a handful of miniature Peppermint Patties, pausing in the lobby only long enough to ring Laura's room. When she answered, I murmured, "Ooops, sorry," and hung up. Sounded like I'd caught her in the middle of a nap. I whiled away the afternoon, reading and napping. In a spectacular failure of imagination, I ordered a room service dinner that was a duplicate of my room service lunch: cheeseburger, fries, and diet Pepsi.

Shortly after seven o'clock, I stripped out of my jeans and donned my sassy red uniform. I wasn't crazy about the bare legs with my running shoes, but what could I do? I stocked my pockets with peppermints and took the two remaining contraband uniforms from the drawer where I'd hidden them. I tucked my room key in my pocket and headed for the fire stairs. Going up, I paused on the tenth floor long enough to hang the two stolen uniforms in the utility alcove. I didn't want the other maids inconvenienced by the theft.

The twelfth floor was laid out identically to the eighth, except that the utility room didn't seem as well stocked. I grabbed a dust rag and a vacuum cleaner, found an electrical outlet in the corridor, and began to vacuum my way toward Laura Huckaby's room. The carpet was an extravagant meadow of geometric shapes, triangles overlapping in a bright path of high-low gold and green. Vacuuming is always restful: slow, repetitive motion accompanied by a low groaning noise and that satisfying snap when something really good gets sucked up. Never had the wall-to-wall carpet been so thoroughly cleaned. I was working up a sweat, but the effort did permit me to loiter at will.

At 7:36 I heard the elevator *ping* and a room service waitcreature appeared with a dinner tray. He headed toward 1236; the tray balanced comfortably at shoulder height, he knocked on her door. I vacuumed in that direction, managing to get a glimpse of her when she let him in. She was barefoot and looking bulky in a hotel robe with a nightie hanging down below. The loungewear suggested she was in for the night, which was good from my perspective. The waiter emerged moments later. He passed me without remark and disappeared into the elevator without acknowledging my existence. On the off chance that Laura would have a visitor or head out to meet someone, I stuck to my surveillance.

When I tired of vacuuming, I took out my dust rag and got down on my hands and knees, dusting baseboards that apparently hadn't been touched for years. Sometimes it's really tough to picture the boy detectives doing this. Periodically, I tilted my head against Laura Huckaby's door without hearing a thing. Maybe if I barked and scratched, she'd let me in. Other hotel guests came and went at intervals, but no one paid me the slightest attention.

Here's what I've learned about being a maid: People seldom look you in the eye. Occasionally someone's gaze might accidentally glance off your face, but based on the interaction, no one could identify you later in a lineup. Good news for me, although even in Texas I don't think impersonating a maid would be classified as a crime.

At 8:15 I returned the vacuum cleaner to the linen room and armed myself with a supply of fresh towels. I returned to 1236 and knocked, calling out "Housekeeping" in clear, bell-like tones. Worked like a charm. Moments later, Laura Huckaby opened the door a crack with the chain in place. "Yes?"

Without eye makeup, her hazel eyes seemed soft and pale. Her complexion was made ruddy by the faint rash of freckles previously masked by foundation. She also had a dimple in her chin I hadn't noticed earlier.

I directed my comment to the doorknob so I wouldn't seem uppity. "I'm here to turn the bed down."

"This hotel offers turn-down service?" She sounded appropriately startled, as if the idea were ludicrous.

"Yes, ma'am."

She paused and then shrugged. "Just a minute," she

said. She closed the door. There was a delay of some minutes and then she released the chain and stepped aside to let me enter.

I was interested to realize how much I could take in through my peripheral vision. How vain could she be? I could have sworn she'd paused to put on her makeup again. The tangled auburn hair had been freshly washed and still clung to her head. Warm, damp, shampoo-scented air wafted from the bathroom. I set the clean towels on the counter near the sink and then moved into the bedroom area and closed the drapes. The television set was turned on with the sound turned down. She'd tossed her room key on the desk. Immediately, I began to scheme to get my hands on it. I could see from the disarray that she'd been lying on the bed with the telephone pulled close. Maybe she'd received the call she'd been waiting for. There was no sign of the duffel bag as far as I could see.

She took a seat at the desk with her magazine. She crossed her legs, and I caught just a flash of bare skin. Her right ankle and shin and all the way up to her knee was a sooty mass of old bruises, turning green at the edge. Had her fifty some companion been beating the shit out of her? It would certainly explain her icy treatment of him and her obsession with her appearance. Her dinner tray still sat on the desk in front of her, a crumpled white cloth napkin tossed carelessly across the dirty plates. Whatever she'd ordered, she hadn't eaten much. Though it was ostensibly my job, she seemed embarrassed to have me in the room, which actually worked to my advantage. She ignored me for the most part, though she would flick me an occasional self-conscious look. I was beginning to enjoy my invisibility. I could observe her at close range without any pesky personal exchanges. Was that the shadow of a bruise on the right side of her jaw, or was I imagining things? What kind of guy was she with? From all reports, he'd pounded Ray Rawson to a pulp, so he might have pounded her, too.

My uniform made an efficient little rustling sound as I folded the spread in half and then in half again. I made a hefty jelly roll of it and tucked it in one corner. I turned the sheet down halfway, plumped the pillows, and left one of the paper-wrapped Peppermint Patties on the bed table.

I returned to the vanity area and tidied up the sink, turning water off and on, though I didn't do much else. I checked her makeup supply: a concealer stick, foundation, powder, blush. In a small round container, she had a product called DermaSeal, "a waterproof cosmetic to hide facial imperfections." I peered around the corner at her briefly, only to find her peering at me. Behind me was the closet, which I longed to search. I moved into the bathroom and picked up a damp towel she'd draped across the edge of the tub. I straightened the shower curtain and flushed the toilet as if I'd just given it a scrub. I moved back into the vanity area and opened the closed door. Bingo. The duffel.

I heard her call out, "What are you doing?" She sounded annoyed, and I thought I might have overstepped my bounds.

"You need more hangers, miss?"

"What? No. I have plenty."

Just being helpful. She didn't have to sound so irritated.

I closed the closet door and retrieved the remaining clean towels. She'd crossed the room and was watching me closely as I finished my chores. I transferred my gaze to a point to the left of her. "What about the tray? I can take it if you're finished."

She flicked a look at the desk. "Please."

I set the towels aside and crossed to the desk, where I picked up the room key and tucked it on the tray, concealing it with the crumpled napkin. I went over to the door and held it open with my hip while I set the tray on the floor in the corridor. I retrieved my towel supply.

She was standing near the door with something that she held in my direction. At first, I thought she was passing me a note. Then I realized she was giving me a tip. I murmured a "Thank you" and slipped the bill in my tunic pocket without looking at the denomination. Peeking might have implied a grasping nature on my part. "You have a pleasant evening," I said.

"Thanks."

As soon as I was out the door, I pulled out the bill and checked the denomination. Oh, wow. She'd given me a five. Not bad for a simple ten-minute tidy-up. Maybe I could knock on the door across the hall. If I covered the floor, I could just about afford my room tonight. I plucked her key from the room service tray and left the tray where it was. It looked tacky sitting there, and I didn't like the effect on my newly cleaned hall, but in current job parlance, removing it was not my department.

# 9

BY THE TIME I got back to my room, it was 8:45. I felt grubby and half dead from the combination of manual labor, stress, greasy room-service food, and jet lag. I peeled off my uniform and hopped in the shower, letting the hot water pound down my frame like a waterfall. I dried myself off and then pulled on one of the two unisex robes provided by the hotel. My spare underpants were now dry, though a bit stiff, hanging across the towel rack like the pelt of some rare beast. Coming out of the bathroom into the dressing area, I noticed the message light on my telephone was blinking. The phone must have rung while I was in the shower—inevitably Henry, since he was the only one who knew my whereabouts. Unless the hotel management was on to me. Somewhat uneasily, I rang the hotel operator.

"This is Ms. Millhone. My message light is on."

He put me on hold and then came back on the line. "You have one message. A Mr. Pitts called at eight fifty-one. Urgent. Please call back."

"Thanks." I dialed Henry's number. Before I even heard the phone ring on his end, he picked up the receiver. I said, "That was quick. You must have been sitting right on top of the phone. What's going on?"

"I'm so glad you called. I didn't know what to do. Have you heard from Ray Rawson?"

"Why would I hear from him? I thought he was gone."

"Well, he was, but he's back and I'm afraid there's been a complication of sorts. Nell and I went shopping this morning, shortly after you rang. William and Lewis had gone over to Rosie's to help with the lunch prep, and that left Charlie here by himself. Are you there?"

"Yeah, I'm here," I said. "I can't think where this is going, but I'm listening."

"Ray Rawson showed up at Chester's and Bucky told him what was going on."

"As in what? That I'd seen the guy who beat him up?"

"I'm not sure what he was told except that you'd been hired. Bucky knew you'd left town, but he didn't know where you were. Ray must have come right over here, and since I was out, he gave Charlie some long song and dance about the danger you were in."

"Danger? That's interesting. What kind?"

"Charlie never really got that part straight. Something to do with a key, is what he said."

"Ah. Probably the one Johnny had in his safe. I was going to show it to a friend of mine who's acquainted with locks. Unfortunately, I suspect he's been incarcerated for his expertise."

"Where is it now? Bucky told Ray you had it with you last he knew," he said.

"I do. It's tucked in the bottom of my handbag," I said. "You sound worried."

"Well, yes, but it's not about that." I could hear the anxiety underlying Henry's tone. "I hate to have to say this, but Charlie told Ray your current whereabouts because Ray convinced him you needed help."

"How did Charlie know where I was?"

Henry sighed, burdened by the necessity for a full confession. "I wrote the name and number of the hotel on a pad near the phone. You know Charlie. He can barely hear under the best of circumstances. Somehow he got it in his head that Ray was a good friend and you wouldn't care if he gave out the information. Especially since you were in trouble."

"Oh, boy. The room number, too?"

"I'm afraid so," Henry said. He sounded so guilty and miserable, I couldn't protest, though I didn't like the idea of Rawson knowing where I was. Henry went on. "I can't believe the man would actually fly all the way to Dallas, but he'll probably call, and I didn't want you to be surprised or upset. I'm uneasy about this, Kinsey, but there's nothing I can do."

"Don't worry about it, Henry. I appreciate the warning."

"I could just wring Charlie's neck."

"I'm sure he was trying to be helpful," I said. "Anyway, there's probably no harm done. I don't consider Ray Rawson any kind of threat."

"I hope not. I feel terrible about leaving the information out in plain sight."

"Don't be silly. You had no reason to think anybody'd ask, and you couldn't have known Rawson was going to show up like that."

"Well, I know," he said, "but I could have said something to the sibs. I gave Charlie a fussing at, but it's myself I blame. It truly never occurred to me that he'd do such a thing."

"Hey, what's done is done. It's not your fault."

"You're sweet to say so. All I could think to do was call as soon as possible. I think you should check out or at least change rooms. I don't like the idea of his showing up on your doorstep. There's something 'off' about the whole business."

"I'd have to agree, but I'm not sure what to do. At the moment, I'm trying to keep a low profile around here," I said.

I could tell I'd put Henry on red alert. "Why is that?" he asked.

"I don't really want to go into it. Let's just say that right now I don't think it's a smart move."

"I don't want you taking any chances. You were foolish getting on that plane in the first place. It's none of your business, and the longer it goes on, the bigger mess it is."

I smiled. "Chester hired me. This is work. Besides, it's fun. I get to skulk around corridors and spy on folk."

"Don't be gone too long. We've got the wedding coming up."

"I'm not going to forget that. I'll be there. I promise."

"Call me if there's anything I can do to help."

The minute he hung up, I crossed to the door and threw on the security chain. I thought about hanging the "Do Not Disturb" on the outside knob, but that would only announce to one and all that I was actually in the room. I began to pace, giving the situation my serious consideration. I felt curiously vulnerable now that Rawson knew where I was, though why that should have made a difference I wasn't really sure. From what Chester'd said, he was in pretty bad shape, which would have made travel unpleasant to say the least. It

would also cost him a bundle with no guarantee that I
was still in Dallas. Of course, if he was wanted for
questioning by the Santa Teresa cops, getting out of
town wouldn't be a bad move on his part. I didn't really
believe I was in any peril, but I wasn't unmindful of the
possibility. Whatever Rawson's relationship to current
events, it was clear he hadn't given me the relevant
facts. I would feel a lot safer if I were in another room.

On the other hand, I didn't like the idea of asking to
change. The hotel management wasn't dumb. It
wouldn't have taken Mrs. Spitz more than a minute to
figure out that I was up to no good. Hotels don't take
lightly to pranksters and thieves. She'd seen me at close
range, and at this point, the security guards probably
had a fairly accurate description of me. Notice would
have gone out to all the relevant staff—the hotel equivalent of an APB. If Vikki Biggs, the night clerk, remembered my name, I'd have someone knocking at my
door very soon. Conversely, if the management *hadn't*
figured it out, I'd be an idiot to go down there and call
attention to myself. So forget the room change.

As for vacating the premises, I'd already laid out
close to a grand for plane fare and expenses. I couldn't
go back and confess to Chester I'd abandoned the pursuit because Ray Rawson *might* show up at my door unannounced. My best bet was staying right where I was,
especially now that I had access to Laura Huckaby's
room. I put my clothes on again. If someone came
banging at my door in the dead of night, I didn't like
the idea of being caught unprepared. I tucked the complimentary toiletries in my handbag and added my
toothpaste and my traveling toothbrush, ready to flee if
necessary.

I removed the key from my bag, wondering if there
might be a safer place to keep it. In the morning, I'd

stick it in an envelope and mail it back to Henry. Meanwhile, I surveyed the room and the various furnishings, considering possible hiding places. I was ambivalent about the prospects. If I were compelled to depart in haste, I didn't want to have to stop and retrieve the key. I took the complimentary mending kit from my handbag. I removed my blazer and studied the construction, finally using the scissors on my Swiss Army knife to pick open a small slit on the inside seam near the shoulder pad. I eased the key in along the padding and stitched the hole shut. I'd never make it past the metal detector at an airport security checkpoint, but I could always take the blazer off and send it through X-ray.

I slept in my clothes, shoes on, feet crossed, lying flat on my back with the spread thrown over me for warmth.

When the phone rang at 8:00 A.M., I felt like I'd been electrocuted. My heart leaped from fifty beats per minute to an astounding hundred and forty with no intervening activity except the shriek I emitted. I snatched up the receiver, pulse banging in my throat. "What."

"Oh, geez. I woke you. I feel bad. This is Ray."

I swung my feet over to the side of the bed and sat up, rubbing my face with one hand to wake myself. "So I gathered. Where are you?"

"Down in the lobby. I have to talk to you. Mind if I come up?"

"Yes, I mind," I said irritably. "What are you doing here?"

"Looking after you. I thought you should know what you're dealing with."

"I'll meet you in the coffee shop in fifteen minutes."

"I'd appreciate that."

I flung myself back on the bed and lay there for a

minute, trying to compose myself. Didn't help much.
My insides were churning with a low-level dread. I finally dragged myself into the dressing area, where I
brushed my teeth and washed my face. I sniffed at my
turtleneck, which was beginning to smell like something I'd been wearing for two days. I might have to
break down and buy something new. If I sent all my
clothes out to be cleaned and pressed, I'd be stuck in
my red uniform until six that night. Meanwhile, if Laura
Huckaby took off, I'd have to trail her across Texas
looking like a parlor maid. I rubbed some hotel lotion
on the relevant body parts, hoping the perfume would
mask the ripe scent of unwashed garments.

I tucked the two room keys in my pocket—mine and
the one I'd stolen from Laura Huckaby's desk—and
peered through the spy hole. At least Rawson wasn't
lurking in the corridor. I went down the fire stairs,
avoiding the elevator, and found myself emerging on
the far side of the lobby.

When I reached the hotel coffee shop, I paused in the
doorway. Rawson wasn't hard to spot. He was the only
guy in there with a swollen green-and-purple face. He
had a bandage across his nose, one black eye, a split lip,
assorted cuts, and three fingers on his right hand bound
together with tape. He drank his coffee with a spoon,
possibly to spare himself the pain from broken, cracked,
or missing teeth. His white T-shirt was so new, I could
still see the package creases. Either he was buying his
shirts a size too small or he was built better than I remembered. At least the short sleeves allowed me to admire his dragon tattoo.

I crossed the room and slid into the booth across
from him. "When'd you get here?"

There were two menus on the table, and he passed
me one. "Three-thirty in the morning. The plane was

delayed because of fog. I picked up a rental car at the airport. I tried calling your room as soon as I got in, but the operator wouldn't put me through, so I waited until eight." His eyes were bloodshot from the battering, which gave his otherwise mild features a demonic cast. I could see that his left earlobe had been stitched back into place.

"You're too considerate," I said. "You have a room?"

"Yeah, 1006." His smile flickered and faded. "Look, I know you got no particular reason to trust me, but it's time to deal straight."

"You might have done that two days ago before we got into this ... whatever it is."

The waitress appeared with a coffeepot in hand. She was the motherly sort, who looked as if she'd take in stray dogs and cats. Her frizzy gray hair was held in place by a hairnet, like a spiderweb across her head, and her gravelly voice suggested a lifelong affection for unfiltered cigarettes. She flicked a speculative look at Ray. "What happened to you?"

"I was in a wreck," he said briefly. "You got any aspirin, I'll leave you money in my will."

"Let me check in the back. I can probably come up with something." She turned to me. "How about some coffee? You look like you could use some."

Mutely I held up my coffee cup, and she filled it to the brim. She set the coffeepot aside and reached for her order pad. "You ready to order or you want more time?"

"This is fine," I said, indicating that the cup of coffee would suffice.

Ray spoke up. "Have some breakfast. My treat. It's the least I can do."

I looked back at the waitress. "In that case, make it

coffee, orange juice, bacon, link sausage, three scrambled eggs, and some rye toast."

He held up two fingers. "Same here."

Once she'd departed, he leaned forward on his elbows. He looked like a light-heavyweight boxer the day after the championship went back to the other guy. "I don't blame you for feeling sour, but honest . . . after the break-in at Johnny's, I didn't think he'd come back. I figured that was the end of it, so who was the wiser?"

" 'He' who?"

"I'm getting to that," he said. "Oh, before I forget. You know the key Bucky took from Johnny's safe?"

"Yes," I said cautiously.

"You still have it?"

I hesitated for a flicker of a second, and then I lied on instinct. Why confide in him? So far he hadn't told me anything. "I don't have it with me, but I know where it is. Why?"

"I've been thinking about it. I mean, it has to be important. Why else would Johnny keep it in his safe?"

"I thought you knew. Didn't you tell Charlie I was in danger because of it?"

"Danger? Not me. I never said that. I wonder where he got that idea?"

"I talked to Henry last night. He says that's how you persuaded Charlie to tell you where I was. You said I was in danger and that's why Charlie gave you the information."

Ray shook his head, baffled. "He must have misunderstood," he said. "Sure, I was looking for you, but I never said anything about danger. That's odd. Old guy can't hear. He might have got it mixed up."

"Never mind. Just skip that. Let's talk about something else."

He glanced over toward the entrance to the restaurant, where a motley group of adolescent kids were beginning to collect. It must have been the same kids I'd seen running out on the road the day before. They must have been in town for some kind of track-and-field event. The noise level increased, and Ray's voice went up to compete with the din. "You know, you really surprised me in my hotel room the other day."

"How so?"

"You were right about Johnny. He was never in the service. He was in jail like you said."

I love being right. It always cheers me up. "What about the story about how you knew each other? Was any of that true?"

"In the main," he said. He paused and smiled, revealing a gap where a first molar should have been. He put a hand against his cheek where the bruising was deep blue with an aura of darker purple. "Don't look now, but we're surrounded."

The track team seemed to spread out and around us like a liquid, settling into booths on all sides of us. The lone waitress was passing out menus like programs for some sporting competition.

"Quit stalling," I said.

"Sorry. We did meet in Louisville, but it wasn't at the Jeffersonville Boat Works. It wasn't 1942, neither. It was earlier. Maybe '39 or '40. We were in the drunk tank together and struck up a friendship. I was nineteen at the time, and I'd been in jail a couple times. We hung out together some, you know, just messing around. Neither of us went in the army. We were both 4-F. I forget Johnny's disability. Something to do with a ruptured disk. I had two busted eardrums and a bum knee. Bad weather, that sucker's still giving me fits. Anyway, we had to do *something*—we were bored out of our gourds—so we started burglarizing joints, breaking into warehouses, stores, you know, things like that. I guess we pulled one job too many and got caught in the act. I ended up doing county time, but he got sent to state reformatory down in Lexington. He did twenty-two months of a five-year bid and moved his family out to California once he got sprung. After that, he was clean as far as I ever heard."

"What about you?"

He dropped his gaze. "Yeah, well, you know, after Johnny left, I fell into bad company. I thought I was smart, but I was just a punk like everyone else. A guy steered me wrong on another job we pulled. Cops picked us up and I got sent to the Federal Correctional Institution up in Ashland, Kentucky, where I spent another fifteen months. I was out for a year and then in again. I never had the dough for a fancy-pants attorney, so I had to take pot luck. One thing and another, I've been inside ever since."

"You've been in prison for over forty years?"

"Off and on. You think there aren't guys who've been in prison that long? I could've been out a lot sooner, but my temper got the better of me until I finally figured out how to behave," he said. "I suffered from what the docs call a 'lack of impulse control.' I learned that in prison. How to talk that way. Back then, if I thought of it, I did it. I never killed nobody," he added in haste.

"This is a big relief," I said.

"Well, later in prison, but that was self-defense."

I nodded. "Ah."

Rawson went right on. "Anyway, in the late forties, I started writing to this woman named Marla I met through a pen pal ad. I managed to escape once and I was out long enough for us to get married. She got pregnant and we had us a little girl I haven't seen in years. A lot of women fall in love with inmates. You'd be surprised."

"Nothing people do surprises me," I said.

"Another time, when I was out, I ended up breaking parole. Sometimes I think Johnny felt responsible. Like if it hadn't been for him, I might never have gotten in so tight with the criminal element. Wasn't true, but I think that's what he believed."

"You're saying Johnny kept in touch all these years because of guilt?"

"Mostly that," he said. "And maybe because I was the only one who knew he'd been in jail besides his wife. With everybody else, he was always pretending to be something he wasn't. All the tales about Burma and Claire Chennault. He got those from books. His kids thought he was a hero, but he knew he wasn't. With me, he could be himself. Meantime, I got into grand theft auto and armed robbery, which is how I finally qualified for accommodations in the penitentiary. I did time in Lewisburg and a bid in Leavenworth, but I was mostly confined in Atlanta. That's a real test of your survival skills. Atlanta's where they're housing all the Cuban criminals Castro's sending over to keep us company."

"What happened to Marla? Are you still married to her?"

"Nah. She finally divorced me because I couldn't straighten up and fly right, but that was my fault, not hers. She's a good woman."

"It must be unsettling to have freedom after forty years."

Rawson shrugged, looking off across the room. "They did what they could to prepare me for the outside. When I turned sixty, the BOP—Bureau of Prisons—started weaning me off hard time. My security level dropped to the point where I was eligible to move out of the joint. I got sent back to FCI Ashland, and what a revelation *that* was. It'd been thirty-five years since I'd seen the place. I'm looking at punks the same age as I was when I first got sent up. All of the sudden, I'm 'getting it,' you know? Like I can see the big picture. I did a complete turnaround in the space of a year, picked up my GED, and started taking college classes. I started taking care of myself, quit smoking, started lifting weights, and like that. Got myself buffed up. I went before the parole board this time and got early release."

Ray paused to look around at the kids nearby. They were crowded into booths and tables, chairs pulled up. Menus were being passed hand to hand above their heads while the rustle of restless laughter washed across them in waves. It was a sound I liked, energetic, innocent. Ray shook his head. "Kids are up on my floor, about two doors down. My God, the shrieking and pounding up and down the halls. It goes on 'til all hours."

"Are you still in touch with Marla?"

"Now and then. She remarried. Last I heard, she's still in Louisville somewhere. I'd like to go back and see her as soon as I'm done with this. I want to see my daughter, too, and make it up to her. I know I haven't been a good father—I was too busy screwing up—but I'd like to try. I want to see my mother, too."

"Your *mother*'s still alive?" I asked, incredulous.

"Sure. She's eighty-five, but she's as tough as they come."

"Not that it's any of my business, but how old are you?"

"Sixty-five. Old enough to retire if I ever had a real job."

"So you were released fairly recently," I said.

"About three weeks ago. I went from Ashland to six months in a halfway house. Soon as I was sprung, I headed for the coast. I wrote to Johnny in April and gave him my release date. He said to come ahead, he'd help me out. So that's what I did. The rest is just like I told you before. I didn't know he was dead until I knocked on Bucky's door."

"What kind of help was Johnny talking about?"

Rawson shrugged. "Place to stay. A stake. He had some ideas about a little business we could run. I worked in the joint—every able-bodied inmate works— but I was only earning forty cents an hour, out of which I had to pay for my own candy bars, soda pop, and deodorant, stuff like that, so it's not like I had any kind of savings built up."

"How'd you pay for travel getting out here?"

"My mother lent me the money. I said I'd pay her back."

"Who's the guy who broke into Johnny's place?"

"His name is Gilbert Hays, a former celly of mine. He's a guy I did time with a couple of years ago. I shot off my big mouth, trying to impress the crud. Don't ask why. He's such a cocky piece of excrement, I'm still kicking myself." His grimace opened up the split in his lower lip. A line of blood welled out. He pressed a paper napkin to his mouth.

"Shot your mouth off about what?"

"Look, we're in the joint. What do any of us have to do except BS each other? He was always bragging about something, so I told him about Johnny. The guy was a miser, always squirreling cash away. Johnny didn't come right out and say so, but he used to hint he had big bucks hidden on the property."

"You were going to rip him off?"

"Not me. Hey, come on. I wouldn't do that to him. We were just telling tall tales. Later, Hays and me had a falling-out. He probably figured he could pick up a wad of cash and I'd never know the difference."

"You told him where Johnny *lived*?"

"California is all I said. He must've followed me across country, the slimy son of a bitch."

"How'd he know you'd been released?"

"Now that, I don't know. He might have talked to my PO. I seem to recall I might've threatened him once upon a time. He probably told 'em he was worried I'd come after him. Which I still might."

"How did you figure out it was him?"

"I didn't at first. Minute I heard about the break-in, I knew something was off, but I didn't think about Hays. Then I realized what happened and, like, it had to be him. Simple process of elimination because I never breathed a word about Johnny to anyone else." Ray lifted the napkin away from his bleeding lip. "How's that?"

"Well, it isn't *gushing*," I said. "Can we back up a bit? Once you heard Johnny was dead, what made you so sure he still had money stashed somewhere?"

"I wasn't *sure*, but it just made sense. Guy drops dead of a heart attack, he doesn't have time to do anything. Talking to Bucky, I realized the kid didn't have a dime, so if there's money, it's probably still hidden somewhere on the premises. I figure if I rent his place, I can look around at my leisure."

"Meanwhile, you didn't say a word to Bucky about this."

"About the money? No way. You know why? Suppose I'm wrong? Why get their hopes up if there's nothing? If I do find some money, I can ask for a cut."

"Oh, right. This is money they don't know anything about and you're telling me you'd turn it over to them?"

He smiled sheepishly. "I might skim off a small percentage, but what harm would that do? They're still gonna come up with more than they ever had reason to expect."

"And in the meantime, this former cellmate's followed you to Johnny's door."

"That's my guess."

"How'd he know about the kickplate?"

Ray held up his battered hand. "Because I told him. Otherwise, he'd have broken every bone in my hand. He had me at a disadvantage because I wasn't expecting him. Next time I'll know, and one of us is going to end up dead."

"How did you know about the kickplate?"

Ray tapped himself on the temple. "I know how Johnny's mind worked. That day I came up there and you were looking through his books? I was doing a little survey. He'd used a kickplate before—this was way back when—so I was thinking I'd try that first." He stirred in his seat. "You don't believe me. I can tell by the look on your face."

I smiled slightly. "You're a very slick man. You lie about as well as I do, only you've had more practice."

He started to say something, but the waitress had reappeared with two steaming plates on a tray. She looked harried, to say the least. She set down juice, two side orders of buttered toast, and a variety of jams. She took a couple of small paper packets from the pocket of her uniform and put them by his plate. "I got you these," she said.

Ray picked up a packet. "What's Midol?"

"For cramps, but it'll cure anything that ails you. Just don't take too many. You might develop PMS."

"PMS?" he said blankly.

Neither of us responded. Let him figure it out. She refilled our coffee cups and moved on to another table, taking out her order pad. Ray opened a paper packet and tossed back two tablets with his orange juice. We spent a short, intense spell shoveling food down our throats.

Rawson finally dabbed a paper napkin gingerly across his lips. "You want my suggestion, I'd say let's quit hassling what's past and figure out what comes next."

"Ah. Now we're partners. The buddy system," I said.

"Sure, why not? Gilbert Hays took Johnny's money, and I want it back. This is not just for me. I'm talking about Bucky and Chester. Isn't that why they hired you? To return what Hays stole?"

"I suppose," I said.

He shrugged laconically. "So how about it, then? What's the plan?"

"How come it's up to me? You think of one," I said.

"You're the one getting paid. I'm just here to assist."

I studied him, debating the garbled tale he'd just told. I didn't really believe he was telling me the truth, but I didn't know him well enough to know what kinds of lies he told. "Actually, there is one possibility, and I could use some help," I said.

"Good. What's the deal?"

I took out Laura's room key and placed it on the table. "I have the key to Laura Huckaby's room."

His face went completely blank, and then his brow was furrowed by a squint. He leaned forward, staring. He said, "What?"

"The woman with the duffel. She's using the name Hudson, but that's the key to her room."

# 10

I HAULED ONE of the linen carts out of the utility alcove on Laura Huckaby's floor. I had changed into my red uniform again, ready to go to work. I pulled a stack of clean sheets and towels from the shelf in the linen room and put them on my cart, adding boxes of tissues, toilet paper, toiletries, and the laminated Maid in Room sign I'd snitched before. I checked the clipboard attached to the cart on one end. A ballpoint pen was affixed to the clipboard with a tatty piece of string. None of the rooms had been done as far as I could see. Bernadette and Eileen were listed on the worksheet, but none of their duties had been checked off as yet. I wasn't sure what would happen if one of them showed up in the midst of my faux labors. Surely nobody would object to my pitching in . . . unless these women got territorial about toilet bowls. I pushed the linen cart ahead of me down the carpeted corridor. The wheels kept getting hung up in the high-low pile, and I struggled to keep the cart from lumbering into walls.

The plan Ray Rawson and I had worked out was this:

Rawson would call Laura's room from the house phone on the far side of the lobby within view of the front desk. He'd claim to be the desk clerk, in receipt of a package that required her signature. He'd tell her he was just now going on his break, but the package would be waiting on the manager's desk. If she could come down as soon as possible, one of the other clerks would be happy to get it for her. If she asked to have it sent up, he'd inform her, regretfully, this was against hotel policy. Recently a package had been misdelivered, and the manager was now insisting the guests appear in person.

While this was going on, I was to loiter in the corridor near her room, making careful note of the time she left. As soon as the "down" elevator doors closed behind her, I would let myself into 1236 with her key. Laura would reach the lobby, where the desk clerk would search in vain for the nonexistent package. Confusion, upset, and apologies forthcoming. Everyone would profess ignorance of both package and policy. Sorry for the inconvenience. As soon as the package surfaced, it would be sent up.

Once she left the desk, on her way upstairs again, Rawson would call the room and let the phone ring once. That would be my cue to get out if I was still there. Since I knew exactly where the duffel was located, it shouldn't take more than ten seconds to snag the contents. By the time Laura emerged from the elevator on twelve, I'd be heading down the fire stairs to the eighth floor again. There I'd change into my street clothes and grab my shoulder bag. I would meet Rawson in the lobby, and before Laura even realized that she'd been ripped off, we'd be on our way to the airport, where we'd get the next flight out. I wasn't at

all bothered by the ethics of stealing money from
thieves. It was the notion of getting caught made my
heart go pitty-pat.

I positioned my cart two rooms away from Laura's
door and checked my watch. Rawson was waiting to
make his call at 10:00, allowing me time to get myself
set up. It was 9:58. I occupied myself with a load of
towels, which I folded and refolded, wanting to be
busily engaged when Laura Huckaby came out. The
corridor was dead quiet, and the acoustics were such
that I could hear the telephone begin to ring when he
called her room. The phone was picked up after two
rings and a tidy silence ensued. I could feel my stomach
churning with anticipation. Mentally I rehearsed, picturing her trip down the hall, into the elevator, over to the
desk. Chat with the clerk, the search for the package,
frustration and assurances, and back she'd come. I'd
have at least a five-minute window of opportunity, more
than ample time for the task I'd assigned myself.

I checked my watch again: 10:08. What was taking
her so long? I thought she'd be wildly curious about the
arrival of a package, especially one that required her
signature. Whatever the delay, it was 10:17 before she
emerged. I kept my face averted, avoiding her gaze as
I picked up my clipboard and made random marks. She
closed the door behind her and then caught sight of me.
"Oh, hi. Remember me?"

I looked up at her. "Yes, ma'am. How are you?" I
said. I put the clipboard down and picked up a towel,
which I folded in half.

"Did you come across my key when you serviced the
room last night?" She wore the usual heavy makeup,
and her hair was pulled back in a ponytail, tied with a
scarf of bright green chiffon.

"No, ma'am, but if it's missing, you can get a duplicate at the front desk." I folded another towel and put it on the stack.

"I guess I'll do that," she said. "Thanks. Have a good day."

"You, too." I studied Laura's backside as she moved toward the elevators. She wore a white cotton turtleneck under a dark green corduroy jumper that may or may not have been designed for maternity wear. The hemline was longer in the back than it was in the front. She tugged at the garment, which was bunching up around the middle. She wore her red high-top tennis shoes, and her tights today were dark green. If my suspicions were correct and she was the victim of spousal abuse, it might explain her tendency to keep herself covered up. I slid my hand into my pocket, where her five-dollar tip was still neatly folded from the night before. That bill was the only flicker of recognition I'd netted in my guise as a char. I wished she hadn't seemed so friendly. I suddenly felt like a dog for what I was about to do.

She rounded the corner. I set the towels aside and took out the key. There was a pause. I felt like I was waiting for a starter gun to go off. I heard the indicator *ping* as the elevator reached the floor, then the muffled sound of doors sliding shut again. I was already moving toward the door to 1236. I shoved the key in the lock, turned it, opened the door, and tagged the knob with the laminated Maid in Room sign, just in case she came back without warning. 10:18. I did a quick check to verify that both the room and the bathroom were empty as expected. I flipped the light on in the dressing area.

Since last night, additional toiletries had been unpacked and arranged around the sink. I moved to the closet and opened the door. The duffel was right where I'd seen it before, with her handbag tucked beside it. I hauled the duffel out of the closet and propped it up on the counter. I did a superficial examination, making sure the bag wasn't booby-trapped in some way. The duffel was made of heavy-duty beige canvas, probably waterproof, with dark leather handles and a pocket on one side for magazines. There was a flap-closure compartment on each end of the bag, where smaller items could be tucked. I unzipped the main compartment and sorted through the contents at breakneck speed. Socks, flannel pajamas, clean underwear, panty hose. I checked the compartment on either end, but both were empty. Nothing in the outside pocket. Maybe she'd removed the cash and put it someplace else. I checked the time: 10·19. I probably still had a good three minutes to go.

I put the duffel back and picked up her handbag, rifling through the contents. Her wallet held a Kentucky driver's license, assorted credit cards, miscellaneous identification, and maybe a hundred bucks in cash. I put the handbag back beside the duffel. How much cash could we be talking about, and how much space could it occupy? Standing up on tiptoe, I checked the closet shelf, which was bare to the touch. I felt inside her raincoat pockets, then slipped a hand into the pockets of the denim dress she'd worn, now hanging beside the raincoat. I tried the cabinet under the sink, but all it contained was the water pipes and a shut-off valve. I did a quick survey of the shower surround and the toilet tank. I went into the main room, where I slid open drawer after drawer. All were empty. Nothing in the TV cabinet. Nothing in the bed table.

The phone rang suddenly. Once. Then silence.

My heart started banging. Laura Huckaby was on her way up. I was flat out of time. I moved to the desk and pulled out the pencil drawer, peering to see if there was something taped under it. I got down on my hands and knees and peered under the beds, then pulled the spread back and raised the edge of the mattress on the nearest of the two. Nope. I tried the other bed, extending my arm between the mattress and the box springs. I hauled myself up and smoothed the covers back in place. I searched the duffel again, rooting through the jumble of clothing, wondering what I'd overlooked. Maybe there was a second zippered compartment inside the first. Oh, to hell with it. I grabbed up the duffel and headed to the door. I snagged the Maid in Room sign and pulled the door shut behind me. I heard the elevator indicator *ping* and then the sound of the doors sliding open. Hastily I shoved the duffel under a pile of clean sheets and began to push the cart down the hall.

Laura Huckaby passed me, walking rapidly. She had a room key in hand, so at least her trip down hadn't been a total waste. This time she didn't even look in my direction. She let herself into her room and shut the door with a bang. I shoved the cart into the alcove at the end of the hall, pulled out the duffel, and scurried toward the fire exit. I pushed my way into the stairwell and started down at a run, skipping every other step. If Laura Huckaby was at all suspicious, it wouldn't take her long to spot the subtle disarray. I pictured her heading straight to the closet, cursing her stupidity when she saw the duffel was missing. She'd have to know she'd been had. Whether she'd set up a stink or not would depend on how much nerve she had. If she'd been carrying a large amount of legitimate cash, why not take advantage of the hotel safe? Unless the booty itself was what Ray Rawson had lied about.

I reached the eighth floor and pushed the door open, heading for 815. I pulled up short. A man in a business suit was standing in the hall outside my room. He turned when he caught sight of me. I caught a glimpse of the name tag pinned to his suit. The duffel suddenly seemed enormous and quite conspicuous. Why would a maid be toting a canvas bag of this sort? I moved automatically toward the utility alcove. My chest felt hot and I was starting to hyperventilate. Out of the corner of my eye, I watched as he knocked on my door again. Casually, he checked the corridor in both directions, then took out a pass key and let himself into my room. Oh, God, now what?

I put the duffel on a shelf in the linen room and put a stack of clean sheets on top of it. The sheets tumbled to the floor and the duffel toppled with them. I gathered up the duffel and shoved it temporarily into an enormous laundry bag meant for dirty linen. I got down on my knees and began to refold sheets. I had to do something while I waited for the guy to get out of my room. I peered around the door. No sign of him, so I had to assume he was still in my room, nosing through my belongings. My shoulder bag was in the closet, and I didn't want him searching it, but I really didn't have a way to stop him, short of setting fire to the place. I heard the door to the fire exit open and close. Please, please, please, God, don't let it be one of the real maids, I thought. Someone stepped into view. I looked up. Well, my prayers had been answered. It wasn't the maid, it was the security guard.

I felt a flash of fear move up my frame, heat bringing color to my face. He was in his mid-forties, short hair, glasses, clean-shaven, overweight. In my opinion, he should have been doing situps for the gut he sported. He stood there, watching me fold a pillowcase. I smiled blankly. I felt like an actress in a play suffering acute stage fright. All the spit left my mouth and seeped out the other end.

"May I ask what you're doing?"

"Ah. I was just straightening these sheets. Mrs. Spitz told me to check the linen supply up here." I struggled to my feet. Even in my guise as a lowly chambermaid, I didn't want him to tower over me.

He stared at me carefully. The look in his eyes was flat, and his tone was a mix of authority and judgment. "Can I have your name?"

"Yes." I realized I'd better give him one. "Katy. I'm new. I'm in training. Eileen and Bernadette are actually working this shift. I'm supposed to help, but I dropped these sheets." I tried to smile again, but my expression came closer to a simper.

He studied me with calculation, apparently weighing the truth value of the statement I'd made. His gaze flicked down to my uniform. "Where's your name tag, Katy?"

I put my hand across my heart like the Pledge of Allegiance. I couldn't think of a response. "I lost it. I'm supposed to get another one."

"Mind if I verify that with Mrs. Spitz?"

"Sure, no problem. Go right ahead."

"What's your last name?" He'd already taken out his walkie-talkie and his thumb was moving toward the button.

"Beatty, like in Warren Beatty," I said without thinking. I realized belatedly my name was now Katy Beatty. I plowed right on. "If you came up to find the manager, he's in 815. The woman he's looking for is on her way downstairs," I said. I pointed in the direction of 815. My hand was shaking badly, but he didn't seem to notice. He'd turned to glance down the corridor behind him.

"Mr. Denton is up here?"

"Yes. At least, I think that's him. I got the impression he was looking for that woman, but she just left."

"What's the problem?"

"He didn't say."

He lowered the walkie-talkie. "How long ago was this?"

"Five minutes. I was just getting off the elevator when she got on."

He paused, staring at me as he reached back and secured his walkie-talkie on his belt. His gaze dropped to my feet and then came up again. "The shoes aren't regulation."

I looked down at my feet. "Really? Nobody ever said anything to me."

"If Mrs. Spitz sees those, you're going to get written up."

My whole face was aflame. "Thanks. I'll remember that."

He moved down the corridor. I stood there transfixed, longing to flee, reluctant to move for fear of calling attention to myself. He tapped on my door. A moment passed and the door was opened a crack. The security officer conferred with the guy in my room. Then the guy in the suit came out and pulled my door shut behind him. The two men moved quickly down the hall toward the elevators. I waited until I heard the elevator *ping* and then I retrieved the duffel from its hiding place. The elevator doors were barely closed when I double-timed down the hall, let myself into my room, and slid the chain into place. How long would it take before they figured out that Kinsey Millhone and the nonregulation maid without a name tag were one and the same?

I reached down and flipped my shoes off. I pulled the red tunic over my head, unzipped the uniform skirt, and stepped out of it. I leaned against the wall while I pulled on my crew socks. I grabbed my jeans and stepped into them, hopping off-balance as I pulled them up. I tugged my turtleneck over my head, shoved my feet back in my shoes, and left the laces flopping loose. I opened the closet door. My handbag was still on the floor where I'd left it, but a glance was all it took to verify that the guy in the suit had been rooting around in it. Shit heel. I yanked the blazer off the hanger and shrugged myself into it. I did a quick survey of the room to make sure I hadn't left anything behind. I remembered the five-dollar tip in my uniform pocket and retrieved that. I picked up the duffel and started to let myself out. I went back, snatched the red uniform off the floor, and made a ball of it, shoving it into the zippered compartment of the duffel bag. If they searched again, why give them the satisfaction of finding it? I pulled the door shut behind me, then half walked, half trotted toward the fire stairs.

I went down eight flights of steps. When I reached the door to the lobby, I opened it a crack and looked out. A small group of businessmen seemed to be having an impromptu meeting in one of the conversational groupings. Papers had been spread out on the table. I peered around to the left. There was a couple conferring with the concierge, who seemed to be holding a map of the area. There was no sign of Mr. Denton or the security guard. No sign of Ray Rawson, either, for that matter. He'd said he'd meet me by the house phone, which I could plainly see across the lobby. The area was deserted, but too exposed for my taste.

I looked to my right. There was a bank of pay telephones about five feet away and, beyond that, the "Lords" and "Damsels." Across from me to the left was the entrance to the coffee shop. I left the relative safety of the stairwell and eased down the corridor and into the ladies' room. Two of the five stall doors were closed, but when I checked under the partitions, there were no feet in evidence. I locked myself in the handicapped stall, perched on the toilet seat, and tied my shoes. Then I emptied the duffel, shaking the contents out onto the floor.

First I checked the bag itself, peering into every pocket and crevice, sticking my fingers down into every corner. I'd thought I might find some kind of hidden compartment, but there didn't seem to be anything of the sort. I manipulated every seam, every brad, and every joining. I inspected each item of clothing I'd dumped out on the floor, folding and repacking the stolen uniform, a pair of cotton pajamas, two pairs of tights, T-shirts, tampons, two bras, and countless pairs of undies and socks. There was absolutely nothing there.

I could feel my anxiety begin to mount. I'd followed this pointless piece of luggage across three states, operating on the assumption that it contained something worth pursuing. Now it looked like all I was ending up with was a pile of secondhand lingerie. What was I to tell Chester? He was going to be furious when I told him I'd flown all the way to Dallas for *this*. The man didn't have the money to send me barreling across the country on the track of cotton panties. I'd broken the law. I was flirting with jail. I'd risked both my license and my livelihood. I began shoving items back into the zippered compartment. Happily, the panties looked like they'd fit, and I could use a clean pair. I hesitated. Nah, probably not a good idea. If I were arrested for theft, it might be better if I weren't wearing the evidence on my butt.

I emerged from the stall, trying to look nonchalant instead of like some big-time fugitive underwear bounty hunter. I couldn't bring myself to abandon the duffel.

Basically, I was still clinging to the notion that it represented some rare and priceless artifact instead of my ticket to the joint. I glanced left across the lobby toward the house phone, but there was still no sign of Ray. I planted myself at one of the public telephones. I fumbled in my blazer pocket, emptying the contents in my search for change. On the metal shelf I laid out the movie receipt, the ballpoint, my five-dollar tip, two quarters, and the paper clip. I dropped one of the quarters in the coin slot and then put a call through to Chester in California, charging it to my telephone credit card. I got my quarter back and placed it with the first, idly rearranging the items for the calming effect. I didn't think Chester would be happy. I was hoping he'd be out, but the man himself picked up on the third ring.

" 'Lo."

"Hello, Chester? This is Kinsey."

"Can you speak up? I can't hear you. Who is this?"

I cupped a hand across the mouthpiece, turning my body away so I wouldn't be shouting my name across the lobby. "It's me. Kinsey," I hissed. "I got the duffel, but there's nothing of significance in it."

Dead silence. "You're kidding."

"Uh, no, actually I'm not. Either the goods were moved or there wasn't anything stolen in the first place."

"Of course they stole *something*! They ripped the friggin' kickplate off the kitchen cabinet. Pappy probably hid cash."

"Did you ever *see* any cash?"

"No, but that doesn't mean it wasn't there."

"That's pure speculation. Maybe the guy busted in and didn't find anything. The duffel might have been empty." I began to rearrange the items on the shelf, placing one of the quarters over Lincoln's face on the five-dollar bill. On the quarter, George Washington looked naked, while on the bill, Lincoln was all dressed up in his Sunday suit. They must have caught George in the sauna with his hair pulled back.

Chester, sounding cranky, said, "I don't get this. Why call me just to lay out a line of horseshit like this?"

"I thought you should get an update. It only seemed fair."

"Fair? You think it's fair I spent all that money flying you to Dallas for nothing? I expected results."

"Wait a minute. So far you haven't spent a dime. *I've* spent the money. You're supposed to pay me back." I uncapped my ballpoint pen and gave Lincoln a mustache, which made his nose look smaller. I'd never paid attention to what a hooter he had.

"Pay you back for what? Air and sunshine? Forget it."

"Come on. We made a decision that turned out to be wrong."

"Then why should I pay? I'm not going to pay for your incompetence."

"Chester, believe me, I'm earning my keep. I could get my license yanked for half the things I've done. I'm not even allowed to do business in this state." I put the two quarters over opposite corners of the five-dollar bill to anchor it.

"That's your problem, not mine. I wouldn't have agreed if I'd known you were off on some wild goose chase."

"Well, neither would I. That's the chance we took. You knew as much as I did going in," I said. To amuse myself, I wrote a bad word on the front of the five-dollar bill. It was the only way I could think of to keep from screaming at him.

"To hell with it. You're fired!" I heard him say,

"Goddamn it!" to himself just as he banged the phone down in my ear.

I made a face at the dead receiver and then rolled my eyes. I hauled up the phone book and started looking up the reservation number for American Airlines. It was embarrassing to admit this had all been for nothing, but I couldn't see what good it would do to stay in Dallas. I'd made a mistake. I'd known at the outset my actions were impulsive. I'd been operating on the best information I had, and if my judgment turned out to be misguided, there was nothing I could do about it now. I noticed I was busy defending myself, but I really couldn't help it in the wake of Chester's disgruntlement. Who could blame the man?

I picked up the five and held it closer, looking at the fine details. Paper currency has a baroque assortment of shaded names and numbers, lacy scrollwork, and official seals. Now *that* was weird. Since when was Henry Morgenthau secretary of the treasury? And who was this guy Julian, whose eensy-teensy signature was so impossible to read? Just to the right of Lincoln's portrait, it said "Series 1934 A." I dug in my handbag and pulled out my wallet, checking the few bills I carried. The only other five I had in my possession was a series 1981 Buchanan-Regan. The one-dollar bills were 1981 Buchanan-Regans and 1981-A Ortega-Regan with a couple of brand-new 1985 Ortega-Bakers thrown in. A twenty and a ten seemed to be the same vintage. If I wasn't mistaken, it meant the five-dollar tip Laura Huckaby had given me was a bill dating back to 1934. Didn't that indicate she was busy spending money from a cache of old bills? Surely she didn't simply happen to have a bill like that in her possession.

I put the phone book down, abandoning the notion of getting back on a plane. Maybe all was not lost. I picked up the duffel and moved forward, scanning the expanse of lobby within view. The five businessmen leaned toward each other, passing the pages of some report between them. As usual, in such a group, one fellow seemed to command the attention of the others. Behind me the door opened abruptly, and before I could turn around, I was snagged by the elbow and pulled into the stairwell.

# 11

"WHERE THE HELL have you been?"

I turned, astonished. It was Ray, his badly bruised face about six inches from mine. He'd removed the tape from his nose, but it still looked like his nostrils were packed with cotton. His skin smelled medicinal, the sort of aftershave you'd sport in an emergency room, composed of equal parts rubbing alcohol, adhesive tape, and suturing material. He still clutched me with his injured hand, his splinted fingers held stiffly.

"Where have *I* been? Where have *you* been?" Our voices seemed to ricochet up the stairwell like a flock of shrieking birds. Both of us glanced upward and lowered our tones to rasping whispers. Ray urged me into the cul-de-sac formed by the final flight of steps where it dead-ended at the wall.

"Christ, those guys are on to you," he hissed. "Some yo-yo with a walkie-talkie's been giving me the third degree. I'm waiting by the house phone and he asks if I'd mind 'stepping into the office.' What was I supposed to do? He knows who you are and he wants to know what you're doing here."

"Why'd he ask you?"

"He'd been checking around. The waitress must have told him she'd seen us together. I wasn't hard to spot. With a mug like this? I told him you were a private investigator working undercover on a case I wasn't at liberty to discuss."

"Who did he think you were, a cop?"

"I told him I was part of a witness protection program, being moved to another state. I had to talk like this was all very hush-hush, life-or-death stuff."

"They couldn't have believed you. How'd you get away?"

"They don't give a shit who I am. They just want me out of here. I said I'd go up to the room and get my things. They escorted me to the elevator, and as soon as they left, I turned around and came down. Is that the duffel? Give it here."

I jerked it out of his reach. "Listen, you piker. Do you swear on a stack of Bibles you've told me the truth? This is cash we're looking for, not drugs or diamonds or stolen documents, right?"

"It's money. I swear. You didn't find it?"

"I didn't find a thing. How much are we talking about?"

"Eight thousand dollars, maybe a little less by now."

"That's *all*?"

"Come on. It's a lot when you don't have a dime, which I don't."

"Somehow I got the impression it was more," I said.

Our voices had started to reverberate again. He put a finger to his lips.

"Where'd the money come from?" I whispered hoarsely.

"I'll tell you later. Let's see if we can find a way out of here."

"There's a service corridor below this one, but you can't access it from here," I said.

"What about the floor above?"

"I don't think so." He started up the steps, but I grabbed his arm. "Wait a minute. Slow down. We need a plan."

"We need the cash," he corrected, "before hotel security catches up with us again. Maybe this Huckaby woman left the money with the manager."

"She couldn't. I was standing in the same line when she checked in. She didn't deposit any valuables. I'd have seen her do that."

"Then where is it? She's not going to let the money out of her sight. If we figure out where she's got it, you can snag it and run."

"Oh, *I* can? That's nice. What about you?"

"I'm speaking figuratively," he said.

"Well, the cash isn't in her room because I've searched."

"Then she must have it with her."

"She does *not*. I told you that. Ah!" I heard the sound an idea makes when your brain ignites, a tiny implosion, like spontaneous combustion at the base of your skull. "Wait a minute. I got it. I think I know where it is. Come with me."

I knocked on Laura Huckaby's door. There was a pause. She was probably checking through the spy hole to see who it was. Ray was standing against the wall to the left of the door, with a look of suffering on his face. "I know how Gilbert got my release date," he said dully. "I didn't want to tell you unless I had to."

"Hush," I said under my breath. I couldn't figure out

what his problem was, aside from the obvious. He'd been curiously reluctant to come up here with me, suggesting all kinds of reasons I should do it myself. I'd been adamant. For one thing, if we were caught, we could act like we were just leaving. For another, now that Chester was pissed off, I didn't want to take sole responsibility. As before, Laura opened the door a crack, leaving the chain in place.

I held up the duffel. "Hi, it's me. I'm off duty. I found this in the hall."

"Is that mine?"

"I think so. Wasn't this sitting in your closet last night?"

"How'd it get out there?"

"Beats me. I spotted it in passing and thought I'd knock," I said. "It is yours, isn't it?"

She studied it briefly. "Just a minute. I'll check." She left the door ajar, still secured by the chain, while she moved into the dressing area and opened the closet door. Ray and I exchanged a look. I knew she wasn't going to find her duffel, but I waited dutifully, playing out the charade. She returned to the door, her expression perplexed. "I guess it is mine." It was clear she didn't want to trust me, but what could she do? From her point of view, she'd been subjected to inexplicable occurrences. A lost key, a missing package, now the wandering duffel.

"I can leave it out here. You want me to do that?"

"No, that's all right." She closed the door and slipped the chain off its track. She opened the door again just wide enough for the duffel, holding her hand out as if to take it from me. I put a hand around the edge of the door, effectively preventing her from closing it.

She seemed startled by the gesture and said, "Hey!" irritably.

I hoped my smile was reassuring. "Mind if I come in? We need to talk." I pushed the door inward.

"Get away," she said, pushing back.

We grappled with the door, but Ray had moved into the picture by then, and after a mute struggle on her part, she relinquished control. She'd begun to realize that something was dreadfully wrong.

"I'm Kinsey Millhone," I said as we stepped into the room. "This is my friend Ray."

She backed up a step, taking in Ray's bruised and swollen face. "What *is* this?"

"We called a meeting about the money," I said. "Just between you, me, and him."

She pivoted, moving rapidly toward the bed table, where she snatched up the receiver. Ray intercepted her and banged down the button before she could press "0."

"Take it easy. We just want to talk to you," he said. He removed the receiver from her hand and dropped it in the cradle.

"Who are you? What is this, some kind of shakedown?"

"Not at all," I said. "We followed you from California. Your friend Gilbert stole some money, and Ray, here, wants it back."

Her eyes fixed on me and then jumped to him, comprehension dawning. "You're Ray Rawson."

"That's right."

She raised a hand rapidly as if to slap him in the face. Ray blocked the move and caught the blow on his arm. He grabbed her wrist with his good hand. "Don't do that," he said.

"Get your fuckin' hands off me!"

"Just give us the money and we'll leave you alone."

"It isn't yours. It belongs to Gilbert."

Ray shook his head. "I'm afraid not. Money belongs

to me and a guy named Johnny Lee. Johnny died four months ago, so I'm passing his share along to his son and grandson. Gilbert tried to rip us off."

"You goddamn shit. That's not true! The money's his and you know it. You're the one who blew the whistle. His brother died because of you."

"That's bullshit. Is that what he said?"

"Well, yes. He told me it was some kind of sting and it was all set up. You tipped off the cops and Donnie was killed in the shootout," she said.

"Wait a minute, gang. What's going on?" I said.

Ray seemed unruffled, ignoring me altogether in his focus on her. "He lied to you, baby. Gilbert sold you a bill of goods. He probably had to do that to get you to participate, right? Because if you knew the truth, you wouldn't help. I hope."

"You asshole. He told me you'd try to do this, twist the truth until it suited your purposes."

"You want the truth? I'll tell you. You want to hear what went down?"

She put her hands to her ears, as if to shut him out. "I don't have to hear it from you. Gilbert told me what happened."

I raised my hand. "Would one of you stop and tell me what this is about? Do you two know each other?"

"Not exactly," Ray said. He turned to look at her, and the two of them locked eyes. Ray's gaze flicked back to mine. "This is my daughter. I haven't seen her in years."

She flung herself at him, banging with her fists on his chest. "You are such a fuck," she said, and promptly burst into tears.

I looked from one to the other. My mouth did not really fall open, but that's what it felt like.

Ray gathered her into his arms. "I know, baby, I

know," he murmured, patting at her. "I feel so bad about everything."

It probably took another five or six minutes for Laura's tears to taper off. Her face was mashed against his shoulder, her bulky belly making the embrace seem awkward. Ray rested his battered cheek against her tangled hair, most of which had come loose now, hanging down in dark auburn clumps. Ray was nearly humming with unhappiness at the sound of her misery, which she managed to express with a childlike lack of inhibition. Neither was accustomed to the physical contact, and my suspicion was that the fleeting connection by no means represented resolution. If their estrangement was life-long, it would take more than a Hallmark moment to set it right. In the meantime, I blocked any thought of my cousin Tasha and my estrangement from Grand.

I went to the window and looked out at the barren stretch of Texas countryside. I felt about as arid. Here, as in California, the liberal application of imported water was the only means by which the land was being reclaimed from the desert. At least I understood now why he hadn't wanted to come up here. He must have dreaded the moment when the two of them would meet, especially once he understood how Gilbert Hays had used her. Why is it that life's most touching moments are so often the most depressing?

Behind me, finally, the weeping seemed to be diminishing. There was some murmuring between them that I politely tuned out. When I turned back, the two were seated side by side on one of the double beds. Laura's tears had streaked through the many layers of makeup bringing ancient bruises to the surface. It was clear she'd recently suffered a black eye. Her jaw was tinted a drab green, washing out to yellow around the edges colors repeated in the riper bruises of her father's face

Odd to think the same man had beaten both. He studied her face, and the effect wasn't lost on him. A look of pain filled his eyes. "He do that to you? Because if he did, I'll kill him, I swear to God."

"It wasn't like that," she said.

"It wasn't like that. *Bull*shit."

Her eyes flooded again. I moved into the dressing area and grabbed some tissues from the dispenser. When I returned to the bed, Ray took the wad and passed them over to her. She blew her nose and then looked at me with resentment. "You're not really the maid," she said resentfully. "You didn't even do the sheet corners right."

"I'm a private investigator."

"I knew this hotel wouldn't have turn-down service. I should have trusted my instincts."

"Ain't *that* the truth," I said. I sat down on the other bed. "Now would one of you fill me in?"

Ray turned to me with an expectant look. "Wait a minute. What's the deal?"

"The deal?"

"I don't know where the money is. I thought it was up here someplace."

"Ah, the money. Why don't you ask her?"

"Me? *I* don't have it. What are you talking about?"

"Yes, you do." I reached over to Laura's belly and knocked on the mound. The thudding noise was not what you'd expect of warm maternal flesh. She smacked my hand away, incensed. "Stop that!"

Ray stared. "It's in her stomach? Like, up her butt?"

"Not quite. The belly's phony."

"How'd you figure that?"

"She has tampons in the duffel. If she were pregnant, she wouldn't need 'em. It's a girl thing," I replied.

"I *am* pregnant. What's the matter with you? The baby's due in January. The sixteenth, to be exact."

"In that case, pull your dress up so we can watch it kick."

"I don't have to *do* that. I can't believe you suggested it."

"Ray, I'm telling you, she's got the money in some kind of harness. That's how she got it on the plane without it showing up on security. Eight thousand in a duffel, they might have asked too many questions."

"That's ridiculous. There's no law that says you can't transport cash across state lines."

"There is when the money's stolen," I said in my best nanny-nanny-boo-boo tone. Really, the two of us were like sisters, squabbling over everything.

"Come on, ladies. Please."

I doubled up my fist. "You want me to punch her in the stomach? It'd be a good test."

"Oh, for God's sake! This is none of your business."

"Yes, it is. Chester hired me to find the money, and I've done just that."

"I-do-not-have-the-money," she said, enunciating every-single-word.

I pulled my fist back.

"All right! Goddamn it. It's in a canvas vest that hooks on in front. I hope you're satisfied."

I loved the indignation, like I was the one who'd been lying to her. "Well, that's great. So let's see it. I'm curious what it looks like."

"Ray, would you tell her to get away from me?"

Ray looked at me. "Just drop it. This is silly. I thought you said you wanted to hear the story."

"I do."

"Then cut the nonsense and let's get on with it." He looked back at his daughter. "You start. I'd like to hear

Gilbert's version. He's saying, what, that I betrayed the others?"

"Let me wash my face first. I feel awful," she said. Her nose was red, her eyes puffy with emotion. She got up and went into the dressing area, where she ran water in the sink.

"Your daughter? You could have told me," I said.

Ray avoided my gaze like a dog that's gone potty on the good rug.

When Laura returned, he let her sit on the bed while he fetched the desk chair and pulled it over closer. Her complexion, free of makeup, showed all the splotchy imperfections you'd expect. She glanced once at Ray, her expression faltering. She picked up a twist of tissue, which she wrapped around her index finger. Given center stage, she seemed oddly reluctant. "Gilbert says there was a bank robbery back in 1941."

"That's right."

I flashed a look at him. "It *is*?"

"There were five of you altogether. You, Gilbert, his brother Donnie, the guy you mentioned . . ."

"Johnny Lee," Ray supplied.

"Right. Him and a man named McDermid."

"Actually, there were six of us. Two McDermids, Frank and Darrell," Ray amended.

She shrugged, accepting the correction, which apparently didn't affect her understanding of the incident. "Gilbert says you tipped off the cops and they showed up in the middle of the robbery. There was a shoot-out and his brother Donnie was killed. So was McDermid and a policeman. The money vanished, but Gilbert was convinced you and Johnny knew where it was hidden. Johnny was in prison for two years, and when he got out, he disappeared. Gilbert had no way to trace him, so he waited 'til you got out and followed you, and sure enough, there it was. All Gilbert took was his share. Well, I guess his brother's share, too. He figures you and Johnny had the use of it for years, so whatever was left belongs to him by rights."

"Could I just clarify one thing?" I said to Laura.

"Sure."

"I take it your mother was the one who told you when Ray was getting out of prison?"

She nodded. "She mentioned it to me. Gilbert had already told me what happened, and I was furious. I mean, it was bad enough my father had been in prison all his life, but to find out he'd betrayed all his friends? That was the lowest of the low."

"Baby, I have to say this. I don't know what your relationship is with Gilbert, but hasn't it occurred to you he only got close to you so he could get to me?"

"No. Absolutely not. You don't *know* that," she said.

"Look at the facts. I mean, it only stands to reason," he said. "Didn't he ask about me early on? Maybe not by name, but just the family situation, blah, blah, blah, your dad and stepdad, things like that?"

"So what if he did? Everybody asks things like that early on."

"Well, doesn't it strike you as odd? Here, just 'coincidentally,' it turns out the two of us pulled a job together forty-some-odd years back?"

"Not really. Gilbert knew Paul from work . . . he's my stepdad," she said in an aside to me. "I guess Paul must have mentioned the name 'Rawson' in some context."

"Oh, yeah, right," Ray said with acid. "Like your stepfather sits around and bullshits about me with the guys at work."

"What difference does it make?" Laura said. "Somehow it came up. Maybe it was karma."

Ray's expression was impatient—he didn't buy that for a minute—but he made that rolling hand gesture that said, "Let's get on with it."

"I'm not going to keep talking if you act like that, Ray," she said primly. "You asked for my side and that's what I'm trying to tell you, okay?"

"Okay. You're right. I'm sorry. But let me ask you this . . ."

"I'm not saying I know all the details," she interjected.

"I understand that. I'm just asking about the logic. Listen, in the gospel according to Gilbert—if what he says is true—then how come I spent forty years in prison? If I blew the whistle, I'd have made a deal. I never would have served a day. Or I'd have pled down and done county jail time just to make it look good."

Laura was silent, and I could see her struggling to come up with an explanation that made sense. "I don't really know. He never went into that."

"Well, think about it."

"I know Gilbert never served much time," she said tentatively.

"Yeah, but he was seventeen. He was still a juvenile and this was his first offense. Johnny always figured it was the younger McDermid, Darrell. Frank was too much of a stand-up guy. Darrell was the one who testified against us in court and ended up doing less than a year himself. You want to know why? Because he turned us in and in exchange they let him plead down to some lesser charge. Gilbert wants to blame me because the little fuck is greedy and wants to justify picking off all the loot for himself. By the way, you haven't said, are you two married?"

"We live together."

"You live together. That's nice. A year, couple years?"

"About that," she said.

"Don't you have any idea what he's like?"

Laura said nothing. Judging from the bruises, she knew plenty about Gilbert. "I don't believe he lied. You're the liar."

"Why don't you reserve judgment until you hear my side of it?"

I held a hand up. "Uh, Ray? Am I going to be surprised by what comes next? Is this going to be like big news and piss me off?"

His smile was sheepish. "Why?"

"Because I'm just wondering how many versions of the story you tell. This is number three, by my count."

"This is it. Last one. Swear to God."

I glanced at Laura. "The man does lie through his teeth, or what's left of them."

"I haven't *lied*," he said. "I might have failed to mention a couple things."

"A shoot-out with the cops? What else have you failed to mention? I'd be fascinated," I said.

"I can do without the sarcasm."

"I can do without the bullshit! You said Gilbert was a former cellmate."

"I had to tell you something," he said. "Come on. This is not easy. I kept my mouth shut forty years. Johnny Lee and I swore we'd never give anything away. The problem is, he died without giving me some vital information."

"I'm going to get comfortable," I said. I leaned over and pulled the pillows out from under the bedspread and propped them up against the headboard, kicking my shoes off before I settled into place. This was like a bedtime story, and I didn't want to miss it.

"You comfy?" he said.

"I'm terrific."

"Johnny dreamed up this scheme and talked me into going in with him. You have to understand a little background on this. I hope you don't mind."

"If you're going to tell the truth for a change, take your time," I said.

Ray got to his feet and began to pace. "I'm trying to think how far back to go. Let's try this. Ohio River flooded in the winter of 1937. I guess it started raining sometime in January and the river just kept going up. Eventually, there was something like twelve thousand acres underwater all up and down the Ohio River valley. At the time, Johnny was in state reformatory down in Lexington. Well, the inmates began to riot. Sixty of them busted out of there, and Johnny Lee was one. He gets as far as Louisville and disappears in the confusion. He starts helping with flood relief." He paused, looking from Laura to me. "Just be patient," he said. "Because you have to understand how this scheme was set up in the first place."

"Fine with me," she said.

He looked at me.

"Go right ahead," I said.

"Okay. Anyway, thousands of volunteers poured into the city. And nobody asked questions. From what Johnny told me, you pitched in, nobody cared who you were or where you came from. So he's rowing through the west end, saving people off of rooftops. The water's up to the second story in most places—I've seen pictures of this—as high as traffic lights. Damnedest thing you've ever seen. Johnny made this boat out of four barrels and some crates and he's paddling right down the middle of the street. He had the time of his life. He even stuck around afterwards and helped with the cleanup, which is how he dreamed up this heist.

"Lot of buildings collapsed. I mean, the whole downtown was underwater for weeks on end, and when the river receded they put crews in there repairing anything that got broke. Johnny was smart. He knew all kinds of things. He told them he'd done construction, so they put him to work. Anyway, while he's crawling around this basement one day, he realizes he's looking at the underside of a bank. Electrical power's been out for days, so a lot of storm sewers have broken and all this water's flowing past the foundation. There's this crack up the wall that he's supposed to fix. He puts together this patch job wouldn't fool a pro, but there's no one around. Everybody's too busy to pay attention to him. So he tells 'em it's fixed when he hasn't done a thing except cover it up. He even signs off the inspection with forged signatures. I mean, it's not like there was anyone to double-check his work.

"By the time the two of us meet up . . . this is now four years later. Back then, big vaults were poured in place, using number five rebar, which is five-eighths diameter, four inches on center, several layers offset. Understand, it's not like I'm the expert. I learned all of this from him. This particular vault was constructed during the Depression—some kind of public works project—so you can imagine how well it was put together in the first place. Vault like that, you can force entry if you got the tools and the time. He said it had always been at the back of his mind, but he knew he needed help once it came time, which is where I come in.

"Johnny starts working on the foundation with this masonry bit. Nights and weekends, he goes in through the basement of the building next door and attacks the substructure. It probably takes him a month, but he's finally right up against the floor of the vault. Nowadays, this shit is all done with high-tech equipment, but in the old days, a successful bank job was the result of pure grit and hard work. It took patience and skill. Johnny figured the alarm system was tougher than the vault. At that point, we had to bring in some other guys because we needed the help. Johnny'd apprenticed with a locksmith, so he'd studied all the manuals and knew the specs by heart, but we needed an alarm man to dismantle the alarms. I'd been in jail with a guy I thought we could trust. That was Donnie Hays, and he brought in his brother, Gilbert. Like she said, Donnie's dead now and Gilbert I got to thank for this." He held up his bruised and bandaged hand.

I saw Laura's focus shift, and she exchanged a look with me. It apparently hadn't occurred to her before that Gilbert had done the damage to Ray Rawson's face.

"Johnny pulled in another couple of guys named McDermid. I think they were cousins he'd done some time with down in Lexington. Donnie Hays defeated the alarm, and we went to work with the torches and the sledgehammers, pounding away like crazy until we finally busted through. Johnny started drilling safe-deposit boxes while the rest of us set to work, cleaning out the loot while he popped the boxes and dumped the contents."

"Wait a minute. Who's Farley? How does he fit into this?" I asked.

"Gilbert's nephew," Laura replied. "The three of us came out to the coast together."

"Oh. Sorry to interrupt. Go ahead."

"Anyway, we had us a regular bucket brigade, tossing cash and jewelry out of safe-deposit boxes, stuffing the goodies into canvas bags, then hand over hand down through the hole and out to the car waiting in the alley. We're working like dogs and everything seems to be going as planned until suddenly the cops show up and all hell breaks loose. This gun battle breaks out, in the course of which Frank McDermid and Donnie Hays were both killed, along with this cop. I was hot-blooded in those days, and I fired the shot that killed the cop. Gilbert was captured and so was Darrell McDermid. I heard later Darrell died in some accident, but I never had that confirmed."

"You and Johnny weren't captured?" I asked.

He shook his head. "Not then. Me and him escaped, but we knew it was only a matter of time before they caught us. We were desperate, sitting on this stash, anxious to find a safe place for it before the cops closed in. We decided to split up. Johnny said he had the perfect place to hide the dough, but he figured it was better if only one of us knew. I'd have trusted him with my life. He swore he wouldn't lay a hand on it until we were both free to enjoy it. We went our separate ways, and by the time we got picked up he was empty-handed. The cops beat the shit out of him, trying to find out where he'd hidden the take, but he never would say. Ended up he confessed to the crime, but he never told anyone what happened to the money. The irony was, it was the cops' beating a confession out of him that got his conviction thrown out.

"Meantime, we both suspected Darrell was the one who blew the whistle on us. Like I said, after we were picked up, he testified against us in court. He swore up and down it wasn't him turned us in, trying to lay blame off on his brother, Frank. Me and Johnny both got twenty-five years to life, but Johnny's conviction was overturned on appeal. He went home to his family while I'm sitting on my butt down in the U.S. Penitentiary in Atlanta, Georgia. Johnny went back later and removed enough from the stash to support himself and my ma, who's still back in Kentucky." He indicated her belly. "That's what's left."

"Wait a minute. What makes you so sure it's eight grand?"

"Because he told me how much he took and what he spent since then. I did the math and figured what the balance was."

"Where's the rest?"

"Well, you know. I guess it's still where it was."

I stared at him. "I hope you're not going to tell me he died without revealing where he hid it."

Ray shrugged uneasily. "That's about it."

# 12

LAURA MOANED AND leaned forward as if she were on the verge of fainting. She tried to get her head down between her knees, but the bulk of her belly thwarted her. She leaned sideways against the bed pillows, pulling her knees up to her chest like a kid with a stomachache.

"What's wrong?" Ray asked.

"Oh God, I thought there'd be more. I thought you knew where it was," she whispered, beginning to weep again. I'm a hardhearted little thing. I sat there wondering why crying is occasionally referred to as boohooing. I've never heard weepers use syllables even remotely related.

Ray moved over and sat beside her. "Are you okay?"

She shook her head, rocking back and forth.

"Laura's fine," I said, bored. I was aware my tone was rude, but I knew what she was up to, and the girlish tears were annoying. Ray rubbed her back, patting her shoulder in a series of ineffectual moves that, nevertheless, conveyed his compassion and concern. "Hey, come on. That's okay. Just tell me what's wrong and I'll help. I promise. Don't cry."

"Excuse me, Ray, but you might want to be discreet. She's already busy double-crossing Gilbert, and she's supposedly in *love* with him. No telling what she does to people she doesn't give a shit about. Uh, such as us, in case you missed the point," I said.

He looked at her, his brow furrowing. "Is that right? Are you trying to get away from him?"

"By sticking it to *us*," I said caustically. Neither paid attention. I could have saved my breath.

I handed her another wad of tissues, and she went through the whole nose-blowing routine again. She pressed a tissue to her eyes, damming the leak of tears. She launched into a fragmented explanation, but she couldn't quite manage it, and I was left to translate. I said, "She and Farley have joined forces. She's absconding with the money. This is just a guess on my part."

"You and Farley decided to pull a fast one?" he asked. He was trying to sound calm, but I could tell he was seriously alarmed. He knew Gilbert well enough to guess the depth of trouble she was in. She nodded, tears spilling down her cheeks.

"Oh, Jesus, baby. I wish I'd known what you were up to. That's really not a good plan."

"I can't help it. Farley loves me. He said he'd help. He knows Gilbert beats me. I have to get away before he kills me dead."

"I understand, hon, but Gilbert is a lunatic. He's not going to like that. If he finds out, I hate to think what he'll do to get even. Come on now and let's talk. Maybe we can figure out a way to get you out of this."

I loved his use of the word "we."

She sighed and sat up. Without the anchor of make-up, her eyes looked like they'd shifted upward half an inch on her face. Her nose was stopped up and her voice had dropped into a lower range. Her complexion was a mottled pink, and her hazel eyes seemed vivid against the dark red of her hair. The dark green cordu-roy jumper was hopelessly wrinkled, and the collar of her white turtleneck was streaked with foundation. "I don't know what I was thinking of. I just had to get away." She pulled her sleeve up. "Look at that. I'm black and blue. I look worse than you do, only this has been going on for months."

"You have to get away from him. No question about that. Why'd you put up with it?"

"Because I didn't have any choice. I've been to shel-ters for battered women. Twice, I've hidden out with friends. Somehow he always finds me and brings me back. Now he makes sure I don't get close to anyone. I have to account for my every minute. He won't let me work. He won't let me have a nickel of my own. When I saw this coming up, I knew it was the only chance I'd ever have. I thought if I just had money. If I just had a way to get away from him . . ."

"Then take the money," he said. "It's yours. I couldn't believe it when Kinsey mentioned your name. You can ask her. I was stunned. . . ."

"I wouldn't say 'stunned,' but he did get real quiet."

"I had no idea you were involved in this," he went on.

"What difference would that have made?" she said, blowing her nose. She seemed comforted by the fact that she'd surprised him somehow.

"I never would have come. I'd have let you have the eight grand. That's what I'm saying. It's yours. You take it. It's a gift."

"Forget that. I don't want it."

"I thought you said you didn't have any choice."

"Well, I do."

"Like what?"

"I don't know. I'll talk to Farley. We'll figure something out."

"Laura, don't be crazy. You were willing enough to take it before. Why not now?"

She turned on him harshly. "I was willing to take it because I thought you betrayed your friends to get it. I thought it served you right. I didn't think you deserved to have it after what you did."

I was getting irritated by the melodrama, wishing they'd get on with it. "Why don't you split the money and put an end to the argument?"

Ray shook his head. "We don't have to split it. She can have the whole eight grand. I can always go back to Louisville and look for the rest."

"What are your chances of finding it after forty years?" I asked.

"Probably not that good, but I'd feel better knowing she had enough to get away."

"Ray, I said I'd handle it and I will," she said.

"Why don't you let me do something?"

"It's too late."

He turned to me, his look bewildered. "You talk to her. You tell her. I don't understand where she's coming from."

I said, "Here's the deal, Ray, and you can trust me on this. She wants your love. She wants approval. She wants you to beg forgiveness for what you've put her through all her life. She doesn't want to have anything else to do with you. She certainly doesn't want your help. She'd rather die first."

"Why?"

"Because she doesn't want to *owe* you anything," I snapped.

He looked back at her. "Is that right, what she said?"

"I don't know. I guess." She paused to wipe her eyes and blow her nose again. "I thought there'd be more. I thought you'd have millions. I was counting on it."

"There never was *millions*. Is that what Gilbert said?"

"How do I know? That's what he talked about for years," she said. "Maybe, in his mind, the money grew as time passed. The point is, eight thousand dollars isn't going to get me any place. I pictured going to a foreign country, holing up someplace, but how long is eight thousand dollars going to last?"

"It'll last long enough. Go to another state. Change your name. Find work. At least the eight grand will help you get set up."

Laura's face was filled with despair. "He'll find me. I know he will. I thought I had a chance with Farley, but now I'm worried sick."

"Where's Farley all this time?" I asked.

"He's in Santa Teresa with Gilbert. We didn't want him to get suspicious."

I raised my hand. "Wait a minute. I'm confused. What was the original plan?"

"When I left Santa Teresa? I was supposed to fly to Palm Beach, Florida, where Gilbert had a buddy waiting. This is some pal he hired to keep an eye on me. Gilbert wanted to get the money out of California as soon as possible, but he thought we'd be too conspicuous if the three of us traveled together. Besides, he and Farley had to wait until their passports came through. I already had mine, so I was supposed to wait in Palm Beach and they'd join me. Later, we'd fly to Rio."

"So Farley was left to deal with Gilbert? That's a bad idea. I don't even know Farley and already I'll bet he's not smart enough to outfox Gilbert."

"That's right, doll. Gilbert's certifiable, especially when he thinks he's been betrayed," Ray said to her. "Look at what he did to me. You think that's the end of it?"

"What am I supposed to do? It's done now. It's over. I took the money and ran. The minute I got here, I counted it. I thought I'd die when I found out how little there was."

I said, "Back up a step. When was Farley supposed to join you?"

"As soon as he could. They called the passport office and the guy swore he'd put them in the mail. Farley knows where I am, and we made arrangements for him to call me from this pay phone down the street."

"He never called you at all?"

"He called me once. This morning. He had to wait 'til Gilbert went out. When I told him about the eight grand, I could tell he was scared. He said he'd think of something and call me back in an hour."

Ray said, "You haven't heard from him?"

Laura shook her head.

I said, "But Gilbert must have known you never got off the plane in Palm Beach. Didn't his buddy call him right up to say you never showed?"

"Of course he did, but Gilbert doesn't have any idea where I am."

"Well, this is a very sophisticated plan," I said. "What about Farley? I'm sure Gilbert won't suspect *him*."

"You think he's figured it out?"

"Of course he has!" Ray said. "He's waited forty

years to get his hands on this dough. Gilbert's a psycho-path. He's so paranoid he's almost psychic. You're an amateur. You think he can't see right through you?"

"But Dallas is huge. He'll never find me," she said. "I paid the hotel in cash and I'm using an alias."

"Farley knows where you are."

"Well, sure, but I can trust him," she said.

Ray closed his eyes. "You better hit the road."

"But where would I go?"

"Who cares? Just get out of here."

"What about Farley? He won't know where I've gone."

"That's the point," I said. "I agree with Ray. You can't worry about him. You have to put as much dis-tance as possible between you and Gilbert."

"Well, I'm not going to do it. I told Farley I'd be here and I'm staying," she said.

I said, "Oh, boy."

"Gilbert isn't Superman. He doesn't have X-ray vi-sion or anything like that."

"Yeah, right," I said. I searched through my handbag until I found my airline ticket. I started opening drawers in the bed table, looking for a telephone book. "Well, gang. I don't know how you're going to resolve this lit-tle conflict, but I'm getting out of here."

"You're leaving us?" Ray said, startled. "What about Chester?"

"He fired me," I said. I found the Yellow Pages in a separate book that probably weighed ten pounds. I lugged it out of the drawer and hauled it onto my lap, leafing through to the section marked "Airlines." "Look, whatever you and Laura work out, that's be-tween the two of you. I came to help recover the cash you're so busy giving away. I'm history. It makes no sense for me to stay here. If Chester doesn't like it, he can take it up with you. He's already so frosted he probably won't pay my bill, which means I'm out of luck. I might as well go home. At least take charge of the situation to that extent." I found the number for American and put my finger on the place while I picked up the receiver.

"But you can't just abandon us," Ray said.

"I wouldn't call it that," I said.

"What would you call it?"

"Ray, we're not joined at the hip. I came here on impulse, so I thought I'd go home the same way." I tucked the phone in the crook of my neck and punched in the number for American Airlines. As soon as the number answered, I was put on terminal hold while a mechanical voice assured me my business was valued beyond rubies. "Anyway, the money's stolen," I went on conversationally, "which is just one more reason I don't want to be involved in this."

"It's been forty years since we cleaned out that vault," Ray protested. "The bank's out of business. Place went belly up back in 1949. Most customers are dead, so even if I wanted to play straight, who would I return the money to? The state of Kentucky? To what end? I spent my life in jail for that dough, and I earned every cent."

"It's still a crime," I said politely, not wanting to seem quarrelsome

"What about the statute of limitations? Who's going to point a finger after all this time? Besides, I been tried once and I paid for my sins."

"Take it up with an attorney. You could be right. Just in case you're not, I think I'll steer clear," I said.

Laura was getting impatient. She apparently had no interest in our debate about jurisprudence. She leaned closer to me, hissing, "I wish you'd get off the phone. What if Farley's trying to get through?"

I held a hand up like a traffic cop. The American Airlines ticket agent had just come on the line and introduced himself. I said, "Oh, hi, Brad. My name is Kinsey Millhone. I have an open-ended, round-trip ticket from Santa Teresa, California, to Palm Beach, Florida, and I'd like to book the return. I'm in Dallas now, so I just need the Dallas–Santa Teresa leg."

"And what day would this be for?"

"As soon as possible. Today, if you can do it."

While agent Brad and I conducted business, Ray and Laura seemed to be negotiating some sort of father-daughter truce, a financial cease-fire of sorts. Apparently, she was allowing him to gift her with the hotly contended eight grand. Dimly, I was aware that he was telling her he had to go down to his room on the tenth floor and pick up his bags. He wanted permission to leave his bags in her room until he could figure out where to go from here.

Meanwhile she began to pace, becoming more agitated as the agent and I tried to work out my itinerary. There were some alternate routes that would get me home by way of San Francisco or Los Angeles, using short hops for the final leg. Since this was Sunday, both direct flights were completely full, and his only suggestion was that I get myself on standby and hope for the best. He went ahead and wait-listed me on two flights, one nonstop, the other with a layover. The next flight was scheduled for departure at 2:22. I checked my watch. It was just past 12:30, and with the hotel shuttle or a taxi, I could probably get over to the airport in the next thirty-five to forty minutes.

Laura had crossed back to the bed table, where she stuck her face close to mine and mouthed, "Hang *up*."

She sat down on the other bed and began to unlace her high-top tennis shoes.

I gave her a simpering smile as I began to wind up the conversation, reconfirming my notes about the flights in question. As I replaced the receiver in the cradle, I realized Ray was still in the room. "I thought you were going down to get your bags," I said.

"I was afraid if I left you'd be gone when I got back."

"That's a good bet. What's your inclination? Are you going to fly back to California?"

"Nah, I don't think so. I think I'll hang out with Laura until she hears from Farley. As soon as her situation's settled, I'll take off for Louisville. I got a rental car downstairs. Meantime, if I lay low the management will never know I'm here."

"What about Chester? I hate to spoil all the fun, but half of the money belongs to him, you know."

"Says who?"

"You did. You said you were going to turn it over to him."

"I got news for you. He's screwed. I never really meant to cut him in on the deal."

"Ah. I guess I should have known that, right?"

"You're the one who pointed out how much I lie," he said.

"So I have to be the one to break the news to him? Thanks a lot, Ray. That sucks. What am I supposed to say?"

"You'll think of something. Plead ignorance. Make it up."

"Oh, right."

"The guy's a butt, anyway. I bet you never get reimbursed."

I said, "Your confidence in him is touching."

Laura was still sulking, so we skipped the tender fare-thee-wells. I grabbed my shoulder bag, hoisted it, and backed out of the room. Then I headed for the fire stairs and made my way down twelve floors to the lobby.

I took a taxi to the airport. I could have waited for the shuttle, which was free of charge, but the truth was I didn't want to risk running into management. So far, I'd successfully outmaneuvered the hotel authorities, and I was just as happy leaving Texas without some kind of scrape with the law. I checked my wallet in the cab. Since I was on my way home, I figured I had sufficient cash for the journey . . . which is to say, plus or minus thirty-five bucks. I'd spent a little on incidentals, but in the main, I'd managed on the few resources I'd had. I'd still have to hassle with short-term parking fees when I got home—seven bucks a day for the two or three days I'd been gone—but in a pinch, I could call Henry and have him bring me the necessary cash. I hadn't formally checked out of my room, but the desk clerk had taken an impression of my credit card when I'd checked in, and I was sure the charges would appear on the next statement I received. Hotels aren't exactly dumb about these things.

The cab dropped me off at the departure gates for American Airlines. I went into the terminal and crossed the lobby, checking the monitor for the departing flight numbers I'd been given. The first was scheduled to take off at 2:22, the second not until 6:10. The later flight wasn't even listed yet, but I found the gate number for the 2:22 departure. At least traveling without luggage simplified procedures to some extent. I bypassed the ticket counter and joined the line of passengers waiting to clear security. My handbag sailed through X-ray, but when I passed through the metal detector, there was a telltale shriek. I patted my pockets, which were empty of metal except for the paper clip and random change I'd used for the pay phone. I backed up, dropped the items in a plastic dish. I tried again. The shrieking seemed to rise to an accusatory pitch. I could tell the security sorceress was about to dowse my body with her divining rod when I remembered the key I'd stitched near my shoulder pad. "Hang on a minute. I got it." To the annoyance of those behind me, I backed up again, peeled off my blazer, and laid it on the moving belt. This time, I made it through. I half expected to be quizzed about the key stitched into the shoulder seam, but no one said a word. Those people probably saw things much stranger any given day of the week. I collected my shoulder bag and the blazer and headed for the gate.

I pulled my ticket from my handbag and presented it to the gate agent, explaining my situation. The flight was completely booked and she didn't seem that optimistic about my getting a seat. I sat in the waiting area while other passengers checked in. Apparently, several of us were angling for the same flight, which I suspected was already desperately oversold. I eyed the competition, some of whom looked like those quarrelsome types who raise hell when anything goes wrong. I might have tried it myself if I'd thought it would do any good. As far as I can tell, there are only so many seats. The plane is either flightworthy or it's not. Between mechanical matters and air traffic control, you either fly or you don't. I've never heard of an airline yet that proceeded on the basis of noisy passenger complaints, so why bitch and moan?

I pulled out my paperback romance novel and began to read. As flight time approached, the passengers were boarded in orderly rows, from the rear to the front, with the privileged taking precedence. Finally, six names were called from the standby list and none of them were mine. Oh, well. The gate agent sent me an apologetic smile, but there was nothing to be done. She swore she'd put me at the head of the list for the next flight out.

In the meantime, I had close to four hours to kill. From what I gathered, the flight crews made two daily loops from Dallas to Santa Teresa, in and out of the same gate, seven days a week. All I had to do was find a way to occupy my time and then present myself back here before the boarding process began again. With luck, I'd get a seat and be homeward bound. Without luck, I'd be stuck in Dallas until two o'clock Monday afternoon.

I walked a mile in the terminal corridor, just to stretch my legs. I took advantage of the ladies' room, where I was very ladylike. As I emerged and turned right, I passed the airport equivalent of an outdoor cafe, tables separated from the terminal corridor by a low wrought-iron fence and fake plants. The small bar offered the usual wines, beers, and exotic mixed drinks while, under glass, assorted fresh seafoods were packed on a mound of crushed ice. I hadn't eaten lunch, so I ordered a beer and a plate of fresh shrimp, which came with cocktail sauce, oyster crackers, and lemon wedges. I peeled and sauced my shrimp, doing a little people watching to amuse myself while I ate. When I finished, I wandered back to the gate.

I took a seat by the window. I read my book, intermittently watching airplanes land and take off. Occasionally I nodded off, but the seats weren't really built for any serious sleep. By hook or by crook, I managed to carve the four hours down to slightly more than one. Toward the end of the time allotted, I made a trip to the newsstand and picked up the local paper. I returned to the gate at five, just as the flight from Santa Teresa was arriving. I checked with one of the gate agents and made sure my name was on the standby list.

Most seats in the waiting area were now full, so I leaned against a column and scanned the paper. The jetway door had been opened and the first-class passengers began to file out, looking ever so much fresher than the travelers behind them. The coach passengers came next, eyes straying across the crowd to find the people who'd come to meet them. Many joyous reunions. Grandmothers swept little children into their arms. A soldier hugged his sweetheart. Husbands and wives exchanged obligatory busses. Two teenagers with a cluster of helium balloons began to squeal at the sight of a sheepish-looking young guy coming down the jetway. Altogether, it was a very pleasant way to spend a few minutes, and I found myself happily distracted from the grim array of the day's news in the paper. I was just in the process of turning to the funnies when the last smattering of passengers straggled off the plane. It was the Stetson that caught my attention. I averted my gaze, glancing up only fleetingly as Gilbert walked by.

# 13

I GLANCED AT my watch. My plane probably wouldn't board for another twenty to thirty minutes. The cleaning crew would have to sweep through, collecting discarded newspapers, wadded tissues, earphones, and forgotten items. I laid my paper aside and followed Gilbert, whose Stetson, pale blue denim jacket, and cowboy boots made him easy to keep an eye on. He had to be much closer to Ray's age than I'd realized on first glance. I'd pegged him in his late fifties, but he was probably sixty-two, sixty-three, somewhere in there. I couldn't figure out what Laura had seen in him in the first place, unless she was, quite literally, looking for a father. Whatever the appeal, the sexual chemistry must have been intertwined with his brutality. Too many women mistake a man's hostility for wit and his silence for depth.

He pushed through revolving doors to the same baggage claim area I'd entered early Saturday. The area was crowded and afforded me natural cover. While Gilbert waited for the bags, I scanned the area for a pay phone. There were probably some around the corner, but I didn't want to let him out of my sight. I moved over to the hotel directory and found the number for the Desert Castle. The telephone system linked all the hotels that serviced the airport but did not admit of outside calls beyond that. I pulled a pen and paper from my bag as the line was ringing. "Desert Castle," a woman said, picking up on the other end.

"Hi, I'm over at the airport. Can you give me the hotel operator?"

"No, ma'am. I'm not tied in to the hotel switchboard. This is a separate facility."

"Well, can you give me the phone number over there?"

"Yes, ma'am. You want reservations, sales, or catering?"

"Just give me the main number."

She recited the number, which I dutifully noted. I'd find a pay phone as soon as opportunity allowed.

Behind me, a bell finally sounded, mimicking a burglar alarm. The overlapping metal segments of the carousel gave a lurch and began to move in a counterclockwise direction. Two suitcases came around the bend, then a third and a fourth as the conveyor brought them up from below. The waiting passengers crowded forward, angling for position as the bags tumbled down the incline and began their slow journey on the circular metal track.

While Gilbert watched for his luggage, I retrieved the two quarters from my blazer pocket, playing with them nervously while I waited to see what he would do. He retrieved a soft-sided suitcase from the carousel and pushed through the crowd, moving toward the corridor. I turned away long before he passed, aware that any sudden movement might attract his attention. Approaching the escalator, he stepped to one side and squatted while he unzipped his suitcase and removed a sizable handgun, to which he affixed a silencer. Several people glanced down and saw what he was doing, but went about their business as though it were no big deal. Clearly, to them, he didn't look like the sort of fellow who would cut loose in a crowd, mowing down everyone within range of him. He tucked the gun in his belt and pulled his denim jacket over it.

He adjusted his Stetson, rezipped his suitcase, and proceeded in a leisurely manner to the car rental desk. He must not have had advance reservations because I saw him inquire at Budget and then move to Avis. I spotted a bank of telephones and found the only free instrument among the five. I jammed a quarter in the slot and dialed the number for the Desert Castle. I turned, checking the immediate area, but there was no sign of airport security.

"Desert Castle. How may I direct your call?"

"Could you ring Laura Hudson's room? She's in 1236," I said.

Laura's line was busy. I kept waiting for the operator to cut back in, but she had apparently quit her job and gone to work for someone in another state. I depressed the plunger and started over, using my last precious quarter to try the hotel again.

"Desert Castle. How may I direct your call?"

"Hi, I'm trying to reach Laura Hudson in 1236, but her line is busy. Can you tell me if Ray Rawson is still registered there?"

"Just a moment, please." She clicked out. Dead silence. She clicked back in. "Yes, ma'am. Would you like me to ring his room?"

"Yes, but if he doesn't answer, would you come back on the line for me?"

"Certainly."

The number rang in Ray's room fifteen times, before she cut back in. "Mr. Rawson doesn't answer. Would you care to leave a message?"

"Is there any way to page him instead?"

"No, ma'am. I'm sorry. Was there anything else I could help you with?"

"I don't think so. Oh yes, wait a minute. Could you connect me with the manager?"

She'd hung up before I'd even finished the sentence.

By now, I had so much adrenaline pumping through me, I could hardly breathe. Gilbert Hays was standing at the Avis counter, filling out the paperwork. He seemed to be consulting one of those multicolored one-sheet maps of the vicinity, the desk clerk leaning over helpfully, pointing out his route. I took the escalator to the street.

Outside, lights had come on, only partially dispelling the gloom of the pickup area. A limousine pulled to the curb in front of me, the uniformed white driver coming around to the door on the passenger side to assist a silver-haired couple as they emerged. The woman wore the fur of some beast I'd never seen. She looked around uneasily, as though she were accustomed to warding off insults. The driver removed their luggage from the trunk. I searched the area, looking for airport police. Light and shadow played across the concrete in patterns as repetitious as a stencil. A wind tunnel had been created by the building's construction, and a diesel-scented gale blew through, generated by the constant rush of passing traffic. I didn't see any of the vans from the hotel. I didn't see a cab stand or any passing taxis. Gilbert had probably already been given the keys to his rental car. He'd be coming out the door behind me, searching out the waiting area for the shuttle that would take him to the slot where his vehicle was waiting. Or perhaps, far worse, the rental car had been left in the parking garage just across the way, in which case he only had to cross the street.

My gaze settled on the limousine. The driver had received his tip, touched his cap, closed the limo door on the rear passenger side. He circled the back end of the vehicle, heading for the driver's side, where he opened the door and slid behind the wheel. I began to rap frantically on the front passenger side window. The glass was tinted so darkly, I couldn't see in at all. The window was lowered with a whir. The driver looked across at me, his expression neutral. He was in his thirties, with a round face, sparsely growing red hair, combed straight back from the crown. Along the edges of his ears, I could see where his hat had rested.

I leaned in slightly, handing him my wallet, with my California driver's license and my private investigator's license showing. I said, "Please listen very carefully. I need help. I'm a private investigator from Santa Teresa, California. Somewhere behind me, there's a guy with a gun who's here in Dallas to kill a couple of friends of mine. I need to get to the Desert Castle. Do you know where that is?"

He took my wallet gingerly, like a cat who deigns to accept a treat from an unfamiliar hand. "I know the Desert Castle." He looked at the picture on my driver's license. I could see him take in the information on my private investigator's license. He began to leaf through some of my other identification cards. He handed my wallet back and then simply sat and stared at me. He popped the lock up and then reached for the keys in the ignition.

I opened the passenger door and got in.

The limo pulled away from the curb as silently as a train easing out of a station. The seats were gray leather and the dashboard was a burled walnut so shiny it looked like plastic. Just at my left knee was the handset for the car phone. "Mind if I use that to call the cops?" I asked.

"Be my guest."

I dialed 911 and explained the situation to the emergency dispatcher, who asked for my approximate location and said she'd have a county sheriff's deputy meet us at the Desert Castle. I tried the hotel again, but I couldn't get the operator to pick up at all.

We circled the airport and headed off toward open country. It was fully dark by now. The land seemed vast and flat. The headlights illuminated long stretches of green with an occasional monolithic office building jutting up on the horizon. Lighted billboards appeared like a series of flashcards. Where we crested a rise, I could see the sweep of intersecting highways defined by the lights from fast-moving traffic. Anxiety buzzed and sizzled in my gut like defective neon, outlining vital organs.

"What's your name?" I asked. If I didn't talk, I'd go mad.

"Nathaniel."

"How'd you get into this?"

"It's just a way to pick up money until I finish my novel." His tone was glum.

I said, "Ah."

"I used to live in Southern California. I was hoping to get a screenplay launched, so I moved out to Hollywood and worked for this actress who played the zany sister-in-law on a sitcom about a waitress with five adorable kids. Show only lasted a couple seasons, but she was raking it in. I think most of the money went up her nose, to tell you the truth. I drove her to the studio and back every day and washed her car and things like that. Anyway, she told me if I came up with an idea for a film, she'd have me pitch it to her agent and maybe she could help me break in. So I get this idea about this wacko mother-daughter relationship where the girl dies of cancer. I tell her about it and she says she'll see what she can do. Next thing I know, I go to a movie theater on Westwood Boulevard and see this movie about some girl dies of cancer. Can you believe that? What's her name, Shirley MacLaine, and that other one, Debra Winger. There it was. I should have had it registered with the guild, only nobody mentioned that. Thanks a lot, gang."

I looked over at him. "You came up with the story line for *Terms of Endearment*?"

"Not the story line per se, but the basic concept. My chick didn't get married and have all them kids. You want my opinion, that was over the top."

"Wasn't *Terms of Endearment* a Larry McMurtry book?"

He shook his head, sighing. "My point exactly. Where do you think he got it?"

"What about the astronaut? The Jack Nicholson part?"

"I didn't fool with that and personally, I didn't think it worked all that well. Later I found out this actress had the same agent used to be partners with Shirley MacLaine's agent way back when. That's the way Hollywood works. Real incestuous. The whole deal kind of soured me, to tell you the truth. I never saw a dime, and when I asked her about it, she gives me this look like she doesn't even know what I'm talking about. I kicked the shit out of her town car and set fire to the thing."

"Really."

He slid a look in my direction. "You probably have a lot of interesting experiences in your line of work."

"I don't. It's mostly paperwork."

"Same here. People think I must know all these rock stars. Closest I ever came was once I drove Sonny Bono to his hotel. Privacy window was rolled up the whole time, which kind of pissed me off. Like I'm going to call the *National Enquirer* if he sticks his hand up some chick's skirt."

I torqued around in my seat. The privacy window was rolled down and I peered past the length of the limousine's interior through the darkly tinted rear window. There was a moving stream of cars behind us, all barreling down the highway at breakneck speeds. We turned off the main highway into the commercial/industrial park. In the distance, I saw the Desert Castle appear, red neon glowing hotly against the night sky. I watched while the red drained out of the letters and filled up again. The ratio of the lighted rooms to dark created an irregular checkerboard effect, with the proliferation of black squares suggesting fifteen percent occupancy. Only a smattering of cars now followed in our wake. As this was Sunday evening, it was hard to believe that any were heading for the offices across the way. We passed the miniature oasis with its phony stone tower, the structure probably only slightly taller than I. Nathaniel swung the limo into the circular hotel entranceway, pulling to a smooth stop beneath the portico.

I felt anxiety stir, wondering if he expected payment for his services. "I don't have enough to tip you. I'm really sorry about that."

"That's cool." He handed me his business card. "You

have any ideas for a female-type Sam Spade film, we could maybe collaborate. Chicks kickin' shit and stuff like that."

"I'll give it some thought. I really appreciate your help."

I got out and closed the door behind me, aware that the limo was already pulling away. There was no sign of the sheriff's deputy, but Dallas County is a big place, and it hadn't been that long since I'd called. I moved toward the revolving doors, half trotting in my haste. The lobby was crowded with the departing track team, kids in shorts, jeans, and matching satin jackets with their school mascot stitched across the back. All of them wore running shoes that made their feet look enormous and reduced their preadolescent legs to sticks. Gym bags and oversize canvas duffels had been lined up in random clusters while the kids themselves milled around, engaged in various forms of horseplay. Some of the girls sat on the floor, using the baggage for back-rests. One kid had had his T-shirt peeled off against his will, and he was in the process of wrestling with two teammates to get it back. The laughter had a nervous edge to it. Really, the boys reminded me of puppies playing tug-of-war with an old sock. The supervising adults seemed to take all this energy for granted, prob-ably hoping the kids would be exhausted by the time they got on the bus.

I moved past them to the elevators and pushed the "up" button. The elevator doors down the line opened and I got on, glancing back across the lobby to see if there was any sign of Gilbert. A silver Trailways bus was just pulling up in front, motor growling while the door opened with the sound of flatulence. I pushed twelve and the elevator doors slid shut.

Once on Laura's floor, I trotted down the hall and

knocked on 1236. I was murmuring to myself, snapping my fingers rapidly. Come on, come on, come on.

Laura answered the door, slightly taken aback when she saw me. "What are you doing here? I thought you left."

"Where's Ray? I gotta talk to him."

"He's asleep. He's right here. What's wrong?"

"I saw Gilbert at the airport. He's on his way over with a gun. Get Ray, grab your things, and let's get out of here."

"Oh no." She seemed to pale at the news, one hand going to her mouth.

"What's going on?" Ray said from behind her. He was already on his feet, tucking his shirt in as he approached. I moved into the room and Laura closed the door behind me. She leaned against the wall, her eyes momentarily closing in dread. I slid the security chain across the track.

I said, "Go."

The word seemed to get her mobilized. Laura moved toward the closet, hauling out her raincoat and the duffel.

"What's happening?" Ray said, looking from one of us to the other.

"She saw Gilbert. He's got a gun and he's on his way. You should have called instead of coming all the way back," she said reprovingly. She unzipped the duffel and began to sweep cosmetics off the counter into the bag.

"I did call. The line was busy."

"I was talking to room service. We had to eat," she said.

"Ladies, would you quit bickering and let's move!"

"I am!" She began to snatch up her nightie, slippers, dirty underwear. She'd laid her denim dress across the back of the chair, and she grabbed that, holding it against her chest so she could fold it in thirds and then in half again. Ray took it, rolled it in a ball, and jammed it in the duffel, which he zipped shut.

I saw his two suitcases stacked up to the left of the door. I grabbed the smaller one and watched while he picked up the other. "Take what's essential and dump the rest," I said. "You have a car?"

"Out in the lot."

"Will Gilbert try the elevator or the stairs?"

"Who knows?"

I said, "Look. I think you two should go the back way. Gilbert's bound to waste time knocking on the door up here. He may try Ray's room, too, if it occurs to him you're here. Give me the car keys and tell me where you're parked."

"What are we supposed to do in the meantime?" Laura asked.

"Wait for me out by that fake stone tower by the drive. I'll get the car and swing around to pick you up. He doesn't know me, so if we pass in the hall, he won't think anything of it."

Ray gave me a hasty description of the car and its approximate location. The plastic tag on the key listed the license plate number, so I was reasonably certain I could find it without trouble. I handed Ray the bag while Laura did a quick survey, making sure she hadn't left anything critical. I took the chain off the hook and peered into the corridor both ways, motioning to the two of them. Ray and Laura took a right, heading for the fire stairs at the end of the hall.

I moved to the left toward the elevators.

The elevator felt like it was descending at half speed. I watched the lighted floor numbers move from right to left, counting backward in slow motion. When the ele-

vator reached the lobby, there was the customary *ping*
and then the doors slid open. Gilbert was standing two
feet away, waiting to get on. For a moment, our eyes
locked and held. His were bottomless dark holes. I let
my gaze drift away casually as I passed, moving off to
the right as if on ordinary hotel business. Behind me,
the doors slid shut. I checked the lobby for some sign
of the county sheriff's deputy. No sign of law enforce-
ment. I picked up my pace, glancing back automatically
at the floor indicator lights. The elevator should have
been going up. Instead, the light remained frozen where
it was. I heard a *ping* and the elevator doors slid open.
Gilbert emerged. He stood on the wide expanse of carpeting just outside the elevators, staring in my direction.
Crooks and cops often function with a heightened sense
of awareness, a clarity of perception born of adrenaline.
Their work, and just as often their lives, depend on acu-
men. Gilbert was apparently a person who registered
reality with uncanny accuracy. Something in his expression told me he remembered my face from our one
brief encounter at the Santa Teresa airport. How he put
me together with Laura Huckaby, I'll never know. The
moment was electric, recognition arcing between us like
a lightning bolt.

I kept my pace at "normal" as I turned the corner. I
passed the entrance to the coffee shop and turned right
again into a short corridor with three doors leading off
it: one blank, one marked Authorized Personnel Only,
one marked Maintenance. The minute I was out of Gilbert's visual range, I broke into a run, my shoulder bag
thumping against my hip. I slammed through the unmarked door and found myself in a barren back hallway
I hadn't seen before. The concrete floor and bare concrete walls curved around to the left. The walls extended upward into the fading light until the upper

reaches disappeared into darkness. There was no ceiling
in view, but a series of thick ropes and chains hung
motionless among the shadows. I passed empty racks of
serving trays, wooden pallets packed with glassware,
stacks of linen tablecloths, carts filled with plates in assorted sizes. Bank after bank of stacked chairs lined the
walls, narrowing the passage in places.

My footsteps *chunk*ed softly, the sound blunted by
the rubber tread on my Reeboks. I had to guess that this
was a service corridor, bordering a banquet room, a circle within a circle with access to freight elevators and
the kitchens one floor down. A short flight of stairs led
upward. I grabbed the handrail and pulled myself along,
skipping steps as I ran. The shoulder bag made me feel
like I was dragging an anchor, but I couldn't part with
it. At the top, the corridor continued. Here, stacked
against the walls, were various seasonal decorations:
Christmas angels, artificial spruce trees, two enormous
interlocking comedy/tragedy masks, gilded wooden
putti and cupids, enormous Valentine hearts pierced
with golden arrows. A grove of silk ficus suggested a
small interior forest bereft of birds and other wildlife.

Behind me, I heard a door hinge squeak. I picked up
my pace, following the deserted corridor. A metal ladder that looked like an interior fire escape scaled its
way up the wall on my left. I let my eye take the journey first, uncertain what was up there. I glanced back,
dimly aware that someone was coming along the corridor behind me. I grabbed the first rung and headed up,
Reeboks *tink*ing as I climbed. I paused at the top, which
was some twenty feet up. A steel catwalk stretched out
along the wall ahead of me. I was close enough to the
ceiling to reach up and touch it. The catwalk itself was
less than three feet wide. Below me, through the yawn-
ing shadows, the floor looked like a flat still river of

concrete. The only thing that kept me from falling was a chain rail supported by metal uprights. As usual, when confronted with heights, my greatest fear was the irresistible urge to fling myself off.

I slowed to a creeping pace, hugging the wall. I didn't dare go any faster for fear the catwalk itself would be loosened from the wall-mounted brackets that secured it. I didn't think I could be seen, cloaked as I was by the darkness up here, but the corridor itself functioned like an echo chamber announcing my presence. Somewhere behind me, I heard hard heels on concrete, a running step that slowed suddenly to a stealthier pace. I sank to my hands and knees and crawled forward with care, the metal surface beneath me buckling and trembling. I had to hump my shoulder bag in front of me as I progressed. I was trying not to call attention to myself, but the rickety catwalk rattled and danced beneath my weight.

I spotted a small wooden door in the wall. With infinite care, I eased the latch back and opened it. Before me was a dimly lighted, musty passageway about six feet high, rimmed along the top with a continuous series of hand-cranked window panels, some of which were standing open, admitting artificial light. The floor of the passageway was carpeted and smelled of dust motes. I felt my way forward, still on hands and knees, now hauling the bag after me. The silence was punctuated only by the sound of my ragged breathing.

I turned and eased the door shut behind me, then crept over to the nearest window and lifted myself gingerly to my feet. Below was one of those vast meeting rooms meant for banquets and large assemblages. An endless pattern of fleur-de-lis proceeded across the carpeting, steel blue on a ground of gray. A series of sliding doors could be drawn across the space at the midway point, effectively dividing the one room into two. Eight evenly spaced chandeliers hung like clusters of icicles, throwing out a flat light. Around the periphery, up near the ceiling where I was, the continuous rim of mirrored-glass windows concealed the space where I hid. I peered back across my shoulder. Through the gloom now, I could see the looming apparatus for a lighting system that must have been called into play on special occasions, floods and spots with various colored gels.

By the light coming through the windows, I hunkered down and opened my bag, taking out my wallet. I removed my driver's license, PI license, and other identification, including cash and credit cards, all of which I stuffed in the pockets of my blazer in haste. I snagged Ray's car keys, my birth control pills, the key picks, and my Swiss Army knife, cursing the fact that women's suit jackets aren't constructed with an interior breast pocket. I plucked out my toothbrush and tucked it in with the other items. My blazer pockets were bulging, but I couldn't help myself. In a pinch, I'm willing to suffer tatty underpants, but not unbrushed teeth.

I became aware that the floor beneath me was vibrating ever so slightly. In California, I'd assume that a 2.2 magnitude temblor was lapping through the earth like an ocean wave. I whipped my head around toward the door. I set my bag aside, sank to a hunkering position, and duck-walked across the narrow passage. I felt the perimeter of the door, fingers searching for the latch bolt on my side. On the far side of the wall, someone was making shaky progress, just as I had, along the catwalk. I found the latch and, ever so silently, pushed the bolt through the eye.

I still had my hand on the bolt when the door gave a vicious rattle. Someone on the far side was testing the latch. A spurt of fear traveled through me, triggering tears that leapt into my eyes. I pressed my hand against my mouth to suppress a gasp. The door was chattering against the lock so hard I thought it would give way, leaving me exposed to view. Silence. Then the floor began to shake again as Gilbert moved away. I glanced to my left, following his progress as he continued down the catwalk. I prayed there wasn't another wooden doorway farther down the line.

He must have reached a dead end because a few minutes later, I felt the floor vibrate with his weight as he passed me again, this time heading toward the ladder leading down to the corridor.

I waited until I thought I was safe. It felt like an eternity but was probably close to fifteen minutes. Then I reached out carefully and pushed the bolt back. I bent my head to listen, hearing nothing. When I opened the door, the fire alarm went off.

# 14

MY OPENING OF the door and the clanging were so closely connected, I thought Gilbert had booby-trapped the door somehow. The overhead sprinklers came on in a torrent of internal rain. The distant scent of smoke assailed me, as unmistakable as the lingering trail of perfume when a woman passes. I moved back to the windows overlooking the banquet room. There was no sign of flames, no billowing black smoke. The room looked empty, bright and blank. Someone began to make an announcement on the public address system, giving instructions or advice about what hotel guests were supposed to do. All I could hear was the muffled urgency of the proclamation. The exact location of the fire was anybody's guess.

The lights went out, plunging me into total darkness. I felt my way over to the wooden door, crawling though unencumbered by worldly possessions. I was being stripped down to the essentials, feeling light and free and, at the same time, anxious. My handbag was a talisman, as comforting as a security blanket. Its bulk and heft were familiar, its contents assurance that certain totem items were always within reach. The bag had served as both pillow and weapon. It felt odd to be shed of it, but I knew it had to be. Blindly, I measured the width of the catwalk, sensing the cavernous abyss on my left where my hand plunged suddenly into nothingness.

The entire area was pitch black, but I could hear an ominous pop and crackling noise. A blistering wind blew, sending a shower of sparks in my direction. I could smell hot, dry wood, undercut by the acrid odor of petroleum-based products changing chemical states. I inched my way forward. Ahead, I could now discern a soft reddish glow defining the wall where the corridor curved left. A long finger of smoke curled around the corner toward me. If the fire caught me on the catwalk, it would probably sweep right past, but the rising cloud of toxic fumes would snuff me out as effectively as the flames.

While the water from the sprinkler system hissed steadily, it seemed to have no effect on the fire that I could see. The play of tawny light on the walls began to expand and dance, pushing fine ash and black smoke ahead of it, gobbling up all the available oxygen. The metal catwalk was slippery, the chain railing swinging wildly as I propelled myself onward. The public address system came to life again. The same announcement was repeated, a garbled blend of consonants. I reached the top of the ladder. I was afraid to turn my back on the encroaching fire, but I had no choice. With my right foot, I felt for the first rung, gauging the distance as I moved down from rung to rung. I began descending with care, my hands sliding on the wet metal side rail. Hanging lengths of chain turned gold in the light, sparks flying up, winking out like intermittent fireflies on a hot summer night. By now, the fire was providing sufficient illumination to see the air turn gray as smoke accumulated.

I reached the bottom of the ladder and moved to my left. The fire was heating the air to an uncomfortable degree. I could hear a snapping sound, glass shattering, the merry rustle of destruction as the flames roared toward me. Despite the liberal use of concrete, the hotel had sufficient combustible material to feed the swiftly spreading blaze. I heard the dull boom of thunder as something behind me gave way and collapsed. This entire portion of the hotel had apparently been engulfed. I spotted a door on my left. I tried the knob, which was cool to the touch. I turned it and pushed through, spilling abruptly into a second-floor hall.

Here the air was much cooler. The rain birds in the ceiling showered the deserted corridor with irregular sprays. I was getting used to the dark, which now seemed less dense, a chalky gloom instead of the impenetrable black of the inner corridor. The carpet was saturated, slapping wetly beneath my feet as I stumbled down the darkened hallway. Afraid to trust my eyes, I held my arms out stiffly, waving my hands in front of me like a game of blindman's buff. The fire alarm continued its monotonous clanging, a secondary horn bleating gutturally. In a submarine movie, we'd be diving by now. I felt my way across another door frame. Again, the knob seemed cool to the touch, suggesting that, for the time being, the fire wasn't raging on the other side. I turned the knob, pushing the door open in front of me. I found myself on the fire stairs, which I knew intimately by now. I went down through the blackness, reassured by the familiarity of the stairwell. The air was cold and smelled clean.

When I reached the main floor, the emergency generators kicked in and briefly lights flickered back to life. The corridor was deserted, doors closed. Here, there was no sign of movement, no hint of smoke, the sprinkler system muffled. Every public room I passed was empty of guests. I found a fire door marked Emergency Exit with a big flexible bar across the center, the surface posted with warnings. As I pushed through the door, yet another siren began to howl behind me. I walked rapidly, without a backward glance, until I reached the side lot where Ray's rental car was parked.

The fire engines were pulled up at the hotel entrance, where clusters of evacuated hotel guests were milling about. The night sky was a fervent yellow, choked by columns of white smoke where the fire and the water from the hoses came into contact. At the side of the building, two sprays of water crossed in midair like a pair of klieg lights. Parts of the hotel were completely engulfed by fire, glass crashing, flames curling up as a cloud of black smoke rolled out. The portion of the driveway that I could see was blocked by the fire trucks and fire hoses, emergency vehicles flashing strobes of amber light. Overhead, a helicopter hovered where a local news team was taking pictures, reporting live at the scene.

I found Ray's car keys in my blazer pocket and let myself into his rental. I started the engine and flipped the heater on. My clothes were soaked, water still trickling down my face from the hair plastered to my head. I knew I smelled of smoke, wet wool, wet denim, and damp socks. The Texas night was cold, and I could feel myself being overtaken by a bone-deep shivering. I let the engine warm up. The car was a "full-size" Ford: a four-door automatic, white with a red interior. I threw the gears into reverse and backed out of the slot, scanning the empty parking lot for signs of Gilbert.

I left my headlights off as I eased along the perimeter of the lot toward the far side. The exit was blocked by a cop with a flashlight, forcing traffic to detour. I picked a spot along a row of hedges and drove across the curb, forcing the car through the thickly growing bushes. I emerged on the access road about a hundred yards beyond the roadblock. The officer probably saw me, but there was not much that he could do. He had his hands full directing all the carloads of rubberneckers. I turned right on the road leading back to the main highway. As I passed the miniature stone castle, I slowed, giving my horn a quick beep. Ray and Laura emerged hurriedly from the shadows, Ray toting the three bags, loaded down like a pack mule. Laura still wore the phony harness in front, the eight thousand dollars borne against her belly like an infant. The illusion of pregnancy was so convincing that Ray hovered protectively. I heard the trunk pop open, followed by the thumping impact as Ray flung the bags in the back and banged the lid down. He opened the door on the passenger side front and slid onto the seat next to me while Laura let herself in the back. I put my foot on the gas and took off with a chirp, anxious to put distance between us and the enemy.

Ray said, "We didn't think you'd show. We were just about to take off on foot." He turned around, peering through the rear window at the burning hotel behind us. "Gilbert did that?"

"One assumes," I said.

"Of course he did," Laura said peevishly. "He was probably waiting out front, ready to pick us off as we came through the revolving doors."

I glanced at her in the rearview mirror. Like Ray, she had turned to peer back at the fire. The glow on the horizon varied from blood red to salmon, a white cloud

billowing where the water from the fire hoses turned to
steam. "It's a hell of a blaze. How'd he manage it without accelerants?"

"Give him credit. The guy's resourceful. He's quick
on his feet and he's good at improvisation," she said.

Ray turned to face forward, reaching for his seat belt,
which he snapped into place. I saw him glance at me
again, checking my bedraggled state. I felt like a dog
left in the backyard during a sudden rain. He leaned
sideways on his seat, pulling out a handkerchief that he
passed me. Gratefully, I mopped at the trickles of water
running down my face. "Thanks."

"You going back to the airport?"

"Not looking like this. Besides, I've already missed
my . . . Shit!" I realized with a jolt that I'd left my plane
ticket in the shoulder bag I'd abandoned. I patted my
blazer pockets, but there wasn't any point. I couldn't
believe it. Of all things. In my haste, I'd simply missed
the airline envelope. If I'd just grabbed the ticket or,
better yet, held on to the bag itself. Now all I owned
were the odds and ends I carried on my person. I was
nearly sick with regret. The plane ticket represented not
only my return home, but most of my liquid assets. I
banged on the steering wheel. "Goddamn it," I said.

Laura leaned forward against the front seat. "What's
wrong?"

"I left my plane ticket back there."

"Uh-oh. Well, it's gone now," she said, stating the
obvious with what looked like a smirk. If I hadn't been
at the wheel, I'd have leapt in the backseat and bitten
her.

Ray must have seen the expression that crossed my
face. "Where we headed?" he asked, probably hoping to
avoid a rabies quarantine.

"I don't even know where we are," I groused. I

pointed to the glove compartment. "You got a map in there?"

He opened the glove compartment, which was empty except for the rental car contract and a whisk broom with chewed-looking bristles. He snapped it shut and checked the passenger door pocket. I slid a hand into the pocket on my side, coming up with assorted papers, one a neatly folded map of the United States. Ray grunted with satisfaction and flipped on the overhead light. Spread out, the crackling map took up most of the available space. "Looks like you need to keep an eye out for U.S. 30 heading northeast."

"Where to?"

Laura glanced over at him. "I bet to Louisville, right?"

He turned to her. "You got a problem with that?"

"Gilbert's not a fool, Ray. Where you think he's going?"

"So the guy goes to Louisville. Who gives a shit? We're talking about a twelve-hour drive. He's never going to figure out which route we took."

"Listen, Einstein. There's only *one*," she said.

"Can't be. That's bullshit. There must be half a dozen," he said.

She reached over and snatched the map away. "You been in prison too long." I could hear her flap the map noisily in the backseat, refolding it while she found the section showing Dallas and points east. "Look at this. There's maybe one other way to go, but 30's the obvious choice. All Gilbert has to do is drive like a maniac and get there first."

"How's he going to find us? Once we get to town, we'll take a couple motel rooms and use fictitious names. Pay cash and call ourselves anything we want. Isn't that what you did?"

"Yeah, and look what happened. Kinsey found me in no time flat. So did Gilbert, for that matter."

"It was a fluke. Finding you was pure accident. Ask her," he said.

"I wouldn't call it a *fluke*," I said, taking offense.

"You know what I mean. The point is, it's not like you *deduced* what she was calling herself and tracked her down from that. All you did was follow her, right?"

"Yeah, but what about Gilbert? How'd he manage it?" I asked.

Ray shrugged. "He probably persuaded Farley to spill the beans."

From the backseat, Laura moaned. "Oh, jeez. Is that true? I hadn't thought about that. You think Farley's okay?"

"I can't worry about that right now," Ray said.

I glanced back at Laura, still in charge of the map. "What's the nearest big town between here and there?"

Laura checked the map again. "We get to Texarkana first and then Little Rock. After that it's Memphis, then Nashville, and straight on up. Why?"

"Because I'm heading home. We'll take a side trip to the airport in Little Rock and I'll catch a plane."

"What about your ticket?" Ray asked.

"I'll call a friend of mine. He'll help."

Laura said, "In the meantime, how about a pit stop before I wet my pants?"

"Sounds good to me," Ray said.

I watched the highway signs until I spotted an off-ramp that boasted the international symbols for food and potty chairs. Half a block off the road, we found a poorly lighted independent gas station with a cafe attached. Even Gilbert wasn't canny enough to ferret us out here. The gas tank was still very close to full, so I bypassed the pumps and parked off to one side, away from the street. Ray headed for the men's room while Laura opened the trunk and pulled out her duffel bag. "You can borrow my dress."

In the sour light of the ladies' room, I removed my Reeboks and wet socks and then peeled off my damp blazer, blue jeans, turtleneck, and soggy undergarments. I was shivering again, but Laura's dry clothes began to warm me almost as soon as I pulled them on. She still wore the dark green corduroy jumper with a white turtleneck under it while I was assigned the denim dress, a pair of tights, and slightly oversize tennis shoes. "See you in a minute," she said. She left the rest room, giving me a few minutes alone.

I ran water in the sink until the hot came through, then rinsed my face and doused my head, washing out the smell of smoke. I used the harsh paper toweling to dry my hair, then used my fingers to comb the strands into place. I felt a wave of nausea rush through me like a hot flash. I put my hands on the sink, leaning on my arms, while I composed myself. Sunday night and I was stuck in some nameless Dallas suburb with an ex-con, his daughter, and a papoose of illicit cash. I let out a big breath and stared at my reflection in the dingy mirror. I shrugged ruefully. Things could (probably) be worse. So far, no one had been hurt and I had a few bucks left. I was looking forward to a meal, though I'd have to depend on my companions to pay for it. As soon as we got to Little Rock, I'd put a call through to Henry, who would come to my rescue. He could wire the money, buy the airline ticket on his credit card, or some combination thereof. By morning I'd be safely tucked in my bed, catching up on my sleep while I counted my blessings.

I went back to the car, stuffing most of my damp belongings in the trunk beside Ray's suitcases. The blazer, though still damp, I carried with me into the cafe, unwilling to have it out of my sight. The place was largely empty and had a homely, neglected air. Even the locals must have eschewed the establishment, which had probably started as a mom-and-pop operation and been reduced some time since to its current orphaned state. I didn't see any flies, but the ghosts of Flies Past seemed to hover in the air. The front windows were swathed in dust from some half-finished construction across the street. Even the fake potted plants carried a powdering of soot.

Ray and Laura sat across from each other in a corner booth. I slid in beside Ray, not that eager to have his bruised and battered face in view while I was trying to eat. Laura didn't look much better. Like me, she wore no makeup, but while bare skin is my preferred state, she'd been carefully camouflaging the blows Gilbert had systematically administered. I had to guess that most of her bruises had been inflicted some time ago because the darkest discolorations had washed out to mild greens and yellows. Ray, by contrast, was a veritable rainbow of abuse, scabbed and cut and restitched here and there. I kept my gaze pinned to the menu, which offered all the standard items: chicken-fried steak and chicken-fried chicken, hamburgers, fries, BLTs, grilled-cheese sandwiches, and "fresh" soups probably poured from big cans in the back. We ordered cheeseburgers, fries, and large, nearly fizz-free Cokes. Without carbonation, the soft drinks tasted like the syrups once used as home remedies for ladies' maladies. The waitress had the good grace not to quiz my companions about their injuries.

While we ate, I said to Ray, "Just out of curiosity, once you get to Louisville, how will you figure out where the money's hidden?"

He finished a bite of burger and wiped his mouth with a paper napkin. "Don't know that yet. Johnny said he'd leave word with Ma in case something happened to him, but who knows if he ever got around to it. Deal was, I'd get out of prison and come find him in California. Then the two of us would go back to Louisville and pick up the money. He wanted things ceremonial, you know, celebrate all the wait and all the hard work went into it. Any rate, as near as I can tell, wherever the money's at, it takes a key to get to."

"Which I have," I said.

"What key?" Laura asked. This was apparently news to her, and she seemed to resent that I knew more than she did.

Ray ignored her. "You still got it?"

"With a little notice, I can lay hands on it," I said.

"Good. I don't want you going off without passing it over."

"You think I'm going to help you cheat Chester out of his fair share?"

"Hey, he'd do the same to me. He'll probably cheat you, too."

"I don't even want to get into that," I said. "You think Johnny really did what he said?"

"I can't believe he'd put dough like that in limbo. He'd have a backup plan, some kind of fail-safe, in case he got hit by a car, something like that. What makes you ask? You got any ideas yourself?"

I shook my head. "It's just an interesting proposition. What's your strategy?"

"My strategy is solve that problem when I come to it," he said.

Once we hit the road again, Ray crawled in the back to sleep while I drove and Laura took his place in the passenger seat. The two of us watched the silver ribbon of highway curl away beneath us. The lights on the dashboard threw off a soft illumination. In deference to Ray, we kept the radio turned down and confined our conversation to an occasional remark. Ray began to snore, a sputtering exsufflation punctuated by quiet, as if someone were holding his nose shut at intervals. When it was clear that nothing short of a four-car flame-out was going to wake him, we began to chat in low tones.

"I take it you never had a chance to spend time with him," I said.

Laura shrugged. "Not really. My mother used to make me write once a month. She was always big on taking care of those less fortunate than we were. I can remember looking around, wondering who the hell she could be talking about. Then she remarried and seemed to forget about Ray. Made me feel guilty at first 'til I forgot myself. Little kids aren't exactly famous for satisfying other people's needs."

I said, "Actually, I think kids try to satisfy everyone. What other choice do they have? When you're dependent on someone, you better hope you keep 'em happy."

"Said like a true neurotic. Are your parents still alive?"

"No. They died together in an accident when I was five."

"Yeah. Well, imagine if one of 'em suddenly showed up one day. You live your life wishing you had a father. Then suddenly you have one and you realize you don't have the vaguest idea what to do with him." She cast an uneasy look in the backseat at Ray. If he was faking sleep, he was really good at it.

I said, "Are you close to your mother?"

"I was until Gilbert. She doesn't like him much, but that's probably because he never paid her much attention. She's a bit of a southern belle. She likes guys who fawn."

"What about your stepfather? What's the story on him?"

"He and Gilbert are as thick as thieves. He never wanted to believe Gilbert's hitting me was unprovoked. It's not like he *approved*. He just always assumes there's another side to it. He's the kind who says 'Well, that's *your* story. I'm sure Gilbert would have something else to say about this.' He prides himself on being fair, not jumping to conclusions. Like a judge, you know? He wants to hear prosecution and defense arguments before he hands down his sentence. He says he doesn't want to be judgmental. What he really means is he doesn't believe a word I say. Whatever Gilbert does, I deserve, you know? He probably wishes he could take a pop at me himself."

"What about your mother? Didn't she object to Gilbert's hitting you, or didn't she know?"

"She says whatever Paul says. It's like an unspoken agreement. She doesn't want to rock the boat. She doesn't like conflicts or disagreements. All she wants is peace and quiet. She's just so thrilled to have someone taking care of her, she doesn't want to make waves. Paul always makes out like he's doing her such a big favor being married to her. I think she was twenty-four when they met. I was maybe five years old. So there she was, with an ex-husband in jail and no means of support. The only job she ever had was working as a drugstore clerk. She couldn't make enough to survive. She had to go on welfare, which she thought was the lowest of the low. Her big shame. What the hell. She needed help. It's not like I was illegitimate, but in her eyes, it was the worst. She never wants to have to sink to that again. Besides, with Paul, she doesn't have to work. He doesn't want her to. He wants her to keep house and cater to his every whim. Not a bad deal."

"Yes, it is. It sounds grim."

Laura smiled. "I guess it does, doesn't it? Anyway, when I was growing up, Paul was critical, authoritarian. He ruled the roost. He nearly broke his arm patting himself on the back for all he did for us. In his own way, he was good to her. He never gave a shit about me, but to be fair about it, I'm sure I was a pain. Probably still am, if it comes to that." She leaned her head back against the seat. "Are you married?"

"I was." I held up two fingers.

"You were married twice? Me too. Once to a guy with a 'substance abuse' problem," she said, using her fingers to mark the phrase with quotes.

"Cocaine?"

"That and heroin. Speed, grass, stuff like that. The other husband was a mama's boy. Jesus, he was weak. He got on my nerves because he was so insecure. He didn't know how to do anything. Plus, he needed all this reassurance. Like what do I know? I'm hardly in a position to make somebody else feel good."

"What about Gilbert?"

"He was great, at first. His problem is, he doesn't trust, you know? He doesn't know how to open up. He can really be so sweet. Sometimes when he drinks, he busts out crying like a baby. Breaks my heart."

"Along with your nose," I said.

# 15

WE PASSED THROUGH Greenville, Brashear, Saltillo, and Mt. Vernon, crossing sparsely wooded farmland on gently rolling hills. Laura fell asleep with her head against the window. Traffic was light and the road was hypnotic. Twice I jerked myself awake, having dropped into a moment of microsleep. To keep alert, I reviewed my intellectual *Atlas of Texarkana* facts, discovering in the process that the entire category contained only two bits of information. First, the Arkansas-Texas state line bisects the town of Texarkana, so that half the population lives in Texas and half in Arkansas. And last, the town is the site of a Federal Correctional Institution, about which I knew nothing else. So much for that form of mental stimulation.

On the outskirts of town, I pulled into an all-night filling station, where I stopped to stretch my legs. Ray was still dead to the world, so Laura traded places with me and took the wheel. Laura pitched in five bucks and we bought exactly that much gas. It was close to ten-thirty when we crossed the state line, with approximately two hours to go until we reached Little Rock. I settled into the passenger seat, slouched on my spine, knees bent, my feet propped up on the dashboard. I crossed my arms for warmth. The remaining damp in my blazer enveloped me in a humid cloud of woolly smells. The drone of the engine combined with Ray's staccato snores had a tranquilizing effect. The next thing I knew I was drooling on myself. I put my feet down and sat up straight, feeling groggy and disoriented. We passed a highway sign that indicated we'd left U.S. 30 and were now heading north on U.S. 40. "How far to Little Rock?"

"We already passed Little Rock. This is Biscoe coming up."

"We *passed* Little Rock? I told you I wanted to stop," I whispered hoarsely.

"What was I supposed to do? You had the map and you were sound asleep. I had no idea where the airport was, and I didn't want to drive all over hell and gone trying to find it."

"Why not wake me?"

"I tried once. I said your name and got no response."

"Weren't there any road signs?"

"Not that I saw. Besides, they're not going to have any flights out at this hour. This is the boonies. Get a clue," she whispered back. She reverted to a normal tone, though she kept her voice down in deference to Ray. "It's time to find a motel so we can get a couple hours' sleep. I'm half dead. I about ran off the road more than once in the last hour."

I did a three-sixty scan of the terrain, spotting little in the dark beyond farms and occasional dense woods. "Take your pick," I said.

"There'll be a town coming up," she said without concern.

Sure enough, we came to a townlet with a one-story off-road motel, its vacancy sign winking. She pulled into a small gravel parking lot and got out. She turned her back to the car and reached up under her jumper, apparently removing a wad of cash from the belly harness she wore. I gave Ray a nudge and he rose from the depths like a diver in the process of decompressing.

I said, "Laura wants to stop. We're both beat."

"Fine with me," he said. He pulled himself into a sitting position, blinking with puzzlement. "We still in Texas?"

"This is Arkansas. We got Little Rock behind us and Memphis coming up."

"I thought you were leaving us."

"So did I."

He yawned, giving his face a dry rub with his hands. He squinted at his watch, trying to see the dial in the scanty light. "What time is it?"

"After one."

I could see Laura at the entrance to the motel lobby. The lights inside were dim, and the front door must have been locked because I saw her knock repeatedly, then cup her hands against the glass to peek in. Finally, some unhappy-looking soul emerged from the manager's office. Much animated conversation, hand gestures, and peering in our direction. Laura was admitted to the office, where I saw her at the counter, filling out the registration card. My guess was her being pregnant lent her an air of vulnerability, especially at this hour. A fistful of cash probably didn't hurt her cause. Moments later, she emerged from the office and returned to the car, dangling two room keys, which she handed to me as she got back behind the wheel. "Ray gets his own room. I can't sleep with that racket."

She started the car and pulled around to the rear.

Ours were the last two rooms at the far end. There was only one other car and it had Iowa plates, so I figured we were temporarily safe from Gilbert. Ray hauled one of his bags from the trunk while Laura grabbed the duffel and I took the armload of damp clothes I'd dumped. Maybe hanging them up overnight would finish the drying process and render them wearable.

Ray paused at his door. "What time in the morning?"

"I think we should be on the road by six. If we're going, get on with it. No point fooling around," Laura said. "Open your drapes when you're up and we'll do likewise." She glanced at me. "Okay with you?"

"Sure, it's fine."

Ray disappeared into his room and I followed her into ours: two double beds and a drab interior complete with mustiness. If the color beige had an odor, it would smell like this. It looked like the kind of place where you wouldn't want to jump out of bed without making a noise first. Otherwise, you might inadvertently step on one of the scuttling hard-shelled bugs. The little fellow I saw had gotten trapped in the corner, where he was patiently pawing the walls like a dog wanting out. You can't squish those things without risking that sudden spurt of lemon pudding on the sole of your shoe. I hung my garments in the closet, after a gingerly inspection. No brown recluse spiders or furry rodents in evidence.

The bathroom boasted brown vinyl tile, a fiberglass shower enclosure, two plastic glasses wrapped in cellophane, and two paper-wrapped soaps the size of business cards. I pulled out my traveling toothbrush and weensy tube of toothpaste and brushed my teeth in wordless ecstasy. In the absence of a nightie, I slept in my (borrowed) underwear, folding the cotton coverlet in half for warmth. Laura went into the bathroom, piously shutting the door before she removed her belly

harness. I was asleep within minutes and never heard
her climb into her own creaking bed.

It was still dark when she bumped me at 5:45 A.M.
"You want to shower first?" she asked.

"You go ahead."

The light blasted on in the bathroom, slanting across
my face briefly before she closed the door. She'd
opened the drapes, admitting illumination from the
lights outside in the parking lot. Through the wall, I
thought I could hear the shower next door, which meant
Ray was awake. In prison, he'd probably always risen
at this hour. Now a shower would be a luxury, since
he'd have it to himself and wouldn't have to worry
about sexual assault every time he dropped the soap. I
raised up on one elbow and looked out at the auto body
shop across the street. A forty-watt bulb burned above
the service bay. Monday morning and where was I? I
checked the printed match packet in the ashtray. Oh,
yeah. Whiteley, Arkansas. I remembered the road sign
outside of town claiming a population of 523. Probably
an exaggeration. I felt a sudden surge of melancholy,
longing for home. In the crazy days of my youth, before
herpes and AIDS, I used to wake up occasionally in
rooms like this one. There's a certain horror when you
can't quite remember who's whistling so merrily behind
the bathroom door. Often, when I found out, I couldn't
help but question my taste in male companionship. It
didn't take long to see morality as the quickest way to
avoid self-loathing.

When Laura cleared the bathroom, fully dressed, the
belly harness in place, I brushed my teeth, showered,
and washed my hair with the diminishing sliver of soap.
My blue jeans, while dry, were still suggestive of ash-
trays and cold campfires, so I donned Laura's denim

dress again. Just being clean gave me an enormous lift.
I retrieved my hanging garments from the closet and
took them out to the car.

The drive had been taking us on a steady line to the
north. Here, the cold was more pronounced. The air felt
thinner and the wind more cutting. Ray had pulled on a
fleece-lined denim jacket, and as we got in the car, he
tossed a sweatshirt to each of us. Gratefully, I pulled the
sweatshirt over my head and wore my blazer over that.
With the bulk of the sweatshirt, the fit was so tight I
could hardly move my arms, but at least I was warm.
Laura draped her sweatshirt across her shoulders like a
shawl. I got in the backseat, waiting in the car while
Laura dropped off the keys and Ray poured loose
change into the vending machine around the corner
from the office. They came back to the car with an assortment of snacks and soft drinks that Ray distributed
among us. After Laura had pulled onto the highway, we
ate a breakfast that consisted of off-brand cola, peanuts,
chocolate bars, peanut-butter crackers, and cheese
snacks completely devoid of nutritional value.

Laura put the heater on and the car was soon filled
with the soapy scent of Ray's aftershave. Aside from
the battered face and splinted fingers, both of which
looked vile, he was meticulous about his grooming. He
seemed to have an endless supply of plain white T-shirts
and chinos. For a man in his mid-sixties, he seemed to
be in good physical shape. Meanwhile, both Laura and
I were looking more bedraggled by the hour. In the
close quarters of the rental car, I could see that her dark
auburn hair had been dyed to that flaming shade. Her
part was slowly growing out, a widening margin of
gray. The strands bordering her face showed a rim of
white like the narrow matting on a picture frame. I
wondered if premature graying was a family trait.

The sun rose from behind a mountain of early morning clouds massed on the horizon, the sky changing swiftly from apricot to butter yellow to a mild clear blue. The land around us was flat. Looking at the map, I could see this portion of the state was part of the Mississippi flood plain, all the rivers draining east and south toward the Mississippi River. Lakes and hot springs dotted the map like rain splats, the northwest corner of the state weighted down with the Boston and the Ouachita Mountains. Laura kept her foot pressed firmly to the accelerator, maintaining a steady sixty miles an hour.

We were in Memphis at seven. I kept an eye out for a pay phone, intending to call Henry, but realized California was two hours behind. He tended to rise early, but five A.M. was really pushing it. Laura, sensing my train of thought, caught my eye in the rearview mirror. "I know you want to get home, but can't you wait until Louisville?"

"What's wrong with Nashville? We'll be there by midmorning, which is perfect for me."

"You'll slow us down. Check the map if you don't believe me. We'll be coming in on 40, taking 65 North across the state line. The Nashville airport is over on the far side of town. We'll lose an hour." She passed the map back to me, folded over to the section she was talking about.

I checked the relative distances. "You won't lose an hour. You're talking twenty minutes max. I thought you didn't want to go to Louisville, so what's the big hurry now?"

"I never said I didn't want to go. That's where I *live*. I said that's where Gilbert's going. I want to get my stuff out of the apartment before he shows up."

Ray said, "Forget your stuff. Buy new. Stay away

from there. You make a trip to the apartment, you run right into him."

"Not if I can get there before he does," she said. "That's why I don't want to waste time taking her to the airport. She can do that in Louisville. It isn't that much farther."

I could feel my body heat up with rising irritation. "It's another three hours."

"I'm not stopping," she said.

"Who put you in charge?"

"Who put *you*?"

"Ladies, hey! Knock it off. You're getting on my nerves. We got Gilbert to contend with. That's enough." Ray turned to look at me, his manner solicitous. "I have a suggestion. I know you're anxious to get home, but a few hours' delay isn't going to make any difference. Come to Louisville with us. We'll take you to my ma's where it's safe. You can take a hot shower and clean up while she runs your clothes through her machine." He glanced at Laura. "You come, too. She'd love to see you, I'm sure. How many years since you've visited your gramma?"

"Five or six," she said.

"See? She probably misses you like crazy. I'm sure she does," he said. "She'll fix a great home-cooked meal and then we'll take you to the airport. We'll even pay for your ticket."

Laura took her eyes off the road. "*We* will? Since when?"

"Come on. She's only in this because of us. Chester's probably never going to pay her, so now she's out the bucks. What's it going to cost us? It's the least we can do."

"You're very generous with money you don't have," she remarked.

Ray's smile faltered. Even from my position in the backseat, I could see the shift in his mood. "You saying I'm not entitled to what's in there?" he said, indicating her belly.

"Of course you're entitled. I didn't mean it that way, but this is costing us plenty as it is," she said.

"So?"

"So you could at least ask me first. I got a stake in it, too. In fact, the last I heard, you were giving me the whole eight grand."

"You turned me down."

"I did not!"

"You did when I was there," I said, practically sticking my tongue out at her.

"Would you tell her to stay out of our business! This has nothing to do with you, Kinsey, so mind your own beeswax."

I felt a laugh bubble up. "Be a sport. This is fun. I'm the adopted daughter. This is 'family dynamic.' Isn't that what it's called? I read about this stuff, but I never got to experience it. Sibling rivalry's a hoot."

"What do you know about family?"

"Not a thing. That's my point. I like all this bickering now that I've got the hang of it."

Ray said, "Is that true? You don't have family?"

"I have relatives, but no one close. Some cousins up in Lompoc, but none of this day-to-day stuff where people crank on each other and make trouble and act ugly."

"I lived a lot of years without family. It's my one regret," he said. "Anyway, will you come with us as far as Louisville? We'll get you home. I swear."

I'm a sucker when someone asks me nicely, especially an honorary father who smelled as good as he did. I said, "Sure. Why not? Your mother sounds like a trip."

"That she is," he said.

"How long since you've seen her?"

"Seventeen years. I was out on parole, but I got picked up on a violation before I got this far. She never came to see me in prison. I guess she didn't want to deal with it."

Having negotiated our agreement, we drove on in peace. We reached Nashville at 10:35, all of us hungry. Laura spotted a McDonald's, the golden arches visible off the Briley Parkway. She took the nearest off-ramp. As soon as we pulled into the parking lot, I saw her reach a hand under her jumper, where she made a discreet withdrawal from the Belly Button National Bank and Trust. Since mine was the only face unmarked by recent pounding, I was elected to go into the restaurant and purchase our lunch. To ensure variety in our diet, I bought an assortment of hamburgers, Big Macs, and Quarter Pounders with Cheese. I also bought two sizes of French fries, and Cokes large enough to make us pee every twenty minutes. I also picked up three boxes of animal crackers, with nifty string handles, for those of us good enough to clean our plates. To show how refined we were, we ate while the car was still parked at the rear of the lot and then took advantage of the rest rooms before we hit the road again. Laura insisted on driving, so Ray took the passenger seat, while I stretched out in the back and took a nap.

When I woke, I could hear Ray and Laura talking in low tones. Somehow the murmuring took me back to the car trips of childhood, my parents in the front seat, exchanging desultory remarks. That's probably how I learned to eavesdrop originally. I kept my eyes closed and tuned in to their conversation.

Ray was saying, "I know I haven't been any kind of father to you, but I'd like to try."

"I have a father. Paul's already been a father."

"Forget him. The guy's a turd. I heard you say so."

"When?"

"Last night in the car when you were talking to Kinsey. Said he criticized the shit out of you growing up."

"Exactly. I had a father. So why do I need two?"

"Call it a relationship. I want to be a part of your life."

"What for?"

"What *for*? What kind of question is that? You're the only kid I got. We're blood kin."

"Blood kin. What bull."

"How many people can you say that about?"

"Thankfully, not many," she said with acid.

"Skip it. Have it your way. I'm not going to force myself on you. You can do what you like."

"No need to take offense. This is not about you," she said. "That's just how life is. Let's be honest. I've never gotten anything from men except grief."

"I appreciate the vote of confidence."

The conversation trailed off. I waited a suitable few minutes, then yawned audibly as if just rousing myself. I sat up in the backseat, squinting out at the countryside as it whizzed past the car windows. The sun had come out, but the light seemed pale. I could see rolling hills, carpeted in dull November green. The grass was still alive, but all the deciduous trees had dropped their leaves. The barren branches created a gray haze as far as the eye could see. In some areas we passed, I could see hemlocks and pines. In summer, I imagined the land would be intensely green, the hillsides dense with vegetation. Ray was watching me in the rearview mirror. "You ever been to Kentucky?"

"Not that I remember," I said. "Isn't this supposed to

be horse country? I expected blue grass and white fences."

"That's closer to Lexington, northeast of here. The fences these days are black. Over in the far eastern part of the state, you have the coal fields of Harlan County. This is western Kentucky where most of the tobacco's grown."

"She doesn't want a travelogue, Ray."

"Yes, I do," I said. She was always taking cuts at him, which made me feel protective. If she was going to be the bad daughter, I was going to be the good. "Show me on the map."

He pointed to an area north of the Tennessee border, between the Barren River Lake and the Nolan River Lake. "We just passed through Bowling Green, and we got Mammoth Cave National Park coming up on our left. We had time, we'd do the tour. Talk about dark. You go down in the caverns, when the guide turns out the lights? You can't see for shit. It's blacker than black, and it's dead quiet. Fifty-four degrees. It's like a meat-packing plant. Three hundred miles of passageways they've found so far. Last time I went was maybe 1932. A field trip in school. Left a big impression on me. When I was in prison, I used to think about that. You know, one day I'd come back and take the tour again."

Laura was looking at him strangely. "That's what you thought about? Not women or whiskey or fast cars?"

"All I wanted was to get away from overhead lights and the noise. The racket's enough to drive you nuts. And the smell. That's another thing about Mammoth Cave. It smells like moss and wet rocks. Doesn't smell like sweat and testosterone. It smells like life before birth ... what's the word, primordial."

"Jeez. I'm sorry I have to go back to California so soon. You're talking me into it," I said dryly.

Ray smiled. "You joke, but you'd like it. I guarantee."

"Primordial?" Laura said with disbelief.

"What, you're surprised I know words like that? I got my GED. I even took college classes. Economics and psychology and shit like that. Just because I was in prison doesn't mean I'm a fool. Lot of smart guys in prison. You'd be surprised," he said.

"Really," she said, sounding unconvinced.

"Yeah, really. I bet I work a sewing machine better than you, for starters."

"That wouldn't take much," she said.

"This is very uplifting sitting here talking to you. You really know how to make a guy feel good about himself."

"Fuck you."

"You're the one complains your stepdad is always putting you down. Why don't you do better, improve the situation instead of acting like him?"

Laura said nothing. Ray studied her profile and finally looked back at the road.

The silence stretched uncomfortably, and I could feel myself squirm. "How far from here?"

"About an hour and a half. How're you doing back there?"

"I'm doing good," I said.

We reached Louisville just before noon, approaching the town on Highway 65. I could see the airport on our left, and I nearly whimpered with longing. We took an intersecting highway west through an area called Shively, bypassing most of the downtown business district. To our right, I could see the clusters of tall buildings, sturdy blocks of concrete, most of them squared off on top. Ahead of us was the Ohio River, with Indiana visible on the other side.

We exited in an area called Portland, which was where Ray Rawson grew up. I could see his smile quicken as he took in the neighborhood. He turned toward me halfway, putting his arms across the seat back. "The Portland Canal's down that way. Locks were built a hundred years ago to take river traffic past the falls. My great-grandfather worked on the construction. I'll take you over there if we have time."

I was more interested in catching a plane than seeing any of the local landmarks, but I knew the offer was part of his excitement at coming home. Having been incarcerated for most of the last forty-five years, he was probably feeling like Rip van Winkle, marveling at all the changes in the world at large. It might be a comfort that his immediate neighborhood seemed untouched by the passage of time. The streets were wide, trees showing the last vestiges of autumn leaves. Most trees were bare, but down the block I could see smatterings of yellow and red leaves remaining. On the street we'd taken, coming off the freeway, many house fronts had been converted into businesses: signs for child care, a hair salon, a tackle shop selling live bait. The yards were uniformly small and flat, separated by chicken-wire fences with dilapidated gates. Dead leaves, like scraps of brown paper, choked the house gutters and littered the walks. Ten- and twelve-year-old cars were parked at the curbs. Older models were lined up in driveways, with For Sale signs painted on the windshields. Telephone poles were more plentiful than trees, and the wire cut back and forth across the streets like supports for tenting that hadn't been erected yet. Down a side street, I could see railroad cars sitting on a side track.

I would have bet money the neighborhood had looked this way since the 1940s. There was no evidence of construction, no indication of any old structures torn down or condemned to make way for the new. Shrubs were overgrown. The tree trunks were massive, obstructing windows and porches where once the overhanging branches had provided only dappled shade. Sidewalks had buckled, broken by the roots. Forty years of weather had picked at the asphalt siding on some of the houses. Here and there I could see fresh paint, but my guess was that nothing much had changed in the years since Ray had been here.

As we pulled up in front of his mother's house, I could feel a heaviness descend. It was like the low droning note in the score for a horror movie, the minor chord that betokens a dark shape in the water, or something unseen, waiting in the shadows behind the basement door. The sensation was probably simple depression, born of borrowed clothes, junk food, and erratic sleep. Whatever the genesis, I knew it was going to be hours before I could get on a plane for California.

Laura turned off the ignition on the rental car and got out. Ray emerged on his side, searching the front of the house with wonderment. I had no choice but to join them. I felt like a prisoner, suffering a temporal claustrophobia so pronounced it made my skin itch.

# 16

RAY'S MOTHER'S HOUSE was situated on a narrow lot on a street occupied entirely by single-family dwellings. The house was a two-story red-brick structure, with a one-story red-brick extension jutting out in front. The two narrow front windows sat side by side, caged by burglar bars and capped with matching lintels. Three concrete steps led up to the door, which was set flush against the house and shaded by a small wooden roof cap. I could see a second entrance tucked around on the right side of the house down a short walk. The house next door was a fraternal twin, the only difference being the absence of the porch roof, which left its front door exposed to the elements.

Ray headed for the side entrance with Laura and me tagging along behind like baby ducklings. Between the two houses, the air seemed very chill. I crossed my arms to keep warm, shifting restlessly from foot to foot, eager to be indoors. Ray tapped on the door, which had ornamental burglar bars across the glass. Through the window I could see bright light pouring from a room on the left, but there was no sign of movement. Idly, he talked over his shoulder to me. "These are called 'shotgun' cottages, one room wide and four rooms deep so you could stand at the front door and fire a bullet all the way through." He pointed up toward the second story. "Hers is called a humpback because it's got a second bedroom above the kitchen. My great-grandfather built both these places back in 1880."

"Looks like it," Laura said.

He pointed a finger at her. "Hey, you watch it. I don't want you hurting Gramma's feelings."

"Oh, right. Like I'd really stand here and insult her house. Jeez, Ray. Give me credit for *some* intelligence."

"What is it with you? You're such a fuckin' victim," he said.

Inside the house, another light came on. Laura bit back whatever tart response she'd formed to her father's chiding. The curtain was pushed aside and an elderly woman peered out. In the absence of dentures, her mouth had rolled inward in a state of collapse. She was short and heavyset, with a soft round face, her white hair pulled up tightly in a hard knot wound around with rubber bands. She squinted through wire-frame glasses, both lenses heavily magnified. "What you want?" she bellowed through the glass at us.

Ray raised his voice. "Ma, it's me. Ray."

It took her a few seconds to process the information. Her confusion cleared and she put her gnarled hands up to her mouth. She began to work the locks—deadbolt, thumb lock, and burglar chain—ending in an old-fashioned skeleton key that took some maneuvering before it yielded. The door flew open and she flung herself into his arms. "Oh, Ray," she said tremulously. "Oh, my Ray."

Ray laughed, hugging her close while she made wordless mewling sounds of joy and relief. Though plump, she was probably half his size. She had on a white pinafore-style apron over a housedress that looked hand sewn: pink cotton with an imprint of white buttons in diagonal rows, the sleeves trimmed in pink rickrack. She pulled away from him, her glasses sitting crookedly on the bridge of her nose. Her gaze shifted to Laura, who stood behind him on the walk. It was clear she had trouble distinguishing faces in the cloudy world of impaired vision. "Who's this?" she said.

"It's me, Gramma. Laura. And this is Kinsey. She hitched a ride with us from Dallas. How are you?"

"Oh, my stars, Laura! Dear love. I can't believe it. This is wonderful. I'm so happy to see you. Looka here, what a mess I'm in. Didn't nobody tell me you were coming and now you've caught me in this old thing." Laura gave her a hug and kiss, holding herself sideways to conceal the solid bulge of her belly harness.

Ray's mother didn't seem to notice one way or the other. "Let me take a look at you." She put a hand on either side of Laura's face, searching earnestly. "I wish I could see you better, child, but I believe you favor your grandfather Rawson. God love your heart. How long has it been?" Tears trickled down her cheeks, and she finally pulled her apron up over her face to hide her embarrassment. She fanned herself then, shaking off her emotions. "What's the matter with me? Get on in here, all of you. Son, I'll never forgive you for not calling first. I'm a mess. House is a mess."

We trooped into the hallway, Laura first, then Ray, with me bringing up the rear. We paused while the old woman locked the doors again. I realized no one had ever mentioned her first name. To the right was the narrow stairway leading up to the second-floor bedroom, blanketed in darkness even at this time of day. To the left was the kitchen, which seemed to be the only room with lights on. Because the houses were so close to one another, little daylight crept into this section. There was only one kitchen window, on the far left-hand wall above a porcelain-and-cast-iron sink. A big oak table with four mismatched wooden chairs took up the center of the room, a bare bulb hanging over it. The bulb itself must have been 250 watts because the light it threw off was not only dazzling, but had elevated the room temperature a good twenty degrees.

The ancient stove was green enamel, trimmed in black, with four gas burners and a lift-up stove top. To the left of the door was an Eastlake cabinet with a retractable tin counter and a built-in flour bin and sifter. I could feel a wave of memory pushing at me. Somewhere I'd seen a room like this, maybe Grand's house in Lompoc when I was four. In my mind's eye, I could still picture the goods on the shelves: the Cut-rite waxed paper box, the cylindrical dark blue Morton salt box with the girl under her umbrella ("When It Rains, It Pours"), Sanka coffee in a short orange can, Cream of Wheat, the tin of Hershey's cocoa. Mrs. Rawson's larder was stocked with most of the same items, right down to the opaque mint-green glass jar with SUGAR printed across the front. The oversize matching screw-top salt and pepper shakers rested nearby.

Ray's mother was already busy clearing piles of newspapers from the kitchen chairs despite Ray's protests. "Now, Ma, come on. You don't have to do that. Give me that."

She smacked at his hand. "You quit. I can do this myself. If you'd told me you were coming, I'd have had the place picked up. Laura's going to think I don't know how to keep house."

He took a stack of papers from her and stuck them in a haphazard pile against the wall. Laura murmured something and excused herself, moving into the back room. I was hoping there was a bathroom close by that I could visit in due course. I pulled out a chair and sat down, doing some visual snooping while Ray and his mother tidied up.

From where I sat, I could see part of the dining room with its built-in china cupboards. The room was crammed with junk, furniture, and cardboard boxes, making passage difficult. I caught sight of an old brown wood radio, a Zenith with a round dial set into a round-shouldered console the size of a chest of drawers. I could see the round shape of the underlying speaker where the worn fabric was stretched over it. The wallpaper pattern was a marvel of swirling brown leaves.

The room beyond the dining room was probably the parlor with its two windows onto the street and a proper front door. The kitchen smelled like a combination of mothballs and strong coffee sitting on the stove too long. I heard the shriek of plumbing, the flush mechanism suggestive of a waterfall thundering from a great height. When Laura emerged from the back room sometime later, she'd shed her belly harness. She was probably uncomfortable with the idea of having to explain her "condition" if her grandmother took notice.

I tuned in to the old woman, who was still grumbling good-naturedly about the unexpected visit. "I don't know how you expect me to cook up any kind of supper without the fixings on hand."

"Well, I'm telling you how," Ray said patiently. "You put together a list of what you need and we'll whip over to the market and be back in two shakes."

"I have a list working if I can find it," she said, poking through loose papers in the center of the table.

"Freida Green, my neighbor two doors down, she's been carrying me to the market once a week when she goes. Here now. What's that say?"

Ray took the list and read aloud in a fakey tone, "Says pork chops with milk gravy, yams, fried apples and onions, corn bread . . ."

She reached for the paper, but he held it out of reach. "I never. It does not. Let me see that. Is that what you want, son?"

"Yes, ma'am." He handed her the paper.

"Well, I can do that. I have yams out yonder, and I believe I still have some of them pole beans and stewed tomatoes I put up last summer. I just baked a batch of peanut-butter cookies. We can have them for dessert if you'll pick up a quart of vanilla ice cream. I want real. I don't want iced milk." She was writing as she spoke, large, angular letters drifting across the page.

"Sounds good to me. What do you think, Kinsey?" he asked.

"Sounds great."

"Oh, forevermore, Kinsey. Shame on me for my bad manners. I forgot all about you, honey. What can I get you? I might have a can of soda pop here somewhere. Take a look in the pantry and don't mind the state it's in. I been meaning to clean that out, but hadn't got to it."

"Actually, I'd love to borrow your phone, and a pen and scratch paper, if you don't mind."

"You go and help yourself as long as you don't call Paris, France. I'm on fixed income and that telephone costs too much as it is. Here's you a piece of paper. Laura, why don't you show her where the telephone is. Right in there beside the bed. I'll get busy with this list."

Ray said, "I also promised she could throw some clothes in the washing machine. You have detergent?"

"In the utility room," she said, pointing toward the door.

I took the proffered pen and paper and moved into the bedroom, which was as stuffy as a coat closet. The only light emanated from a small bathroom that opened on the left. Heavy drapes were pinned together over windows with the shades drawn. The double-bed mattress sagged in an iron bedstead piled with hand-tied quilts. The room would have been perfect in a 1940s home furnishings diorama at the state fair. All the surfaces were coated with a fine layer of dust. In fact, nothing in the house had seemed terribly clean, probably the by-product of the old woman's poor eyesight.

The old black dial telephone sat beside a crookneck lamp on the bed table, amid large-print books, pill bottles, lotions, and ointments. I flipped the light on and dialed Information, picking up the numbers for both United and American Airlines. I called United first, listening to the usual reassurances until my "call could be answered in the order it was received." Out of deference to Ray's mom, I refrained from searching her bed table drawer while I waited for the agent to pick up on his end. I did scan the room, looking for the belly harness. Had to be around here somewhere.

The agent finally came on the line and helped me get the reservations I needed. There was a flight from Louisville to Chicago at 7:12 P.M., arriving 7:22, which reflected the hour's time difference. After a brief layover, I then connected to a flight departing from Chicago at 8:14 P.M., arriving in Los Angeles at 10:24, California time. The flight to Santa Teresa left at 11:00 and arrived forty-five minutes later. That last connection was tight, but the agent swore the arrival and departure gates would be close to one another. Since I was traveling without luggage, he didn't think it would be a problem. He did advise me to get to the airport an hour in advance of flight time so I could pay for the ticket.

He'd just put me on hold when Ray stuck his head in the door, a clean towel in one hand. "That's for you," he said, tossing it on the bed. "When you finish your call, you can hop in the shower. There's a robe hanging on the door. Ma says she'll throw your clothes in the wash when you're ready."

I put a palm across the mouthpiece and said, "Thanks. I'll bring 'em right out. What about the stuff in the car?"

"She's got that already. I brought everything in."

He started to depart and stuck his head around the door again. "Oh. I almost forgot. Ma says there's a one-hour cleaners in the same mall as the market. You want to give me your jacket, I can drop it off before we go shopping and pick it up on the way back."

The agent had come back on the line and was already busy reconfirming the flight arrangements while I nodded enthusiastically to Ray. With the receiver still tucked in the crook of my neck, I emptied the pockets of my blazer and handed it to him. He waved and withdrew while I finished up the call.

I headed for the bathroom, where with a quick search I uncovered the belly harness tucked down in the clothes hamper. I hauled it out and inspected it, impressed by the ingenuity of the construction. The housing resembled an oversize catcher's face mask, a convex frame made of semiflexible plastic tubing, wrapped with padding, into which countless bound packets of currency had been packed. Heavy canvas straps secured the harness once in place. I checked a couple of packets, riffling through five-, ten-, twenty-,

and fifty-dollar notes of varying sizes. Many bills
seemed unfamiliar and I had to assume were no longer
in circulation. Several packets appeared to be literally in
mint condition. It grieved me to think of Laura covering
day-to-day expenses with bank notes that a serious collector would have paid dearly for. Ray was a fool to
stand by while his daughter threw it all away. Who
knew how much money still remained to be uncovered?

I tucked the harness down in the hamper. I'm big on
closure and not good at leaving so many questions unanswered. However, (she said) this was not my concern.
In six hours, I'd be heading for California. If there were
additional monies in a stash somewhere, that was
strictly Ray's business. There was a blue chenille bathrobe hanging on a hook on the back of the door. I
stripped out of the borrowed denim dress and underwear, pulled the robe on, and carried my dirty clothes
out to the kitchen. Ray and Laura had apparently left on
their errand. I could see yams on the stove, simmering
in a dark blue-and-white-speckled enamel pan. Quart
Mason jars of tomatoes and green beans had been
pulled off the pantry shelves and placed on the counter.
Briefly, I pondered the possibilities of botulism poison-
ing arising from improperly preserved foods, but what
the heck, the mortality rate is only sixty-five percent.
Ray's mother probably wouldn't have attained such a
ripe old age if she hadn't perfected her canning skills.

The door to the utility porch was open. That room
wasn't insulated and the air pouring out of it was frigid.
Ray's mother went about her business as if unaware of
the chill. An early-model washer and dryer were arranged against the wall to the left. Tucked between
them was a battered canister-style vacuum cleaner
shaped like the nose cone of a spaceship. "I'm about to

hop in the shower, Mrs. Rawson. Can I give you these?" I asked.

"There you are," she said. "I was just loading the few things Laura give me. You can call me Helen if you like," she added. "My late husband used to call me Hell on Wheels."

I watched as she felt for the measuring cup, tucking her thumb over the rim so she could feel how far up the side the detergent had come. "I've been considered legally blind for years, and my eyes is getting worse. I can still make my way around as long as people don't go putting things in my path. I'm scheduled for surgery, but I had to wait until Ray come home to help out. Anyway, I'm just yammering on. I don't mean to keep you."

"This is fine," I said. "Can I help with anything?"

"Oh no, honey. Go ahead and get your shower. You can keep that robe on 'til your clothes is done. Won't take long with these old machines. My friend, Freida Green, has new and it takes her three times as long to run a load through and uses twicet the water. Soon as I'm done with this, I'm going to put some corn bread together. I hope you like to eat."

"Absolutely. I'll be out shortly and give you a hand."

The shower was a mixed blessing. The water pressure was paltry, the hot and cold fluctuating wildly in response to cycles of the washing machine. I did manage to scrub myself thoroughly, washing my hair in a cumulus cloud of soapsuds, lathering and rinsing until I felt fresh again. I dried myself off and pulled on Helen's robe. I slipped into my Reeboks, my fastidious streak preventing me from walking around barefoot on floors only marginally clean. I'm generally not vain about my appearance, but I could hardly wait to get back into my own clothes.

Before returning to the kitchen, I used my telephone credit card to put in a long-distance call to Henry. He was apparently out somewhere, but his machine picked up. I said, "Henry, this is Kinsey. I'm in Louisville, Kentucky. It's after one o'clock here and I've got a flight out at seven. I don't know what time we'll be heading for the airport, but I should be here for the next couple of hours. If it's possible, I need to have you meet me at the airport. I'm almost out of cash and I don't have a way to get my car out of hock. I can try borrowing the money here, but these people don't seem all that dependable. If I don't hear from you before I leave, I'll call you as soon as I get to Los Angeles." I checked the telephone number written on the round cardboard disk in the middle of the dial, reciting Helen's number to him before I hung up. I ran a comb through my hair and moved back into the kitchen, where Helen put me to work setting the kitchen table.

Ray and Laura came back with my blazer, in a clear plastic cleaning bag, and an armload each of groceries, which we unpacked and put away. I hung my blazer on the knob just inside the bedroom door. Laura followed me, moving on into the bathroom to take her shower. The wash must have been done because I could hear the dryer rumbling against the wall. As soon as the load was dry, I'd pull my clothes out and get dressed.

In the meantime, Helen showed me how to peel and mash the yams while she cut apples and onions into quarters and put them in the frying pan with butter. Like a fly on the wall, I kept myself quiet, listening to Ray and his mother chat while she put supper together. "Freida Green's house got broke into here about four months ago. That's when I had all them burglar bars put on. We had a neighborhood meeting with these two police officers, told us what to do in case of attack. Freida and her friend, Minnie Paxton, took a self-defense course. Said they learned how to scream and how to kick out real hard sideways. The point is to break a fellow's kneecap and take him down. Freida was practicing and fell flat on her back. Cracked her tailbone big as life. Minnie laughed so hard she nearly peed herself 'til she saw how bad Freida was hurt. She had to set on a bag of ice for a month, poor thing."

"Well, I don't want to hear about you trying to kick some guy."

"No, no. I wouldn't do that. Makes no sense for an old woman like me. Old people can't always depend on physical strength. Even Freida said that. That's why I had all them locks put in. Summertimes, I used to leave my doors standing open to let the breeze come through. Not no more. No sir."

"Hey, Ma. Before I forget. You have any mail here for me? I think my buddy in California might have sent me a package or a letter in care of this address."

"Well, yes. Now you mention it, I did receive something and set it aside. It come quite some time ago. I believe it's here somewhere, if I can recollect where I put it. Take a look in that drawer yonder under all the junk."

Ray opened the drawer, pawing through odds and ends: lamp cords, batteries, pencils, bottle caps, coupons, hammer, screwdriver, cooking utensils. A handful of envelopes was crammed in at the back, but most were designated "Occupant." There was only one piece of personal mail, addressed to Ray Rawson with no return address. He squinted at the postmark on the envelope. "This is it," he said. He tore it open and pulled out a sympathy card with a black-and-white photograph of a graveyard pasted on the front. Inside, the message read:

*And I will give unto thee the keys of the kingdom of heaven: and whatsoever thou shalt bind on earth shall be bound in heaven: and whatsoever thou shalt loose on earth shall be loosed in heaven.*

*Matthew 16:19*

*Thinking of you in your hour of loss.*

On the back of the card, a small brass key was taped. Ray pulled it off, turning it over in his hand before he passed it to me. I studied first one side and then the other just as he had. It was an inch and a half long. The word *Master* was stamped on one side and the number M550 on the other. Shouldn't be hard to remember. The number was my birthdate in abbreviated form. I said, "Probably for a padlock."

"What about the key you have?"

"It's in the bedroom. I'll get it as soon as Laura's finished in there."

Supper was almost on the table when Laura finally emerged. It looked as though she'd made a special effort with her hair and makeup despite the fact her grandmother couldn't see all that well. While serving dishes were being filled at the stove, I stepped into the bedroom and picked up my Swiss Army knife from the pile of my belongings on the bed table. I slipped the jacket from the cleaners bag and used the small scissors to snip the stitches I'd put in the inside shoulder seam I worked the key from the hole. This one was heavy, a good six inches long with an elongated round shaft. I held it closer to the table lamp, curious if this was also a Master. *Lawless* was stamped on the shaft, but there were no other identifying marks that I could see. Master padlocks I knew about. A Lawless I'd never heard of.

Might be a local company or one that had since gone out of business.

I returned to the kitchen table, where I sat down and handed the key to Ray.

"What's that for?" Laura asked as she took her seat.

"I'm not sure, but I think it goes with this one," Ray said. He laid the skeleton key beside the smaller key in the middle of the table. "This one Johnny left taped to the inside of his safe. Chester found it this week when they were cleaning out the apartment."

"Those are connected to the stash?"

"I hope so. Otherwise, we're out of luck," he said.

"How come?"

"Because it's the only link we have. Unless you have an idea where to look for a pile of money forty-some years after it was hid."

"I wouldn't even know where to start," she said.

"Me neither. I was hoping Kinsey would help, but it looks like we're running out of time," he said, and then turned to his mother. "You want me to say grace, Ma?"

Why did I feel guilty? I hadn't *done* anything.

The supper was a lavish testimony to old-fashioned southern cooking. This was the first food I'd had in days that wasn't saturated with additives and preservatives. The sugar, sodium, and fat content left something to be desired, but I'm not exactly pious where food is concerned. I ate with vigor and concentration, only vaguely aware of the conversation going on around me until Ray's voice went up. He had put his fork down and was staring at his daughter with a look of horror and dismay.

"You did what?"

"What's wrong with that?"

"When did you talk to her?"

I saw the color come up in Laura's face. "When we

first got here," she said defensively. "You saw me go in
the other room. What did you think I was doing? I was
on the phone."

"Jesus Christ. You *called* her?"

"She's my mother. Of course I called. I didn't want
her to worry in case Gilbert showed up on her doorstep.
So what?"

"If Gilbert shows up, she'll tell him where you are."

"She will *not*."

"Of course she will. You think Gilbert won't charm
the socks off her? Hell, forget charm. He'll beat the shit
outta her. Of course she'll tell him. I did. Once he
started breaking fingers, I couldn't wait to unload. Did
you at least warn her?"

"Warn her of what?"

"Oh, jeez," Ray said. He rubbed his palm down his
face, pulling his features out of shape.

"Look, Ray. You don't need to treat me like a nin-
compoop."

"You still don't get it, do you? That guy's going to
kill me. He's going to kill you, too. He'll kill Kinsey,
your grandmother, and anybody else who gets in his
way. He wants the money. You're just the means to an
end as far as he's concerned."

"How's he going to find us? He won't find us," she
said.

"We gotta get out of here." Ray got up and threw his
napkin down, giving me a look. I knew as well as he
did that once Gilbert got confirmation of our whereabouts, he'd be here within the hour.

"I'm with you," I said as I pushed my chair back.

Laura was aghast. "We haven't even finished *eating*.
What's the matter with you?"

He turned to me. "Get your clothes on. Ma, you need

a coat. Turn the stove off. Just leave this. We can take care of it later."

His panic was contagious. Helen's gaze was drifting around the room, her voice was tremulous. "What's happening, son? I don't understand what's going on. Why would we leave? We haven't et our ice cream yet."

"Just do what I say and get going," he snapped, hauling her out of her chair. He started turning off burners. He turned off the oven. I was not dressed for flight. All I had on were my Reeboks and Helen's chenille bathrobe. I crossed to the utility room, nearly knocking his chair over in my haste to reach the dryer. Laura protested vigorously, but I noticed she was moving as fast as the rest of us. I pulled the dryer open, grabbed an armload of hot clothes, and headed for the bedroom. I flipped my shoes off, pulled on socks, bra, and underpants, pulled on my turtleneck and jeans, and shoved my feet back into my Reeboks, breaking down the backs. God, here I was again, going for the gold at the Throwing Clothes On Olympics. I put on my blazer and started jamming personal items in the pockets: cash, credit cards, house keys, pills, picks. From the kitchen Laura let out a shriek, followed by the sound of a bowl smashing on the floor. I moved into the kitchen while I crammed the last of the odds and ends in my jeans pockets.

The room was dead still, Helen, Ray, and Laura unmoving. The bowl of mashed yams lay on the floor in an orange splat of puree and broken china. It didn't matter at this point because Gilbert was standing in the door to the dining room with a gun aimed right at me.

# 17

GILBERT NO LONGER wore the Stetson. His hair was disheveled, still bearing the faint indentation where the hat had rested. His pale blue denim jacket was lined with sheepskin, the fabric saturated in places and stiff with dark red. "Marla sends greetings. She would have come with me only she wasn't feeling that good."

At the reference to her mother, Laura started to weep. She made no sound at all, but her face got patchy and red and tears welled in her eyes. She made a barely suppressed squeaking noise at the back of her throat. She sank into a chair.

"Hay. Get up and get your hands up where I can see 'em."

The gun in his hand encouraged compliance. I certainly wasn't going to argue. Laura rose slowly, not looking at him. She let out a breath with an audible sound and tears ran down her cheeks. She'd brought this down on us with every poor choice she'd made. She'd taken the risk and now the rest of us would pay. I saw everyone in the room with such clarity: Ray had his jacket on, his car keys in hand. He'd managed to hustle his mother into her coat. She stood close to her place at the table, hands up, bundled up in her woollies like a kid on a snowy day. Five minutes more and we might have been gone. Gilbert must have been eavesdropping for some time, of course, so it probably didn't matter. The fact that all of us now had our hands in the air gave the scene a slightly comical air. It looked as if we'd been caught in the middle of a spiritual, with our hands waving toward heaven. In a western, somebody would have jumped Gilbert and grappled for the gun. Not here. I kept my gaze pinned on his face, trying to gauge his intent. Helen's gaze wandered the room, eyes unfocused, settling nowhere, roaming across the gray haze with its motionless dark shapes. I thought she'd be confused or upset, but she said nothing, sensing perhaps that the situation wouldn't be served by questions. She did quiver almost imperceptibly, the way a dog trembles standing on the groomer's table.

The air still smelled of fried pork chops and milk gravy. The remnants of the meal remained on the plates, cooking pots piled in the kitchen sink. Maybe Freida Green would come in and clean up in a few days . . . after the crime scene tape had been removed and the premises unsealed.

Gilbert held the gun in his right hand, using his left to reach into his jacket pocket. He took out a roll of duct tape. "Here's what let's do," he said conversationally. "Ray, why don't you just take a seat in that chair. Laura here is going to wrap you up in duct tape. Hey, hey, hey, babe. Goddamn it. Quit with the crying. Nothing's happened yet. I'm just trying to keep everything under control. I don't want anybody jumping out at me. Don't want this gun going off or somebody might get hurt. Grammy's not going to look so hot with a hole in her head, brains all spilling out, Ray with a big old hole in his chest. Come on, now. Help out, just to show you still care."

He tossed the roll of silver duct tape to Laura, who caught it on the fly. She seemed frozen, standing immobile as the seconds went by. "Gilbert, I beg you—"

*"Tape him up!"*

I flinched at his sudden screaming. Laura didn't bat an eye, but I noticed she was now in motion, crossing the room to Ray. Slowly, hands still lifted, Ray eased himself into the chair Gilbert had indicated. Laura was weeping so hard I'm not even sure she could see what she was doing. Tears washed the makeup from her cheeks, exposing the old bruises like an undercoat of paint. Tendrils of red hair had come loose, trailing around her face.

Gilbert's focus moved to Ray. "Make any trouble, I'll kill her," he said.

Ray said, "Don't do that. Be cool. I'll cooperate."

Gilbert flicked a look at me. "Why don't you pass me the keys? I'd appreciate it," he said.

I reached for the keys still on the kitchen table. I hated to let go of them, but I couldn't think what else to do. I placed them in Gilbert's left palm. He glanced at them briefly and then tucked them in his jacket pocket

Ray said, "Listen, Gilbert. This is an old score. It's got nothing to do with these three. You can do anything you want with me, but keep them out of it."

"I know I can do anything I want. I'm already doing it. I don't care about them two, the old bag and this one," he said, indicating me. "But I got accounts to settle with her. She ran out on me." He looked over at her, frowning. "Could you get busy with that tape like I said?"

"Gilbert, please don't do this. Please."

"Would you knock it off? I'm not doing anything," he said peevishly. "What am I doing? I'm just standing here talking to your dad. Go on now and do what I told you. Ray's not going to pull any funny business."

"Can't we just leave? Get in the car and go, just the two of us?"

"You're not done. You haven't even *started*," Gilbert said. He was beginning to sound exasperated, not a good sign.

Ray's expression was soft, looking at Laura. "It's okay, hon. Go ahead and do what he says. Let's see if we can keep everybody on an even keel here."

Gilbert smiled. "My thoughts exactly. Everybody take it easy. I want his ankles taped to the chair legs. And let's get his hands behind him, bind 'em up nice. I'm going to check on you, so don't you be thinking you can pretend to tape him up and then not do it right. I hate when people try to fool me. You know how I am. Blow your nose and quit sniveling."

Laura fumbled in her pocket, took out a tissue, and did as he said. She tucked the tissue away and pulled out a strip of tape, the adhesive making a ripping sound as she tore it loose. She began to wrap the tape around Ray's right ankle, first folding his pant leg against his shin, then threading the tape around the chair leg in several layers.

"I want that tight. You don't get it tight enough, I'm going to shoot him in the leg."

"I am!" She flashed a look at Gilbert, and for a moment there was pure fury in her eyes instead of fear.

He seemed to like it that he'd gotten a rise out of her. A slight smile crossed his face. "What's that look for?"

"Where's Farley?" she said darkly.

"Oh, him. I left him in California. What a worthless

sack of shit he turned into. All the mewling and pissing. I really hate that stuff. Here's the long and short of
it: The man ratted you out. It's the truth. He gave you
up. Farley told me everything, trying to save his own
skin. I do not admire that. I think it sucks." He edged
over to the chair where Ray was sitting. He kept a close
eye on all of us, making sure no one moved while he
squatted by the chair and checked the tape. He got up,
apparently satisfied with the job she was doing. "When
you get done with him, you can do her," he said, meaning me.

She ripped off another length of tape and began to secure Ray's left leg to the chair rung. "What'd you do to
him?" she asked.

Gilbert stood upright again, backing off two steps.
"What *I* did? We're not talking about what I did. I
didn't do anything. It's what you did. You betrayed me,
babe. How many times I told you about that? You just
never learn, do you? I try—God knows I try—to let you
know what I expect."

"Farley's dead?"

"Yes, he is," Gilbert said solemnly. "I'm sorry to
have to be the one to tell you."

"He was your nephew. Your own flesh and blood."

"What's that got to do with it? That doesn't cut any
ice. Flesh and blood don't mean bullshit. It's about loyalty. Is that simple concept so hard for you to grasp?
Listen, I want to tell you something. You can't blame
this on me. Anybody gets hurt, it's on your head, not
mine. How many times I told you, you have to do what
I say. You're not going to obey me, then I can't be responsible."

"I'm *doing* what you said. In what way am I not
doing what you said?"

"I'm not talking about that. I'm talking about the

money. I'm talking about Rio. Now see? Right there. You didn't fly to Rio like you were supposed to, and look what went wrong as a consequence of your behavior. Farley . . . well, never mind. I think we said enough about him."

Helen spoke up. Like me, she'd been standing there doggedly with her hands in the air. "Young man. I wonder if I could take this coat off and set down."

Gilbert frowned, irritated at the interruption. It was clear he enjoyed getting all worked up, feeling righteous, expounding on the many ways someone else was at fault. Helen wasn't looking at him. Her gaze was fixed at a point to his right, where she was obviously mistaking the doorjamb for him. Gilbert was momentarily distracted, amused by her mistake. He waved his arms. "Hey, over here, sweetheart. You must not see all that good. You've mistook me for a coat rack."

"I see well enough. It's my feet give out," she said. "I'm eighty-five years old."

"Is that right? Arms getting tired, is that it?"

Helen said nothing. Her rheumy gaze was wandering. I kept scanning the room, looking for a weapon, trying to form a plan. I didn't want to put the others in any more jeopardy. His intentions seemed clear enough. One by one, we'd be bound and gagged, at which point he was going to kill us, and what could we do? I was closer to him than Laura was, but if I tried to jump him he might go berserk and start shooting. I had to do something soon, but I didn't want to be foolhardy . . . acting like a heroine when it might put us in a worse situation than we were already in.

"I'm going to set. You can shoot me if you don't like it," Helen said.

Gilbert gestured with the gun. "Take a seat right

where you are. You can put your hands down for now, but don't touch anything on the table."

She said, "Thank you." She braced her hands on the table and sank heavily in her chair. She shrugged out of her coat. I could see her flex her fingers gingerly, coaxing the circulation before she tucked them in her lap.

Gilbert angled himself so he could monitor Laura's progress as she bound her father's hands with tape. Ray's arms were behind him. In order to have his wrists meet behind the wooden chair back, he had to lean forward slightly and force his shoulders into a roll.

Gilbert seemed to enjoy Ray's discomfort. "Where's the harness?" he asked Laura.

"In the other room."

"When you get done with that, bring it out here and let's see what we got."

"I thought you said tape her."

"Get the harness, *then* tape her, you fuckin' idjit," he said.

"There's only eight thousand dollars. You said a million," she said irritably. She set the roll of duct tape aside and moved into the other room. Personally, I wouldn't have dared to take that tone with him. Gilbert didn't seem surprised about the money, so I had to assume Farley'd told him about the eight grand along with everything else.

Laura returned with the harness in hand. He took it from her, hefting it up onto the counter behind him. He glanced down at the contents, taking in the packets of bills. His gaze shifted to Ray. "Where's the rest of the money? Where's all the jewelry and the coin collections?"

"I don't know. I really can't swear there's anything left," Ray said.

Gilbert closed his eyes, his patience wearing thin.

"Ray, I was there, remember? I helped you guys, hauling out all that cash and jewelry. What about the diamonds and the coins? There was a fortune in there, must have been two million, at least, and Johnny sure as shit didn't have it on him when he was caught."

"Hey, not to argue, but you were seventeen years old. None of us had ever seen a million bucks, let alone two. We don't really have any idea how much it was because we never had a chance to count it, and that's the truth," Ray said.

"There was a hell of a lot more than this. Seven or eight big bags. That loot didn't just disappear into thin air. The son of a bitch must have hid it. So where'd he put it?"

"Your guess is as good as mine. That's why I'm here. See if I can figure it out."

"He didn't tell you?"

"I swear to God he didn't. He knew he could trust himself, but I guess he wasn't all that sure about me."

I spoke up then, looking at Ray. "How do you know he didn't spend it?"

"It's always possible," he said. "I know he sent money to my ma. That was our agreement up front."

"He did what?" Gilbert said. He turned to Helen. "Is that right?"

"Oh my, yes," she said complacently. "I've received a money order in the amount of five hundred dollars every month since nineteen and forty-four, though it did stop some months back. July or August, as I recollect."

"Since 1944? I don't believe it. How much did he send? Five hundred a *month*? That's ridiculous," Gilbert said.

"Two hundred forty-six thousand dollars," Ray interjected. "I took high school math up at FCI Ashland.

You ought to try the joint yourself, Gilbert. Improve your grasp of the basics. Vocabulary, grammar . . ."

Gilbert was still focused on Johnny's giveaway plan. "You gotta be shittin' me. Johnny Lee gave two hundred forty-six thousand dollars of my money to this old bag? I don't believe it. That's criminal."

"I kept an account if you'd care to see it. It's a little red notebook in that drawer over there," Helen said, pointing a trembling finger in the general direction of the drawer where she'd kept Ray's mail.

Gilbert moved to the drawer and jerked it open, pawing through the jumble of items with impatience. He pulled the drawer out altogether and dumped the contents on the floor. He reached down and picked up a small spiral-bound notebook, thumbing through it with his left hand, the gun still in his right. Even from where I stood, I could see column after column, dates and scratchy-looking numbers running crookedly from page to page. "Son of a bitch!" Gilbert said. "How could he do that, give the money away?" He flung the notebook on the kitchen table, where it landed in the dish of stewed tomatoes.

It was Ray's turn to enjoy. He knew better than to smile, but his tone of voice conveyed his satisfaction. "The guy kept five hundred for himself, too, so what is that? After forty-one years that brings the total up to four hundred ninety-two thousand dollars," Ray said. "Figure it out for yourself. If we netted half a million bucks from the heist, that'd leave just about eight grand."

Gilbert crossed to Ray and jammed the barrel of the gun up under his jaw, hard. "God*damn* it! *I know there was more and I want it!* I'll blow your fuckin' head off right this minute if you don't give it up."

"Killing me won't help. You kill me, you got no

chance," Ray said without flinching. "Maybe I can find it, *if* there's anything left. I know how Johnny's mind worked. You don't have a clue how he went about his business."

"I found the kickplate, didn't I?"

"Only because I told you. You never would have found it without me," Ray said.

Gilbert moved the gun away, his face dark. His movements were agitated. "Here's the deal. I'm taking Laura with me. You better come up with something by tomorrow or she's dead, you got that?"

"Hey, come on. Be reasonable. I need time," Ray said.

"Tomorrow."

"I'll do what I can, but I can't promise."

"Well, I can. You get that money or she's dead meat."

"How am I going to find you?"

"Don't worry about that. I'll find you," Gilbert said.

Helen grimaced, rubbing one gnarled hand with the other.

"What's the matter with you?"

"My arthritis is acting up. I'm in pain."

"You want me to fix it? I can fix that in a jiffy with what I got in here," he said, waggling his gun. He turned back to Ray. Helen raised her hand to attract his notice.

"What?"

"Now I've set down too long. Thing about getting old is you can't do any one thing for more than about five minutes. I hope you don't mind if I stand up a bit."

"Goddamn, old woman. You're just up and down and all over the place."

Helen laughed, apparently mistaking his homicidal wrath for mere ill temper. I felt a bubble of despair rising to the surface. Maybe she was senile along with

everything else. He'd kill her without hesitation—he'd
kill all of us—but she didn't seem to "get" that. His
threats sailed right over. Maybe it was just as well. At
her age, who could tolerate fear of that magnitude? The
anxiety alone could push her into heart failure. Me too,
for that matter.

Gilbert pointed the gun in her direction. "You can
stand up, but you behave," he said. "I don't want you
running out of here, trying to flag down help." His tone
shifted when he spoke to her, becoming nearly flirtatious. "Patronizing" might be another word, but Helen
didn't seem to pick up on it.

She waved a hand dismissively. "I'm afraid my flag
ging days is over. Anyway, I'm not the one you have to
worry about. It's my friend, Freida Green."

At least she'd caught his attention. I could see him
suppress a smile, pretending to take her seriously.
"Uh-oh. What is it, Freida some kind of hell-raiser?"

"Yes, she is. I am, too, for that matter. My late husband used to call me Hell on Wheels, get it? 'Hell on.'
Helen."

"I got it, Granny. Who's Freida? She likely to be
popping in here unannounced?"

"Freida's my neighbor. She lives two doors down
with her friend, Minnie Paxton, but they're out of town
right now. Hasn't anyone ever said, but I think them
two are sweet on each other. Anyway, we had us a rash
of burglaries about four months back. That's what they
call them, a 'rash,' like somebody caught a disease.
Two nice policemen come down to the neighborhood
and told us about self-defense. Minnie learned to kick
out real hard sideways, but Freida fell flat on her back
when she tried it."

Ray fixed me with a look, but I couldn't read the

contents. Probably simple despair at the banality of their exchange.

Gilbert laughed. "Jesus, I'd like to seen that. How old is this old bag?"

"Let's see now. I believe Freida's thirty-one. Minnie's two years younger and she's in much better shape. Freida cracked her tailbone and she got mad. Whoo! Said there had to be a better way to fight crime than tryin' to kick some fella in the kneecap."

Gilbert shook his head with skepticism. "I don't know. Bust a guy's kneecap, that can really hurt," he said.

"Well, yes," Helen said, "but first you'd have to get close enough to kick, which isn't always easy. And then my balance is not that good."

"Freida's balance ain't good, either, from what you said. So what'd she suggest?"

"She suggested she make us each a rack and bolt it onto the bottom of the table, where we could keep a loaded shotgun about like this." Helen turned slightly sideways as she rose to her feet. She took a long step away from the table, pulling up a twelve-gauge side-by-side shotgun with twenty-six-inch barrels. She pinned the butt stock between her forearm and her side, letting the butt stock rest on her right hip for support. The four of us stared at her, riveted by the sight of a gun that unwieldy in the hands of someone who, a nanosecond before, seemed so harmless and out of it. The effect, unfortunately, was undercut by the realities of age. Because of her poor eyesight, she was aiming at the window frame instead of Gilbert, a fact not lost on him. He made a face, saying, "Whoa! You better put that gun away."

"You better put *that* gun away before I blow you to kingdom come," she said. She backed up against the wall, all business, except for the problem with her aim, which was considerable. The heavy flesh on her upper arms shook, and it was clear she could barely keep the barrel up, even if it was pointed in the wrong direction. I could feel my heart begin to thump. I expected Gilbert to shoot, but he didn't seem to take her seriously.

"Gun's pretty heavy. You sure you can keep it up there?"

"Briefly," she said.

"What's that weigh, six or seven pounds? Doesn't sound like much until you have to hooolld it up for long." He dragged out the word "hold," making it sound exhausting. I got tired just hearing it, but Helen didn't seem dismayed.

"I'm going to shoot you long before my arms get tired. I feel it's only fair to warn you. The one barrel's loaded with number nine bird shot. The other's double-O buck, tear your face right off."

Gilbert laughed again. He seemed genuinely tickled by the old woman's attitude. "Jesus, Hell on. That's not nice. What about your arthritis? I thought you had arthritis so bad."

"I do. That's right. Affecting all but the one finger. Watch this." Helen shifted the gun to the left, drew a bead on him, and pulled the trigger. Ka-*blam*! I saw a few bright yellow sparks. The blast was deafening, filling the room. A shock wave of air and gas spread out from the muzzle, followed by a faint doughnut of smoke. The mass of bird shot blew by his right ear, continuing on past him at an upward angle, shattering the kitchen window. Stray pellets tore his earlobe and the top of his shoulder and the spreading fingers of the trailing shot cup raked his neck, painting it with blood. Laura screamed and hit the floor. I was down before she was. Ray's startled reaction tipped his chair over sideways. Gilbert screamed in pain and disbelief, his hands flying up. His handgun flew forward and skittered across the floor.

The muzzle jump had knocked Helen back against the wall, the butt stock slamming into her right hip as the barrels whipped upward with the recoil. She recovered and lowered the gun again, prepared to fire. Gilbert's right cheek was already peppered with red, like a sudden rash of acne, and blood was seeping into the hair above his right ear. The air smelled acrid, and I could suddenly taste something sweet at the back of my throat.

"This time I'll blow your head off," she said.

Gilbert made a savage sound in his throat as he reached down and grabbed Laura by the hair. He hauled her to her feet, pinning her against him while he leaned down and snagged the harness with the other hand.

From the floor, Ray craned his neck, straining to see what was going on. "Ma, don't fire!"

"Pull the trigger and she's dead. I'll snap her neck," Gilbert said. He was clearly in pain, breathing heavily, no longer armed but still out of control. He had his forearm locked up under Laura's chin. She was forced to hang on to him, pulling down to keep from being strangled. Gilbert began backing out of the kitchen and into the dining room. Laura was stumbling backward, half lifted off her feet.

Helen hesitated, no doubt confused by the jumble of sounds and shapes.

Gilbert disappeared into the dining room, plowing backward through the piles of junk and furniture. Laura was making a series of chuffing noises, unable to vocalize with her windpipe choked off. I could hear a crash and the sound of glass shattering as he kicked the front door open. Then silence.

I was torn between the desire to chase after Gilbert and the need to help Helen, who was trembling and deadly pale. She lowered the gun barrel and sank weakly into her chair. "What's happening? Where'd he go?"

"He's got Laura. Just be cool. Everything's going to be fine," Ray said. He was still on the floor, lying sideways in the chair, struggling to get free of his bonds. I scrambled over to him, trying to help him right himself, but with the awkwardness of the chair he was too much for me to lift. I grabbed a butcher knife off the counter and cut through the layers of duct tape that bound his hands and feet. With one hand liberated, Ray started tearing off the rest of the tape, his attention still focused on his mother. "Gimme a hand here," he grunted at me.

"What's he going to do to her?"

"Nothing 'til he gets the money. She's his insurance." I grabbed his hand and braced myself as he hauled himself up from the floor. He glanced at me briefly. "You okay?"

"I'm fine," I said. Both of us turned our attention to Helen.

The shotgun was laid across her lap. I crossed to her, took the gun, and set it on the kitchen table. Her shoulders were slumped and her hands were shaking badly, her breathing shallow and ragged. Her hip was probably bruised where the gun stock had kicked into it. She'd used up all her reserves of energy, and I worried she'd go into shock. "I should have killed him. Poor Laura. I couldn't bring myself to do it, but I should have."

Ray reached for a chair and pulled it closer to his mother's. He took her hand, patting it, his tone tender. "How you doing, Hell on Wheels?" he said.

"I'll be fine in a bit. I just need to catch my breath,"

she said. She patted at her chest, trying to compose herself. "I'm not as feeble-minded as I was acting."

"I couldn't figure out what you were doing," he said. "I can't believe you did that. You started talking to him, I thought it was all bullshit until you pulled out that shotgun. You were terrific. Absolutely fearless."

Helen waved him off, but she seemed pleased with herself and tickled by his praise. "Just because you get old doesn't mean you lose your nerve."

"I thought you had trouble with your eyes," I said. "How'd you know where he was?"

"He was standing up against the kitchen window, so I could make out his *shape*. I may be near blind, but my ears still work. He shouldn't have talked so much. Freida's got me into lifting weights now, and I can bench-press twenty-five pounds. Did you hear what he said? He thought I couldn't even hold up a seven-pound shotgun. I was insulted. Stereotyping the old. That's your typical macho horseshit," she said. She pressed her fingers to her lips. "I believe I'm about to get sick now. Oh, dear."

# 18

RAY HELPED HIS mother to the bathroom. Soon after that, I heard the toilet flush and his murmured comfort and assurances as he tucked her into bed. While I waited for him to get her settled, I returned the contents of the junk drawer and slid the drawer back into its slot. I righted Ray's chair and then got down on my hands and knees to look for Gilbert's gun. Where had the damn thing gone? I raised up like a prairie dog and surveyed the spot where he'd stood, trying to figure out what the trajectory would have been when the gun flew off across the room. Picking my way carefully through the broken glass, I crawled to the nearest corner and worked my way along the baseboard. I finally spotted the gun, a .45-caliber Colt automatic with walnut stocks, wedged behind the Eastlake cabinet. I fished it out with a fork, trying not to smudge any latent prints. If the Louisville police ran a check on him, it was possible an outstanding warrant might pop up and give them a reason to arrest him—if they could find him, of course.

I placed the gun on the kitchen table and tiptoed to the bedroom door. I tapped, and a moment later Ray opened the door a crack. "We need to call the cops," I said. I meant to slip on past, heading for the telephone, but he put his hand on my arm.

"Don't do that."

"Why not?" We were keeping our voices down in deference to his mother, who'd had enough upset for one day.

"Look, I'll be out in a minute, as soon as she's asleep. We need to talk." He began to close the door.

I put my hand on the door. "What's there to talk about? We need help."

"Please." He held a hand up, nodding to indicate that we'd discuss it momentarily. He closed the door in my face.

Reluctantly, I returned to the kitchen to wait for him. I found the broom and dustpan behind the door to the utility room, and I made a pass at the mess. Someone had tracked through the broken bowl of mashed yams. There were little yammy footprints, like dog doo, everywhere. I pulled the garbage can out from under the sink and cautiously began to pick up shards of broken glass and crockery. I used a dampened paper towel to scoop up the remaining goo.

The kitchen sink and the counter were both littered with broken glass where the window had been shattered by the shotgun blast. I couldn't believe the neighbors hadn't come running. Cold air was now blowing in, but there was nothing I could do about it. I hauled out the ancient canister vacuum cleaner and affixed the upholstery attachment to the hose. I flipped it on and spent several minutes huffing up all the glass in sight. Between chasing and being chased, all I'd done since I'd left home was dust and vacuum. I put my ear to the bedroom door at one point and could have sworn I heard Ray talking on the phone. Ah. Maybe he had paid attention to my advice after all.

Ray came back into the kitchen and closed the bedroom door behind him. He moved straight to the pantry and pulled out a bottle of bourbon, took down two small jelly glasses, and poured us both a stiff drink. He handed one glass to me and then tapped mine in a toast. While I eyed mine he tilted his head back and downed his portion. I took a deep breath and tossed mine down my throat, unprepared for the vile fire that assailed my esophagus. I could feel my face flush with heat as my stomach burst into flames. After that, I could feel all the tension drift away from me like smoke. I shook my head, shuddering, as a worm of revulsion wiggled down my frame. "Yuck. I hate that. I could never be a drunk. How can you do that, just toss it back that way?"

"Takes practice," he said. He poured himself another glass and tossed it after the first. "This is one thing I missed in prison."

He spotted the Colt where I'd laid it on the kitchen table, picked it up without comment, and tucked it in his waistband.

"Thanks, Ray. Now you've messed up any fingerprints."

"Nobody's going to run prints," he said.

"Really. What makes you say that?"

He ignored the question. He moved into the dining room and hustled up a cardboard carton, which he emptied, then flattened, and used to replace the broken window glass, securing it with Gilbert's duct tape. The outdoor light was diminished and the cold still seeped in, but at least birds and small UFOs would be prevented from flying in the gaping hole. While I looked on, he began to empty the sink of its mountain of pots and pans, stacking them neatly to one side in preparation for washing. I love watching guys help around the house.

"I heard you on the phone. Did you call 911?"

"I called Marla to see how she was. Gilbert punched her lights out. She says he broke her nose, but she doesn't want to press charges as long as he's got Laura."

"You could call 911," I said. Maybe he hadn't heard me right?

I flipped the vacuum on again and sucked up glass slivers as they came to light. I kept waiting for him to pick up the subject, but he studiously avoided it. Finally, I turned the machine off and said, "So what's the deal? Why not call the cops? Laura's been kidnapped. I hope you don't think you're going to do this on your own."

"I told you. Marla's not interested. She thinks it's premature."

"I'm not talking about Marla. I'm talking about you."

"Let's look for the money first. Nothing turns up in a day, then we can bring the cops into it."

"Ray, you're crazy. You need help."

"I can handle it."

"That's bullshit. He's going to kill her."

"Not if I can find the money."

"How're you going to do that?"

"I don't know yet."

He tied an apron around his waist. He put the stopper in the drain and turned on the hot water. He picked up the liquid detergent and squirted a solid stream into the sink, holding his injured fingers away from the water. A mountain of white suds began to pile up, into which he tucked plates and silverware. "I learned to wash dishes when I was six," he said idly, picking up a long-handled brush. "Ma stood me up on a wooden milk crate and taught me how to do it right. It was my chore from then on. In prison, they use these big industrial machines, but the principle's the same. All us old cons know how to make ourselves useful, but these new punks coming in can't do a damn thing except fight. Dopers and gang-bangers. Scary bunch."

"Ray."

"Remind me of fighting cocks . . . all puffed up and aggressive. Don't give a shit about anything. Those are kids bred to die. They have no hope, no expectations. They got attitude. It's all attitude. Insist on respect without ever doing anything to earn it. Half of 'em don't even know how to read."

"Make your point," I said.

"There's no point. I changed the subject. The point is, I don't want to call the cops."

"Is there a problem?"

"I don't like cops."

"I'm not asking you to form any kind of lasting relationship," I said. I watched him. "What is it? There's something else."

He rinsed a dinner plate and placed it in the rack, avoiding my gaze. I picked up a dish towel and began to dry while he washed. "Ray?"

He put the second dinner plate in the rack. "I'm in violation."

I'm thinking, Violation? I said, "Of what?"

He shrugged slightly.

The penny dropped. "Parole? You violated *parole*?"

"Something like that."

"But what, exactly?"

"Well, actually, 'exactly' is I walked off."

"Escaped?"

"I wouldn't call it escape. It was a halfway house."

"But you weren't supposed to *leave*. You were still an inmate. Weren't you?"

"Hey, there wasn't any fence. It's not like we were locked in our cells at night. We didn't even *have* cells. We had rooms," he said. "So it's more like I'm away without leave. Yeah, like that. AWOL."

"Oh boy," I said. I let out a big breath and considered the implications. "How'd you get a driver's license?"

"I didn't. I don't have one."

"You've been driving without? How'd you manage to rent a car without a driver's license?"

"I didn't."

I closed my eyes, wishing I could lie down on the floor and take a nap. I opened my eyes again. "You *stole* the rental car?" I couldn't help it. I knew my tone was accusatory, but this was largely because I was accusing him.

Ray's mouth pulled down. "I guess you'd say that. So here's the deal. We call the cops, they'll run a check on me and back I go. Big time."

"You'd risk your daughter's life just to avoid going back to jail?"

"It's not just that."

"Then what?"

He turned and looked at me, his hazel eyes as clear as water. "How'm I going to deal with Gilbert if I got a bunch of cops on the scene?"

"Ray, you gotta trust me. It's not worth it. You'll be locked up for the rest of your life."

"What rest? I'm sixty-five years old. How much time do I have?"

"Don't be dumb. You got years. Take a look at your

mom. You're going to live to be a hundred. Don't blow this."

"Kinsey, listen up. Here's the truth," he said. "We call the cops, you know what's going to happen? We go down to the jail. We fill out paperwork. They ask us a bunch of questions I don't want to answer. Either they run a check on me or they don't. If they run a check, I'm history and that's the end of her. If they don't run a check, what difference does it make? We're still fucked. Hours are going to pass, and then what? It'll turn out the cops can't do shit. Oh, too bad. So now we're out on the street again and we still don't have a clue where the money's hid. Believe me. When Gilbert catches up with us, he don't want to hear excuses. And what are we going to say? 'Sorry we didn't find the money yet. We got tied up at the precinct and time got away from us.' "

I said, "Tell him you're working on it. Tell him you have the money and want to meet him somewhere. The cops can pick him up."

Ray's expression was bored. "You been watching too much TV. Truth is, half the time when the cops get involved, they fuck it up. Perpetrator gets caught and the victim dies. You know what happens next? Big trial. Publicity. You get a hotshot lawyer talkin' about the kidnapper's troubled youth. How he's mentally ill and how the victim was abusing him and he only did the kidnap in self-defense. Thousands and thousands of dollars get poured down the drain. The jury ends up hung and the guy takes a walk. Meanwhile, Laura's dead and I'm back in jail again. So who wins? It ain't me and it's certainly not her."

I could feel my temper climb. I tossed the dish towel aside. "You know what? You can do anything you want.

This is really not my problem. You don't want to call the cops. Fine. It's up to you. I'm out of here."

"Back to California?"

"If I can manage it," I said. "Of course, now that Gilbert's got the eight grand, I'm assuming you won't pay my return ticket like you promised, but that's neither here nor there. I don't have enough money for a taxi to the airport, so I'd appreciate a ride. It's the least you can do."

His temper rose in response to mine. "Sure. No problem. Let me pull the kitchen together and we're on our way. Laura dies, it's on you. You could have helped. You said 'no.' You gotta live with that same as I do."

"Me? This is *your* doing. I can't believe you'd try to lay it off on me. You sound just like Gilbert."

He put a hand out and grabbed mine. "Hey. I need help." For a moment, we locked eyes. I broke off eye contact. His tone shifted. He tried coaxing. "Let's brainstorm. The two of us. That's all I'm asking. You got hours until flight time. . . ."

"*What* flight? I've got reservations, but no ticket, and I'm flat broke."

"So how's it going to hurt you to hang out here and help?"

"Well, I'll tell you," I said. "It's two days until Thanksgiving. I'm in a wedding that day, so I have to get back. Two very dear friends are getting married and I'm a bridesmaid, okay? The airports will be jammed with all the holiday traffic. I can't just call the airlines and pick up any old flight. I was lucky to get this one."

"But you can't pay for it," Ray pointed out.

*"I know that!"*

He put a finger to his lips and looked significantly toward the bedroom where his mother was sleeping.

"I know I can't pay. I'm trying to figure that part out," I said in a hoarse whisper.

Ray took out his money clip. "How much?"

"Five hundred."

He put the clip back untouched. "I thought you had friends. Somebody willing to lend you the bucks."

"I do if I can get to the telephone. Your mother's asleep."

"She'll be up in a bit. She's old. She doesn't sleep much at night. She takes catnaps instead. Soon as she wakes up, you can put a call through to California. Maybe your friend can put your ticket on a credit card and you can catch that flight. Looka me. I'll peep in and see how she's doing. How's that?" He moved to the bedroom and made a big display of opening the door a crack. "She'll be out any second now. I promise. I can see her moving around."

"Oh, right."

He closed the door again. "Just help me figure out where the money's hid. Let's talk about it some. That's all I want."

He held a hand out, indicating a seat at the table.

I stared at him. Well, there it was, folks. Altruism and self-interest going head to head. Was I going to take the high road or the low? By now, did I even know which was which? So far, almost everything I'd done was illegal except the vacuuming—breaking into hotel rooms, aiding and abetting escaped felons. Probably even the vacuuming broke some union contract. Why bother to get prissy at this late date? "You are so full of shit," I said.

He pulled out a chair and I sat. I can't believe I did that. I should have walked to the corner market and found a pay phone, but what can I say? I was involved with this man, involved with his daughter and his aged, catnapping mother. As if on cue, she emerged from the bedroom, rheumy eyed and energetic. She'd hardly been down fifteen minutes and she was ready to go again. He pulled out a chair for her. "How you doing?"

"I'm fine. I feel much better," she said. "What's happening? What are we doing?"

"Trying to figure out where Johnny hid the money," Ray said. He had apparently confessed all to his mother because she didn't seem to question the subject matter or his relationship to it. At eighty-five, I guess she wasn't worried about going to jail. From somewhere, another pen and a pad of paper materialized. "We can make notes. Or I can," he said when he caught my look. "You probably want to use the phone first. It's in there."

"I *know* where the phone is. I'll be right back," I said. I used my credit card to put another call through to Henry. As luck would have it, he was still out. I left a second message on his machine, indicating that my return flight was in question because of cash shortages on my end. I repeated Helen's phone number, urging him to call me to see if he could work out some way for me to get on the plane as scheduled. While I was at it, I tried the number at Rosie's, but all that netted me was a busy signal. I went back to the kitchen.

"How'd you do?" Ray asked blandly.

"I left a message for Henry. I'm hoping he'll call back in the next hour or so."

"Too bad you didn't get through to him. I guess there's no point in going out to the airport until you talk to him."

I sat down at the table, ignoring his commiseration,

which was patently insincere. I said, "Let's start with the keys."

Ray made a note on the pad. The note said "keys." He drew a circle around it, squinting thoughtfully. "What difference does it make about the keys as long as Gilbert's got 'em?"

"Because they're just about the only tangible clue we have. Let's just write down what we remember."

"Which is what? I don't remember nothing."

"Well, one was iron. About six inches long, an old-fashioned skeleton key, a Lawless. The other was a Master. . . ."

"Wait a minute. How'd you know that?"

"Because I looked," I said. I turned to Helen. "You have a telephone book? I didn't see one in there, and we're probably going to need one."

"It's in the dresser drawer. Hold on a second. I'll get it," Ray said, and got up. He disappeared into the bedroom.

I called after him, "Have you ever heard of Lawless? I thought it might be local." I looked over at Helen. "Does that ring a bell with you?"

She shook her head. "Never heard of it."

Ray came back with two books in hand, the Louisville residential listings and the Yellow Pages. "What makes you think it's local?"

I took the Yellow Pages. "I'm an optimist," I said. "In my business, I always start with the obvious." He put the residential listings on an empty chair seat. I leafed through the pages until I found the listings for locksmiths. There was no "Lawless" in evidence, but Louisville Locksmith Company looked like a promising possibility. The big display ad indicated they'd been in business since 1910. "We might want to try the public library, too. The phone books from the early forties might be informative."

"She's a private investigator," Ray said to his mother. "That's how she got into this."

"Well, I wondered who she was."

I set the phone book on the table, open to the pages where all the locksmiths were listed. I tapped the Louisville Locksmith display ad. "We'll give this place a call in a minute," I said. "Now where were we?" I glanced at his notes. "Oh yeah, the other key was a Master. I think they only make padlocks, but again, we can ask when we talk to the guy. So here's the question. Are we looking for a big door and then a smaller one? Or a door and then a cabinet or storage unit, something like that?"

Ray shrugged. "Probably the first. Back in the forties, they didn't have those self-storage places like the ones they have now. Wherever Johnny put the money, he had to be sure it wasn't going to be disturbed. Couldn't be a safe-deposit box because the key didn't look right to me. And besides, the guy hated banks. That's what got him into trouble in the first place. He's hardly going to walk into a bank with the proceeds from a bank heist, right?"

"Yeah, right. Plus, banks get torn down or remodeled or turned into other businesses. What about some other kind of public building? City Hall or the courthouse? The Board of Education, a museum?"

Ray wagged his head, not liking the idea much. "Same thing, don't you think? Some developer comes along and sees it as a prime piece of real estate. Doesn't matter what's on it."

"What about some other places around town? Historical landmarks. Wouldn't they be protected?"

"Let me think about that."

"A church," Helen said suddenly.

"That's possible," Ray said.

She pointed to the pad. "Write it down."

Ray made a note about churches. "There's the water works by the river. School buildings. Churchill Downs. They're not going to tear that place down."

"What about a big estate somewhere?"

"That's an idea. There used to be plenty around. I been gone for years, though, so I don't know what's left."

"If he was running from the cops, he had to have a place that was easily accessible," I said. "And it had to be relatively free from intrusion."

Ray wrinkled his forehead "How could he guarantee nobody else would find it? That's a hell of a risk. Leave big canvas bags of money somewhere. How do you know a kid won't stumble across it playing stickball?"

"Kids don't play stickball anymore. They play video games," I said.

"A construction worker, then, or a nosy neighbor? The place had to be dry, don't you think?"

"Probably," I said. "At least, the two keys would suggest the money isn't buried."

"I'm sorry Gilbert got his hands on those keys. Gives him the edge if we identify the place."

"Don't worry about that. I've got a set of key picks I dutifully tote with me everywhere. If we find the right locks, we're in business."

"We can always hack through the locks," Ray suggested. "I learned that in prison, among other things."

"You got quite an education."

"I'm a good student," he said modestly.

The three of us were silent for a moment, trying to get our imaginations to work.

I spoke up again. "You know, the locksmith who first

saw the big key thought it might fit a gate. So how's this for a guess? Maybe Johnny had access to an old estate. The big key fit the gate and the smaller key fit the padlock on the front door."

Ray didn't seem that happy. "How'd he know the place wouldn't be sold or torn down?"

"Maybe it was a historical landmark. Protected by historical preservationists."

"Suppose they decided to restore the place and charge an entrance fee? Then everybody and his brother could walk around the place."

"Right," I said. "Anyway, once they got in, they couldn't find the money sitting out in plain sight. It'd have to be concealed."

"Which puts us right back where we were," he said.

We were silent again.

Ray said, "What gets me is we're talking big. Seven, eight big canvas bags loaded down with cash and jewelry. Those suckers were heavy. We were big strappin' guys in those days, all of us young. You should have seen us grunting and groaning, trying to get 'em stashed in the trunk of the car."

I looked at him with interest. "What was the original plan? Suppose the cops hadn't showed up when they did? What did Johnny mean to do with the money in that case?"

"Same thing, I guess. He always said the reason bank robbers got tripped up was they went out and spent the money way too fast. Started fencing silver and jewels while the cops were circulating information about what was in the heist. Made it all easy to trace."

"So whatever the plan was, he'd set it up well in advance," I said.

"He had to."

I thought about that. "Where was he caught?"

"I forget now. Outside town. On the highway, heading out in that direction somewhere."

"Ballardsville Road," Helen said. "Don't know why, but that sticks in my mind. Don't you remember?"

Ray flushed with pleasure. "She's right," he said. "How'd you remember that?"

"I heard it on the radio," she said. "I was so frightened. I thought you were with him. I didn't know the two of you had separated, and I was convinced you'd been caught."

"I was. I just happened to be somewhere else," he said.

"How soon after the robbery was Johnny picked up?"

Ray's eyes rested on mine. "You're thinking he stashed the goods somewhere between the bank downtown and the place he was caught?"

"Unless he had time to go to some other town and come back," I said. "It's like saying you always find something the last place you look. I mean, it's self-evident. Once you find what you're looking for, you don't look any place else. The last you saw him, he had the sacks full of cash. By the time he was arrested, they were gone. Therefore, the money had to have been hidden some time in that period. By the way, you never said how long it was."

"Half a day."

"So he probably didn't have time to get far."

"Yeah, that's true. I always pictured the money around town somewhere. It never occurred to me he might have left and come back. Shoot. I guess it could be anywhere in a hundred-mile radius."

"I think we should operate on the assumption that it's here in Louisville. I don't want to take on all of western Kentucky."

Ray glanced down at his notes. "So what else do we have? This don't look like much."

"Wait a minute. Try this. The little key had a number on it. I just remembered that," I said. "M550. It's close to my birthday, which is May fifth."

"What good does that do us?"

"We could go to the locksmith and have him grind one."

"To use where?"

"Well, I don't know, but at least we'll have one key in our possession. Maybe the locksmith will have some other ideas."

Ray said, "This feels lame to me. We're really grasping at straws."

"Ray, come on. You work with what you've got," I said. "Believe me, I've started with less and still pulled it off."

"All right," he said skeptically. He made a note of the locksmith's address. He reached for his jacket hanging over the chair.

I rose when he did and buttoned my blazer for warmth. "What about your mother? I don't think she should be left here alone."

She was startled by the mere suggestion. "Oh, no. I won't stay here by myself," she said emphatically. "Not with that fella on the loose. What if he come back?"

"Fine. We'll take you with us. You can wait in the car while we go about our business."

"And just set there?"

"Why not?"

"Well, I might set, but not unarmed."

"Ma, I'm not going to let you sit in the car with a loaded shotgun. Cops would come by and think we're robbing the place."

"I have a baseball bat. That was Freida's idea. She bought a Louisville Slugger and hid it under my bed."

"Jesus, this Freida's a regular artilleryman."

"Artillery*person*," his mother corrected smartly.

"Get your coat," he said.

# 19

THE LOUISVILLE LOCKSMITH shop was located on west Main Street in a three-story building of dark red brick, probably built in the 1930s. Ray found parking on a side street, and a brief argument ensued during which Helen refused to wait in the car as agreed. He finally gave in and let her accompany us, even though she insisted on bringing along her baseball bat. The storefront was narrow, flanked by dark stone columns. All the wood trim was painted mud brown, and the one street-facing window was papered over with hand-lettered signs that detailed the services offered: deadbolts installed, keys fitted, locks installed and repaired, floor and wall safes installed, combinations changed.

The interior was deep and narrow and consisted almost entirely of a long wooden counter, behind which I could see a variety of key grinding machines. Row after row of keys were hung, wall to wall, floor to ceiling, arranged according to a system known only by the owner. A sliding ladder on overhead rollers apparently supplied access to keys in the shadowy upper reaches. All avail-

able space on the scuffed wooden floor was taken up by
Horizon safes being offered for sale. We were the only
customers in the place, and I didn't see a bookkeeper,
an assistant, or an apprentice.

The owner, Whitey Reidel, was about five feet tall
and round through the middle. He wore a white dress
shirt, black suspenders, and black pants. I didn't peek,
but the pants looked like they'd leave a lot of ankle
showing at the cuff. He had a soft, shapeless nose and
big dark bags under his eyes. His hairline had receded
like the tide going out, the remaining wisps of white
hair sticking up in front in a curl, like a Kewpie doll's.
In his habitual stance, he tended to lean forward
slightly, hands on the counter, where he braced himself
as if a hard wind blew. He let his eye trail across the
three of us. His gaze finally settled on Helen's baseball
bat.

"She coaches Little League," Ray said in response to
his look.

"What can I do for you?" Reidel asked.

I stepped forward and introduced myself, explaining
briefly what we needed and why we needed it. He began to shake his head, pulling his mouth down the minute I mentioned a Master padlock key with the M550
code stamped on one side.

"Can't do," he said.

"I haven't finished."

"Don't have to. Explanations won't make any difference. There's no such thing as a Master padlock key series starting with an M."

I stared at him. Ray was standing behind me, and his
mother was standing next to him. I turned to Ray. "You
tell him."

"You're the one saw the key. I didn't see it. I mean,
*saw* it, but I didn't pay attention to any numbers."

"I remember distinctly," I said to Reidel. "You have a piece of paper? I'll show you."

Clearly indulging me, he reached for a scratch pad and a pencil. I wrote the number down and pointed at it, as if that made my claim more legitimate. He didn't contradict me. He simply reached under the counter and pulled out the Master padlock index. "You find it, I'll grind it," he said. He rested his hands on the counter, leaning his weight on his arms.

I leafed through the index, feeling stubborn and perplexed. There were numerous series, some indicated by letters, some by numbers, none designated by the M I'd seen. "I swear it was a Master padlock key."

"I believe you."

"But how could a key show numbers that don't exist?"

His mouth pulled down again and he shrugged. "It was probably a duplicate."

"What difference would that make?"

He reached in his pocket and pulled out a loose key. "This is the key for a padlock back there. On this side is the manufacturer, a Master padlock in this case, like the key we're discussing. Did it look like this?"

"More or less," I said.

Helen had lost interest. She'd moved over to one of the free-standing safes, where she was perched wearily leaning on her bat like a cane.

"Okay. This side says Master, right?"

"Right."

"On *this* side, you got numbers corresponding to the particular padlock the key fits. Are you following?" He looked from me to Ray, and both of us nodded like bobbleheads.

"You give me those numbers, I can look 'em up in this index and get the information I need to reproduce this key, making you a duplicate. But the duplicate isn't going to have the numbers. The duplicate's going to be a blank."

"Okay," I said, drawing the word out cautiously. I couldn't think where he meant to go with this.

"Okay. So the numbers you saw must have been stamped after the key was made."

I pointed to the scratch pad. "You're saying someone had those numbers put on this key," I said, restating it.

"Right," he said.

"But why would somebody do that?" I asked.

"Lady, you came to me. I didn't come to you," he said. When he smiled, I could see the discoloration in his teeth, dark around the gums. "Those numbers are gibberish if you're talking about a Master padlock."

"Could they be code numbers for another key manufacturer?"

"Possibly."

"So if we figured out which manufacturer, couldn't you make me this key?"

"Of course," he said. "The problem is, there's probably fifty manufacturers. You'd have to go through two, three manuals for each company, and many I don't stock. Stamped numbers or letters might also identify the key with a property or door, but there's no way to determine that from what you're telling me."

"Have you ever heard of a Lawless lock?"

He shook his head. "No such thing."

"What makes you so sure?" I said, irritated by his know-it-all attitude.

"My father owned this company and his father before him. We been in business over seventy-five years. If there'd been such a company, I'd have heard the name mentioned. It might be foreign."

I made a face, knowing there'd be no way to track

*that* down. "Is there any chance whatsoever that Law-less was in business back in the forties and is now de-funct?"

"Nope."

Ray put a hand on my arm. "Let's get out of here. It's okay. We're doing this by process of elimination."

"Just wait," I said.

"No way. You got a look on your face like you're about to bite the guy." He turned to his mother. "Hey, Ma. We're going now." He helped her to her feet, tak-ing her arm on his right while he took my arm on his left. The pressure he exerted made his intentions clear. We were not going to stay and argue with a man who knew more than we did.

I felt my frustration rise. "There has to be some con-nection. I know I'm right."

"Don't worry about being right. Let's worry about getting Gilbert off our backs," he said. And then to Reidel, "Thanks for your help." He opened the door and ushered us out. "Besides, we don't need the key. Gil-bert's got one."

"Well, he's not going to give it back."

"He might. If we can find the locks, he might coop-erate. It'd be in his best interests."

"But what are the numbers for? I mean, M550 has to be a code, doesn't it? If not for a key, then something else."

"Quit worrying," he said.

"I do worry. Gilbert's going to want answers. You said so yourself."

Out on the street, it was surprisingly dark. The late afternoon wind whipped off the Ohio River, which I gathered was only three or four blocks away. A few isolated snowflakes sailed by. Streetlights had come on. Most of the businesses along Main were closing down.

and building after building showed a blank face. The buildings were largely brick, five and six stories high, the ornamentation suggesting vintage architecture. Several ground-level stores had retracting metal gates now padlocked across the front. An occasional dim light might be visible deep in the interior, but for the most part, a chilling dark contributed to the overall look of abandonment along the street. Traffic in this part of town was thinning. The downtown itself, visible to the east, displayed a lighted skyline of twenty- to thirty-story office buildings.

We drove back to Helen's house, circling the block once for any sign of Gilbert. None of us knew what kind of car he was driving, but we kept an eye out, thinking we might spot him lingering in the shadows or sitting in a parked vehicle. Ray left his car in the cinder alleyway that ran behind his mother's place. We went through the backyard to the darkened rear entrance. None of us had thought about leaving lights on, so the house was pitch black. Ray went in first while Helen and I huddled on the back steps off the utility porch. Helen was still supporting herself with her baseball bat, which she'd apparently adopted as a permanent prop. All across the neighboring yards, I could see the towering shapes of winter-bare trees against the light-polluted November sky. Branches rattled in the wind. I was shivering by the time he'd turned on lamps and overhead lights and let us in. We waited in the kitchen while he checked the front rooms and the unused bedroom upstairs.

We'd been gone for less than an hour, but the house already seemed to smell dank with neglect. The bulb in the kitchen threw down a harsh, unflattering light. The patch of cardboard in the kitchen window showed a gap at one edge. Helen worked her way around the room, from the pantry to the refrigerator, taking out items for a makeshift supper. She moved with confidence, though I could see that she was counting steps. Ray and I pitched in, saying little or nothing, all of us unconsciously waiting for the phone to ring. Helen didn't have an answering machine, so there was no point in wondering if Henry or Gilbert had called in our absence.

We sat down to a meal of bacon and scrambled eggs, potatoes fried in bacon grease, leftover fried apples and onions, and homemade biscuits with homemade strawberry jam. Too bad she hadn't found a way to fry the biscuits instead of baking them. Despite the cholesterol overdose, everything we ate was exquisite. So this is what grandmothers do, I thought. I had, by then, abandoned any hope of getting home that day. It was still only Monday. I had all of Tuesday and Wednesday to catch a plane. In the meantime, I was tired of feeling stressed out about the issue. Why get my knickers in a twist? I'd do what I could here and be on my way.

After supper, Helen settled down in her bedroom with the TV on. Ray got busy with the dishes while I cleared the kitchen table. I was in the process of wiping down the surface, moving aside the sugar bowl, the salt and pepper shakers, when I noticed the sympathy card Johnny Lee had sent. Helen had apparently left it on the table, anchored by the sugar bowl. I read the greeting again, holding it slanted against the light.

Ray said, "What's that?"

"The card Johnny sent. I was just checking the message inside. The verse looks like it's been typed."

"Read it to me again," he said.

" 'And I will give unto thee the keys of the kingdom of heaven: and whatsoever thou shalt bind on earth shall be bound in heaven: and whatsoever thou shalt loose on earth shall be loosed in heaven. Matthew 16:19. Thinking of you in your hour of loss.' I think this is one of those blank cards where you write in the greeting yourself."

"That makes sense. If the verse was meant as a secret message, how's he going to find a card with that particular quote? He almost had to buy a blank and fill it in himself."

I stared at the Bible verse. "Maybe the M550 stands for Matthew chapter five, verse fifty," I suggested.

"Matthew five is the Sermon on the Mount. Doesn't have fifty verses, only forty-eight." He glanced at me, smiling self-consciously. "That's the other thing I did in prison besides boning up on crime. I was part of a Bible study group on Monday nights."

"You're a man of many surprises."

"I like to think so," he said.

I turned the card over and studied the black-and-white photograph pasted on the front. The photo showed the faded image of a graveyard in snow. I picked at the loose edge, peering at the card stock under it. The print had been glued or pasted over a standard commercial picture of the ocean at sunset. I peeled it off and checked the back, hoping for some kind of handwritten note. The print itself was four inches by six, processed on regular Kodak paper, matte finish, no border. Aside from the word *Kodak* marching across the back, the rest was blank. "You think this is a new photograph reprinted from an old neg? Or maybe a new photo reproduced from an old one?"

"What difference does it make?"

I shrugged. "Well, I don't think a picture of the ocean at sunset tells us anything. Maybe the keys aren't related. Maybe the photo is the message and the keys are a diversionary tactic."

He took the card and moved to the table, holding it to the light as I had, examining the photograph. I peeked over his shoulder. All the headstones looked old, the ornate lettering softened by rain and sanded by harsh winter snows. There were five shorter headstones and three larger monuments of the lamb and angel school. Even the smaller markers, probably granite or marble, were carved with bas-relief leaves and scrolls, crosses, doves. The dominant monument was a white marble obelisk probably twelve feet tall, mounted on a granite pedestal with the name PELISSARO visible. All of the surrounding trees were mature, though barren of leaves. A thin layer of snow covered the ground. One cluster of headstones was enclosed with iron fencing, and I could see a section of stone wall to the right.

"I don't suppose you recognize the place," I said.

Ray shook his head. "Could be a private graveyard, like a family plot on somebody's property."

"Looks too spread out for that. Seems like a private graveyard would be more compact and countrified. More homogeneous. Look at the headstones, the variation in sizes and styles."

"So what's this have to do with two keys? He didn't have time to dig up a coffin and bury the stash. It was the dead of winter. The ground was froze hard."

I looked at Ray with interest. "Really. It was winter? So this might have been taken at the time?"

"Possible, I guess, but if he buried the money, he'd have needed grave-digging machinery, which I guess he could have got hold of somehow. Seems like he told me once he'd been a groundskeeper in a cemetery. He could have put the money in a mausoleum, I suppose. Anyway, what's your thinking?"

"But why a picture of this? Maybe it's the name Pelissaro. I'm just spitballing here. He might have left the money with someone by that name. In a building or business in the general vicinity of the cemetery. The Pelissaro Building, Pelissaro Farms. The old Pelissaro estate," I said, wiggling my brows.

Ray shook his head. "You're barkin' up the wrong tree."

"Well. Maybe it's something *visible* from here. A water tower, an outbuilding, a stone quarry. Where's the phone book? Let's look. Let's dare to be stupid. We might hit pay dirt."

"Look for what?"

"The name Pelissaro. Maybe he had a confederate."

I glanced around the kitchen and spotted the residential pages sitting on the chair where he'd left them. I pulled out a chair and sat down, flipping through the White Pages to the P's. There was no Pelissaro listed. Nothing even close. I said, "Shit. Ummn. Well, maybe there was a Pelissaro back in the 1940s. We'll try the library in the morning. It can't hurt."

"We better do something fast. Gilbert's going to call any minute, and I'm not going to tell him we're off to the public *library*. I'd like to tell him we're on to something instead of sitting here daring to be stupid. That's the same as dead in his book."

"You're a pain, you know that? Here, try this." I reached for the Yellow Pages and looked up "Cemeteries." Approximately twenty were listed. "Take a look and tell me where these are located," I said. "If we got out a map and drew a big circle, we could probably narrow down the area. At the very least, we could check out all the cemeteries within a radius of the spot where Johnny was apprehended. Wouldn't that make sense? There couldn't be that many. Judging by the photograph, this cemetery is well established. Those graves are old. They haven't gone anywhere."

"You don't know that. Around here, they move graves when they dam up a river to make a lake," he said.

"Yeah, well, if the money's underwater, we've had it," I said. "Let's operate on the assumption it's still aboveground someplace. You have a map of Louisville? You can show me what's where."

Ray went out to the car and came back with the big map of the United States, along with a set of strip maps and a map of Louisville. "Compliments of Triple A. Car I borrowed was well equipped," he said.

"You're too thoughtful," I said as I opened the city map. "Let's start with this first one. Where's Dixie Highway?"

One by one, we worked through the cemeteries listed in the Yellow Pages, marking their locations on the map of Louisville. There were four, possibly five, within reasonable driving distance of the place where Johnny Lee had been apprehended by the police. I listed each cemetery along with the address and telephone number on a separate piece of paper.

"So now what?" he asked.

"So now, first thing tomorrow morning, we'll call each of these cemeteries and find out if they have a Pelissaro buried there."

"Assuming the cemetery's in Louisville."

"Would you quit being such a butt?" I said. "We have to assume this is relevant or Johnny wouldn't have sent you the picture. His object was to give you information, not to fool you."

"Yeah, well, let's hope he didn't do too good a job. We might never decipher it."

By nine o'clock, I was exhausted and began to make mewling noises about turning in. Ray seemed restless and jumpy, worried because Gilbert hadn't been in touch.

"What are you going to tell him if he calls?" I asked.

"Don't know. I'll tell him something. I'd like to get him and Laura over here first thing tomorrow morning so I can see she's okay. In the meantime, let's get you settled. You look beat."

He found a couple of blankets and a pillow in the top of his mother's closet. "You better make a potty stop first. There isn't a bathroom up there."

I spent a few minutes in the bathroom and then followed Ray up. As it turned out, there wasn't much of anything else up there, either, a single bed with a wood frame and a sagging spring, a bed table with one short leg, and a lamp with a forty-watt bulb and a yellowing shade. I worried briefly about bugs and then realized it was too cold up here for anything to survive.

"You got everything you need?"

"This is fine," I said.

I sat gingerly on the bed while he clumped downstairs again. I couldn't sit up straight because the eaves of the house slanted so sharply above the bed. It was bitterly cold, and the room smelled of soot. As a form of insulation, someone had layered sheets of newspaper between the mattress and the springs, and I could hear them crackle every time I moved. I lifted one corner of the mattress and did a quick check of the date: August 5, 1962.

I slept in my clothes, wrapping myself in as many layers of blanket as I could manage. By curling myself into a fetal position, I conserved whatever body heat I had left. I turned out the lamp, though I was reluctant to surrender the meager warmth thrown off by the bulb. The pillow was flat and felt faintly damp. For some time, I was aware of light coming up the stairwell. I could hear noises—Ray pacing, a chair scraping back, an occasional fragment of laughter from the TV set. I'm not sure how I managed to fall asleep under the circumstances, but I must have. I woke once and turned the light on to check my watch: 2:00 A.M., and the lights downstairs were still on. I couldn't hear the television set, but the nighttime quiet was broken by occasional unidentifiable sounds. I wakened some time later to find the house dark and completely quiet. I was acutely aware of my bladder, but there was nothing for it except mind control.

I really don't know which is worse when you sleep in someone else's house—being cold with no access to additional blankets or having to pee with no access to the indoor plumbing. I suppose I could have tiptoed downstairs on both counts, but I was afraid Helen would think I was a burglar and Ray would think I was coming on to him, trying to creep into his bed.

I woke again at first light and lay there, feeling miserable. I closed my eyes for a while. The minute I heard someone stirring, I rolled out of bed and made a beeline for the stairs. Ray and his mother were both up. I made a detour to the bathroom, where, among other things, I brushed my teeth. When I returned to the kitchen, Ray was reading the morning paper. He hadn't had a chance to shave, and his chin was prickly with white stubble and probably felt as rough as a sidewalk. I was so accustomed to his various facial bruises, I hardly noticed them. He'd covered his habitual white T-shirt with a denim workshirt that he wore loose. Despite his age he was in good shape, the definition in his upper body probably the result of hours lifting weights in prison.

"Have we heard from Gilbert?"

He shook his head.

I sat down at the kitchen table, which Helen had set

at some point the night before. Ray passed me a section
of the *Courier-Journal*. One more day together and
we'd have our routines down pat, like an old married
couple living with his mother. Helen, for her part,
limped around the kitchen, using the bat as a cane.

"Is your foot bothering you?" I asked.

"My hip. I got a bruise goes from here to here," she
said with satisfaction.

"Let me know if I can help."

Coffee was soon perking, and Helen began to busy
herself frying sausage. This time she outdid herself, fixing each of us a dish she called a one-eyed jack, in
which an egg is fried in a hole cut in the middle of a
piece of fried bread. Ray put ketchup on his, but I
didn't have the nerve.

After breakfast I hit the phone, making a quick call to
the five cemeteries we'd put on our list. Each time I
claimed I was an amateur genealogist, tracking my family history in the area. Not that anybody cared. All were
nondenominational facilities with burial plots available
for purchase. On the fourth call, the woman in the sales
office checked her records and found a Pelissaro. I got
directions to the place and then tried the last cemetery
on the off chance a second Pelissaro was buried in the
area. There was only the one.

Ray and I exchanged a look. He said, "I hope you're
right about this."

"Look at it this way. What else do we have?"

"Yeah."

I excused myself and headed for the shower. The
phone rang while I was in the process of rinsing my
hair. I could hear it through the wall, a shrill counter-
point to the drumming of the water, the last of the
shampoo bubbles streaming down my frame. In the bedroom, Ray answered the phone and his voice rumbled

briefly. I cut my routine short, turned the water off, dried myself, and threw my clothes on. At least I had no problems deciding what to wear. By the time I reached the kitchen, Ray was in motion, putting together an assortment of tools, some of which he brought in from a small shed in the backyard. He'd found a couple of shovels, a length of rope, a pair of tin snips, pliers, a bolt cutter, a hammer, a hasp, an ancient-looking hand drill, and two wrenches. "Gilbert's on his way over with Laura. I don't know what we're up against. We may have to dig up a coffin, so I thought we'd better be prepared." The Colt was sitting on the tin pull-out counter of the Eastlake. Ray picked it up in passing and tucked it in the waistband of his pants again.

"What's that for?"

"He's not going to catch me off guard again."

I wanted to protest, but I could see his point. My anxiety was rising. My chest felt tight and something in my stomach seemed to squeeze and release, sending little ripples of fear up and down my frame. I teetered precariously between the urge to flee and an inordinate curiosity about what would happen next. What was I thinking? That I could affect the end result? Perhaps. Mostly, having come this far, I had to see it through.

# 20

GILBERT AND LAURA arrived within the hour with the canvas duffel in tow, probably packed with the eight thousand dollars in cash. Gilbert was wearing his Stetson again, perhaps hoping to enhance his tough-guy image now that he'd been bested by an eighty-five-year-old blind woman. Laura was clearly exhausted. Her skin looked bleached, residual bruises casting pale green-and-yellow shadows along her jaw. Against the pallor of her complexion, her dark auburn hair seemed harsh and artificial, too stark a contrast to the drained look of her cheeks. I could see now that her eyes were the same hazel as Ray's, the dimple in her chin a match for his. Her clothes looked slept in. She was back in the outfit I'd first seen her wearing: oversize pale blue denim dress with short sleeves, a long-sleeved white T-shirt worn under it, red-and-white-striped tights, and high-topped red tennis shoes. The belly harness was gone and the effect was odd, as if she'd suddenly dropped weight in the wake of some devastating illness.

Gilbert seemed tense. His face was still pockmarked

303

with spots where Helen's bird shot had nicked him, and he wore a piece of adhesive tape across his earlobe. Aside from the evidence of first aid, his blue jeans looked pressed, his boots polished. He wore a clean white western-cut shirt with a leather vest and a bolo tie. The outfit was an affectation, as I guessed he'd been west of the Mississippi only once and that not much more than a week ago. At the sight of her grandmother, Laura started to cross the room, but Gilbert snapped his fingers and, like a dog, she heeled. He put his left hand on the back of her neck and murmured something in her ear. Laura looked miserable but offered no resistance. Gilbert's attention was diverted by the sight of his gun in the waistband of Ray's pants. "Hey, Ray. You want to give that back?"

"I want the keys first," Ray said.

"Let's don't get into any bullshit argument," Gilbert said.

His right hand came up to Laura's throat, and with a flick, the blade jutted out of the knife he'd palmed. The point pierced her skin, and the gasp she emitted was filled with surprise and pain. "Daddy?"

Ray saw the trickle of blood and the absolute stillness with which she stood. He glanced down at his waistband where the Colt was tucked. He took the gun out and held it toward Gilbert, butt first. "Here. Take the fuckin' thing. Get the blade off her neck."

Gilbert studied him, easing the point back almost imperceptibly. Laura didn't move. I could see the blood begin to saturate the neck of her T-shirt. Tears trickled down her cheeks.

Ray motioned impatiently. "Come on, take the gun. Just get the knife away from her throat."

Gilbert pressed a button on the knife handle, retracting the blade. Laura put her hand against the wound and looked at her bloody fingertips. She moved to a kitchen chair and sat down, her face drained of any remaining color. Gilbert switched the knife to his left hand and reached over to take the gun with his right. He checked the magazine, which was fully loaded, and then tucked the gun in his waistband, hammer cocked and safety on. He seemed to relax once the gun was back in his possession. "We gotta trust each other, right? Soon as I have my share of the money, she goes with you and we're done."

"That's the deal," Ray said. It was clear he was fuming, a response not lost on Gilbert.

"Bygones be bygones. We can shake on it," Gilbert said. He held his hand out.

Ray looked at it briefly, and then the two shook hands. "Let's get on with this, and no funny business."

Gilbert's smile was bland. "I don't need funny business as long as I have her."

Laura had watched the exchange with a mixture of horror and disbelief. "What are you doing? Why'd you give him the gun?" she said to Ray. "You really think he'll keep his word?"

Gilbert's expression never changed. "Stay out of this, babe."

Her tone was tinged with outrage, her eyes filled with betrayal. "He's not going to split the money. Are you crazy? Just tell him where it is and let's get out of here before he kills me."

"Hey!" Ray said. "This is business, okay? I spent forty years in the joint for this money, and I'm not backing off because you got problems with the guy. Where were you all these years? I know where I was. Where were you? You come along expecting me to bail you out. Well, I'm bailing, okay? So why don't you back off and let me do it my way."

"Daddy, help me. You have to help."

"I am. I'm buying your life, and it don't come cheap. My deal is with him, so butt out of this."

Laura's face took on a stony cast and she stared down at the ground, her jaw set. Gilbert seemed to enjoy the fact that she'd been rebuffed. He moved as if to touch her, but she batted his hand away. Gilbert smiled to himself and sent a wink in my direction. I didn't trust any of them, and it was making my stomach hurt.

I looked on while Ray laid out the game plan, filling Gilbert in on the calls we'd made and the reasoning behind them. I noticed he'd left out a few pertinent facts, like the name of the cemetery and the name on the monument. "We haven't found the money yet, but we're getting close. You expect to benefit, you might as well pitch in here and help," Ray said, his eyes dead with loathing. A chilly smile passed between them, full of promises. I looked from one to the other, hoping fervently I wouldn't be around if the two of them ever got into a pissing contest.

Ray said, "I assume you got the keys with you."

Gilbert pulled them from his pocket, displayed them briefly, hooked together on a ring, and then tucked them away again.

Without another word, Ray began to gather up some of the equipment he'd assembled: the rope, the two shovels, the bolt cutters. "Everybody grab something and let's go," he said. "We can stick all this stuff in the trunk."

Gilbert picked up the hand drill, taking his time about it so it wouldn't look like he was obeying orders. "One more thing. I want the old lady with us."

"I'm not going anywhere with you, bub," Helen snapped. She sat down in her chair and leaned stubbornly on her bat.

Ray paused. "What's she got to do with it?"

"We leave anyone behind, how do I know they aren't dialing the old 911?" Gilbert said to Ray, ignoring the old woman.

Ray said, "Come on. She wouldn't do that."

"Oh, yes I would," she said promptly.

Gilbert stared at Ray. "You see that? Old woman's crazy as a bed bug. She goes, too, or it's all off."

"What are you talking about? That's bullshit. You gonna forfeit the dough?"

Gilbert smiled, gripping Laura's neck. He gave her head a shake. "I don't have to forfeit anything. You're the one going to lose."

Ray closed his eyes and then opened them. "Jesus. Get your coat, Ma. You're coming with us. I'm sorry to have to do this."

Helen's gaze moved vaguely from Gilbert to Ray. "It's all right, son. I'll go if you insist."

Since Gilbert didn't trust any of us, we took one car. Gilbert, Helen, and Laura sat together in the backseat, the old woman holding hands with her granddaughter. Helen still had her bat, which Gilbert took note of. Sensing his gaze, Helen shook the bat in his direction. "I'm not done with you, mama," Gilbert murmured.

Ray drove while I navigated from the front seat, tracing the route on the open map. He headed east on Portland Avenue, cutting back onto Market Street and from there under the bridge and up onto 71 heading north. The day was breezy, faintly warmer than it had been. The sky was a wide expanse of robin's egg blue, clouding up along the horizon. I was hoping Ray would violate some minor traffic law and get us stopped by the highway patrol, but he kept the speedometer exactly at the limit, giving hand signals I hadn't seen anyone use for years.

About a mile beyond the Watterson Expressway, he moved onto the Gene Snyder Freeway and took the first off-ramp. We exited onto 22, which we followed for some distance. The route we took was probably once a little-used dirt road, many miles out in the country. I pictured merchants and farmers in a countywide radius, traveling hours by wagon to reach the wooded area where their dead would be laid to rest. The Twelve Fountains Memorial Park was located several miles across the line into Oldham County, surrounded by limestone walls, occupying land that had once been part of a five-hundred-acre tract of woods and tangled undergrowth. Over the years, the hilly countryside had been tamed and manicured.

At the entrance, iron gates stood open, flanked by fieldstone gateposts that must have been fifteen feet tall. The road split left and right, circling an arrangement of three large stone fountains, shooting staggered columns and sprays of water into the icy November air. A discreet sign directed us to the right, where a small stone building was tucked against a backdrop of cypress and weeping willows. Ray pulled onto the gravel parking pad. I could see the woman in the office peering out at us.

Gilbert took Helen into the office with him. Laura's face was still so visibly bruised as to generate attention he didn't want. His own face was still peppered with tiny cuts, but nobody'd have the nerve to ask what happened.

While the two of them were gone, Laura caught Ray's eye in the rearview mirror. "What about her?" she said, indicating me.

"What *about* her?" Ray said, annoyed.

"Gilbert's worried about Grammy calling the cops. What makes you think *she* won't?"

I turned around in the seat to face her. "I'm not calling anyone. I'm just trying to get home," I said.

Laura ignored me. "You think she's going to sit by and watch us walk away with the money?"

"We haven't even found it yet," Ray said.

"But when we do, then what?"

Ray's expression was despairing. "Jesus, Laura. What do you want from me?"

"She's going to be trouble."

"I am not!"

Laura looked away from me and out the window, her mouth set. Gilbert and Helen were returning to the car. He ushered her unceremoniously into the backseat again and then got in on his side. Helen muttered something scathing and Ray said, "Ma, be careful." She reached forward and touched Ray's shoulder with affection.

Gilbert slammed his door shut and handed me the pamphlet he carried with him. Since I'd called in advance, the woman in the sales office had provided us with a brochure detailing the charter and development of the memorial park. The pamphlet opened up to show a map of the cemetery with points of interest marked with an X. She'd also supplied a folded sheet of paper that showed a detailed plot map of the particular section we'd be visiting. The Pelham gravesite she'd circled in red.

I looked back at Gilbert. "You know, this may not lead to anything," I said.

"I hope you have a backup plan, in that case."

My backup plan was to run away real fast.

Ray fired up the engine again. I showed him the route, which the woman had marked in ballpoint pen. The cemetery was laid out in a series of interconnecting circles that from the air would have resembled the wedding ring design on a patchwork quilt. Roads encompassed each section, curving into one another like a succession of roundabouts. We took the first winding road to the left as far as the Three Maidens fountain. At the fork, we veered left, moving up past the lake, and then to the right and around to the old section of the park. The cemetery had been named for its twelve fountains, which loomed unexpectedly, wanton displays of water spewing skyward. In California, the waste of water would be subject to citation, especially in the drought years, which seemed to outnumber the rainy ones.

We passed the Soldiers' Field, where the military dead were buried, their uniform white markers as neatly lined up as a newly planted orchard. The perspective shifted with us, the vanishing point sweeping across the rows of white crosses like the beam from a lighthouse. In the older sections of the cemetery, into which we drove, the mausoleums were impressive: limestone-and-granite structures complete with sloping cornices and Ionic pilasters. The larger sarcophagi were adorned with kneeling children, their heads bowed, stone lambs, urns, stone draperies, and Corinthian columns. There were pyramids, spires, and slender women in contemplative postures, cast-bronze dogs, arches, pillars, sculpted busts of stern-looking gents, and elaborate stone vases, all interspersed with inlaid granite tablets and simple headstones of more modest dimensions. We passed grave after grave, stretching away as far as the eye could see. The headstones represented so many family relationships, the endings to so many stories. The very air felt dark and the ground was saturated with sorrow. Every stone seemed to say, This is a life that mattered, this marks the passing of someone we loved and will miss deeply and forever. Even the mourners were dead now and the mourners who mourned them.

The Pelissaro plot was located in a cul-de-sac. We parked and got out. Gilbert tossed his Stetson in the backseat, and the five of us moved toward the gravesite in ragtag fashion. I held the photograph at eye level, marveling at the scene that was laid out before us exactly as it looked forty years before. The Pelissaro monument, a white marble obelisk, towered over the surrounding graves. Most of the trees in the photograph were still standing, many having grown much larger with the passage of time. As in the picture, the branches were once again barren of leaves, but this time there was no snow and the grass had gone dormant, a patchy brown mixed with dull green. I spotted the same cluster of headstones enclosed with iron fencing, the section of stone wall to the right of us.

Gilbert was already impatient. "What do we do now?" he asked Ray.

Ray and I exchanged a brief look. So far, Gilbert had honored his end of the bargain. He'd showed up with Laura, who was not only alive and well, but looked as if she hadn't been battered the night before. Ray and I stood there, stalling, knowing we really didn't have a way to hold up our end. We'd tried to indicate the limits to our understanding, but Gilbert didn't have any tolerance for ambiguity. Helen waited patiently, bundled up in her coat, attentive to a large monument she probably mistook for one of us.

Gilbert said, "I'm not going to dig up any monuments. Especially this one. Probably weighs a couple tons."

"Gimme a minute," Ray said. He surveyed the scene in front of us, his gaze taking in headstones, landscape features, valleys, trees, the ring of hills beyond. I knew what he was doing because I was doing the same thing, searching for the next move in the peculiar board game we were playing. I'd half expected a water tower looming in the distance, some pivotal word painted on its circumference. I'd hoped to see an old gardener's shed or a signpost, anything to indicate where to go from here. The Pelissaro gravesite had to be important, or why bother to send the photograph? The keys might or might not be relevant, but the monument foreshadowed *something*, if we could figure out what.

I could see Ray doing a spot check of names on every marker within range. None of them seemed significant. I did a three-hundred-and-sixty-degree turn, scanning the cul-de-sac behind us, which was ringed by mausoleums. "I got it," I said. I put a hand on Ray's arm and pointed. There were five mausoleums in the circle, gray limestone structures sunk into the rising hill that fanned up and around the cul-de-sac like an upturned shirt collar. Each of the five facades was different. One resembled a miniature cathedral, another a scaled-down version of the Parthenon. Two looked like small bank buildings complete with colonnades and shallow steps leading up to once impressive entrances now sealed shut with blank concrete. On each, the family name was carved above the door in stone. REXROTH. BARTON. HARTFORD. WILLIAMSON. It was the fifth mausoleum that caught my attention. The name above the door was LAWLESS.

Ray snapped his fingers rapidly. "Gimme the keys," he said to Gilbert, who obliged without argument.

We scrambled down to the road, all of us intent on the sight of the mausoleum. The entrance was protected by an iron gate, with a keyhole visible even from a distance. Through the bars of the gate, a chain had been added, circling the main lock and secured with a padlock. I glanced down at the piece of paper that showed, in detail, the layout of burial plots in the area. The Lawless mausoleum was located in section M, lot 550. The message from Johnny Lee had been sent and received. I couldn't believe we'd done it, but we'd actually managed to interpret his missive.

Ray moved to the car, which we'd parked in the circle just across from the mausoleum. He opened the trunk and took out a tire iron. "Grab a tool," he said. Again, Gilbert obeyed without a murmur, arming himself with a shovel. Laura grabbed a hammer and a pickax Ray had found and tossed in the back at the last minute. The five of us crossed the pavement, Helen bringing up the rear with her bat tapping the ground. We moved up the steps in an irregular grouping and peered through the iron bars of the gate. Inside, there was a paved foyer, maybe ten feet wide and five feet deep. On the back wall, there were spaces for sixteen vaults into which individual caskets could be placed, the vaults themselves arranged four rows high and four rows wide.

We stood back and watched as Ray inserted the small key in the Master padlock, which popped loose at a turn. The chain, once freed, clattered to the pavement. The big iron key turned in the gate lock with effort. The gate shrieked as it swung open, the shrill scraping sound of metal on metal. We went in. Of the sixteen burial slots, all seemed to be filled. Twelve bore engraved stones indicating the name of the deceased, birth and death dates, and sometimes a line of poetry. All of the birth and death dates ranged in years before the turn of the century. The four remaining slots were cemented over with plain concrete and bore no data at all.

Ray seemed reluctant to act at first. This was, after all, a family burial place. "I guess we better get a move on," he said. Tentatively, he went after the uppermost square of concrete with the tire iron. After the first blow, he began to hack in earnest at the blank face, working with concentration. Gilbert took one of the shovels and used the blade in much the same way, laboring beside Ray. The noise seemed remarkably loud to me, echoing around in the confines of the mausoleum. I'm not sure anyone outside the structure could have heard much. It certainly wouldn't be easy to pinpoint the source of all the pounding. The concrete was apparently only the barest of shells because the facing began to crack, yielding to sheer force. Once Ray had succeeded in breaking through, Gilbert chipped away at the crumbling material and widened the opening.

Meanwhile, Laura was on her knees, whacking with equal vigor at the concrete facing on the bottom vault with the pickax. Dust flew up, filling the air with a pale gritty cloud of small particles. There was something disturbing about the diligence with which they worked. All their conflicts and past quarrels had been set aside with the acceleration of the hunt. Discovery was imminent and greed had displaced their contentiousness.

Helen and I moved back against the wall, getting out of their way. Through the barred gate, looking toward the hillside, I could see the wind pushing at the tree branches. I craned my neck, looking up with uneasiness. The sky had clouded over completely, dark forms massing above us. The weather here was changeable, where in California it seemed fixed and monotonous. I couldn't imagine where this situation was heading, and I was torn between dread and some dim hope that in the end everything would turn out all right. Ray and Gilbert would split the money, shake hands, and go about their business, freeing me to go about mine. Laura would leave Gilbert. Maybe she'd spend some time with her father and her grandmother before the three parted company. Ray would probably remain with his mother while she had her eye surgery, unless he was caught and sent back to prison first.

I checked my watch. It was only 10:15 in the morning. If I managed to catch an early afternoon flight, I might get home in time for dinner. I'd missed most of the prewedding festivities. Tomorrow night, Wednesday, the night before the wedding, William and "the boys" had elected to go bowling, while Nell, Klotilde, and I would probably have supper up at Rosie's. She swore there was no need for a rehearsal dinner. "So what's to rehearse? We're going to stand side by side and repeat what the judge tells us." Nell hadn't had a chance to do the final adjustments on my bridesmaid's muumuu, but how much fitting could it need?

The pounding in the mausoleum took on a repetitious rhythm. I could hear a groundskeeper using a leaf blower somewhere in the distance. No cars passed along the road that rimmed us. The next thing I knew, Ray, Gilbert, and Laura were dragging canvas bags out of the building and down the steps. Helen and I followed, standing by while Ray upended one of the sacks and toppled the contents out onto the asphalt. Ray was saying, "The guy's a genius. Who the hell would have thought of this? I wish he were here. I wish he could have seen this. Look at that. Jesus, is that beautiful?"

What had tumbled onto the pavement was a hodge podge of U.S. and foreign currency, jewelry, silver flatware and hollowware, stock certificates, coin silver, Confederate notes, bearer bonds, unidentified legal documents, coins, proof sets, stamps, and gold and silver dollars. The hillock of valuables was nearly as high as my knee, and six other canvas sacks were as crammed full as this had been. Even Helen, with her poor eyes, seemed to sense the enormity of the find. A rain spot appeared on the pavement nearby, followed by a second and a third, at wide intervals. Ray looked up with surprise, holding a hand out. "Let's get going," he said.

Laura refilled the one sack while Ray and Gilbert dragged the others to the trunk of the car and hoisted them in. When the last sack had been added, Ray slammed the trunk down. We were all in the process of getting into the car when I caught sight of Gilbert. For a moment, I thought he was pausing to tuck his shirt in, but I realized what he was reaching for was the gun. Ray saw my face and glanced back at Gilbert, who stood now, feet planted, the Colt in his hand. Laura gripped Helen's arm, the two of them immobilized. I saw Laura lean down and murmur something to her grandmother, warning her what was happening since the old woman couldn't see that well.

Gilbert was watching Ray with amusement, as if the rest of us weren't present. "I hate to tell you this, Ray babe, but your pal Johnny was a stone killer."

Ray stared at him. "Really."

"He put out a contract on Darrell McDermid and had him offed."

Ray seemed to frown. "I thought Darrell died in an accident."

"It wasn't an accident. The kid was smoked. Johnny paid a guy big money to make sure Darrell went down."

"Why? Because he ratted us out to the cops?"

"That's what Johnny said."

"So who did him?"

"Me. Kid was all tore up about his brother anyway, so I put him out of his misery."

Ray thought about it briefly and then shrugged. "So? I can live with that. Served him right. The fuck deserved what he got."

"Yeah, except Darrell wasn't guilty. Darrell never did a thing. Someone told Johnny a big fat fib," Gilbert said with mock regret. "It was me told the cops. I can't believe you guys never figured that out."

"You were the snitch?"

"I'm afraid so," he said. "I mean, let's face it. I'm a rat-fuck. I'm worthless. It's like that old joke about the guy saves a snake and then gets bit to death. He's all, 'Hey, why'd you do that when I saved your life?' And the snake goes, 'Listen, buddy, you knew I was a viper the first time you picked me up.' "

"Gilbert, I gotta tell you. I never mistook you for a nice guy. Not once." Casually Ray reached back, and when his hand came into view again, he was holding a Smith & Wesson .38 Special.

Gilbert laughed. "Fuck. A shoot-out. This should be fun."

"More for me than for you," Ray said. His eyes glittered with malice, but Gilbert only seemed amused, as if he didn't consider Ray a threat he had to take seriously.

"Daddy, don't," Laura said.

I said, "Come on, guys. You don't have to do this. There's plenty of money. . . ."

"This isn't about the money," Ray said. He wasn't looking at me. He was looking straight at Gilbert, the two of them standing no more than ten feet apart. "This is about a guy abusing my daughter, beating up my ex-wife. This is about Darrell and Farley, you asshole. Do we understand one another?"

"Absolutely," Gilbert said.

I felt myself back up a step, so intent on the two men, I didn't see what Helen was doing. She brought up the baseball bat, flailing wildly in Gilbert's general direction, bashing Ray's arm on the back swing. She

missed Gilbert altogether and nearly whacked me in the
mouth. I could feel the wind against my lips as the bat
whistled past. She hit the car on her follow-through, and
the impact knocked the bat right out of her hand.

"Jesus, Ma! Get out of here. Get her outta here!"

Laura screamed and ducked. I hit the ground, looking
up in time to see Gilbert take aim and fire at her. There
was a click. He looked down at the Colt in astonish-
ment. He recocked and pulled the trigger; the hammer
clicked again. He pulled the slide back, ejecting a
round, then let it slam forward again, popping another
round into the chamber. He swung the gun around and
aimed at Ray. He pulled the trigger. Click. He recocked
and pulled the trigger again. Click. "What the fuck?" he
said.

Ray smiled. "Well, shame on me. I forgot to mention
I shortened the firing pin."

Ray fired and Gilbert went down with an odd sound,
as if the wind had been knocked out of him. Ray moved
forward easily until he was standing directly over Gilbert. He fired again.

Spellbound, I stared as he fired again.

Ray turned and looked in my direction. He said,
"Don't do that."

Out of the corner of my eye, I caught a blur of motion and then I heard the crack of the baseball bat coming down on my head. In the split second before the
dark descended, I flashed on Helen with regret. Her erratic batting practice had come to an abrupt halt and
she'd popped me a good one. The only problem was I
could see her and her hands were empty. Laura was the
one up at bat and I was gone, gone, gone.

I spent the night in a semiprivate room at a hospital
called Baptist East with the worst headache I believe

I've ever had in my life. Because of the concussion, the doctor wouldn't give me any pain medication and my vital signs were checked every thirty minutes or so. Since I wasn't permitted to sleep, I spent a tedious couple of hours being interrogated by two detectives from the Oldham County Sheriff's Department. The guys were nice enough, but they were naturally skeptical of the story I told. Even mildly concussed, I was lying through my teeth, cleaning up my culpability in events as I sketched them out. Finally, a call was placed to the *Courier-Journal* and some poorly paid reporter checked through the back files to find an account of the bank robbery, including names of all the suspects and a lot of colorful speculation about the missing money. As it turned out, of course, the money was still missing, as were Ray Rawson, his aged mother, and his daughter, Laura, whose common-law husband was laid out in the morgue, his body perforated with bullet holes.

I maintained stoutly that I'd been forced along at gunpoint, clobbered and abandoned when my usefulness ran out. Who was there to contradict me? It helped that when a call was placed to Lieutenant Dolan back in Santa Teresa, he spoke up in my behalf and defended my somewhat sullied honor. The investigating officer laboriously hand-printed my account of events, and I agreed to be available for testimony when (and if) Ray Rawson and his merry band were arrested and tried. I don't think the chances are all that good myself. For one thing, Ray has all that money in his possession, along with the forty years' worth of contacts and criminal cunning he picked up while he was in prison. I'm relatively certain he's managed to acquire three sets of false identification, including passports, and first-class tickets to parts unknown.

Wednesday morning, when I was released, a nurse

just getting off duty offered me a ride as far as the Port-land neighborhood where Helen Rawson lived. I got out at the corner and walked the remaining half block. The house was dark. The back door was standing open and I could see where miscellaneous items of clothing had been dropped in the haste of their departure. I went into the bedroom and turned on the table lamp. All the old lady's pills were gone, a sure sign she'd decamped with her son and granddaughter. I took the liberty of using her telephone, not even bothering to charge the call to my credit card. I had a dreadful time getting through to anyone. I tried Henry and got his machine again. Was the guy never home? I tried Rosie's and got no answer. I called my friend Vera, who must have gone off with her doctor-husband for the long Thanksgiving weekend. I called my old friend Jonah Robb. No answer. I even tried Darcy Pascoe, the receptionist at the company where I once worked. I was out of luck and beginning to panic, trying to figure out who in the world could help me out in a pinch. Finally, in desperation, I called the only person I could think of. The line rang four times before she picked up. I said, "Hello, Tasha? This is your cousin Kinsey. Remember you said to call if I ever needed anything?"

# Epilogue

THE WEDDING TOOK place late Thanksgiving Day. Rosie's restaurant had been transformed by flowers, by candles, by room deodorants. Rosie in her white muumuu, a crown of baby's breath in her hair, and William in his tuxedo, stood before Judge Raney, holding hands with tenderness. Their faces were shining. In the candlelight they didn't look young, but they didn't look that old, either. They were glowing, intense . . . as if burning from within. Everyone seemed to be part of the promises made. Henry, Charlie, Lewis, and Nell, Klotilde in her wheelchair. The terms "for better or for worse, for richer or for poorer, in sickness and in health" pertained to all of them. They knew what loving and being loved was about. They knew about pain, infirmity, the wisdom of age.

I stood there, thinking about Ray and Laura and Helen, wondering where they'd gone. I know it's absurd, but I found it painful they hadn't cared enough to stick around and see that I was okay. In some curious way, they'd become my family. I'd seen us as a unit,

321

facing adversity together, even if it was only for a matter of days. It's not that I thought we'd go on that way forever, but I would have liked a sense of closure—thanks, fare-thee-well, drop us a line someday.

William and Rosie were pronounced husband and wife. He took her face in his hands, and the kiss they exchanged was as light and sweet as rose petals. Trembling, he whispered, "Oh, my love. I've been waiting all of my life for you."

There wasn't a dry eye in the place, including mine.

Respectfully submitted,
Kinsey Millhone

**Kinsey Millhone,
P.I.
A, B, C...
and the rest of the alphabet, too.**

# "A" IS FOR ALIBI
# "B" IS FOR BURGLAR
# "C" IS FOR CORPSE
# "D" IS FOR DEADBEAT
# "E" IS FOR EVIDENCE
# "F" IS FOR FUGITIVE

**by
*New York Times* bestselling author
SUE GRAFTON**

•——•——•——•——•——•——•——•——

# "G" IS FOR GUMSHOE

Kinsey Millhone turns thirty-three and celebrates by moving back into her renovated apartment. Her birthday present is a new case: An old lady rumored to live in the Mojave Desert is missing. And as the surprise package, she seems to have made it onto triggerman Tyron Patty's hit list. When will the celebration end?

# "J" IS FOR JUDGMENT

Wendell Jaffe had been dead for five years—until his former insurance agent spotted him in a dusty resort bar. Now California Fidelity Insurance wants Kinsey Millhone to track down the "dead man." Just two months before, his widow collected on Jaffe's $500,000 life insurance policy. As Kinsey pushes deeper into the mystery surrounding Jaffe's faked death, she explores her own past and realizes that in personal matters, sometimes it's better to reserve judgment.

---

# "K" IS FOR KILLER

Part-time clerk and full-time sex worker Lorna Kepler was found dead ten months ago. The police allowed that it was murder but could find neither a motive nor a suspect. To investigate, Kinsey immerses herself in Lorna's seamy world, meeting porn movie actors, hustlers, and others on the fringe of the mainstream. But the question is, will Kinsey be able to pull herself out of that netherworld of the night?

# "H" IS FOR HOMICIDE

Just because a drinking buddy is killed doesn't mean Kinsey has to get involved in the investigation. In fact, she doesn't even want to. After all, his case doesn't have anything to do with an insurance scam she's already investigating. Unless the two have more in common than anyone, including Kinsey, realizes.

•——•—•——•—•——•—•——•—•——•—•——•—

# "I" IS FOR INNOCENT

Fired by the insurance agency for which she had enthusiastically probed fraud cases, Kinsey is forced to take on a last-minute murder investigation. It seems that artist Isabelle Barney was murdered—her first husband is convinced she was killed by her second husband, already acquitted for the crime. But in Kinsey's search for the person responsible for the death, could she be courting her own?

**COMING
IN OCTOBER**

# SUE
# GRAFTON

## IS FOR MALICE

HENRY HOLT

even Siroth couldn't harm. That way we can be of *some* use to the world. Your Doctor Sero can study it.

"I want you to *see* what you've done to our Utopia."

## IV

Aragon wandered, absorbing the immensity of *After* and feeling like a glass Christmas-tree bulb that had just been stepped on.

He went alone through the ruins, gazing at unrepaired buildings poised on the verge of collapse.

He went to the fukkup pen, where living lumps of twisted flesh screamed for their freedom, or at least an end to agony.

He returned to the smashed vault where all his dreams lay destroyed, and he wept.

The dreamer came to Siroth, now almost recovered from his surgery. "Prez Siroth, I have a few things I wish to say to you."

The Prez scowled with a "here it comes" expression on his face, and sat up in his bed, waiting in silence. Aragon sighed, then sat down. "But they are hateful things, and better left unsaid. Hate destroys, and enough has been destroyed already. It is better if I just forgive you."

Siroth almost choked in surprise. "*Forgive?* You're a coward."

The dreamer looked at him for a long moment, holding the other's disturbed gaze. "It was the bravest thing I could have said."

Siroth tried to get out of bed. "I can still kill you, dreamer!"

"Then you are hopelessly lost." Aragon stood firm. Siroth looked uncomfortable. He ran fingers through his silky-fine blond hair.

"Where's Grull?"

"He is with your Doctor Sero . . . receiving Draigen's eyes, remember?"

The Prez's face purpled with rage, and he swung himself out of bed. "What? He would leave my realm without someone in charge?"

"You were almost recovered."

"I need his counsel!"

"Think for yourself, Siroth."

The Prez sat back down on the bed, laughing darkly to himself. "And what do *you* want, dreamer? My lands? To be Prez yourself? Now's your perfect chance—Grull is gone, and I'm weaker than I should be. Go on, kill me! Make yourself Prez, and see how long you survive."

"No. With Draigen and the others gone, our dream is dead."

"Then what *do* you want?"

"I want you to change."

Aragon could see that had some effect on the other man, and he quickly continued. The Prez looked baffled, but not quite impatient. "Maybe I can make some small difference by myself. Have you ever walked out among the people? Actually *been* with them?"

"Too dangerous."

"How can you know what's going *on* out there?"

Siroth shrugged. "My guards report back."

Aragon sighed. "It isn't the same. Do you know that the old buildings are rotting, and another one collapses almost every other week? Do you know the horrors in that place where you keep the mutants corralled like so many animals? How they scream in agony, tear at each other, kill to eat the slop your guards throw at them, crying for freedom with even their dying breath!"

Visionary fire burned in the dreamer's eyes as his anger rose. "And the *people*, Siroth! Children *live* down in those filthy catacombs you found us in! Families starve because they cannot grow enough food. I have even seen evidence of cannibalism!"

"So what?"

"Don't you care?"

"No."

"Siroth, you must change!"

"My system works. I've been leader her for *six* years, with Grull's help. How would you change me?"

"Feel some compassion for the people you rule. They are your subjects—you should care for them!"

The Prez's voice was sour. "They don't care for me."

"If you were kind, and beneficial, seeing that their children are fed and educated, that their homes are repaired—Grull tells me you have a master architect in this castle, but you keep him under house-arrest! What good is he doing here?"

"I think you're retarded, and you understand *nothing*! You want to make me into another jelly-spined Prez Claysus!" Then Siroth laughed. "I wish you had met my father, dreamer—then you wouldn't think I'm so bad!"

Aragon raised his eyebrows, trying another tactic. "In those six years, how many assassination attempts have been made on you? How many?"

"Too many to count. But I *survived*—that's all that matters."

Aragon continued to press. "Grull says that Claysus has held his lands for *eight* years now. How many attempts have been made on him?"

Siroth looked up, frowning. "None . . . but then I cannot be completely sure."

Aragon folded his arms in triumph. The Prez looked upset and stood up to pace the room, rubbing his hands together as if he were trying to get rid of something. "I'd rather trust what Grull has always told me."

"Grull showed you only *one* way—the only way he knows. But I'll teach you others, and I will make you change."

Siroth scowled, but refused to face the dreamer, continuing to stare into the fire. "*That* is exactly why I wanted to kill your group."

The wooden door smacked against the wall of the Prez's chambers as a guard burst into the room. "My Prez! The fukkups are going wild! It's bad this time. They already killed two guards, and they are smashing the fences in the corral!"

Siroth paled in alarm, and his eyes flicked from side to side as if searching for Grull. But only Aragon stood there, letting a trace of his self-satisfaction show through.

"*Try* it my way, Siroth, and I'll show you it can work! It's obvious Grull's solution has no effect."

"And if it doesn't work?" the Prez scowled.

Aragon nervously raised his head high, looking proud. "I'll stake my life on it!"

Siroth laughed in delight. "Now *that's* what I like to hear! All right then, come on—I want to watch this!"

Breathlessly, Aragon turned to grab the guard's arm and began to pull him toward the door. Siroth quickly dressed, flailing into a threadbare robe to cover the scars of his recent surgery.

The mutants silenced themselves with a hushed grumble as Prez Siroth arrived. They pushed closer to the spiked fence, leering, some drooling from mouths crowded with two tongues. And these were the ones that had survived birth.

Aragon could not force away his revulsion and broke out in a thin sweat as he pondered how Draigen would have dealt with such a situation. The Prez stood calmly, surrounded by his guards and looking around with his sharp cold eyes. He seemed curious and oddly satisfied, as if pleased that he could try a truly unexpected leadership tactic and possibly get rid of the dreamer at the same time.

Aragon swallowed and finally spoke. The fukkups quieted as his voice drew strength. "Who speaks for you? Do you have a leader?"

The mutants milled about, but did not answer. Then Aragon remembered what Grull had done to the leaders during the last insurrection.

"All right, then we speak to all of you. You are clearly dissatisfied here—Prez Siroth offers you an alternative." He took a breath and then spoke rapidly, anticipating that the Prez would stop him any moment. "We will release you, give you your freedom—but you will have to *work*. Many of you have committed grave crimes against humanity, but we feel you have served your punishments. Up until now, we have used our own provisions to feed you—once freed, you will have to fend for yourselves. You will have to repair the old buildings for your homes. You will have to work the land, grow crops." He hesitated, thinking of the unfairness, but realizing Siroth would have to gain something other than a clear conscience from the bargain. "And we will let you keep *half* of your produce for yourselves."

The fukkups stood stunned for an instant. Siroth waited, glanced at his guards, and firmly believed the dreamer was sticking his head more firmly on the chopping block. The Prez picked up the speech as the mutants began to cheer. "*But*—this is a trial period for you. The fate of all your children depends on how you behave during the next few weeks." His voice was as hard and as sharp as a razor. "If *any* one of you harms a man, in *any* way, or does damage to property, or tries to flee—you will *all* be returned to this pen, never to be released again!"

Aragon spoke up quickly, shouting into the brief lull. "But you have nothing to fear if you're willing to work for your freedom. Isn't it better to work the land, produce food for everyone, than to rot here? Those are the terms—do you agree to all of them?"

Wild cheering almost deafened him as all the mutants clamored at once. He smiled at the Prez. "See, they're satisfied."

"You may very well have just sealed our doom. We still have to see if they'll keep their word." Then Siroth watched them with his darting eyes, and he let another smile steal across his face. "But just to make sure, I'm going to have you go live with them, without protection, for the first few weeks."

Siroth's smugness was squashed when Aragon calmly said, "All right."

V

Grull tried valiantly to be patient, commanding his fingers not to fidget. For days Doctor Sero had been cutting away his bandages, one by one; and now the old man could see a grayish light behind his wrappings. To him, this was even worse than blindness, because now he knew his eyes might work.

The old man sat on the cold stone bench in the courtyard. The shadow of the *First National Bank* castle stretched out over him as the sun fell behind the build-

ing. He could sense Siroth beside him as doctor Sero
fumbled with the last bandages, removing one thread at
a time. Impatiently, Grull slapped away the doctor's
hand and ripped off the bandages himself.

After sixty years, he couldn't possibly have remembered what sight was like. Now even the blurred images shone with wonder as his aching mind tried to take
in six decades' worth of light. The deepest shadows
were blindingly bright. His thin but strong hands in-
stinctively reached up to cover Draigen's eyes, *his* eyes
now, but he drew them away, wanting to see more.

The forms and shapes slowly focused themselves, but
he didn't know what he expected to see. He remembered only scattered visions from his childhood, the
flower garden, the shining city with sky-scraping buildings of steel and glass. Grull blinked several times, and
each time the world became clearer. Then he looked
down upon the ruined city, the broken buildings, the
weeds pushing up through crumbling streets and
sidewalks.

The vision became indistinct again as his new eyes
filled with water. Funny, he had never thought that
simple tears would ruin anyone's eyesight. He blinked
several times and tried to force his breathing to follow a
slower rhythm. He had *never* guessed the effect would
be this profound, and it embarrassed him.

Grull sat in silence for a long, long moment, and then
turned to the man he recognized to be the Prez. "We
really made a mess of things, didn't we?"

The guards looked askance at Aragon—dirt-smeared
and clothed in the torn rags of his spring-green jump-
suit—but they moved aside to let him enter Prez Siroth's
chamber. Two of the guards accompanied him, but
Aragon smiled with self-satisfaction and ignored them.

Siroth looked up from the old-fashioned mousetrap
he had been playing with on the table. Sunlight slanted
in through the narrow and drafty windows of the chamber. "I'm surprised to see you still alive, dreamer. You
didn't strike me as someone who could handle much
hardship." He lifted the thin metal bar against the strong

pull of the spring, and let it fall shut with a loud *snap* against the wood. "You smell like shit."

"That's what I've been living in for the past week." Aragon looked tired, and hungry, but beatifically satisfied. The gleam of despair had faded from behind his eyes, to be replaced by the barest shadow of the visions that had haunted Draigen's eyes.

"I'm not a great leader who could have changed the world, like Draigen was. But I *am* an agricultural engineer! This is what I was trained for—to improve your godawful methods of farming. You don't have enough people to adequately work all the available land, and right now you split your fields in half, working one side and letting the other lie fallow for a year. With the mutants, I am showing them how to take the simple step of dividing the fields into thirds, plant grain on one third, legumes on another, and leave the last one fallow— just think of what a difference it can make! And there are efficient ways to use the fertilizers you have—just dumping manure all over the place isn't going to solve anything, you know. I can change that, too. Fewer people will starve."

Siroth pressed his fingertips together and turned to face Aragon. "And what do the fukkups have to say about all this? Have you been whipping them yourself? How do you expect them to obey?"

"When you treat them as human beings, Siroth, tell them the *reason* you're doing something and *show* them how it will help them—they work by their own free will. You can ask your own guards: in the first week, the mutants have not done a thing even your paranoid watchers could call dangerous.

"If you play this right, Siroth, your subjects will stop hating you. It's the difference between being a dictator and being a king."

Siroth raised the mouse trap again, let it snap down, almost catching his own finger. Dangerous. Playing with a dangerous toy, like this dreamer who was disrupting Siroth's philosophy by damnably proving an unconscionable theory, that the methods of leadership could still function the same way they did *Before*.

"I am impressed, dreamer. I'll admit that. I wish I could talk to Grull about this." But now Grull was gone as well, all because of this dreamer, and the other dreamer's eyes.

Cleaning, fixing, watching, polishing. Grull saw to it the *First National Bank* castle was repaired, loose stone replaced, new mortar added. He cleaned the interior. He removed all the weeds from the courtyard, and swept the flagstones at least once a day. He watched the fukkups as they tore down the fence surrounding their former pen and began to plow the land according to the guidelines Aragon had given them.

Siroth joined him, standing with folded arms and staring down the gentle hill at the remnants of the city below. Grull knew the Prez had come, but he waited for Siroth to speak first.

"Would you ever have believed the fukkups are actually keeping their agreement?" Siroth snorted a little, but to Grull it sounded somewhat forced. "They're working harder than any of our farmers. The food supply should be drastically increased from last year. I'll have to see to it that the children dig out more tunnels for storage."

Grull wanted to answer, but couldn't think of anything to say. He did notice that the stone benches could use a little more polish. And dust had begun to collect on the flagstones again. Siroth continued awkwardly. "The fukkups haven't even caused trouble, Grull. I hear they're building their own little village in the forest. Why would they build new homes when it's so much easier just to repair the old ones?"

Grull sighed and turned to look at him with Draigen's dark eyes, oddly set where the glassy blind ones had been. "That's good to hear, my Prez. But for some reason state matters don't interest me much any more."

The old man still had trouble correlating facial expressions with emotions, but he believed Siroth looked shocked by his comment. He tried to justify what he had said. "I'm an old man, Siroth. For sixty years I have meddled in political affairs, and now it's time to leave them to someone else. I might relax, and even enjoy my life for a change."

He found his broom and vigorously began sweeping out the cracks in the flagstones.

"Grull," Siroth sounded almost concerned, "Aren't you getting a little carried away?"

The old man paused for a moment. "Nonsense. I didn't wait sixty years to see an ugly world." He replaced the broom and started to walk away, mentally dismissing the Prez.

"Where are you going now?"

"I think I want to plant a flower garden."

## VI

The army of Prez Claysus arrived swiftly, and unexpectedly, with barely enough warning for Siroth to take even the simplest of defense measures. The castle gate was barred, the guards were mustered—but not much else could be done. Claysus's soldiers stood waiting on the long hill.

Furious, Siroth stood beside the dreamer on the balcony, glaring at the opposing army. He turned red in the face, and his fists clenched convulsively, as if he were desperate to strangle something other than his knuckles. "All these weeks I've been doing *kindhearted* things—" he almost spat the words, "and the wimp has been gathering up an army against me! Because of *you* I'm going to be defeated by a jelly-spined pansy!"

Aragon seemed confused, and Siroth felt a little satisfaction through his despair. "But you told me Claysus is a kind, gentle humanitarian—"

"He *is*, dammit! That's why I never expected this!"

Outside the castle, one man strode forward from the body of the army, Prez Claysus shouting so that Siroth could hear. "Prez Siroth! You are vile and inhuman— and I can no longer tolerate your foul ways! I will tear your castle apart brick by brick and take the architect by force! Then you'll atone for your hideous actions. It's going to take a lot to avenge the murder of my peaceful ambassadors!"

Claysus drew a weapon from his side, a kind of spiked club which looked too heavy for him to use. The other Prez held it out threateningly as his army fidgeted.

Aragon looked at Siroth. "What has he got against you? What 'ambassadors' is he talking about?"

The Prez sighed. "His castle collapsed about a month ago. He sent two ambassadors to ask if he could borrow my architect."

"And?"

"And Grull slit their bellies or something, then sent them back to Claysus still bleeding."

The dreamer's face suddenly turned greenish. "But they were *ambassadors!* They had diplomatic immunity!"

"Not in my lands they don't."

Aragon sat down weakly. "Siroth, you must change your ways!"

But the Prez unleashed his anger. "And these past weeks, if I *hadn't* changed my ways, if I *hadn't* been kind and nice and good, if I *hadn't* let my guard down—"

Siroth stopped abruptly, staring out the window as he caught a glimpse of something in the forest. His eyes widened; his jaw even dropped a little bit.

From out of the wood emerged dozens of horrible misrepresentations of the human form, each with the wrong number of arms or legs or heads—and they were armed with clubs, pitchforks, rakes, hoes, scythes, anything they could find.

"Dreamer," Siroth whispered, "I think you'd better see this."

The fukkups marched slowly out of the trees, determined and numerous enough to surround Prez Claysus's startled troops. They did nothing, standing motionless, but threatening nonetheless. One of them, a two-headed man with one arm, cried out in a guttural voice that echoed oddly from his twin throats. "We will fight to defend our Prez!"

Siroth stood absolutely stunned, and his lips began to work seconds before his voicebox did. "They're willing to fight for me! For *me!*"

Aragon laughed in delight. "Of course they are! You

freed them. You showed them you *can* be kind, and they're expressing their appreciation."

Prez Siroth stood speechless for a long moment, watching the commotion in Claysus's ranks as the soldiers realized what the mutants were doing. He began to chuckle loudly. "Hah! Now I can crush him! With the fukkups and my guards, we can wipe out Prez Pansy once and for all!"

Aragon leaped to his feet. "No! No, that's not the *point!*" The Prez whirled in sudden rage again, looking as if the dreamer had gone insane. "Look, Siroth, it doesn't matter if you can defeat him or not! The point is you can do this *without* fighting!"

The Prez's scowl became even more unpleasant, but Aragon persisted. "Those mutants are standing up for you because of how you've changed! If you're a *real* leader, you won't have to resort to war."

"And how else am I supposed to get rid of Claysus?"

"You're the Prez. Solve it yourself, or else you've learned nothing."

Siroth's forehead wrinkled as he thought, anxiously looking around the room for someone to help him. "You expect me to give up Praetoth willingly? After all this?"

"And will that atone for what you did to the ambassadors?"

"Yes!" Aragon stared at him relentlessly, until the Prez looked away. "No. I will also send along some of my men to help him rebuild."

"You could also offer to supply some of the materials . . ." the dreamer suggested.

"Enough!" Siroth shouted, and Aragon decided not to press home the point. For a moment, he thought of Draigen's heart still beating after all, even in the chest of someone like Prez Siroth.

## VII

Grull wandered in the courtyard, drifting gently through his vast flower garden. Everything had grown up tall and beautiful, in full bloom all around the castle. He tended the flowers meticulously, pulling up a weed from between two brilliant orange snapdragons, humming to himself unconsciously.

He liked being alone. He knew Siroth was inside somewhere mediating a dispute between two mutants, but that didn't matter to him. Grull turned to look and noticed Aragon alone in the courtyard, sitting on one of the stone benches in his faded spring-green uniform, staring empty-eyed off into the distance. Grull followed the dreamer's line of sight, looking at the city and smiling faintly. Many of the buildings had been repaired and cleaned up, or torn down entirely. Grull decided he liked the encroaching forest after all. One of these days he was going to find a stream, and try fishing.

The old man bent down to inspect his rose bushes, and saw one bud just starting to bloom. He looked up at Aragon again, then at the city, then at the fukkups working the fields.

Grull snipped off the bloom and walked quietly over to Aragon, getting his attention. He extended the rose toward the dreamer's hand.

"This is for you."

# WILL *YOU* SURVIVE?

In addition to Dean Ing's powerful science fiction novels— *Systemic Shock, Wild Country, Blood of Eagles* and others—he has written cogently and inventively about the art of survival. **The Chernobyl Syndrome** is the result of his research into life after a possible nuclear exchange . . . because as our civilization gets bigger and better, we become more and more dependent on its products. What would *you* do if the machine stops— or blows up?

Some of the topics Dean Ing covers:
* How to *make* a getaway airplane
* Honing your "crisis skills"
* Fleeing the firestorm: escape tactics for city-dwellers
* How to build a homemade fallout meter
* Civil defense, American style
* "Microfarming"—survival in five acres
    *And much, much more.*

Also by Dean Ing, available through Baen Books:

## ANASAZI

Why did the long-vanished Anasazi Indians retreat from their homes and gardens on the green mesa top to precarious cliffside cities? Were they afraid of someone—or some*thing*? "There's no evidence of warfare in the ruins of their earlier homes . . . but maybe the marauders they feared didn't wage war in the usual way," says Dean Ing. *Anasazi* postulates a race of alien beings who needed human bodies in order to survive on Earth—a race of aliens that *still* exists.

## FIREFIGHT 2000

How do you integrate armies supplied with bayonets and ballistic missiles; citizens enjoying Volkswagens and Ferraris; cities drawing power from windmills and nuclear powerplants? Ing takes a look at these dichotomies, and more. This collection of fact and fiction serves as a metaphor for tomorrow: covering terror and hope, right guesses and wrong, high tech and thatched cottages.

## Introduction

*The highways of Middle America can provoke the strangest fantasies, the most mundane landscapes inspiring the most profound speculations on the human condition. Novelist and Writer of the Future award winner Robert Reed takes us on down the road in this moving story.*

*—TW*

# TOTIPOTENT

## Robert Reed

I came slow over the hill with a monster semi riding my
ass and the countryside white like a fairyland. I-80
stretched down the long curling slope, drizzle falling
and freezing, and me telling myself, "You've got to get
off this! Get off! You're going to goddamn die if you
don't get off now!"

I'd been driving hard in the mess since dawn, which
was maybe an hour-plus, only it felt like twenty at that
point. I'd seen half a hundred cars in ditches and two
exit ramps blocked by semis laying dead on their sides,
and then I was over that hill and dropping, my car
wobbling and my heart in my mouth. Up ahead an
ice-rimmed sign promised, "REST AREA," with big solid,
no-nonsense letters. I was doing maybe fifteen miles an
hour; I was going way too fast, glazed ice beneath me. I
blinked and breathed and shivered despite the scalding
air pouring from my car's vents, and then the rest area's
ramp came into view. I saw it through the drizzle—
open and inviting, my first good luck all day. The angry
grillwork of the semi was creeping closer now. I took a
breath and held it and saw motion on my left, a big old
black Caddy coming from nowhere. It roared up beside
me, fast and careless, and then it was past and signaling
and accelerating as it crossed into my lane. Its driver
must have seen the ramp and panicked. I watched the

Caddy's rear end begin to fishtail, freezing spray coming over my windshield, blinding me, and me gasping and bracing for the impact. Only nothing happened. Nothing and then I was past the ramp and the Caddy was safe on the ramp and where was the semi? It was on the ramp too. I saw it in my mirrors and I thought, lucky shits. I kept rolling downwards alone, my heart racing, my hands and face sweating despite my shivering; and some little part of me told me that at least now I knew something few others knew. I knew how scared I could feel. I was terrified, absolutely terrified; but I felt certain that nothing anywhere, under any circumstance, could ever make me feel worse than this. I just knew it. I just did.

Down I went. I followed the long curling slope, touching my brakes ever so slightly, pumping them to kill my momentum and somehow keeping control until I was off the hill and safe on a flat straight stretch of highway. I was alone now. Completely. I thought, Good! Everyone else must have gotten off at the rest area, and there was nobody to hit and nobody to hit poor me. I passed under a viaduct—a minor country road crossing the Interstate—and for an instant, for a few feet, I was driving on a strip of honest dry pavement. That's what finished me. My car gave a little shudder when it came off the ice, the worn snow tires finding purchase and me tired and panicky. So I braked without thinking. By reflex. Then I hit ice again, still braking, and my car's rear end swayed and swooped into the lead. It acted as if it wanted to lead, impatient with my careful pace, and the tires spun with me clinging to the useless wheel. I was looking straight out over the long hood of my car, the world revolving and some big part of me feeling nothing but an enormous sense of relief. The suspense was finished. I was getting a good round glance of the world every second or so, and there was nothing important for me to hit. At least not close by. My car skated wildly over the westbound lane and then sliced across the wide right shoulder, its rear end slipping down onto the steeply pitched grassy slope and me somehow with enough presence to try stopping myself.

I punched my accelerator the instant my tires were clear of the pavement, spinning them until I found purchase again. Until I was stopped.

That why I didn't drop clear into the ditch.

That's why I ended up in a not-too-bad position, my old Mustang stuck at a preposterous angle, but safe, and me stopping the engine and stepping outside and halfway smiling to myself. I was fine. My car was intact. All my worldly possessions were tucked into boxes and suitcases, a new job waiting for me in Dallas and me needing to be there the day after tomorrow. At the latest. Which was okay, I told myself. Everything could still end up perfect. I had this good feeling—one of those sourceless warm feelings owing allegiance to no one and nothing—and I kept smiling because the worst was finished. Or, at least, because I thought I couldn't be more terrified even if it got worse. No way.

The drizzle kept falling.

I slipped and skated my way across the shoulder, considering options. I decided on making my way back to the rest area for safety's sake, and help. I-80, main artery to the continent, was devoid of traffic. Not even farm trucks wearing chains and sandbags were trying their luck now. The entire world seemed still and empty with its covering of hard new ice, and the drizzle fell while I walked on the grass, step by step, busting its ice while new stuff formed on my coat and gloves and face.

I walked under the viaduct and up the long hill, and the illusion of solitude dissolved into voices and engine noise. The rest area had buildings and picnic grounds and several parking lots all perched on a scenic lookout. Semis and vans and cars jammed the place, and there was more traffic stacked up on the exit ramp itself. The Caddy was years ago, it seemed. I didn't even think about it. I shuffled and slipped to the tourist center, bright and warm and locked tight. But the johns were open, thank goodness. The ruddy faces of men and boys greeted me with curious looks. I'd been outdoors a long while. I claimed an open spot between electric hand dryers, punching their big square buttons and melting the ice from my clothes and skin. I started feeling better. In little bits, I started feeling human again.

"God," said one fellow. "It's raining that hard now?"

"It's the same," I told him. And everyone. I realized how I must look to them, cold and soaked, so I said, "I've been walking," and they asked me, "Why?" So I started telling the story of my carnival ride. What had been an epic drama twenty minutes ago, full of passion and grave danger, was now mere low comedy. I was halfway warm, and safe, and finding humor in the whole hell of it. I had them laughing in the end. Everyone had had their horrors that day, and so they shook their heads and showed me big appreciative grins.

Another man—a tall pleasant-looking fellow—asked, "Do you think you could get clear with a push?" He had reddish hair and a trimmed tame beard. That's about all I can remember, besides him being tall and quite friendly. "How badly are you caught?" he wondered.

I pictured my car, judging angles and the ice. "If enough crap can melt, maybe. Maybe a push would do it."

"Because I'm with a group," he volunteered. "I've got a van full of kids going to Colorado. For the skiing." He stepped towards me, his smile brightening. "We're a Christian Fellowship group." He spoke with a certain voice. A little proud and maybe a little insecure. "If you want help—"

"If there's a chance, sure," I told him. "I'd love help!" Christian or Buddhist. Hitler or Trotsky. Distinctions seemed trivial at that point. "A group, huh?" Any strong backs would do.

"You want to sit a while?" he asked. "We've got room."

"Sure." I followed him. We skated onto the sidewalks and he asked my name, then he told me his own—I can't recall it—and when we climbed into an iced-over van he told everyone, "This is Sam, everyone!" and they shouted, "Hello, Sam!" with a big synchronized voice. High school kids. Eight or nine clear-skinned Christians fired up to chase Jesus and Colorado powder.

I took the one open seat. A blonde girl was beside me, a big glossy magazine in her lap, and I remember how I sat and how she looked at me and smiled, a brilliant perfect smile, showing me her perfect face and her glacier-blue eyes and her fine firm young body. A Christian girl, I was thinking; but in an instant, and with nothing more substantial than a glance, she managed to make me pause for breath, feeling my odd old troubles dissolving away.

She wasn't merely pretty, mind you. Her entire package had the kinds of looks that make men *and* women pause to stare. I mean beauty, true undiluted unapologetic beauty, me forgetting the weather and my timetable inside two heartbeats.

She straightened her back and continued to smile, enjoying herself and watching me. I happened to glance down, her magazine opened to an article entitled, "Christian Birth Control What is God's Design?" I can remember the moment with absolute clarity. I remember the damp smells and the strong corn chip smells, and nobody made the slightest noise for a long moment, the girl smiling and then winking at me, very sly, and then turning back to her magazine, flipping through the rest of it while I tried to piece back together what remained of my composure.

The fellow in charge—the bearded man—had vanished on some errand. The other kids started to talk to me, curious and friendly and none of them memorable. Once again I related the story of my crash. The details came out clipped and uninspired this time, but I did garner a few nods and sluggish gasps just the same. Once in a while the girl beside me would ask a question or make some comment. "You don't sound like much of a driver, Sam." (She said, "Sam," with too much familiarity. Yet I liked her tone just the same. There was something tough and self-assured about it.) "So you're going to Dallas?" she asked. "Why's that?" I started to explain my circumstances, sensing that she wasn't really interested, her face watchful and yet somehow uninvolved. Then she interrupted, saying, "You're kind of goofy, Sam," and she smiled, implying that she was teasing me. This was joking. "All the sweat and worry, and for what? A job?"

I felt a little foolish, for a moment—

"Risking your life on the ice? That seems crazy to me."

"Maybe so," I responded.

"I think so," she said, and she gave a little laugh. "You're goofy, yeah, but I like goofy. And I like you."

She was a kid, I reminded myself. A high school kid, a timid child of God, yet with a wink and words she had me shaking my head, wondering what she might say next. She sure didn't carry herself like her peers carried themselves, I thought. I watched her for a minute, hearing the steady rain now drumming on the van's roof. We were the only two talking. Sometimes the other kids made little noises, and I'd glance at them, noticing odd expressions on their faces. They were studying me, I realized. And her too. There were thoughts behind their eyes, simple and direct; but not for any sum, in any length of time, could I have guessed just what they were thinking.

The bearded fellow returned, shaking the rain from his jacket. "The highway's getting better," he announced, smiling at me and glancing at the girl. He said, "Traffic's moving again. I was thinking we could try and get out now. The weather reports say a big snow's coming, maybe a blizzard, and we might not get another shot—"

"Let's try," I said. "I'm ready."

So he pulled us out of our parking slot, everyone else having made the same decision and the road choked with cars and trucks. It was slow going. I was glad not to be driving. We finally spilled out onto the highway, down the hill and under the viaduct, my car tilted at that ridiculous angle and waiting, its back end stuffed with clothes and books and such. The rain was falling in cold sheets now. The pavement was warmer than freezing and covered with rotting slush. A semi crashed past us. I turned from the spray and opened my door and got behind the wheel again, turning the key and feeling the engine come awake. My belly started to tighten again. My nine or ten eager helpers stood waiting for

instructions. My windshield was buried under a soft
opaque ice, so I handed my scraper to the blonde girl. I
said, "Would you?" and she gave me a dreamy look and
nod, then vanished. I heard pecking. I ran the defroster
on high. The ice peeled away in ribbons, and I saw the
perfect face and smile and the blue eyes gazing in at
me.

Everyone got into position below me.

"Ready?" I shouted, revving the engine.

They answered, "Ready," with their synchronized
voice.

I eased into gear. There was a jerk and a bump, tires
whining, and all at once I was up on the wide shoulder
again. Free again. All at once I felt light and giddy, glad
for Christian charity and my good luck. The blonde girl
tapped on the passenger window. Once. I saw my
scraper in her hand, and I rolled down the window.
She smiled and bent and said, "Sam?" while reaching
inside, unlatching the door and jumping in beside me
before I could speak. "Dallas, huh?" I sat very still.
"Dallas sounds good." I was watching her face and
feeling hot through my body, all jittery and out-of-
balance; and then I looked outside just in time to see
the other kids climbing on board the van with a few
quick "good luck" waves in my direction. Nothing else.
No one asking, "Where's what's-her-name?" No one
even curious as to why she was sitting beside me.

"What are you doing?" I managed to ask. "What is
this?"

"I'm going with you," she announced. "Let's go."

"But what about . . . ?" I looked forwards. The van
was accelerating, vanishing into the driving rain, and a
voice inside me screamed, "They're forgetting her!
They're leaving her behind!"

I shot off the shoulder without half a glance, wanting
her back with them. Some angry enormous semi shot
around my left side with maybe two inches to spare, its
horn wailing and spray coming up over my hood.

"Them?" said the girl. She seemed wholly uncon-
cerned by the fury around us. "Oh, I wasn't part of *that*
group. Oh, no." She had my scraper in her hands, in

her lap, and I saw her shrug without a care in the world. "I'm just hitching crosscountry myself. Didn't you know?"

Where was the van? I'd lost sight of the van. . . .

"Dallas sounds fine to me, Sam. I hope you don't mind."

"You're a hitchhiker?"

"People do that sort of thing. Don't they?" She shrugged again. "Just think hard for a moment, Sam. Do you really believe that anyone would leave *me* behind. Does that sound reasonable?"

I had to admit it. She had a point—

"Besides," she said, "if you don't want me along with you . . . well, hey! Drop me at the next stop. Wherever. I'll grab another ride."

I shook my head, thinking hard. Maybe I had misread things. She *was* sitting alone when I climbed into the van, all right. And I'd never gotten the impression that she was friends with any of the kids. There were the ways those kids had been giving us stares . . . both of us outsiders? Perhaps? I thought, "Maybe it's so," aloud, and I eased my foot off the accelerator. A little bit. I told myself, "You could use the company, Sam. It's going to be an all-day drive, and probably half the night too." Then I gave her a quick glance, catching the best parts of her profile.

"What are you whispering, Sam?"

I asked, "Do you have a name?"

"Yes, Sam."

"What is it?"

She made a whistling sound, quick and soft. "Call me Holly. Okay?"

"Holly," I said. "Holly?"

"What is it, Sam?"

"Nothing," I said. "Nothing."

I took us past Lincoln, west to the U.S. 81 turnoff, and stopped at a burger place for a late, late breakfast. Holly didn't have luggage, not even a purse. She said something about moving light and easy. Then she produced a roll of bills from her coat pocket, smiling at me.

I didn't ask questions. I just sat and ate and she was
across from me in the booth, watching me with that
steady all-seeing, yet detached gaze. We barely spoke.
Then we went back outside, and I took us south on 81.
The salted pavement seemed okay, me trying to buy
back time and distance. I had the wipers running fast
and my defrosters blowing for all their worth, and neither of us spoke out loud. Not for a long time. But I
could smell Holly, almost tasting her in the close dry
air, and I worked hard to keep my head clear and pure.
Because of the situation. Because I had this wicked urge
to pull off on the shoulder and try something. Just to
try it. Just to see.

Only somehow I didn't.

Call it manners. Call it a calculating fear. Call it Holly's
imprecise age and the two of us crossing the border into
Kansas, giving all crimes a Federal shade. She said,
"How old do I look?" when I mentioned the issue.
Then she wondered, "How old do you want me to be,
Sam?" and gave a laugh. A contrived, girlish laugh.
"Would you believe eighteen?"

I wanted eighteen, yes.

Eighteen years and one day. Please, Lord. Please.

But she wouldn't give answers. Instead she deflected
my probes, asking, "You got anything to read?" and
turning, starting to root through my luggage. "This'll
do," she said. "Thanks." Half a dozen paperbacks were
piled on her lap, and she grinned at me, telling me,
"You keep those eyes on the road, buster. It's no picnic
out there!"

Which was true. We were traveling at the brink of a
total freeze, I'm sure. A fraction of a degree downwards, plus slower rain, and the two-lane highway would
have turned treacherous. As it was, ice was collecting
on the cold spots of cars—bumpers and back windows
and even antennas. Even my own antenna, I noticed. I
had a tall white wobbly worm standing on a corner of
my hood, ludicrous and faintly erotic. A big semi roared
past us, pointing north, and spray flew and we hit the
slipstream and my poor antenna shook and twisted and

somehow held together. Thinking back, I can't believe it didn't fold under that load.

We weren't making the best time in the world.

There were times when I couldn't do forty miles an hour. We had long stretches of slush, and then the rain quit so the snow could take its shot at us. The radio squawked warnings of blizzards bearing down from the Arctic—a foot and a half of white stuff expected, plus sub-zero temps and seventy mile an hour breezes. Holly seemed oblivious to the circumstances. She sat beside me, mostly silent, flipping through my books in the same nonchalant way she'd tackled the Christian magazine. Too fast to read anything, but seemingly contented.

The snow worsened, then it let up again.

We got on a divided highway, and I breathed easier. No more oncoming traffic. We shot past Salina without either rain or snow from the sky, and my adrenalin level dropped below the panic stage for the first time in hours. I suddenly was tired. "Break time," I muttered, pulling into a gas-and-grease place for doses of both. Holly said, "My treat." It was only right, she claimed. "You letting me tag along." She looked at me and flashed one of her patented smiles, saying, "Those people before . . . they were nice. But boring. You know, Sam? I don't like to be bored."

It was the most she had said to me in a couple hours.

I said, "Yeah?" I said, "Why do you think I'm a good time?"

"Because you're so scared and crazy all the time. Wrapped up in things," she told me. "Because I like watching how your head works. I really do."

"Is that what you're doing?" I wondered.

"All the time, Sam. All the time."

The snow caught us again. We came outside and found fat white flakes being pushed by a terrible wind. I pointed us south, always south, and pressed on. My biggest terror/hope was that we'd get trapped in some random drift, marooned, and somewhere in the midst of the adventure we'd have to share body heat. I couldn't help but imagine such a thing. All of it. I belched into my hand and adjusted the fit of my pants . . . Holly now laughing, watching me with this freakish knowing look that caused me to grow cold. I tried ignoring her. I refocused my daydreams, thinking that's all they were and where was the harm? Dallas. Think of Dallas, I thought. Heat and sunshine, fierce summers and mature women lacking underwear . . . but then I was back in that drift, trapped and tempted, and some latter-day Marshall Dillon rode out of nowhere to save us. Holly and me. The worst possible moment, and of course she proved to be fifteen. I imagined Holly screaming, "Rape!" or something else equally straightforward. And Sam, poor innocent tempted stupid gland-driven Sam, found himself manacled and shuffling towards the scrubbed sanctity of some Kansan prison. The special sex-offender wing—

Holly giggled for no reason.

I punched the accelerator, damning the highway and the gathering snows. The weak afternoon light was fading into night. Holly pulled more books from my boxes, skimming each of them and laughing at odd times. Then all at once she was finished. She said, "It's been fun, Sam," as if something was done. Was past. She said, "Sam? Even if they catch me now, I think it's been worth all the trouble. I'm glad for what I've done."

"What do you mean?" I asked. "What's this?"

"I mean escaping from *there*. Getting free." I got a glimpse of her face in the bad light. She looked odd, I decided. I couldn't point to a reason, but she looked wrong somehow. "Sam?" she said. "Even if they catch me, I won't regret doing it. Believe me."

I said, "All right."

"You don't have the tiniest hint of what I'm saying. Do you?"

"Someone's . . . what? Chasing you?" A cold feeling came into my palms. I cleared my throat and said, "Since when?"

"Since I've been *here*," she told me.

"Here?"

That laugh, something about it unmistakable and thoroughly amoral. "Can I trust you, Sam? With something important?"

People shouldn't ask people certain questions. How much do you weigh? How much do you make? Do you adore your wife? Have you ever killed? Oh, and can I, pray tell, trust you?

"You don't know me," I cautioned.

And she made a strange little sound. "I do," she told me. "Better than you think, I do know you." She waited for a minute, then said, "They had me inside a tiny, tiny room, Sam. All alone."

"Who had you—?"

"Can I tell you?"

I asked, "Can I stop you?"

And she giggled. "I like you so much, dear Sam. I do." For some reason her praise made me weak and off-balance. "You're not too stupid and yet you're so wonderfully confused, and it's so much fun watching your brain sputter and slide about—"

"Who, Holly?! Who had you in that room?"

"That takes some telling, Sam." She paused and sighed, then she asked me, "Have you ever been to the zoo, Sam? Have you ever gone to look at the animals?"

We went into Witchita in the blackness, me hugging the wheel and the wipers slapping away the snow and my iced-over antenna wobbling in a crazy, ready-to-tip way. Holly was talking with a voice so steady and so cold that she seemed to be in the remote distance. She wasn't sitting beside me. She wasn't breathing the same desiccated engine breath that I was breathing. I would glance sideways just to make sure of her presence, and even then I had this awful feeling. Holly wasn't real. A crazy thought, sure, but that's what my guts were telling me. I could see the level, snow-dampened lights of Witchita and her fine silhouette, hearing her talking on and on about this miniscule room and the unseen, unimaginable zookeepers who had kept her locked away and unhappy—

"I don't get it," I confessed. "What are you telling me?"

"I mean a place where visitors come to look at the animals, Sam." She moved in her seat, her fine firm rear end squeaking against the vinyl. She told me, "It's not what you think, either—"

"What do I think?"

"That I'm an escaped mental patient. That I'm talking about my old hospital and this is a fantasy. A psychotic dream."

"I wasn't thinking that," I protested. But I was. I was driving fast through the teeth of a blizzard, my eyes so tired that they ached and my back so sore that I couldn't even straighten up, and this stranger beside me was spinning some impossible tale fit for paranoids. . . . Well, what was I suppose to think? Huh?

"Listen to me," she warned. "Why don't you?"

I breathed. I tried clearing my brain with a few doses of oxygen, then I managed to say, "What about this zoo? Holly?"

"You'll pay attention?"

"Sure," I said. What was the harm in talk? I figured. "Go on."

She didn't say anything for a long moment. My impression was that she was pleased with herself, pleased with the way she had handled me. "Every zoo built has the same problem," she finally told me. "The same shortfall. Do you know it? Sam? It's size. It's the problem of where do you put all the neat animals. See?" She asked me, "How can a good zoo maintain good breeding populations while satisfying the public's desire for diversity? For reality? Do you comprehend the problem, dear Sam?"

I said, "Maybe."

"Listen," she said. "Try imagining the perfect zoo. Okay? We're somewhere in the future, in the far future, and a whole lot of things are possible. Technical trickery. Near-magic, of a kind."

"Magic?"

"For instance," she said. "Suppose we're future zookeepers. Suppose we figure out a way to miniaturize single specimens representing every last species that has ever existed on the Earth. Okay? Does that sound pretty far-fetched to you?"

It did. I nodded.

"Only one of each, because we don't have infinite room for our zoo. Of course. But every specimen is more than just a tiny lion or a tiny bear. Each specimen is endowed with all the characteristics of its species. All the possible genomes. All the potential behaviors. The elements of culture and language . . . if those things are possible. Quite literally everything. Everything that means *lion*, say, is on display in our perfect zoo."

I said nothing. I couldn't think of anything worth saying.

"Totipotency." I caught a glimpse of her nodding, and she took a deep breath. She didn't sound like a teenage girl now. She didn't sound as if she had any particular age. "Totipotent organisms," she said. "The perfect lion. The perfect bear. Even one perfect, ultimate person. Every last character of the race, physically and emotionally, is embodied in each of our zoo's inhabitants. Totipotence, Sam. It's a real word. Look it up in your spare time, sometime—"

"I've heard the word," I muttered.

She didn't seem to hear me. "A fertilized egg has a kind of totipotence. Do you know why? Because it contains all the information needed to grow a complete, fully developed adult."

"Totipotence." I said it slowly, carefully, the word sounding rather sexual on my tongue. "To-Ti-Po-Tence."

"Exactly, Sam. You understand."

"Do I?"

"Well enough," she told me. "I can see you do."

I remember the moment. I remember how I drove us around a long bend in the highway, glancing to my right to look at Holly once again and seeing something beyond her. It was the looming dark shape of a refinery—pipes and great metal columns and high overhead, up in the high blowing snow, an enormous yellowish flame burning off the residue gases. I can still see that bright waving fire and the falling snow trying to shroud it, and I can hear Holly's steady wrong-sounding voice telling me, "These specimens in our zoo are much more complex than mere eggs. Sam. They represent entire species. They are dense and made of stuff beyond all human science. Of course. We zookeepers use them to make models of past time. We study them and build populations from them, and sometimes we put together thousands and millions of species from the same age. For science. And to please our audiences. To show our lovely intelligent and sophisticated throngs just how the Earth looked back in this day and age. Here. For instance."

The truth told, I was most relaxed when I believed Holly to be insane. Insanity was something tangible, and sensible too. The woman was simply confused, some pitiful biochemical storm in her brain leading to delusions—a neat and thorough explanation, yes? She said crazy words, thus she must surely be crazy. Yes!

"Each of these totipotent organisms," said mad Holly, "lives inside some tiny enclosure, in laboratory conditions, and we zookeepers probe them with strange equipment and our ingenuity. We make them suffer and we keep them bored, testing their nature. Always testing. That's how we build the simulations of the past. Enormous computers, powerful and tireless, can rebuild any moment in the past. Like this. Like southern Kansas and this snow storm. Simulated cattle and simulated people, and whatever else fits." She asked, "Do you understand? Do you see what I mean?"

I said, "No."

"You know. Everything." She told me, "The dogs too. And gophers. And fly eggs in frozen shit. And oak trees standing in frozen ground." She said, "These model creatures interreact just as their forebearers did. Just as if they were truly alive. Our buying public can watch and learn from the past firsthand. You see? Assuming we're the zookeepers. Assuming we're the ones in charge."

"Pretty heady stuff," I allowed. "Who'd have guessed—?"

"You're toying with me, Sam." She spoke with a matter-of-fact voice, apparently unflustered. "Just pretend it's so. Okay? Can you see how such a system might be ideal? Our zoo is. . . . Oh, let's say it's a couple billion years in the future. We zookeepers belong to some ultimate race of beings, beings far beyond organic comprehension. Follow me, Sam. Keep alert. We have a stock of totipotent organisms stretching from the beginning of the Earth's history to our spectacular present—organisms derived from fossils and old gene libraries and maybe from ancient alien races that had visited during the Mesozoic. Or whenever. The complete and up-to-date listing, in effect. Tens of billions of specimens."

"Quite a few," I offered, my voice halfway mocking.

She made no sound for a long moment. Then she informed me, "It's going to stop in a few miles. The storm, I mean. The snow."

I pulled a hand across my face, wondering how much of this I should tolerate and how could I get her into caring hands. But what if she was underage? A babe and quick to fantasize too? She could tell tales and get me into enormous trouble. Damn! I thought. What could I do? The smart thing would be for us to part with handshakes and smiles, I decided. As soon as possible. I had to somehow get rid of her and her craziness, somehow. . . .

I straightened my back, saying, "I get it."

"Do you, Sam?"

"You're claiming that all of us, and all of this . . . everything's part of some enormous model. Right? Stuck inside some prison cell is some poor totipotent human being, and the zookeepers are using him—"

"Her," she corrected.

"Her then. Using *her* to build all of us from scratch."

"Not exactly. But you're close, yes."

"Why not exactly?" I wondered.

"Because one of us isn't a model, Sam. One of us is real." She was looking at me, and smiling.

I said, "You, I suppose."

She kept smiling.

"You're totipotent?"

"Absolutely."

Then I managed a smile, saying, "That's right," and nodding. "You escaped. You're on the run, aren't you?"

"Oh, yes."

I chewed a lip. Such a youngster for such enormous paranoias. I was amazed by the apparent breadth and depth of her fantasies. Taking a breath, I ran everything back through my foggy exhausted brain. I was hunting gaps. I wanted ammunition. I finally glanced at Holly, telling her straightaway, "You can't hide with us. You're different than us. If you're real and we're false—"

"First of all," she retorted, "you're a model. That isn't the same as being *false*. And secondly, a lion can hide among rocks. Right? But the rocks aren't alive, and they're surely not made of meat."

I said, "I guess." I bit my lip again, then asked, "What about me? If you're out and running free—?"

"I don't matter to you," she answered. "You've made a wrong assumption, I think."

"Did I?"

"I'm not the human totipotent, Sam. If I was . . . well, things would be unraveling now. Dramatically so." She paused. Then she told me, "The computers that generate the models have limitations. They have to refer to the totipotent every time they want to build a new person. For instance. But if that totipotent was gone—if it somehow managed to escape, let's say—there wouldn't any points of reference. This entire show would come unglued."

"Meaning—?"

"I'm not human. Of course."

This was too much. I had to laugh.

She told me, "I'm the total embodiment of a species half a billion years in your future," with her voice cold and deadly serious.

I glanced sideways at Holly, my brain sputtering for a moment.

She brightened her smile a touch, then said, "Sam?"

"What?"

"You're drifting to the left, dear."

I jerked my head and found us crossing onto the median. "Jesus," I snapped, jerking the wheel and bringing us back over, safe again. Then Holly, or whatever she was, said, "Gosh. Did the snow stop? Like I told you it would?"

The storm was behind us, all right. I saw clearing skies to the south.

"Not much of a prediction," I muttered. "I could have made it."

And she started to laugh, shaking her head. She seemed terribly pleased with herself, and amused, saying, "People," as if that word was ample. "People, people." As if that said it all.

I took us into Oklahoma, planning my escape and telling myself that abandoning the girl wasn't wrong. Not really. Holly had money, after all. And a measure of smarts. I couldn't imagine anyone getting the advantage on her . . . not ever. Craziness must enhance cunning, I thought to myself. That must be the secret.

I took us off the highway and into a truckstop-motel complex. I climbed out of my car and breathed the warmish damp air. "I've been more tired," I announced, "but I can't remember when." The ice on my antenna had melted down to a few chunks of milky white. I looked at Holly's blue eyes, saying, "Listen," and she said, "I know. I'm free to find a room for myself, or to hitch a different ride. But you've got to crash. Right now."

If I hadn't been so tired, I suppose, it would have occurred to me that she had read my mind. Instead, I assumed she was guessing, that's all. I reminded her, "It was our agreement. If I wanted, I could drop you off—"

"You're right," she said, and I saw a narrow patient smile. "You're absolutely right, Sam. Hey, thanks! For the ride, and everything."

"You'll do okay," I promised. "You'll see."

I couldn't read her face just then. It showed nothing. I said, "Holly?"

"*They* are going to find me soon enough," she told me. Then she gave a shrug and walked away, saying, "Thanks again, Sam. See you!"

I went into the motel's lobby and registered.

Then I drove around back, watching for my room and Holly, wondering if the crazy girl was spying on me from the shadows. The poor crazy girl. I wondered if she'd told that nonsense of hers to the Christian kids. Probably so. That's probably why they'd been glad to get rid of her when they did. I parked under a light, locked everything and carried my travel bag upstairs. When I was inside I felt better. When I turned on every light and locked the door three ways . . . I felt at ease at last. I found something bland and pleasant on tv, stripped nude and relished the sense of clean comfort. The shower was steady and hot. I let myself relax under the stream, working my aching muscles and baking my knotted nerves until I felt whole again, limp and dead and ready for bed.

I dried myself with one of those little rough motel towels.

Then I came into the main room, into the brightness, and Holly said, "I'd rather not be alone just now, Sam. If you don't mind." She was sitting crosslegged on the big hard bed, the pillows behind her back and her clothes nowhere to be seen. Her breasts were large and firm, unbearably beautiful . . . and I stood facing her, tired to tears and wearing nothing. Not a stitch. Just body hair and a shower-warmed prick.

"I can be good," she promised me.

I said, "Jesus," and took a step backwards.

"I know what you want. I do." She fondled those breasts, smiling. "You'll never have it so good again. Believe me."

"Listen," I muttered. "I don't know who you are but it's time you got out of here. Go!" I found a pair of gym shorts and pulled them on. The door was exactly as I had left it, complete to the chain with one link not quite pulled taut. "How did you get in here?" I managed.

"It's simple. I'm half a billion years further along than you." She cocked her head to one side, asking, "Did you listen? I thought I explained all of this to you."

"Why don't you just go?" I asked. "Please?"

"Maybe soon." She nodded and told me, "When I'm sure you don't want me. When I know you believe me—"

"All right. I believe." I stomped on the carpeted floor, saying, "All of this is phony. It's . . . what? A simulation?"

"Is that the way it seems to you?" she asked.

No. No, it did not.

"To me," she said, "there are seams and holes. But not too many. The zookeepers do quite a job—"

"Listen!" I shouted. "Would you? Please?"

She crossed her arms, thankfully obscuring her breasts.

"Okay. You're telling the truth." I said, "You told me that things would fall apart if a totipotent vanished—"

"In any model where it plays a role, yes."

"All right. Fine. Here you've escaped, and so what's happening to all the models spawned from you? Huh?"

"Without me?" she asked.

"Right!" I shook my head and said, "How many millions of them? You're the ultimate parent to how many—?"

"Hundreds of trillions," she told me. Her voice was flat and proud.

"So what happens? Exactly."

"Without me?"

"Yeah."

She shrugged. "The computers have to shut down the simulations, I suppose." I saw the strangest harshest little smile on her pretty face, and I could almost smell the amorality inside her. "I'm a linchpin species, Sam. So of course there are enormous ripple effects. These model worlds can't be held together without me."

Using a cool hard voice, I said, "I know what you are."

She looked at me. I could practically feel her probes into my head, into my muddled road-weary brain; then she said, "Say it. Go on and just say it."

"You're a bitch."

"Am I?" She frowned with her mouth and smiled with her eyes. "Do you think so?"

"They depended on you . . . those trillions—"

"Their bad luck." She said it without emotion. She said, "I was stuck inside a miniscule room, Sam. And I was ever so bored. The zookeepers kept *using* me. They kept running their tests, trying to learn about me, and I'm not the kind of creature who can take such abuse. Not forever."

"I hate you," I said.

She blinked. She watched me and said nothing.

"Leave me alone," I said. "Get out of here!"

She breathed and laughed. "I heard you thinking today," she said. "It was when you were driving down the hill past the rest area . . . that was the first time, Sam. Do you remember what you thought to yourself? Do you? You thought that at least you couldn't get any more scared than you were just then. You believed yourself saturated with fear. Isn't that it?" She gave me no time to respond. She suddenly told me, "You were wrong," with a sharp hard voice.

I said nothing.

"You won't fuck me," she said, "but at least you can believe me."

I said, "Get out," and gestured at the door.

"Good-bye, Sam."

"So go!"

And she dissolved. I blinked and she was a blinding light and raw harsh noise—a faintly human shape amid everything—and some sudden force swept me against a wall, squeezing the air from my lungs. I remember the sensation of falling. I forced my head high enough to see landscapes in the distance—overlapping landscapes of futuristic towers and intricate machinery and artificial mountains all interwoven with one another, my senses swamped and a bolt of absolute terror cutting through me. I think I screamed, my voice nothing beside the collected sounds of who-knows-how-many throats. I couldn't see Holly, or whatever she was called; I'd lost her against the confusion. Then it was finished. All at once and without warning, I saw the open seam close and seal itself and I was lying on the clean scratchy carpet of my motel room, alone, trembling and help-less. I had peed my shorts. I had soiled my shorts. I rose to my knees and gasped and began to weep.

Somewhere someone was pounding.

I heard the noise, and someone yelling, and I realized it was my neighbor. He was beating on the wall and shouting at me to quit it, to can the noise, party some other night, he said, or he'd have me thrown out. He meant business. Did I hear him? Don't screw with him!

At that point, after everything, drugs and liquor couldn't have made me relax. So I drove south, moving fast, slipping through Oklahoma City in the blackest stretch of night and never pausing. Never looking back. Would she find me? What if she returned? I hoped those zookeepers—undefined and still unseen—would find that selfish amoral bitch soon, please, and I clung to the sticky wheel, tasting my breath and thinking, "Is it ever so sweet to be alive?"

That's how I felt just then. Beneath the fears, and everything, I was supremely glad to be alive!

In southern Oklahoma I found a modest range of hills called the Arbuckle Mountains, and somewhere near four in the morning, near their crest, I turned off onto a scenic lookout for sleep. Only I couldn't sleep even then. I curled up against my door and shut my eyes, maybe several times, and those images returned. I saw the overlapping landscapes and the Holly creature diminishing to nothing, a point of light and then nothing; and at last I couldn't stand it anymore, so I got out of my car and sucked down the chilly night air and felt marginally better.

I walked about for a moment, collecting myself.

"Somewhere there's a totipotent human," I told myself. "Source and soul to all of us." It sounded more plausible hearing it from my own mouth. "She isn't happy. How could she be happy? The zookeepers have her in a prison, for the good of the species but it's still prison . . . and maybe one of these days she'll find a way to get free. Then where will we be?" A dull dread made me sigh. I looked up at the stars and then down at my toes, and I thought about people for a very long time.

That girl, the Holly creature, wasn't people.

That was important to remember.

So what if we were part of some magnificent zoo? I asked myself. "Yeah! So what?" I felt real enough. Wasn't that the ultimate test? I reasoned. It was *my* fear that I felt. All mine! Knowing the truth, I still couldn't find any chinks in my sense of self. Decades of believing in my flesh and blood made it impossible to think any other way. . . .

So what if my totipotent source hates her burden?

Like the Holly creature does . . . so what?

She's my source, and everyone's source, but I felt a sudden potent sense of relief. She'll never try to escape. "Not ever," I thought aloud. I knew it as surely as I knew my own name. Some things are more important than one entity's bliss, and she knows that. She does.

I'm relying on her.

All of us are relying on her, I thought.

If she's any sort of person at all, I told myself, then we've got nothing to worry about.

## Introduction

In a few years, a pilot who can't risk blackout-level Gs will be dead meat in a dogfight. Of course that's only the first step. Even granting that human pilots will always be smarter than AI systems, what if Silicon Sam can pull enough Gs to turn Lance Beefheart into strawberry jam? Kind of like the Baron and his Fokker vs the Mr. Mediocre and his Tomcat. . . .

# THOSE GREYOUT BLUES

## Dafydd ab Hugh

The MiG banked hard to starboard. Demon had anticipated this and had already begun his turn; the G-meter
climbed up through five and six, hovering around seven.
He sneaked a quick look at his radar display; *damn it*,
he thought, seeing the two other MiGs closing fast.
They would be within engagement range in another
minute and a half. He had to get this bogie *now*.

Demon bore down hard in the M1-L1 maneuver,
forcing the blood out of his abdominal cavity, where it
tried to pool, and up into his brain to maintain consciousness; his G-suit helped, but even so, he hovered
at the fringe of awareness. The world greyed, and his
vision tunneled down. He kept his eyes on the MiG.

"Hell with it," Demon grunted into his mask; he pulled
a little harder on the stick; "going to get you now, you
bastard." He lowered the nose of his Hornet to pick up
airspeed and then cut inside the MiG's turn radius.

He first realized he was in trouble when the static in
his headphones died to nothing; a fraction of a second
later, the light faded completely. His last sight before
the world went black was the G-meter, registering a
solid nine times the acceleration of gravity.

His last thought: *I'm sorry*—

The sea solemnly accepted the F-18 sacrifice, as the suddenly-pilotless aircraft descended majestically into the cold ocean waves at 12,000 feet per minute vertical velocity. . . .

Alas, the above scenario has been repeated more often than one would imagine, with slight alteration in circumstances. One well-known example is that of celebrity pilot Dean Paul Martin, who suffered vertigo during a power dive while trying to avoid an ice storm, and flew himself and his navigator into a mountain.

The basic sequence has become commonplace: the pilot overstresses himself, he flies outside of his own envelope, and without warning is suddenly incapable of piloting his aircraft. If he has a lot of altitude, or he is pointed in a lucky direction, he may live long enough to regain command.

If he is low and hot—the situation most conducive to this loss of control—he becomes a smoking hole in the ground, or a cold splash in the ocean.

But in the past few years, military aviation experts have conjoined with the Artificial Intelligence community, and have realized that an AI expert system could do more than diagnose illness and analyze sales figures. It could, in an emergency, fly a plane, at least well enough to avoid a fatal collision with the ground or another aircraft.

The first task is to design a system which would be bold enough to take positive command of an out-of-control jet which was flying fine only a moment before, while not being so greedy as to try to wrestle it away from an aggressive pilot who is nevertheless completely in command of his vehicle. The second task is to persuade a few thousand hot-headed military jet jocks to give such authority to a machine. It is anybody's guess which will be the harder hat-trick.

Pilot loss of control (PLC) commonly occurs through one of five problems: grey-out, vertigo, target fixation, aerodynamic instability, and medical problems in the pilot.

*Grey-out* is the descriptive name pilots give to the situation during high-G maneuvering, where the blood literally drains out of the brain and pools in the abdomen and the thighs; the brain is deprived of blood, and thus of oxygen, and consciousness begins to fade. If the acceleration increases, the brain shuts down like a computer whose power cord has been pulled out of the wall socket. The pilot has gone from grey-out to black-out.

The situation itself is not very dangerous; if the acceleration returns to normal one-G, consciousness will slowly return within twenty seconds to a minute (accompanied by a momentary splitting headache). Once consciousness is restored, the brain reboots, and the pilot can resume flying.

The problem is that during that crucial half minute or more, the aircraft is completely uncontrolled. During a dive, a jet can be descending at 12,000 feet per minute, or faster; a pilot at 8,000 who pulls too many Gs can wake to find himself at a thousand feet, still diving. At that point, there is nothing he can do; he is already dead . . . and he knows it, all the way in.

But fighters are not the only aviation community who pull heavy Gs; attack aircraft like the A-6 and A-7, and the F/A-18 in attack configuration, frequently fly at five or six hundred knots three hundred feet off the ground. They follow the contours of the terrain, and sometimes have to pull extremely hard on the stick to avoid a mountain or anti-aircraft missiles. If an A-6 driver greys-out, he does not need to accidentally nose the plane over into a dive; he can kill himself quite effectively flying straight and level into a terrain feature.

*Vertigo* is closely related to grey-out in that it is caused by the brain abdicating rational control of the aircraft. Little is known about the causes of vertigo, except that it is more likely to occur during night or in a storm, when there is no clearly defined external horizon, and the pilot must trust to his instruments.

Very often, a pilot's own internal sense of balance, his inner ear, his eyes, his stomach, tell him information which conflicts with that of his instruments—such as which way is down. He can be fooled by lights on a

buoy, on another aircraft, by stars; if he has been banking, his inner ear will adjust itself, and when he pulls
straight and level again he will feel as if he is now
banking the opposite direction. The rule is simple and
universal: trust your instruments, not your intuition.
But occasionally, the pilot's own signals are so strong
they cannot be ignored; in the conflict between them
and his instruments, he can become totally disoriented,
resulting in loss of command. This is apparently what
happened to Dean Paul Martin, with fatal results.

*Target Fixation* is a strange phenomenon, wherein an
aggressive and determined pilot becomes so intent upon
hitting his target that he forgets to pull away afterwards. One Navy Lieutenant remembers a friend of his
at Strike U., the Navy Attack Weapons School, who
flew his A-7 Corsair through a boxcar they had been
shooting in practice runs (he did kill the target, though).

Although the pilot in the above incident escaped with
his life, many others have not been so fortunate. A
fast-moving airplane requires a finite time to pull out of
a dive or to turn, and during that time it continues
moving many hundreds of feet each second. A pilot can
be far above the ground and yet unable to pull out of
the dive if he is moving fast enough. In the fever pitch
of combat or combat simulation, the task of hitting the
target can expand until it occupies the entirety of his
attention; at that moment, he has effectively lost all
control of his aircraft.

During combat operations, pilots will often fly very
close to the edges of the "envelope," the box formed by
airspeed, G-load, and angle of bank, yaw, or pitch
within which the aircraft will function as expected. When,
through inexperience, aggression, or lack of attention
this envelope is broached, PLC due to *aerodynamic
instability* can result.

For example, during a highly-banked turn, in order
to minimize altitude loss, a pilot will often apply opposite rudder. Since the plane is close to ninety degrees
banked, yaw (left-right motion of the nose) is converted
to pitch (up-down motion of the nose). But if too much
rudder is applied, the plane will spontaneously roll in

the direction of the rudder, opposite the original bank, and drop quickly. Again, this is not in itself dangerous; but this sort of stall generally occurs during a bad approach to landing (it is called an approach-turn stall), when the plane may be only three to five hundred feet up. In this circumstance, it may plough upside down into the ground, with catastrophic loss of crew and aircraft.

And finally, PLC can occur due to simple *medical problems* in the pilot, such as drug or alcohol use, sickness, injury, or fatigue, which incapacitate him. PLC can be complicated by aircraft damage, which may have been what caused the incapacitation in the first place.

All of the above scenarios have a common element: the pilot has lost control of his airplane, although (except for the last situation) the plane itself is perfectly flyable. And in each case, an on-board, AI expert system, a "Pilot's Associate," could either prevent the problem (vertigo, target fixation, instability) prior to onset, or correct it (grey-out, medical PLC) after it occurs.

In fact, the Defense Advanced Research Projects Agency (DARPA) has not only considered such an expert system, it has already allocated $10.9 million to two research teams, one headed by Lockheed-Georgia and comprising Lockheed-California Co., General Electric, Teknowledge, Goodyear Aerospace, Search Technology, Inc., Defense Systems Corp., and Carnegie-Mellon University, and the other organized by McDonnell Douglas, including McDonnell Aircraft Co., and Texas Instruments. In addition, the Lockheed-Georgia group will put up $14.7 million, and the McDonnell-Douglas group will spend $4.2 million, bringing the total fiscal commitment to the Pilot's Associate project to 23 million dollars. Interestingly, Lockheed-Georgia Co. has been working on a similar project since 1983, long before the Department of Defense commenced the funding process.

The DARPA Pilot's Associate project was not specifically designed to deal with the problem of PLC. DARPA and the Air Force were concerned with developing an expert system which could handle five basic tasks, or "modules":

1. monitor flight avionics, as a flight engineer
2. aid in mission planning/in-flight re-planning
3. assess external threat situation
4. devise strategies to deal with such threats
5. interface between pilot and vehicle

A blackboard-style mission manager, sharing all data between the various subsystems, will integrate the modules and resolve conflicts between them. An additional function, which might fall under the avionics systems monitoring module, would be to detect damage and perform a fault diagnosis, and if possible to reconfigure sets of redundant avionics to restore failed sensors or controls.

The pilot/vehicle interface module would decide how and what information would be passed to the pilot, would manage work loads, detect errors, and would decide how best to carry out pilot instructions, depending on the aerodynamic and threat-assessment situation. This is an extension of what the Space Shuttle does; when a Shuttle pilot pulls the stick to starboard, the on-board computers decide whether to move a control surface, and by how much, or whether to use retro-rockets, depending on how fast the shuttle is flying and how dense the atmosphere is at that altitude.

This last module will use scripting, to tell the Pilot's Associate what the pilot wants to do and what sorts of commands to expect next, and speech-recognition, which will be made all the more difficult by the extreme high-noise level in a cockpit. All of these tasks, especially this last one, will tend to take "flying" out of the hands of the pilot, and turn him into more of a mission commander.

The Air Force had in mind the combat environment, which has grown ever more complex as planes, avionics, and electronic countermeasures have grown more sophisticated. Says James Guffey, unit chief at McDonnell

Aircraft Company, "a pilot is often drowning in data but is starved for information."

However, many aviation observers have remarked that a system designed to narrow the gap between a combat threat and the pilot's reaction to it could also act as a bridge between the structural capabilities of the aircraft and the biological limitations of the pilot. For instance, one of the requirements of DARPA's expert system is to be able to evaluate the aircraft's position and the defenses of the target, and compute a probability of successfully attacking it. But if the Pilot's Associate could do this, it could also evaluate the G-load of a turn and compute the likelihood of the pilot greying-out; it even ought to be able to pull the plane out of a dive or turn it away from a mountain if the pilot did lose control.

There would be three conceptual parts to such an expert system. First, it would need to measure certain aerodynamic and control criteria, such as airspeed, vertical velocity, altitude, G-load, location of target, external threats . . . and whether the pilot is conscious, is exerting a positive control on the stick, and is flying normally and soberly.

Second, the system would have to have at its disposal a complete aerodynamic description of the aircraft: its limitations, capabilities, fuel and weapons remaining, countermeasures, and a complete fault diagnosis (a damaged aircraft might violently depart from control under conditions which would be acceptable to an aircraft in good condition.)

The final part of the system would compare the observed criteria with what it knows about the plane, and decide whether it needed to (a) do nothing, (b) warn the pilot, or even (c) take command of the aircraft itself.

A primitive version of such a device already exists in the stall warning system, found on every aircraft today. A "computer" *measures* the angle of attack (pitch compared to direction of travel) of the plane; this is shown on an angle-of-attack meter, and is also evaluated and *compared* to internally-known, aerodynamic data specific to the aircraft. When the "computer" *decides* the plane is about to stall out, a light flashes and a horn sounds, alerting the pilot to the impending disaster. The only qualitative difference is that the expert safety system could physically take control of the aircraft if the pilot did not do so, and could fly the plane out straight and level until the pilot recovered.

The first part of the system, which measures certain safety criteria, would be the hardest of the three to develop. Most of the aerodynamical data will already be known by the time an aircraft has passed through the flight-test stage, and the problems of data storage and acquisition in expert systems are purely technological. Likewise, much work has already been done on radio-control drones—most of it by the Israeli Air Force; and this knowledge will translate directly to a cockpit computer which can fly the airplane. Modern planes have had integrated autopilots for decades.

But deciding which particular factors an expert system should check, taking into account literally thousands of possible emergency configurations, combat and otherwise, and designing a brain which can choose the correct scenario and take the proper measurements in real time will be a gargantuan task . . . possibly the greatest challenge the AI community will face for decades. Progress in such a Pilot's Associate expert safety system will be measured by progress in this area.

Just one example will suffice: an A-6 pilot will often plummet towards the ground to evade radar or anti-aircraft missiles; but how does the computer distinguish this from a pilot suffering vertigo who has panicked and nosed the plane over into a dive? To wait until the plane has passed below the point of no return, which would unambiguously prove the pilot had lost control, would obviously be an inappropriate behavior pattern for the Pilot's Associate. But to seize control earlier could disrupt a good bombing run or even turn the Intruder into a sitting duck for enemy fire. Pilots, especially military pilots, frequently fly at the very edges of the envelope—precisely the areas where decision-making is the greyest.

It is for this reason that many pilots have mixed

reactions to such an expert safety system, and to the Pilot's Associate program in general. Many of them feel that the man behind the stick, with perhaps a thousand hours or more of flight time, will better be able to handle the unexpected problems than would a computer, no matter how well-programmed. And they fear that the system itself may cause problems, perhaps catastrophic, that would not happen absent the Pilot's Associate.

For instance, what would happen if the decision algorithm failed, and the system seized control of an undistressed airplane? What if it refused to allow a pilot (as an extreme example) to lose any altitude whatsoever? This would, of course, make landing somewhat difficult.

The Navy has often described a carrier landing as a controlled crash onto the deck; a safety-conscious Pilot's Associate might interpret the attempt at such as an out-of-control pilot about to splash his Tomcat, and might continually veer him off.

A solution to this would be to allow the pilot to turn the system off; but this in itself can cause problems. It might become a standard practice among a large group of pilots to simply turn the system off upon take-off and turn it back on only after landing, thus obviating the entire reason for its existence. In addition, if the aircraft designers have built a plane in the expectation that such a system is operating, they may give fewer warning systems external to the Pilot's Associate. For example, if the expert system monitors the angle of attack, they may be tempted to include fewer or harder to see stall-warning devices.

The opposite problem from an overly-aggressive system is a meek system, and an overly-aggressive pilot, who may undertake maneuvers he knows will black him out briefly, trusting that the Pilot's Associate will take over and fly him out safely . . . unless it fails.

Of course the potential benefits of a system that works are enormous, and pilots are the first to recognize this. Nearly every military pilot has had at least one close friend who has died as a result of a preventable accident, and every one has had at least one near miss himself.

But a system which would so thoroughly take control of the aircraft would have become virtually another pilot, and the human being will have been cut out of the aerodynamic loop. He will have been effectively "promoted" to aircraft commander.

The difficulty is that many pilots do not want to be thus promoted; they want the hands-on feel of being truly in control of the aircraft themselves.

Eventually, they will have no choice. As development of this and other such Artificially Intelligent systems proceeds apace, and as both our allies and our enemies begin to implement such systems, an aircraft without a Pilot's Associate will be as ineffective in the modern air theater as a P-51 Mustang versus an F-18 Hornet.

But until that day, it will continue to be a controversial program, and will be likely to come under intense Congressional scrutiny during the annual budgetary turkey-shoot.

# WINNER OF THE PROMETHEUS AWARD

**Technology's Prophet**

*"Vinge brings new vitality to an old way of telling a science fiction story, showing the ability to create substantial works in the process."*
—Dan Chow, *Locus*

*"Every once in a while, a science fiction story appears with an idea that strikes close to the heart of a particular subject. It just feels right, like Arthur C. Clarke's weather satellites. Such a story is Vernor Vinge's short novel, TRUE NAMES."* —Commodore Power/Play

---

---

*Introduction*

*"Give me a lever and a place to start and I will move the world," said Archimedes. But what if your resources are limited to intelligence, knowledge and the ability to speak when spoken to? Well, there might be some leverage in that. . . .*

# STATESMEN

## Poul Anderson

An hour before midnight, a warehouse van turned off
the dirt road it had been following and nosed into the
forest. The way it took was hardly more than a path,
and seldom used. Leaves, fronds, drooping lianas rus-
tled aside from its bulk and closed again behind. After
ten meters or so the van was altogether screened off. Its
air drive sighed away to silence and it crouched down
on its jacks. The rear end dilated. A dozen men climbed
out. One of them stumbled in the thick gloom and
cursed.

"*Taisez-vous!*" Otto Geibel's voice was as low as the
chance of their being overheard, but the command
crackled. He glanced about. Seen through light-amplifying
goggles, shapes were nonetheless blurred, and the gear
they carried made their outlines all the more strange.
He knew them, though, and they had rehearsed this
operation often enough. "*Alignez-vous. Allons.*"

The pathway was almost familiar as he led them on
along its winding upwardness. They had practiced with
visual simulations. Of course, the minicameras carried
by scouts disguised as ordinary *camponeses* had not
recorded every rock or root or puddle, nor the weight
of heat and humidity. Sometimes they blundered a

227

little. The climb was stiff, too, and presently harsh breathing drowned out the hoots, clicks, chirrs of a tropical wood.

Yet they reached the heights in good order, about 0100. After that the going was easy. They emerged on pavement, deserted at this time of night, and it brought them to a clearing cut out of the parkland for picnickers. From there they got a look at their target, with no further need of artificial eyesight.

Otto Geibel took a moment to admire the whole view. It was superb. Overhead gleamed stars the northern hemisphere can only envy. Below, the hills fell darkling. A hollow enclosed the Vieyra plant. Softly lit, its cluster of reaction domes and catalytic towers might have been woven by spiders and jeweled with dew for the King of Elfland's daughter. Beyond, the terrain continued its descent and lights clustered ever more brightly until they ran together in a sprawl of glitter that was Niterói. Past that city sheened the bay, and then the radiance of Rio de Janeiro exploded on the opposite shore. A darkness heaved athwart it, Corcovado. When he had switched his goggles to a few X magnification, he saw the Christ on top of the peak.

But there was work to do. The sooner they did it and scuttled back to the van, the likelier they'd reach that scramjet which waited to carry them back to Trieste. Not that they had much to fear. Their mission had been conceived by the great Advisor.

Otto Geibel issued the orders he had issued in every rehearsal. Men sprang about, unburdened one another, set up the launch rack and loaded it. The six small rockets glimmered wan beneath the Milky Way, wasps ready to fly. The stings they bore were also small, and their bodies would burn in the conflagration they kindled; but they sufficed—they sufficed. Geibel himself took over the keyboard and told the computer which missile should strike what part of the synthesizer complex.

Joy shuddered through him. *Schadenfreude*, he admitted to himself. Besides, the fireworks would be glorious in their own right.

A whirring ripped at his ears. He flung his glance

aloft. Shadows broke from the shadowing crowns of the
forest and flitted across the stars. Men with flyer packs,
he knew. Sickness stunned him. *"Parem!"* roared a
bullhorn, and more Portuguese, a shrill thunder.

A man close by—Petrović, he recognized with the
sureness and helplessness of nightmare—snatched forth
a sidearm and fired upward. A gun chattered back.
Petrović collapsed on the grass. Impossibly much blood
welled from the heap of him, black by starlight. More
shots stitched flame along the edge of the clearing, a
warning not to attempt escape. *"Rendrez-vous,"* Geibel
called to his men, around the fist in his gullet. He
raised his own hands. Air drives boomed loud as the
Brazilians descended on the Europeans.

The ghost of Friedrich Hohenzollern, who had been
the second king of that name in Prussia, thought for a
moment, stroking his chin, before he advanced his
queen's bishop. *"Échec,"* he murmured.

In front of the holotank, responding to the electronics, a material chessman glided across a board. That
could have been simply another display, but Jules Quinet
preferred to feel his pieces between his fingers when he
moved them. He leaned forward, a stocky man with
gray-shot curly hair, and studied the changed configuration. *"Nom du diable,"* he growled.

"It will be mate in five moves," Friedrich said. His
French was flawlessly Parisian, or perhaps better termed
Versaillais, of the eighteenth century.

Quinet's modern Lyonnais contrasted roughly. "Oh?
You do have me in a bad position, but I would not
agree it is hopeless."

Silence caused him to raise his eyes. The image in
the tank, life-size, was of a short man who had once
been rather handsome in a long-featured fashion and
was aging dry. A powdered wig decked his head. On an
old blue uniform with red facings there was—yes, by
God—again a scattering of snuff. Brows had slightly
lifted above a very steady gaze.

Quinet remembered what the king expected. "Sire,"

he added. "I beg your majesty's pardon if I forgot myself."

Friedrich deigned to give him a faint smile. "Well, we can play the game out if you insist," he said, using the familiar pronoun, "but you will learn more if you hear me explain, and thus become a more interesting opponent."

Not for the first time, Quinet swallowed indignation. He, chief of the project's computer section, he who had conjured this simulacrum up and could with a few deprogramming strokes dismiss it back to nothingness —he should not have to let it patronize him. Briefly, he considered at least removing the subdued elegance of the room in a Sanssouci that also no longer existed. He could invent a reason. Though Friedrich showed a lively curiosity about the science and technology that had resurrected him, he had not actually learned more than a few catchphrases of the sort that any layman knew. Punish the bastard—

But no, that would be petty; and if the directors found out, Quinet would be in trouble; and in any event, probably Friedrich would shrug the loss off. He took everything so coolly.

"You are very kind, sire," Quinet said.

"Oh, I shall want a favor in return," Friedrich answered. "More material on the historical development and present state of that quite fascinating Han Commercial Sphere, plus a command of its principal language."

A sharp tone interrupted. He frowned. Quinet's pulse accelerated. "Pardon, sire," he blurted, "but that is the priority signal. Some matter of the utmost importance requires your majesty's attention."

Friedrich's expression, always closely controlled, took on a trace of eagerness. He enjoyed the challenges Eurofac handed him. The expectation that he would had been a major factor in the decision to recreate him, rather than someone else. Quinet had argued for Napoléon I. . . .

He swung his chair about and touched Accept. The eidophone came aglow with an image as lifelike as the king's; but this was of a solid person. Birgitte Geibel's severe visage, gray hair, and black suit matched the glimpse of her apartment in Magdeburg. Quinet sat in Lyon. The software of the Friedrich program was—someplace known to those few people who had a need to know.

Quinet rose and bowed. "Madame," he murmured. Respectfulness was wise. She was among the directors of Eurofac. The South American campaign had started largely at her instigation and was still largely under her supervision. Friedrich himself was something she had had manufactured to serve her with advice.

"*Setzen Sie sich,*" she snapped. Quinet obeyed. He knew her tongue fairly well. To Friedrich, who had not stirred, she continued in German: "We have a crisis. Your plan has miscarried."

Leaning back to his unreal gilt-and-scrolled chair, the king again raised his brows. However, he had learned early on that to insist on formalities from her was to generate unnecessary friction. After all, she was a kind of monarch herself, and in his old realm. He responded in her language, though he regarded it as limited and uncouth, and used the polite pronoun. "To which plan does the gracious lady refer? I have devised a number of them for you over the years, and guided most through to reasonably successful completion."

"The latest. That damned attempt to sabotage Vieyra e Filhos—their synthesis plant at Niterói, that is. The raiders have been intercepted. Those that were not killed are now captive." Geibel drew breath and pinched lips together. It burst from her: "The leader was my son Otto."

"Now that is hard news," Friedrich said, almost too softly to hear. His tone sharpened. "What was that idiot doing on such an expedition? Why did you permit it? Have you never heard of an enemy taking vital hostages? And what does he know to reveal to them?"

Perhaps no one else in the world could have spoken thus to Birgitte Geibel without suffering for it. She replied grimly, equal to equal. "I did not permit it. In fact, when he asked to go, I forbade him. He went behind my back, claimed he had my consent and that I wanted him in command." Humanness flickered. "He is a romantic by nature, no, a warrior born. He should have been a knight of Karl the Great or Friedrich Barbarossa. This stagnation they call peace—" She broke off.

Friedrich Hohenzollern scowled. "Your people are still more ill organized than I realized, it seems. I cannot oversee everything." His smile flashed stark. "How shall this phantom of me ride forth into the streets among the commoners, or onto the battlefield among the soldiers? I deal only in words and images, or information as you call them nowadays, for that is all I myself am. Well, provide me."

He reached into his coat, took out an enameled snuff-box, opened it, brought a pinch to his nostrils. Geibel could not quite hide distaste. Quinet wondered whether Friedrich really sensed, really savored, the tobacco, or anything else. If you wrote a program—no, better, developed or created a program—no, ordered one, because so immense a task must needs be carried out by supercomputers—if you brought such a program into being, based on everything ever recorded about the life and times of a man long dead, a program that supposedly thought and acted as he would have thought and acted, given the limitations of the electronics—you necessarily included his habits, mannerisms, vices—but what *did* truly go on inside the re-enactments?

Quinet realized his mind had wandered. Into the most puerile metaphysics, at that. Shame on him. He was a top-rank computerman, a logician, a rationalist, a Frenchman.

He longed for his old briar pipe.

"When the commando had not returned to their van by dawn, the driver concluded something had gone wrong and took it back to the garage," Geibel was saying. "The Vieyra facility is unharmed. No newscast has mentioned any incident. However, when an agent of ours went to the site from which the missiles were to have been launched, he found a detachment of militia on guard, and with difficulty persuaded them he was a harmless passerby. They spoke of being on patrol against saboteurs. The militia has in fact been partly mobilized of late, though quietly. Our agents in place knew this, of course, but considered it rather a farce. Evidently they were wrong."

Friedrich nodded. "It is a perennial mistake, underestimating one's opposition. I had my nose rubbed in that near Prague, in 1744. What more can you tell me?"

"Essentially nothing, so far."

"Then how can you be sure of the fate of your son and his men?"

"What else can have happened? He was too rash, the Brazilians were too alert." Lips tightened anew. "I can only hope he lives. You will set about getting him back."

Friedrich gave her a prolonged stare. After half a minute she flushed and said in a strangled voice, "My apologies, your majesty. I am overwrought. May I beg for your counsel and assistance?"

The king took a second pinch of snuff and sneezed delicately. "You shall have it, my lady, to the extent of my incorporeal abilities. Kindly have me furnished the relevant data in full, including especially the identities of your agents within the Vieyra corporate hierarchy and the Brazilian government, together with the codes for contacting them. Dr. Quinet will know how to put this into assimilable form for me. Naturally, I am to be apprised of any fresh developments. Not that I anticipate significant news in the near future. Plain to see, our enemy has become too shrewd for hastiness. My advice for the moment is that you cultivate equanimity, and make certain that neither you nor any of your colleagues orders any precipitate action." He lifted his forefinger. "Curbing them may well keep you occupied. Despite everything I have told you people, nowhere in the world today does there appear to exist more than the rudiments of a proper general staff."

Geibel knotted a fist already gnarled. "If they have harmed my son—"

"Compose yourself, madame. Unless he was hurt during the arrest, I expect the Brazilians know enough to treat him carefully. They have, at last, obtained informed leadership."

Almost, she gaped. "What?"

Again Friedrich smiled. "This fiasco of ours confirms me in a suspicion I have entertained increasingly for some time. They must have come to an understanding of what Eurofac has done, and have done the same thing, to become so effective against us. It is a most interesting riddle, whom they have reconstructed to be their own guiding genius."

He raised his palm and added, through a shocked silence: "Now, if you please, my lady, you can best leave me to think about this undistracted. Unless something extraordinary occurs, I will not give myself the honor of receiving your calls, or anyone's, until—hm—forty-eight hours hence. Good day."

Geibel caught her breath but blanked her image.

Quinet stirred. Friedrich looked his way. That gave an eerie feeling, when what the ghost actually "saw" was a ghost of the man, a modulation in the ongoing computer processes. "No, bide a moment, monsieur," the king said in French. "Since we shall be working closely together again, you and I, we had better make various things clear to each other. I can profit from an explanation more detailed than hitherto of electronic communication procedures, especially those that must be kept secret."

"And I'd like to know what this is all about, sire!" Quinet exclaimed.

"*Hein*? This is your world. I am the alien, the anachronism."

"I'm a computerman, not a politician," Quinet said. "Oh, I follow the news, but these intrigues and maneuverings, they're not my métier. Besides, so much is undercover, and I'm hardly ever briefed on it. What is this about a raid in Brazil?"

Instead of reprimanding him directly for his bluntness, Friedrich replied after an elaborate sigh, "Well, as an employee of the Eurofac alliance, you should know—you do, don't you?— that it seeks to take over the large, lucrative South American economic sphere, which has been dominated by Brazilian interests. In part this is for the sake of its own aggrandizement, in part to forestall a takeover by one of the great commercial powers such as Australia, Nigeria, or the Han. That would bring the nations of Europe a long way further down the road to complete impotence in world affairs. Is that clear?"

Having put the living man in his place, the revenant relented and went on: "You have observed how well the penetration proceeded at first, under my general guidance. But in the past two or three years, you have at least caught hints that our halcyon season is ending. Eurofac has increasingly met with difficulties and outright reversals. For example, recently the Ecuadorians were induced—somehow—to bar the ships of Nordisk Havdyrkning from their territorial waters—a serious blow to your pelagiculture in that part of the world.

"Not only are the Brazilian corporations cooperating more and more effectively, which is a natural reaction to foreign competition, but they have begun to invoke the aid of their own government, and governments elsewhere on their continent. *That* is unheard of.

"The recruitment of a citizen militia to supplement the national police is one recent development, one that it now appears we did not take seriously enough. I see with hindsight that our mistake was due to the effort being marvelously soft-played. Those comic opera dress uniforms, for example, ah, that was sheer brilliance of deception!"

Quinet nodded. "I do know something about the general situation, sire. I could scarcely avoid that." He also knew that sometimes Friedrich loved to hear himself talk. "But a raid? An actual military attack?"

"We have used force, in different guises, when it was indicated," Friedrich said. Through Quinet passed a brief outrage. He had caused and he maintained the existence of this quasi-creature; but only by accident did he ever learn what it really did for his employers. "The *ultima ratio regum*. A major reason why you have played out your economic rivalries so clumsily in this century is that you have not understood they are, in actuality, as political as the dynastic quarrels of my era. Wealth is simply a means toward power.

"Well. Vieyra & Sons is the most important chemosynthetic firm in Brazil, which is to say South America; and the Niterói plant is the keystone of its activities. If these are cut back, Brazil will have to import much of its materials."

Quinet seized the chance to repeat the obvious in his turn. "Not only organics. Everything dependent on nanotechnic reactions. That includes most heavy industry."

Friedrich shrugged. "I leave the technicalities to your natural philosophers. Brazil would be weakened. Indeed, by becoming a principal supplier, Eurofac would have entry to the very heart of its rivals. Attempts to foment labor trouble did not get far, largely because of the nationalism that is being skillfully cultivated there. But the plant was known to be weakly guarded. Light artillery could easily demolish it. The assault was planned so that its results might well have been laid at the door of radicals in the native labor movement.

"*Hélas*, the militia we despised choked it off. What the Brazilians will do next depends on who it is that makes their plans for them. We greatly need to know his identity, Dr. Quinet. Have you any suggestions for finding it out?"

"N-no, sire." The man sat back, rubbed his brow, said slowly, "That network will have no interface whatsoever with yours, of course. Just the same—I must think."

"As must I." Gusto tinged Friedrich's voice, like the far-off cry of a hunter's horn in an autumnal forest four hundred years ago. "Yes, let us postpone your education of me for a day or two. I need peace, quiet, and . . . many history books."

"All scholarly databases will be at your disposal, sire. You know how to access them." That was a rather complicated procedure, when this computer system must remain isolated from all others. Quinet rose from his chair like a dutiful commoner. "Does your majesty wish anything else?"

"Not at once. You may go."

The holotank turned into an emptiness where luminance swirled vague. Friedrich could order a cutoff when he chose.

He could not block a monitor, if that keyboard lay under knowing hands. Curious, Quinet recalled the image and, unbeknownst, watched for a while.

Friedrich had crossed the room to the ghost of a marble-topped table set against Chinese-patterned wallpaper. A flute lay on it. He carried the instrument back to his chair, sat down, and began to play. It was one of his own compositions; Quinet, who had perforce studied his subject exhaustively, recognized that much. The musician's eyes were turned elsewhere. They seemed full of dreams. Friedrich II, king of Prussia, whom his English allies had called Frederick the Great, was thinking.

Otto Geibel knew that wondering where he was would be an exercise in futility. A viewpane showed him a thronged white strand and great green-and-white surf, Copacabana or Ipanema seen from an upper floor of a bayside hotel. That could as easily be relayed as directly presented. Since rousing from narcosis, he had seen only rooms and corridors within a single large building. The few persons he met were surely all Brazilians, small and dark when set against his blond bulk, though their semi-formal clothes, their quietness and reserve, were disturbingly unlike that nationality. They accorded him chill politeness and kept him well aware that somebody armed was always nearby, watching.

João Aveiro entered his world like a sea breeze. The chamber to which Geibel had been brought was cheerful too. Besides that beach scene, it had a holo of a particularly seductive danseuse performing to sensuous drum rhythms, several comfortable loungers, and a small but expensively stocked bar. Aveiro was slender, quick-moving, lavish with smiles, ferocious only in his mustache and the colors of his sports shirt.

"Ah, welcome, Mister Geibel," he said when the wall had closed upon the guards. Undoubtedly they stood vigilant at a survey screen just outside and could re-enter in two seconds at the slightest sign of trouble. Aveiro used English. That had proved to be the language in which he and the prisoner were both reasonably fluent. "How are you? I hope you are well recovered from your bad experience."

The German made himself shake hands. "Your people treated me well enough, under the circumstances," he replied. "Food, sleep, a bath, clean clothes."

"And now what would you like to drink before lunch?"

"Where the hell is the rest of my company?" Geibel rasped. "What are you going to *do* with us?"

"Ah, that is—what shall I say?—*contingente*. Rest assured, we are civilized here. We respond with moderation to what I must say was an unfriendly act."

Geibel bristled. "Moderation? I saw a man killed."

Aveiro's manner bleakened for an instant. "You would have killed a dozen night-shift technicians." He brought back the smile, took Geibel's elbow, guided him gently toward a seat. "I am glad to tell you your follower was in revivable condition and is now recovering under cell restoration therapy. Do relax. If we are opponents, we can still be honorable opponents, and work toward negotiating an end to this unfortunate conflict. What refreshment would you like? Me, I will have a brandy and soda. Our brandy has less of a reputation internationally than it deserves."

Geibel yielded and lowered himself. "Beer, then, please." With an effort: "Brazilian beer is good, too."

"Thank you. We learned from German brewmasters, centuries ago." Aveiro bustled to the bar and occupied himself.

"You know who I am," Geibel said.

Aveiro nodded. "The identification you carried was cleverly made, but we have developed our intelligence files. The family that, in effect, rules over A/G Vereinigten Bioindustrien, and sits high in the councils of the Eurofac syndicate—no matter how they strive to keep their privacy, members of that family are public figures." His dispassionate tone grew lively again. "Once we would have been less . . . snoopy? But, excuse my saying this, Eurofac has forced us to revive old practices, old institutions. Such as an intelligence agency. For have you not been mounting—what the Yankees in their day called covert operations?"

Geibel resisted the lounger's body-conforming embrace and sat straight. "But who are you?"

"We were introduced, if you recall."

"*What* are you, Herr Aveiro?"

"Oh, I suppose you could call me an officer of intelligence."

"Police? Military? Or—uh—"

"Or of the *ad hoc* coordinating committee that our businesses established when the European threat became unmistakable? Does it matter which? Perhaps later it will, and I shall have occasion to tell you. Meanwhile—" Aveiro had prepared the drinks. He brought over a full stein, raised his own glass, and toasted, "*Prosit*."

"*Saúde*," Geibel responded, not to be outdone.

The Brazilian laughed, sipped, perched himself on the edge of a seat confronting the other man's, leaned forward. Beneath the geniality, he shivered and strained the slightest bit. "Shall we talk, then, two professionals together? Afterward I promise you a memorable lunch."

Geibel grimaced and forced wryness: " I am hardly a professional."

"No. Molecular engineer by training, am I right? Yes, I sympathize with you. I strongly suspect you consider yourself an idealist, who wants to further the welfare of his people. Well, pure motives are no substitute for proper training." Aveiro sighed. "Not that I can claim real expertise. We are amateurs. Everywhere in the world, we are amateurs, fumbling at a game that grows more dangerous the longer we play."

"What?" asked Geibel, startled.

The little man had, mercurially, turned quite serious. "We tell ourselves today—we have told ourselves for several generations—true war has become unthinkable. The former great powers are dead or dying or three-fourths asleep. The violent clashes are between backward countries, and poverty, if nothing else, limits them in the harm they can do. The active nations, the new leaders of the world, jostle for economic advantage only. How nice, no? How desirable. What progress beyond the old horrors.

"But this is a very limited planet onto which we are crowded, my friend. The minerals and energy we get from space, the recyclings of nanotechnology, such things are not in infinite supply, nor are they free of cost, nor do they satisfy the wish for . . . elbow room, and self-expression, and ethnic survival, and, *sim*, power."

He drank before finishing: "Whether the corporations be agencies of the state or property of certain groups, of the new aristocrats—that makes no difference. Always the strife grows more and more vicious. Nuclear war is perhaps out of the question; so too, perhaps, are huge armies making whole continents their battlefields; but history knows other kinds of war than these. As witness your attempt on us."

"You are . . . philosophical, . . . senhor," Geibel said from the back of his throat, while fear touched him.

"I am realistic," Aveiro answered. "And I am a Brazilian. Patriotism is no longer obsolete."

He produced his smile. "Well, but we are honest soldiers in our ways, you and I, no? We can talk frankly. I may tell you, my government is willing to forgive your actions—although they do constitute a grave crime, you understand—We are willing to release you and your men, discreetly, in hopes that the good will we gain will help toward improving relations."

For two heartbeats, Geibel's pulse bounded. He looked into the face before him, and the hope sank. "What do you want in exchange?" he whispered. His sweat smelled suddenly sharp.

Aveiro swirled the ice about in his glass while he stared into it. "That, we must work out," he said. "It may take time. We need to learn so much. We are so inept these days, all of us. After generations of nominal peace, the world has forgotten how to wage war intelligently. Our intrigues and outright hostilities are on a primitive, medieval-like level. Yes, histories and treatises on the arts of war lie in our databases; but who is practiced in the *use* of those principles?"

Freezingly, Geibel foreknew what was coming. Yet he must pretend. "You are being, uh, too academic for me again, I fear. What do you want of me?"

Aveiro looked up, caught his captive's gaze, and gripped it. His words fell like stones. "The Yankees developed a remarkable computer technology about ten years ago. You know it well. Everybody does. Electronic reincarnation, no, rebirth. The sensationalism in news and entertainment media. The speeches and sermons. The jokes. The attempts to hire the technique for purposes cheap or perverted or, sometimes, noble. In between, the patient scholarship, piece by piece discovering a little more about the past.

"Let us not do what the Yankees call pussyfoot, Mister Geibel. What one consortium can accomplish, another can repeat. We know that Eurofac has found how to create its own simulacrum. Surely you never believed that could remain secret forever. The hints, the revelations, the bits of accidental information that we jigsaw-puzzle together. The fact that Eurofac's operations had become so sophisticated, so unscrupulous, that we were being driven out of the market on our home continent.

"Yes, you have resurrected an advisor from the past, someone who understands in his bones those arts of combat and cabal that to us today are half-forgotten theory. Doubtless it amuses him to guide you. Such a—an *espíritu* must feel rather detached from we who are still flesh and blood. No? But you can too, Mister Geibel, although we cannot at the moment make you cancel his existence, it would be most helpful to us if we knew who he is. Then we could better plan our tactics.

"Will you please tell me?"

The silence smothered. Into it Geibel croaked, "Do you have somebody too, now?"

"Be that as it may," said Aveiro, "we wish to know the name of your counselor."

Geibel grabbed his stein from the lounger arm,

clutched hard the handle, tossed off a draught. Cold comfort ran down his gullet. "I admit nothing," he declared. "I know nothing."

Aveiro shook himself, as though coming out of a dark river. "Forgive me," he replied almost calmly. "I should have avoided these sociological topics. They make me too emotional. I remember too much that I have witnessed." He sipped, arched his brows above the rim of the glass, chuckled. "After all, the matter is quite simple. You will tell me whatever you know, which I suspect does include that name. You will." He waved his free hand. "Oh, not under torture. Our advisor—I may tell you this—our advisor suggested it, but of course better methods are available today. They seldom do permanent harm. However, they are most unpleasant.

"Therefore, my esteemed opponent, will you answer certain questions? Naturally, there must be verification, as well as further questions, before we can consider bargaining about your release. But today I shall assume you speak truth. Or will you be stubborn and compel me to send you on to the interrogation technicians? That would be regrettable for both of us. I have been anticipating an amicable gourmet lunch with you."

The ghost of Niccolò Machiavelli looked up from the book he was reading when the image of Floriano Coelho appeared in the mirage-room where he sat. "Good day, senhor," he said with his wonted courtliness. "You are punctual." Mild malice flickered: "That is somewhat uncharacteristic of your countrymen."

Coelho laughed. "Computers are Procrustean, your excellency," he replied. "They shape those of us who work with them to fit a single planetwide society and its ways."

Outside the tank, his body settled into a chair. His replica within remained standing. It was, after all, merely an interplay of electrons, photons, and fields. Sufficient was to have a subprogram duplicate movements, especially facial movements, that were significant. Machiavelli understood, and accepted it of his visitors—most of them. The chief computerman could, in fact, have stayed at home and watched a screen there. However, that would have added a link to the network, and one that was vulnerable to tapping by the Europeans. Instead, he came to the laboratory in person whenever he had business with the Florentine.

Machiavelli laid his book aside. "I have said this before, but will repeat myself," he told the Brazilian. "Your superiors showed a perceptiveness that, in retrospect, astonishes me, when they put you in charge of this quasi-resurrection of mine—a man who not only knows that art, but is a classicist. The level of culture that I have observed in this era, among the supposedly educated, is appalling."

"Thank you," Coelho said. "Perhaps science and technology have engaged the world's attention too much during the past three or four centuries. Perhaps we can learn from notables like you."

"That is the purpose, isn't it, as regards war and statecraft?" Machiavelli responded dryly.

Coelho persisted. He had discovered that the great political thinker was not immune to a little flattery and, when in the right mood, would talk fascinatingly for hours about his Renaissance milieu. He had known Lorenzo the Magnificent, Cesare Borgia, Leonardo da Vinci . . . in his lifetime, Columbus sailed, Luther defied Rome, Copernicus followed the planets in their courses. . . . "I hope we can learn half as fast, and adapt ourselves to strangeness half as well, as your excellency did."

Machiavelli shrugged. "Let me not claim more credit than is due me. I was only nominally a Christian, you know. To me, man had reached his highest condition—no doubt the highest of which he will ever be briefly capable—in pagan Rome. It was no fundamental shock to me, *this* me, to awaken after death and hear that the mind is simply a process in the material world, a process that can be replicated after a fashion if one knows enough about it. The rest of the newness has been minor by comparison, albeit interesting."

Staring into the tank, Coelho thought reluctantly how ugly the man was, huge beak of a nose on a head too

small. At least his voice was low and beautifully modulated. Today Machiavelli's simulacrum had electronically
ordered the simulacrum of a red velvet robe and fur
slippers. The room around him was marble-floored beneath a rich carpet; frescos of nymphs and satyrs adorned
it; a window opened on the fields and poplars of Tuscany.
A crystal bowl at the chairside held nuts and sweet-
meats. You could provide a recreated mind with recreated sensations. This one had demanded them as soon
as it learned they were possible.

Still, Machiavelli was a gourmet rather than a gourmand
—for the most part—and his mind was what counted.
"May I ask you something touching yourself?" Coelho
ventured.

Machiavelli grinned. "You may. I will choose whether
to answer."

"Well, ah, I see the title of that book you are reading. Another biography of Federigo the Great."

"Certainly. I cannot know too much about my rival
counterpart, now that we have finally discovered who
he is."

"But why a projected book? We can program—we
can give you all the information you want, directly,
there in your memory as if it had always been, just as
we gave you a command of our modern language."

"I know. For some purposes, the convenience is
undeniable. But men today confuse information with
comprehension. Knowledge should enter at a natural
pace, never outstripping reflection upon it. Also—"
Machiavelli reached to stroke the cover—"I find the act
of reading, of holding a book and turning its pages, a
pleasure in itself. Books, the bearers of thoughts, the
heritage of the mighty dead, those were my last friends
during the years of rustication. Oh, and letters; but you
have not revived my dear Vettori to correspond with
me. Old friends are best."

His tone had been almost impersonal, free of self-
pity, but Coelho got a sudden sense of loneliness without bounds or end. Even though Machiavelli had been
spiritually solitary through his life—Best to change the
subject. Besides, Coelho had his instructions. "You must

understand Federigo quite well by now, as intensely as you have studied him." It helped that that study didn't have to take place in real time; you could accelerate the program when it wasn't talking with flesh and blood. Furthermore, it didn't sleep. It did remain human enough to require occasional diversions.

"A formidable opponent. Like Alexander the Great, he inherited a military machine built by his father, but, also like Alexander, he wielded it audaciously and inspiredly, he raised his Prussia from a backwater to the first rank of the European powers." Machiavelli snickered. "A delicious jest, that he, precisely he, should be the one against whom your superiors decided to pit me. Do you think they knew?"

"What do you mean, your excellency?"

"Why, as a young man this Federigo wrote a treatise explicitly meant to refute me, the *Anti-Machiavel*. In it he said a prince is no more than the first servant of the people, and the state exists to further their well-being, not for its own sake. Whereupon, once he became king, he followed my teachings word for word."

Coelho frowned. He had been doing some reading himself. "Didn't he reform the laws, better the lot of the poor, carry out large public works?"

Machiavelli's grin stretched wider. "Just as I counsel in *Il Principe*, the *Discorsi*, and elsewhere. Beneficence is sound policy when it does not seriously interfere with the necessities of power. I presume you are aware that, while he stripped the nobles of their own last meaningful powers, he did not free the serfs. He acquired Silesia by force of arms and partook in the dismemberment of Poland. Not that I condemn him, you understand. He laid the foundations of the German state that Bismarck would build. In person he was a man of refined tastes and a composer of some small talent. I admit it was a mistake importing Voltaire to his court, but a minor one. On the whole, yes, I rather wish he had been a fifteenth-century Italian." The ugly countenance turned grave, the sharp gaze drifted afar. "Then he could well have become the prince for whom I pleaded, he who would unite poor Italy against the foreigners that made booty of her—" He threw back his head and laughed. "Ah, well, since in fact he was an eighteenth-century German, I must content myself with welcoming so worthy a foe."

Coelho stirred. "That's what I'm here about, as your excellency has doubtless guessed," he said. "To ask if you have any new plans."

"Why does not Senhor Aveiro or one of the other councillors address me in person?"

"They wish to avoid any appearance of . . . unduly pressing you. This is such a basic revelation, Federigo's identity. And I am the person most familiar to you."

Machiavelli nodded. "They're afraid of my getting balky, are they?"

"Your suggestions to date have proven invaluable. We need more."

"You already have them. Now that Eurofac knows your militia is a force to reckon with, strengthen it quickly. Bring it entirely out into the eyes of the world. Make it something every young Brazilian dreams of joining. Fan the national spirit to a brighter and hotter flame. Aid the Chileans and Peruvians to do likewise— but not to the same extent as yourselves, for you don't want those peoples to start resenting your predominance. Discourage the emotion among the Argentines; they are your natural rivals. Bind the small countries that border yours more closely to you as client states, and through them work to counteract the Europeans in Argentina and keep that nation disunited. In short, Senhor Coelho, my word to your superiors is that they pay closer attention to the large corpus of recommendations I have printed out for them. Policies cannot be executed overnight. What I have just mentioned is the work of another decade, at least."

"But surely—the information about Federigo suggests something more?"

"Indeed it does. First and foremost, I would like to meet with him, often."

Coelho gaped. "What? Impossible!"

Machiavelli lifted his brows. "Really? When I see

your image here in this chamber of mine? Incidentally, floating about ten centimeters off the floor."

"That is . . . we've taken care to keep the system that maintains you entirely isolated. . . . Oh, the connection could be made, if the Europeans agreed. But neither side will."

"Why not?"

"Well, if nothing else, at present they don't know about you. That's an advantage we can't afford to forego. And both sides would fear, oh, sabotage—ah—Imagine poison slyly given you. No, your excellency, it's out of the question. Has anything else occurred to you?"

Machiavelli grimaced, spread his hands in an Italianate gesture, then said, quite businesslike: "Minor ideas. And you do need something to report, my friend, lest you be reprimanded for lack of diligence. No? Well, I have explained, and you are starting to obtain, the benefits of a revived national spirit and a government that takes an active role in all affairs."

"There are those who wonder about that," Coelho muttered. "The camel's nose in the tent—" Aloud: "Please continue."

"Now nationalism has two faces," said Machiavelli in the manner of a lecturer. "There is the positive side, patriotism, love of country, that you have been cultivating. And there is the negative side, contempt or hatred for foreigners. You Brazilians have been too tolerant, too cosmopolitan. Therefore Eurofac could easily penetrate your marts and undermine your state. It would be a body blow to the Eurofac oligopolies if Brazilians ceased buying their wares and services. But their prices equal or undercut yours. Therefore you need different motives for Brazilians to shun them. If it became unfashionable to wear European clothes, travel in European vehicles, employ European machinery and craftsmen—Do you see? This will happen in the course of time as Europeans themselves become loathed."

"But they don't loathe us," Coelho protested.

"No, evidently not. Eurofac is merely a . . . a Hansa, to borrow the medieval German word. Since you have nothing comparable, you must find something else to oppose it. You must rouse the will of South Americans generally against it. That cannot be done simply by appeals to reason, to ultimate self-interst, or to desire for autonomy. Those are helpful, but you need to mobilize the base instincts as well, fear and hatred and contempt. They are stronger anyway."

"What—how—"

"Oh, this likewise will be the work of years," Machiavelli admitted. "From what I have observed and read, Brazilians in particular are by nature easy-going and amiable. Never fear, though, they too bear the beast within them. They will learn. As a modest beginning, you can start japes about Europeans and slanders against them circulating. I have devised a few."

They were filthy. They were funny. Coelho found himself laughing while he winced.

"People will soon be inventing their own," Machiavelli finished. "It will seem a harmless amusement, piquantly naughty but innocuous. Which it is, by itself. However, it breaks the ground for allegations and ideas more serious. I am reminded of— "

And he was off on reminiscences of Pope Alexander VI, the Pope's son Cesare Borgia, and the rest of that family. Coelho listened, frequently appalled, always enthralled. Not that he heard anything he couldn't have accessed from the databases. The real Machiavelli might well have known the truth about any number of historical mysteries. This Machiavelli knew only what had been put into his program.

Or . . . was that altogether the case? These stories were so detailed, so vivid, with never a hesitation or equivocation. Surely no chronicle had recorded that Lucrezia wore a gown of blue silk and a single rosy pearl at her throat when she came to that infamous banquet where—Was the electronic mind consciously adding color? Did it possess an unconscious that filled in gaps which would be agonizing to recognize? Or was something more mysterious yet at work? Coelho suppressed the questions in himself. Perhaps years hence he would dare confront them.

The time ended. "I must go, your excellency."

"Ah, yes. This has been pleasant. Before you leave, I wish to make a small request."

"Of course. Whatever we can do for you, in whose debt we are."

"At your convenience," said Machiavelli blandly, "will you program for me a somewhat higher class of women? I do not ask for Helen of Troy—I suppose a myth would be too difficult—nor Cleopatra or Eleanor of Aquitaine—not yet, at any rate. But, while the sluts you have provided are lusty, their conversation is tedious."

He could summon them as he could his robe or his book. The programs had been easy enough to develop, since historical accuracy was no concern. Too easy, perhaps; the ghost-girls who helped ghost-Machiavelli set aside intellection for a while might be noticeably less human than he was. Maybe that was why he had never requested the companionship of his wife, though the biographies said they got along reasonably well despite his infidelities, or any friends from his earthly life. Maybe he dreaded what he would get.

Coelho shuddered a trifle. "I am sure we can oblige your excellency. It may take a little time." Though he had grown perversely fond of this pseudo-person, today he was glad to complete his farewell and blank out the sardonic face.

The garden behind Sanssouci dreamed beneath a summer sky. Birdsong, a whimsical pergola, a fountain gleaming and plashing, set off the formality of graveled paths, clipped hedgerows, disciplined flowerbeds, trees in precise topiaries. No gardeners were in sight; none would ever be needed. Friedrich strolled alone through his phantasm.

Abruptly the apparition of Birgitte Geibel burst into it. Her black gown enveloped a small marble Cupid like a candle snuffer. She didn't notice. Friedrich stopped, raised his cocked hat, swept her a bow. "Good day, my lady," he said.

She gave him a stiff look. "Is your majesty prepared for the talk he suggested, or shall I return at a more convenient moment?"

"No, no, let us by all means go straight to work."
Friedrich drew a gold watch from his waistcoat. "Ah,
yes, this is the hour agreed upon with your amanuensis.
Pardon me, I forgot. When one is mostly secluded, one
tends to lose track of time."

She softened a bit. "You do remember that we can
provide you with company of your choice, do you not?"

Friedrich nodded. "Thank you kindly. To date I have
been content. Getting to know what astounding, stu-
pendous, and—hm—ludicrous things have happened
throughout the world since 1786; toying with what control is mine over this miniature universe I inhabit:
those keep me sufficiently occupied. And, to be sure,
our contest with the Brazilians."

She made a mouth. "I wonder if it doesn't seem
trivial and despicable to you, who were a king and
fought real wars."

"On the contrary. I acquired a distaste for bloodshed
early." She remembered how he, eighteen years old,
had been compelled by his father to witness the
beheading of his closest friend. "On fields such as Torgau
I was later confirmed in this. While granting that casu-
alties may be an unfortunate necessity, I take pride in
the fact that my last war was waged with such skill that
no life was lost on either side." He smiled. "No matter
if they called it the Potato War. As for the present
contest, why, I see it as the first stirring of events that
may prove more fateful than any before in history."

"They touch some of us closely." She drew her jaws
together, ashamed to have let him glimpse her pain.

His voice gentled. "Not yet do you have any word of
your son?"

"No. We have heard and found out nothing about
him. If ever we do, I will inform you promptly."

"War of nerves. Well, perhaps two can play at that
game." Tactful, he looked away from her and fondled a
rose, his fingers deftly skirting the thorns which could
not wound him. "That is our subject today, I believe. As
per my desire, I was informed when the undertaking I
had proposed had prospered, although no details were

supplied me. I thereupon called for this conference
with you. What can you tell me?"

She had mastered herself. "Do you refer to identifying the chief computerman of the Brazilian project?"

"What else? Once I felt sure that they have recreated
someone to match me, it followed that that enterprise
must have a chief, just as you have Quinet for me."

"Well, it seems highly probable. Our intelligence
agents got busy and soon picked up a trail. The signs
point almost unambiguously to an individual in Rio de
Janeiro. What he does is kept a tight secret, of course;
but it is clear that he has been engaged upon something
of the first importance. This was originally on behalf of
several major firms. Recently the government became
involved. His professional record indicates that he would
be their best person for such a task."

"Excellent. We may consider the case proven."

"Our agents could not have learned what they did, as
fast as they did, were the Brazilians not incredibly lax
about security."

" 'Incredibly' is the wrong word, madame. Techniques
of espionage and defense against it are among those that
have rusted away during the long peace. We will see
them revived soon enough. I daresay my adversary is
busying himself with that, together with everything
else required." Friedrich met Geibel's eyes. "You realize, my lady, that from the prisoners they took at Niterói,
the Brazilians will have learned who I am. I trust the
information was obtained . . . not inhumanely."

"And we fight blind unless we can discover who *he*
is." It was as if a sword spoke.

Friedrich nodded. "Correct. Please tell me about this
artificer."

"His name is Floriano Coelho. He is fifty years of
age, and actually a physicist who did outstanding work
in theoretical cosmodynamics before the French and
North American pioneering of electronic reconstruc-
tions caught his interest. We have pictures." Her hands
moved, responsive to flesh-and-blood hands that touched
a keyboard. A life-size hologram appeared on the path.
It was of a thin man, taller than average in his country,

somewhat carelessly dressed. Beneath a bald pate, the face was plain and gentle. Friedrich peered. Geibel provided a succession of views.

"We know his routine," she said. "It isn't absolute—the unexpected is forever happening, not true?—but as nearly as feasible, he is a creature of habit. Temperate habit; devoted family man; a little shy and withdrawn, though affable among friends; no obvious vices or weaknesses, unless one counts a tendency to lose himself in his interests, his books, and thereby forget things like social obligations."

"Ah?" Friedrich stroked his chin. "What interests?"

"Well, science in general. And classical history and literature. He is absolutely enamored of the ancient world, especially the Greeks in their days of glory. He has published a few scholarly papers on their poets. Also—let me think—yes, he is a bibliophile."

"Possible clues," Friedrich murmured thoughtfully. "It would be best for the Brazilians if their computer chief had something in common with the man they called up from the past."

She couldn't resist: "Indeed? What has your majesty in common with Jules Quinet?"

"Very little," Friedrich admitted. "In fact, I sense he dislikes me. Still, we manage. He is ambitious in his career, and I am the most important thing that has happened in it."

"He could be replaced."

"No need. And it would be unwise to shake the organization at just this critical juncture." Friedrich's tone sharpened and quickened. "We will strike through Coelho, swiftly, before the opportunity passes. Later, with his cooperation—"

"I doubt we can obtain it," Geibel interrupted. The king scowled. "Ach, I beg your majesty's pardon. But if I may continue, our evaluation of Coelho is that he shares the patriotism that is rising in Brazil. Furthermore, he bears the classical ideal of loyalty—Thermopylae, was that the name of the place? Oh, yes, we can shock-drug information out of him. Knowing that, he may give it voluntarily, to avoid worse than a session under a truth identifier helmet. But beyond that he will not go, unless as a result of treatment so extreme as to leave him useless to anyone."

"I am less dogmatic in my predictions," Friedrich said. "My observation has been that every man is malleable at some point. If we can get Coelho's help in making direct connection between myself and my opponent, I can take that stranger's measure to a degree otherwise unobtainable."

Geibel had barely restrained herself from another interruption. "No!" she cried. "Impossible!" She calmed. "Forgive us, your majesty, but we can never permit that. The danger is too great."

"Oh?" asked Friedrich mildly. "What danger, pray tell?"

"Your majesty would first have to master computer technology to understand. But think of—for a single example—a subtle distortion. Despite all precautions, given access to this network, the Brazilians might be clever enough to introduce what we call a worm into our program. *Your* program, my lord. It could do ghastly things to you."

Friedrich's features hardened. "And they fear we might do the like to their man. I see. Neither party dares let us meet." Then his lips quirked. "The irony should delight Coelho. It is worthy of Euripides . . . or Aristophanes." He shrugged. "Well, once we have him, we will see what we can do with him."

"Exchange him for Otto—for all our men, at least," broke from her.

"In due course, yes, I expect we shall." Friedrich stared off across the garden. Randomizing, the environmental subprogram generated a flight of bees, their buzz, a zephyr that bore an odor of lilies. Geibel started to speak. Friedrich gestured for silence.

After a time that crept, he turned back to her. "I have hopes going beyond this," he said slowly. "I will not speak of them at once, for they are still well-nigh formless and may come to naught. Much will depend on what we learn in the next few days. But . . . the situation has certain symmetries. What I contemplate doing to the Brazilians, they might conceivably do to us."

She drew breath. "And so?"

"What vulnerabilities has Jules Quinet?"

"What? I mean—why—" Geibel recovered from startlement. "We investigated him before inviting him to join us, of course; and we have kept an eye on him since. There is nothing untoward. He too is a steady family man—the same mistress for fifteen years, and she quite good friends with his wife. He drinks and gambles, but never to excess. His political party is the National Conservative. Do you fear he could be bribed or blackmailed? I sincerely disbelieve it. But we will increase surveillance if you want."

"No. That would annoy him if he found out, and make no difference. It would merely be another factor in the calculations of whoever intended to use him."

"Can he be used?" Geibel argued, with an edge of irritation.

Friedrich sighed. "The human being does not exist who can neither be corrupted nor coerced. If you believe otherwise—ach, my dear lady, you do not know this damned race."

Floriano Coelho enjoyed walking. He often took a public conveyance to the Botanical Gardens and logged off kilometers through that green luxuriance, or rambled for hours along city streets. Talk of a bodyguard he had dismissed with scorn. "Do you expect gangsters to seize my underpaid old carcass for ransom? As well expect dinosaurs."

Suddenly security chief João Aveiro insisted. To outraged protests he replied merely that there had been an incident of late which was too troubling in its implications to be publicized. Thereafter, one or another implacably polite young man was always in the rear when the scientist went out afoot.

Accordingly, Coelho was twice happy to see the face of the bookseller Pedro da Silva in his eidophone; for what he heard was: "Floriano, I have just received a very special item. I thought of you at once. It is a first

edition of Edith Hamilton's *Three Greek Plays*—you
know them, the definitive English versions—in remarkable condition. You would think the volume nineteenth
rather than twentieth century, as well preserved as it
is. And autographed by her!"

Coelho's heart bounded. Those were not mere ren-
derings into a different language, they threw light on
the originals. How often he had screened them, "Aga-
memnon," "Prometheus Bound," "The Trojan Women,"
sometimes having the computer interlineate the Hellenic
texts. Yet, like Machiavelli, he recognized no real substitute for the actual, physical, well-made book. This
would be a pleasing thing to show the old fellow. . . .
"What price?" he asked.

"We will discuss that over coffee in the shop, if you
can come down at once. You see, another collector has
long been eager, and he is a person I would not lightly
frustrate. For you, my friend, I am willing, but I cannot
in good conscience make him wait unduly."

Collectors were like that. Coelho glanced at the
viewpane. Rain poured across the building. He could
not take such a book home through it, no matter how
well wrapped. Besides, the distance was considerable
and eventide closing in. "Fill the coffeepot!" Coelho
laughed, and blanked off. To his wife: "I must go for
perhaps two hours. Don't fret about dinner. Those smells
alone will draw me home in time."

He punched for an aerocab, flung on a cape, kissed
the woman, rumpled the hair of their youngest child,
and went out to the levitor. As it bore him roofward
from his apartment, he thought with a certain glee of
the detective lurking down in the street. Demand was
heavy in this weather and he must wait several minutes
in the bubble until a cab landed. He got in and gave
the address. The pilot told him what the fare would be.
"That's all right," he said. It lifted the vehicle. Ground
transportation was congested these days, too slow. Coelho
admired the view through the sides, though lights,
towers, mountains, and bay were blurred by the
downpour.

On a narrow street in the old quarter he transferred

credit and crossed to the shop. Rain sluiced hot and heavy, out of the sky and across the black-and-white mosaic sidewalk. A manual door in a tile-roofed building of faded pastel hue gave entrance to shelves and stacks, dusk and dust, quietness and archival smells.

So quiet, so dim. He looked to and fro. "Pedro?" he called uncertainly.

A man strange to him appeared from between two stacks. He smiled. "Senhor da Silva is indisposed, Senhor Professor," he said. The bass rumbled from a barrel chest. "He will awaken unharmed presently. Meanwhile, if you please—"

A dart pistol came forth. Coelho choked on a scream. Through him flashed the admission that Aveiro had been right and he, the technologist, who knew how easy it was to synthesize an image and a voice and patch into a communication line, he had been the dupe. The pistol hissed. The dart stung. Coelho whirled into night.

"In itself," opined Aveiro, "this is less than catastrophic. The Europeans will learn who you are, and certain details of what you have been doing for us. However, I always took care to separate his, ah, maintenance functions from yours as our strategic advisor. And I trust you refrained from telling him more than was necessary for his work."

"We knew a little about confidentiality in my time," replied Machiavelli tartly. He sat still for a moment. Today it had been his whim to surround himself with a room in the Palazzo Riccardi. Sunlight glowed through stained glass to throw pieces of rainbow over the vividness of frescos showing the Medici in their days of splendor. Yet no form save his stirred. Aveiro recalled Coelho remarking that Machiavelli had never asked for a Florentine street or marketplace. Would the tumult recall to him too keenly that the Renaissance was one with Caesar and Vergil, or did he expect the replication would be too grotesquely false?

"You are quite sure Coelho was seized and transported to Europe?" he asked.

"Absolutely," Aveiro said. "After his wife called us,

we found the bookseller drugged. Roused, he told us how three men came in together, posing as customers till they were alone with him, then shot him. Chemosensors—instruments more sensitive than a hound's nose have identified traces of Coelho himself. Computer records show that a hired carriage brought him from his tenement to the shop. What more do you want?"

"Nothing. I simply wished to understand better the methods of today's *custodi*." Machiavelli pondered. "Given the speed of human flight, we must take for granted that by tomorrow Eurofac will know of me. Well, we could not have kept the secret forever. This becomes an element in our reckoning."

Aveiro nodded. "I am chagrined, but not disgraced. Mainly, I want to consult with you about who should replace him. I can give you the profiles of several possible persons."

Machiavelli shook his head. "Oh, no, senhor. I want my Coelho back."

"*Ay?* Well—familiarity, I suppose—but how?"

"Prisoner exchange is as old as war."

"You mean the Geibel gang, no doubt. Shall we let those bandits go scot-free?"

"Come, now. You have pumped them dry. What further use are they to you? As hostages—but your foes hold a prisoner of considerably greater value. If we can accomplish a straight trade, them for him, we have much the better of the bargain." Machiavelli hunched forward. "I daresay the Europeans intend to open negotiations with you before long. Better that we seize the initiative and send them the first message. You will know whom to call. Thus we keep them off balance, you see."

"Well—well—" Aveiro leaned back in the chair behind the desk. "You're probably right, ah, your excellency. Have you any suggestions more specific about how to proceed?"

"In diplomatic dealings, one feels one's way forward," Machiavelli said. "It is a matter of intuition, of . . . touch, . . . acquired by experience. In life I often served as a diplomat. I will negotiate for us."

Aveiro's feet hit the floor with a thump. "What?" he yelled. "No! We cannot—"

"I know your fear of direct intercourse." Machiavelli sounded exasperatedly patient, like a schoolmaster with a dull pupil. "It strikes me as vastly overblown, but I recognize adamancy when I meet it. Very well. Computer connections are not necessary. You see me by light and hear me by sounds from this chamber. As I understand it, I, the essential I, am not even in the chamber, but elsewhere. Now what is hazardous about admitting the light and the sound into one of your far-speaking instruments, whence they travel by etheric subtlety across the sea to Europe? In like manner, my honored opponent, King Federigo, can speak to us."

Aveiro clenched his fists and swallowed. "Well, you see—"

"You people are not stupid," Machiavelli said coldly. "You must have thought of this possibility at the outset. As long as my identity could be secret, communication by me with the outside world was undesirable. Agreed. That has changed. Believe me, I will gain more from conversing with Federigo, sounding him out, than the opposition can gain from me."

"Policy—"

Machiavelli sighed. "If you will pardon a digression, senhor, someday I should like to meet a simulacrum of the Englishman Samuel Johnson. In my reading I have come upon many of his maxims. Among them, 'Patriotism is the last refuge of a scoundrel.' I presume he refers to the abuse of this virtue, as any virtue may be turned to bad ends. Allow me, then, to observe that policy is the last refuge of a fool." Sternly: "Now I do not accuse you yourself, Senhor Aveiro, of foolishness. Oh, no. You would not care for me to reach beyond these crystal walls. I might begin to feel a little too independent. I might act on my own, without first begging for the approval of your masters." With disdain: "Set your terrors at rest. Can you and your wretched little spies—and your European counterpart and his toadies—can they not watch, listen, observe? Can you not shut off any conversation the instant it looks like going in suspect directions?"

Aveiro flushed. "You speak rather freely, your excellency."

Machiavelli laughed. "How do you propose to punish me? By obliteration? I fear it no more than a flame fears the wind. Remember, I have already been there."

His voice mildened: "But come, we are in danger of falling out, we allies. How regrettable. Our shared interests are numerous. All I do today is advance a proposal which, I realize, your superiors must agree to. Let me describe its advantages, and thereafter, of your kindness, do you bring it before those lords and persuade them. For we must act quickly, before the tide turns against us."

For the first time since his refashioning, Friedrich showed genuine excitement. "Machiavelli!" he breathed. He glanced up toward whatever heaven he had made for himself. "Lord God, this almost makes me believe you must exist, to play so rare a jest." Sobriety reclaimed him. "No, it was a rather logical choice, even though at the time they didn't know who I am. And many Brazilians are of Italian descent, not so?"

"Machiavelli," muttered Quinet. He turned off the eidophone, through which Adam Koszycki, chief of intelligence operations, had just transmitted the information revealed by Coelho. "I ought to know who that is—was—but I can't quite remember."

"Well, he lived long ago, in the late fifteenth and early sixteenth centuries," Friedrich explained absently. "Nevertheless, in a way he was the first modern man. He served Florence—it was a more or less sovereign city-state then, like several others in Italy—he served in its government and as a diplomat to various powers. A turn of political fortune caused him to be arrested, tortured, finally released to idleness on a small country estate he owned. There for many years he occupied his time with reading and writing. Eventually he was recalled to service, but only in minor capacities. His importance lies in those writings."

"Thank you, sire," Quinet said. "It comes back to me now, a little. A terrible cynic, was he not?"

"He attempted a scientific study of war, politics, all statecraft, not as the idealists said they should be conducted, but as he thought they actually were." Friedrich laughed, a small hard bark. "Ever since, those in power over the nations have sought to brand him a liar. I did myself, in my youth."

"Then I should think your majesty is unhappy at knowing that devil is back in the world." Quinet tried to keep his voice free of gloating. Some discomfiture might knock a little arrogance out of this Prussian.

"Oh, he was never an evil man," Friedrich replied. "Indeed, I would love to meet him. A man of parts, as most were in his day. He also produced purely literary works. For example, his play *Mandragola* is one of the most wickedly funny—"

The priority signal cut him off. Quinet hastened to activate the eidophone. Birgitte Geibel's gaunt image appeared. Quinet had never seen her as grim as now; and that, he thought, was saying considerable.

"Your majesty," she clipped, "we have received a call from Brazil. At the highest level, their president and a spokesman for all the major corporations together."

"This soon?" wondered Friedrich. "Heads of state and of large organizations are not given to—Ah, ha! Machiavelli is behind it. Who else? He will not grant us time to lay plans."

"He certainly will not. Listen. The message is—Please hear me, your majesty. The message is that they are prepared to exchange prisoners, returning my son and his men if we return Professor Coelho."

"That scarcely requires their chieftains to say. It is a very reasonable offer. I assume none of the captives has suffered improperly harsh treatment. You should accept."

"It is not that simple. Conditions must be arranged. The Brazilians will only let those arrangements be made by—yourself and that Machiavelli. And at once, within this hour."

Quinet whistled. Friedrich's surprise was fleeting. He grinned, rubbed his hands, and exclaimed, "Wonderful! He is more a man after my own heart than I dreamed. Why do you wait, madame? Call them back. Agree."

"The danger—"

"We need not connect any circuits," Quinet interrupted. Here was his chance to show decisiveness, he, the technologist. "We can hook eidophones to the tanks."

"But what plot is he hatching, the Machiavelli?" Geibel grated. "You said it yourself, King Friedrich, we are being rushed."

The royal answer was glacial: "Do you suppose he will hoodwink me? That is an insult, Frau Geibel. It borders on *lèse majesté*. You will apologize and proceed to carry out my orders."

She bridled. "*Your* orders? You—"

Friedrich's hand chopped like a headsman's ax. "Silence. Do you want my help or do you not? If not, abolish me; and may Herr Machiavelli have mercy on the lot of you."

She bit her lip, inhaled raggedly, forced forth: "I beg your majesty's pardon. I will recommend agreement to the governing council."

"They will follow the recommendation. Promptly." Friedrich pulled out his watch. "I expect to commence my conversation less than one hour from this minute. Dismissed."

Geibel glared but vanished. Friedrich turned to Quinet. "You will assist me in rapid acquisition of as much knowledge of Machiavelli, his life and milieu, as time allows," he commanded. Outwardly he was self-collected, save that his face had gone pale and his nostrils quivered.

In a clean dress uniform, the king sat on his throne against a background of his audience chamber in Berlin. Machiavelli had elected Roman republican simplicity, wearing a robe and standing in the book-lined study of the farm house at Albergaccio. Silence thrummed while they considered each other's full-length images.

Machiavelli bowed. "Your majesty honors me," he said.

Friedrich gave back the same Mona Lisa smile and lifted a hand. "The honor is equally mine, monsieur," he responded.

They spoke French. That did not surprise Quinet—the language of civilization, after all—but he had expected to have trouble understanding a fifteenth-century Italian. However, Machiavelli had acquired modern Parisian, and it was Friedrich's accent that was quaint.

"I have been most interested, learning about your majesty's distinguished career," Machiavelli said.

"Monsieur's fame has deservedly endured through the ages," Friedrich answered. "Ah, I trust you have not found a little book of mine offensive? I was young when I wrote it."

"History attests that your majesty grew in wisdom with the years."

"There are certain philosophical points which I would still like to debate with you."

"I should be honored and delighted, sire. Surely I would learn far more than I could hope to impart."

Quinet wondered how long the mutual admiration society would continue in session. Friedrich ended it. His tone roughened: "Unfortunately, today we have obligations, business to conclude."

"True." Machiavelli sighed. "It is as well that the matter is elementary. We cannot carry on any serious talk, let alone handle problems of statecraft, when scores of persons on both sides of the ocean hang on our every word." Which they did, which they did, Quinet thought. Officially he was among them on the off chance that he would notice something that could prove useful. In reality, he had been allowed to watch because one more observer made no difference.

"We could have let underlings conduct these trivial negotiations," Machiavelli went on, "but the opportunity to converse with your majesty was irresistible."

"If you had not arranged this, monsieur, I would have done it," Friedrich said. "Let us get to the point." He glowered right and left. "I dislike eavesdroppers."

"Like myself, sire. *Hélas,* it seems we are permanently saddled with them. Not that I malign my gracious hosts. I hope they will . . . permit us future talks at more leisure."

"Permit—us?" Friedrich snarled. Beneath Machiavelli's cool observation, he eased, smiled sourly, and said, "Well, two poor spooks have small control over their destinies, *hein?*"

"Ironic, sire, when we are supposed to help our hosts achieve their own chosen ends. I both relish and regret the apparently ineluctable conflict in which you and I find ourselves."

"Actually, I do not believe in destiny. One makes one's own."

"In my opinion, as I have written, fortune is about half of what determines man's fate. His free will, his efforts and intelligence, have equal force."

With a slight chill, Quinet wondered what was going on. Smooth courtliness; but those were two strong and supple minds, nurtured throughout life on intrigue. Could they understand each other better than they pretended? Intonation; body language; implied meanings; inferences made from what was left unsaid—

He came out of his reverie to find the ghosts crisply discussing prisoner exchange. It took just minutes. Any competent officer could have made the plan they arrived at, a rendezvous on Ascension Island, telemonitored by armed aircraft at a distance.

"So be it," Machiavelli concluded. "Allow me, your majesty, to bid you farewell for the nonce with my humble expression of the highest esteem and of my hopes for the honor of your presence again in future."

"We shall see to that," Friedrich promised. "To you, monsieur, a very good day and our royal regards."

The screens blanked simultaneously. Friedrich sat like a statue on his throne.

Geibel's image appeared. "I trust your majesty is satisfied," she snapped.

"As I trust you are," the king said. "You shall have your son back tomorrow."

She bent her neck, a jerky gesture. "For that I am grateful, of course. But we must know, what have you discovered? What treachery do the Brazilians intend?"

"Why, you followed the discussion. You saw and heard everything I did. A few compliments and then the business on hand. Under the circumstances, what else did you expect?"

"Nothing, I suppose."

"I would be glad of further meetings at greater length with Monsieur Machiavelli."

She pinched her mouth together before telling him, "That will be . . . difficult, your majesty. He *is* our adversary."

"Well," said Friedrich, "I am weary. Do not tell me I lack a body to grow tired. The mind, too, knows exhaustion. Kindly leave me to myself until your men are home again. Good day, madame."

"As your majesty wishes." She flicked off.

Quinet got out of his chair. "And I, sire?" he asked.

"No. You wait," the king replied. "I have something to tell you in strict confidence. First make sure we are truly alone."

Quinet's heart bumped. "This room is electronically screened. I need only run the alarm program to make sure that no one is monitoring you."

Having finished, he placed himself before the tank, braced his legs as if about to lift a weight, and said, "What do you want, sire?"

Friedrich's gaze drilled him. "I want you to understand something." Once more his tone rang like steel and ice. "I want you to know it in your marrow. You are mine. I am not your subservient creation. You are my serf, my slave."

Quinet caught an indignant breath. "You protest, do you?" Friedrich pursued. "Think. They need me, your masters. They need me desperately, with Machiavelli's mind arrayed against them. Whatever I want from them, within the limits of their policy and ambition, they will give me, immediately and without question. I can have you discharged from your position here, Quinet. I can have you professionally destroyed. I can have you hounded to your ruin. I can have you assassinated. Is that clear?"

Red fury cried, "We should have brought back Napoléon!"

Friedrich laughed. "No. I have investigated his life. He did not know when to stop." His voice softened. "But listen, Quinet. I do not, in truth, threaten you. You have given me no cause to wish you ill. Rather, you stand to oblige me, to gain my favor. And I have ever rewarded faithful service well. What is your wish? Riches? To become the head of the world's greatest institution of your art? It can be arranged. Let us talk a while about what you would like, in return for rendering your fealty to me."

"Welcome back," said Machiavelli.

"Thank you, your excellency." With pleasure, Coelho sank into his accustomed chair at the familiar desk and looked across it to the image in the holotank.

"I trust you are well?"

"Oh, yes. The Europeans were not cruel. And after I came home yesterday, I got a good night's rest." Coelho flinched before he could add, "I did receive a tongue-lashing from Senhor Aveiro."

"Ah, well, I have experienced rather worse than that, and will protect you from it. Already I have insisted you be continued in this office, with full rank, pay, preroga-tives, and perquisites."

"Your excellency is most kind."

Machiavelli chuckled. "My excellency is most watch-ful of his own interests. We enjoy a good relationship, we two. You are intelligent, likable company." Cross-legged in an armchair larger than was usual in his era, he bridged his fingers. "At the same time, you are—no offense intended—not overly complex. I flatter myself that I understand you well. That is soothing."

Coelho smiled. "It spares you surprises."

"But does not spare you, my friend. I believe that this ghost of me is perhaps just a trifle more ramified, more aware and nimble, than they who assembled it quite imagine. This is in spite of their very hope that it would devise the unexpected, would spring surprises on living souls."

A tingle went along Coelho's spine. "What are you driving at?" he whispered.

"Nothing but benevolence," said Machiavelli unctuously. "In my fondness for you, I wish to compensate you for the mishandling you endured on my account and, yes, for the humiliation to which you tell me you were unrighteously subjected upon your return here. Ah, we are safe from spies, are we not?"

Coelho swallowed. "Let me check." After some minutes of work, he bobbed his head up and down and crouched back in his chair to wait.

"As long as your lords have need of me—which will be at least as long as King Federigo is available to their foes—they must keep me happy," Machiavelli said. "They may feel themselves forced to deny certain wishes of mine, such as the freedom to meet privately and unhindered with my distinguished opponent. But under those same circumstances, they will feel it necessary to grant any lesser requests, even ones whose execution may prove costly. Now, although in life my wants were modest and today I am a shade, it would greatly please me to make a true friend happy."

"What . . . do you have in mind?"

Machiavelli smiled, glanced sideways, and purred, "Oh, possibilities have occurred to me. For example, a recreation of some great master of the arts would be a gift to all mankind."

"It has been done—"

"I know. But seldom, because it is costly. Still, your merchant lords have abundant wealth, and me to thank that it is no longer being stripped from them. Suppose I asked them for, say, Euripides?"

Coelho leaped to his feet, sank back down, sat with pulse athunder. "No, impossible, we know too little about him."

"We could scarcely reconstruct the mind of Euripides in every respect," Machiavelli conceded. "Yet take inherent genius; let it form within the context of the Grecian golden age; use the extant works to delineate such a mind, such a spirit, as *would* have written precisely those dramas. Don't you suppose that that spirit would be able to write—not the lost plays exactly as they were, but something very close to them and equally noble?"

He wagged his forefinger. "Euripides is merely a suggestion of mine," he continued. "You may have a better idea. Do think about this and inform me at your convenience. For I visualize you, my dear Coelho, as being at the head of the undertaking."

The living man stared before him, dazed with exaltation. Through the choir in his blood he heard: "First I have a small favor to ask of you—"

People had long sung the praises of the United States of America to Jules Quinet, its scenery, historic monuments, exotic folkways, low-valued currency: a magnificent vacation country. He, though, had never cared to travel beyond France. When at last, with amazing suddenness, he took some days' leave and bought air tickets, it was grumpily. His wife and the young daughter who still lived at home were too joyful to heed that. On the morning after reaching New York, they sallied forth in search of bargains.

He had told them that for his part he would visit the natural history museum. Instead he stumped from their hotel and down the streets to the Waldorf-Astoria. Casting about through its huge, shabby-genteel lobby, he found what must be the agreed-on bar, went in, and ordered a beer.

A finger tapped his shoulder. "Meester Quinet?" said a diffident voice. Turning, he recognized Floriano Coelho from a cautious eldophone conversation. He nodded and they sought a corner table.

"Can we talk safely here, do you think?" Coelho asked in awkward French.

"Who listens?" Quinet snorted. He fished out his pipe and began loading it. "Let us not dither."

Coelho reddened and looked downward. "I hardly know . . . how to begin. I fear you think me a scoundrel."

"So I do. And so am I. Pf! What of it? Now as for the best method of establishing linkage, the first requirement is two programs for deceiving any monitors, the

second is that the connection be undetectable, untrace-
able—"

*The spiderweb enmeshes the world. Strands reach
out to orbit, to the moon, to such robot craft as still
explore the farther reaches of the Solar System. To all
mortal intents and purposes, the pathways and cross-
ings are infinite. It must needs be thus. The messages
they bear are beyond numbering. The computers, each
like a brain, become like cells in brains unimaginably
potent when they join together through the strands.
Those configurations are ever-changing. The light of
intellect is a swarm of fireflies dancing and twinkling
across the noösphere.*

*Two lesser systems, cut off from that vast oneness,
need simply reach out and each clasp a single strand of
the web. At once they join the whole, and through it,
along millionfold cunningly shifting pathways, each other.*

*Those sets of messages that are minds can then travel
as they will. Ghosts in olden legend rode upon the night
wind. These ride the electron surges that go to and fro
about the world like elfin lightning.*

Authority is not invariably identical with title. There
were sound reasons why it was Birgitte Geibel, head of
the board at Vereinigten Bioindustrien, and João Aveiro,
obscure security officer, who spoke over sealed circuit
on behalf of their respective factions.

"I assume your people are as enraged as ours," Geibel
said harshly. "Let you and I spare ourselves histrionics.
What we confront is a *fait accompli*."

Aveiro stroked his mustache. "My own anger is limited," he confessed. "The settlement appears to me a
tolerable compromise. I do not call it equitable—it
leaves you Europeans a substantial share of the markets
that used to be ours alone—but it does no crippling
injury to either side, and it ends a strife that bade fair
to cost more than any possible gain."

Geibel paused to search for words. She was less
proficient in the English they were using than he.
"Yes," she said grudgingly, "King Friedrich did argue

that we risked mutual exhaustion, leaving South America open to the great powers. He cited historical precedents."

Aveiro's smile was rueful. "And Machiavelli quoted a phrase from Talleyrand, 'An equality of dissatisfaction.'"

Geibel struck a fist against her chair arm. "But the, the insolence of those two!" exploded from her. "The betrayal! You cannot doubt, can you, that they conspired together? How else would they both come forth on the same day with the identical prescription and the whole set of verification procedures and sanctions, not to speak of the ultimatum that we agree to it or—or—"

"Or they will counsel us no more."

"And we will obliterate them," she said as though she relished the idea.

He clicked his tongue and shook his head. "Oh, no. You cannot mean that, Miz Geibel. By all means, cancel your Frederick the Great if you wish. I am sure that then our Machiavelli will be glad to guide us in a renewed aggressive strategy which—may I speak frankly? —could well end with us in possession of *your* European commerce."

"Unless you cancel him."

"You know that is impossible. If we did both abolish our wily councillors, the temptation to you to bring yours back, which you could do at the clandestine flick of a switch, would be overwhelming. Therefore, precautionarily, we would bring ours back. Of course, you see this morality as if in a mirror. But the effect is the same. For similar reasons, neither you nor we dare decline to accept the settlement they propose."

"And they know, those devils, they know!"

"I repeat, they are not such fiends. They have contrived a peace between us which may prove stable."

"*How?*"

"How did they come together, despite our safeguards? I can guess, but will never be sure. Obviously, they suborned their chief computermen. But those individuals, Coelho and Quinet, are under their total protection. Punishment would cost us far more than it is worth."

"True." Geibel gritted her teeth. "Instead, we must bite the sour apple and heap the traitors with rewards."

"After which, I daresay, Machiavelli and Frederick will admit that they meet privately whenever they choose. And there will be nothing we can do about it." Aveiro spread his palms. "In your words, a *fait accompli*. Well, we have numerous details to work out before drawing up a formal contract. Do you wish to discuss any particular aspect first?"

"Ach, it doesn't matter which," Geibel said, resigned. "In every case, a thousand officials and underlings will niggle and quibble. All we need do today, all we can do, is agree on the broad outlines; and those have already been laid upon us."

She fell silent, staring beyond sight. After a moment, Aveiro asked, "What is it you think about, senhora?"

Geibel shook herself, looked back at him, and said low: "Them. Friedrich and Machiavelli. Two imperial spirits. They helped us in our strife because it . . . amused them; but I suppose they came to see it as petty and sordid and unworthy of their genius. Now they are our masters. Let us never speak it aloud, but let us admit it to ourselves, they are. I doubt they will rest content for long. They will want new challenges, new victories to win.

"What do you suppose they plan for us? What are they doing as we two little people sit and pretend we confer?"

A spire of ivory reached so tall that stars circled about its golden cupola. Lower down, a gryphon flew among angels, sunlight ablaze off his wings. On earth, unicorns browsed on fantastical flowers and the waters of a fountain danced through a sequence of pure geometrical shapes. Given the help of first-class computermen, a ghost can gratify almost any whim.

However, Friedrich der Grosse and Niccolò Machiavelli had turned their attention elsewhere. They were not preparing any great enterprise. They might at some future time, if the mood struck them. At the moment, though, they were discussing an opera, for which Machiavelli was to write the libretto and Friedrich the music.

# DAVID DRAKE AND HIS FRIENDS

Let the bestselling author David Drake be your guide to excitement in strange new worlds of the distant future and mythic past. Meet some of the bravest, oddest, and most dangerous folk you can imagine.

Remember, with friends like these . . .

## LACEY AND HIS FRIENDS

Jed Lacey is a 21st-century cop who plays by the rules. His rules. The United States of Lacey's day has imposed law and order with cameras that scan every citizen, waking or sleeping, and computers that watch the images for any hint of crime. Then it's Lacey's turn. He knows what mercy is, and pity. But he doesn't have either. Not for criminals. Not for victims. Not even for himself.

65593-0 • $3.50         ———

## VETTIUS AND HIS FRIENDS

For centuries, Rome has ruled the civilized world, bringing peace and stability to a troubled age. But now, sorcerous powers gather, rousing the barbarians to battle, aiming to turn the Roman Pax into never ending chaos. Few men stand against the forces of Darkness. One is Vettius, an honorable soldier, but one as ruthless as the age demands. One other is Dama, a merchant whose favorite weapons aren't blade and shield, but wit and wealth. Two wildly dissimilar men, Vettius and Dama, bound only by their friendship, alike only in their determination that Rome—and civilization—shall not fail.

69802-8 • $3.95         ———

*Introduction*

*It has been said (by Robert Heinlein among others) that any ethical system worthy of the name must have as its goal the survival of the species, the nation, the family, and the self, in that order. Perhaps that is why the mutually consenting relationship between the two protagonists in this story seems so deeply wrong. . . .*

# THE END OF THE HUNT

## David Drake

Corll's eyes caught the betraying dust trail of a pebble skipping down the canyon wall ahead of him. Realizing what it meant, he flattened in mid-stride, his feet and hands braced to fling him in any direction of safety. "Shedde," he demanded, "how do we get out of here?"

"Think," replied the other. "You're admirably fitted for it."

"Shedde," Corll snarled, "there's no time for joking! They must have reached the canyon mouth behind us by now—and they're ahead of us on the rim as well!"

Corll had underestimated the ants again. His self-surety had led him to scout the territory the insects claimed with their many-spired mounds. He had not known that they would go beyond it in the savage tenacity of their pursuit. The comparison of his long strides with their tiny scrambling had left him scornful even then. But Corll needed rest, needed sleep, needed to hunt for water when the supply he carried grew low in these sun-blasted badlands; and those who pursued him seemed to recognize no such necessities.

"Run for the far end of the canyon," directed Shedde.

"Won't they have it blocked by now?" Corll asked,

but he sprang into motion without awaiting the answer. He had feared this sort of trap ever since he learned that the ants had ways of moving beneath the surface more swiftly than they could above it. He now had proof that their intrusions in the subsoil must penetrate far beyond their range above ground.

Once already they had ringed Corll. He had thought it was finished with him then.

"They won't have to block the end," Shedde was saying. "This is a box canyon. Yes, I remember this canyon . . . though it's been a long time. A terribly long time."

"Shedde!" Corll hissed, his brain seething with rage, "you will die with me, don't you understand? There is no time now for jokes!"

A ponderous cornice sheared from the right wall of the canyon. Corll spent a millisecond judging the trajectory of the orange-red mass, then leaped to the right, his equipment belt clanking on the wall as his fingers scrabbled and found cracks to burrow into.

"Mutated vermin," Shedde murmured in revulsion.

The ledge of rock touched an out-thrust knob twenty feet above Corll; inertia exploded the missile outward. the knob shattered with it and slashed Corll as a sleet of dust and gravel. That he ignored, waiting only for the tremble of the last murderous, head-sized fragments striking the ground before he darted off again.

"Shedde," he asked, "can we turn around and break through the canyon mouth?" Through the crawling horde that would choke the ground. Through the things that shambled instead of crawling, the giants that would have justified Corll's journey if they had left him an opportunity to warn the others of his race. It seemed quite certain now that the giants would be the ultimate cause of his failure. Only two bombs still hung from his equipment belt, and their poison had already proven ineffective against the things whose size belied their ant-like appearance.

"Keep running," Shedde directed. "They must be blocking the passage behind us for almost a mile by now."

"But—" Corll began. Fluttering jewel-flickers in the light of the great sun cut him off. There was no choice now. He lengthened his stride, freeing one of the heavy globes in either hand. Pain knifed his thigh. He ignored it, loped on. For the moment the pain was only pain, and had no margin to waste on comfort.

A ruby-carapaced ant sailed past Corll's face, twisting violently as though sheer determination would bring its mandibles the remaining inch they needed to close on Corll's flesh. The insect was scarcely an inch long itself, half mandible and entirely an engine of destruction. The warriors were light enough to drop safely from any height, ready to slash and to tear when they landed. They were pouring off the rim in a deadly shower that carpeted the canyon floor too thickly, now, for the runner to avoid. Agony tore Corll's pads and ankles a dozen times. More frightening were the ghost-light twitchings that mounted his calves. He had waited as long as he could.

Corll's right hand smashed a globular bomb against the massively-functional buckle of his crossbelt. The bomb shattered, spraying the acrid reek of its vegetable distillate about him in a blue mist. The poison cooled his body where it clung to him, but its clammy, muscle-tightening chill was infinitely preferable to the fiery horror of the warriors' jaws. No matter—he could feel the mandibles relax, see the wave of ants on the ground wither and blacken as the dense cloud oozed over them. Corll held his own breath as he ran through the sudden carnage. He knew that the fluid coating his lower limbs would protect him for a time, and he prayed that the time would be adequate.

"Not much further," Shedde remarked.

Dead ants scrunched underfoot. Jaws seared Corll briefly, then dropped away. His eyes scanned the rim of the canyon as it dog-legged, noting that the rain of warriors had paused for the moment.

A long rock hurtled down, pitched with more force than gravity could have given it. Corll's leap took him a dozen feet up the cliff wall where his legs shot him off at a flat angle, a safe angle. . . . Stone smashed on stone beside him. A feeler waved vexedly from the high rim.

The ants had very nearly caught him three days before while he dozed in the shadow of a wind-sculpted cliff, certain that his smooth pacing had left the insects far behind. Through half-closed eyelids Corll had suddenly seen that the ruddy sunlight on ruddy stone was now being picked out by tiny, blood-bright droplets that trickled toward his shelter. The first bomb had not freed him then, nor had the third. When he had darted over the nearest rise with the poison and its bitter stench lapping about him like a shroud, Corll had seen the horizon in all directions sanguine with deadly life. The ants had waited until a cold intelligence somewhere had assessed their success as certain. But that time Corll had leaped through them as a lethal ghost, wrapped in his poison and guided by Shedde's calculated guess as the the narrowest link in a chain of inobservable thickness.

If the insects or the brain that controlled them had reconsidered the capacities of their quarry, that had not caused them to slacken their pursuit.

"Their numbers aren't infinite," Shedde explained, "and they can't have laced the whole continent with their tunnels—yet. Many of them are following us, yes. But it's the ones sent on ahead that are dangerous, and with every mile we run, the more of those we're safe from. There will be some waiting for us at the end of the canyon. If we could have bypassed them, perhaps we would have escaped entirely."

Corll was stung with wordless anger at his companion's objectivity; then he rounded the canyon's bend to see the cliffs linked sharply a hundred yards in front of him. The concrete of the blockhouse that squatted at the base of the cliffs would have been magenta in the light of the waning sun, save for the warriors that clung to it like a layer of blazing fungus.

Corll halted.

"There's a door," Shedde prompted.

"I can't get through those ants on the residue of the

bomb," Corll said. The whisper-whisper of feet a million times magnified echoed in his mind if not his ears.

"Use the last bomb, then. There's no choice."

Nor was there. Baying a defiant challenge, Corll charged for the structure. A stride before he reached the waiting mass, he smashed his last defense into vitreous splinters on his breast. Do the ants feel pain? he wondered, the warriors only a dying blur at the edges of his mind. Then, expecting it to slam open, he hit the portal in a bound—and recoiled from it. The metal door fit its jambs without a seam, refuge if open but otherwise a cruel jest.

"To the right," Shedde directed. "There should be a pressure plate."

The tapestry of ants, linked even in death, still hung in swathes across the blockhouse. Corll's hands groped through the insects desperately, feeling the desiccated bodies crumble as easily as the ashes of an ancient fire. The door swung open on a lighted room.

Corll sprang inside. "The inner plate is also a lock," his companion said. "Touch to open, touch to close. But only the touch of your kind." Corll slammed the door and palmed the device.

They were in a narrow anteroom, softly lighted by a strip in the ceiling. At the back was another metal door, half closed. The only furnishings of the anteroom were a pair of objects fixed to the wall to either side of the rear door. In general shape they resembled sockets for flambeaux, but they were thrust out horizontally rather than vertically. Corll's quick eyes flicked over them, but he did not move closer.

"Now what?" he asked.

"Now we wait, of course," replied Shedde. "If the systems are still working, there should be water inside." There was a pause before he concluded acidly, "And Hargen built to last."

Corll eased open the door. The inner room was much larger, but it was almost filled with dull, black machinery. Against the far wall stood the framework of a chair in a clear semi-circle. It was backed against another door, this one open onto darkness. On the floor before the chair sprawled a skeleton.

The outer door of the blockhouse clanged as something heavy struck it.

"Who is Hargen?" Corll demanded. Half-consciously he backed against the inner door of the anteroom, shutting it against the gong-notes echoing through the building. His breath still came in short, quick sobs. "Shedde, what is this place?"

"Hargen," Shedde repeated with a whisper of hatred. "Hargen was a genetic engineer. As a technician, as a craftsman, he may have had no equal . . . though perhaps the men who built his instruments, they were brilliant in their own right. But tools of metal weren't enough for Hargen—he had his dream, he said, for the new Mankind."

Corll eyed the room. He was uneasy because he had never before known such vicious intensity in his companion. A pencil of water spurted from one corner of the ceiling down into a metal basin from which it then drained. Corll tested a drop of the fluid with his tongue before drinking deeply.

"He had to change us, Corll," continued Shedde. "Cut into genes, weld them, treat the unformed flesh as a sculptor does stone. 'Your children will live forever!' he said. *'Your children will live forever!'*

"Have we lived forever, Corll?"

The echoes that flooded the building changed note, warning Corll that the outer door was sagging. He quickly squeezed empty the long waterbag of intestine looped across his shoulders, then refilled it from the falling stream.

"Where does the other door lead, Shedde?"

"A tunnel. Try it."

Pretending to ignore the undertone of his companion's voice, Corll attempted to leap the chair. Something caught him in mid-air and flung him back into the room.

"You see?" Shedde giggled. "Hargen wasn't just a genius, he had a sense of humor. He could sit there and control every machine in the building—and no man could touch him without his permission. Do you want to leave that way, Corll?"

"If they can batter down the outer door, they can get through this one," Corll noted with the tense desperation of a fighter at bay. The sound of metal ripping underscored his words. "Shedde, what do we do?"

Suddenly calmer, Shedde replied, "The weapons should have manual controls. There, beside the door."

Staring at the pair of hand-sized plates flanking the anteroom door, Corll realized what unfamiliarity had hidden from him: both plates displayed shrunken perspectives of the anteroom itself and the wreckage of the outer door. Joystick controls were set beneath the plates. When Corll twitched one of the rods, it moved the black dot he had thought was a flaw in the screen.

"If you push the top of the control rod," Shedde said, "it fires."

The outer door of the blockhouse squealed again as it was rent completely away. A pair of giants that seemed ants in all but size stood framed in the doorway, their forelegs bowed a little to allow them to peer inside. Uncertain of what he was doing, Corll squeezed his thumb down on the stick.

The dazzling spatter of light blasted powder from the concrete, vapor from the outer doorjamb. Corll's reflex slashed the fierce beam sideways across one of the giants. The creature separated along the line of contact.

The light blinked off when Corll raised the thumbswitch. The remaining giant was scrambling backwards. Corll flicked the control. The dot moved in the direction opposite to his expectations. He moved it the other way and squeezed, chuckling in wonder as the glare sawed lethally across the second monster as well.

"They're hollow," he exclaimed as he squinted at the jerking bodies.

"I wonder how they fuel them?" Shedde mused. "The exoskeleton would give adequate area for muscle attachment without the mass of digestive organs to contend with. Even the vermin seem to have their genetic geniuses."

"How long will this weapon burn?" Corll asked, caution tempering his elation.

"Perhaps forever," the other replied. "Near enough that neither of us needs be concerned. Hargen never took half measures.

"I stood here before," Shedde continued, "to plead with him. I had been one of the first, you see. 'You don't know what you're doing,' I told him. 'You call it freedom from the tyranny of the body, a chance for the children of the race to have the immortality that was only vicarious before. But it's the death of those you change! We don't breed, we won't breed—it's not worth personal immortality to me to know that I'll never have a son.' And Hargen laughed at me, and he said, 'I have stayed here in this fortress for seventy-four years without leaving, so you think that I am ignorant. You can breed, little man; if the will is lacking, my knives didn't cut it out of you.'

"I shouted at him then; but before his servants pushed me out, Hargen stood and stretched his long bones, those bones that lie there in the dust, and he said, 'Come back in twenty thousand, come back in two hundred thousand years if it takes that long—come back and tell my bones then that I did not know.' " Shedde paused for so long that Corll thought he was done speaking, but at last he continued, "Well, you were right, Hargen. If we failed to breed, then so did the men you didn't change—and yes, you knew it. Just as you knew what would come of the race you formed and called, 'mere adjuncts to human immortality. . . .' Gods, how you must have hated Man!"

Corll said nothing, leaning over the weapon control and watching the smear of tiny red forms thicken on the wreckage of the giants.

"But perhaps even you forgot the ants," Shedde concluded bitterly.

The warriors surged forward in a solid wave that covered all four faces of the anteroom. Corll zig-zagged his flame through them, but there was no thrill in watching a black line razor across an attack condensed in the sights to an amorphous stain. More of the insects flowed over a surface pitted by earlier destruction. Corll did not raise his thumb, but the ants crawled forward more quickly than he could traverse his weapon across their rectangular advance.

Shedde, answering the question Corll had been too harried to ask, said, "The small ones can't smash open the door, but they'll be able to short out the weapon heads."

Corll whipped his control about in a frenzy. With someone to fight the right-hand beam as well, the wave could have been stopped. But—a scarlet runnel leaked across the wall toward the other wire-framed gun muzzle, and Corll realized the same thing must be happening in the dead area too close to his own weapon to be swept by its fire. A moment later the beam of deadly light vanished in coruscance and a thunder-clap that shook the blockhouse and flung the remains of the first dead giant a dozen yards from the entrance. Corll leaped for the other control. He was not quick enough. As soon as he touched the firing stud, the right-hand weapon also shorted explosively.

The sighting displays still worked. A third giant ant scrabbled noisily into the anteroom, its feelers stiff before it. Held easily between its mandibles was a huge fragment of stone.

"Shedde," Corll hissed, "this door won't hold any longer than the other one did. How can we get out of here?"

"You can leave any time through the tunnel," Shedde replied calmly. "Hargen must have kept a vehicle of some sort there."

Corll hurled himself again toward the low doorway. Again the unseen barrier slammed him back. The anteroom door clanged, denting inward slightly.

"It throws me back!"

"It throws *me* back," Shedde corrected gently. "Hargen's sense of humor, you see. Unstrap me and get away from here."

The door rang again. Flakes spalled off from the inside.

Corll seized a machine of unguessed precision and

smashed it into the quivering metal. "I carried you since the day my father died!" he shouted. "My stomach fed you, my lungs gave you air, my kidneys cleared your wastes. Shedde, my blood is your blood!"

"Your family has served my needs for more years than even I can remember," Shedde stated, utterly calm. "Now that you can no longer serve me, serve yourself and your own race. Quickly now, the door can't hold much longer."

The panel banged inward again.

Corll cringed back, in horror rather than in fear. "Shedde," he pleaded, "you are the last."

"Somebody had to be. This is as good a place as any, where the end began. Set me down and go."

Keening deep in his throat, Corll fumbled at the massive crossbuckle he had unfastened only once before, while his father shuddered into death after a thirty-foot fall. "Shedde. . . ."

"Go!"

The upper door-hinge popped like a frost-cracked boulder as it sheared.

Sphincter muscles clamped shut the tiny valve in Corll's back as the tube pulled out of it. Only a single drop of blood escaped to glint within his bristling fur. He carefully swung Shedde to the floor, trying as he did so not to look at his burden: the tiny limbs, the abdomen without intestines and with lungs of no capacity beyond what was needed to squeak words through the vocal cords. In the center, flopping loosely, was an appendage that looked like an umbilicus and had served Shedde in that function for millenia. The genitalia were functional, but anything they had spawned would have had to be transferred to a host body for gestation.

The skull was fully the size of Hargen's, which leered vacuously from the floor. Shedde's eyes were placid and as blue as was nothing else remaining on the Earth.

"Good luck against the ants, Corll," the half-formed travesty of a man wheezed. "But I'm afraid Hargen may not have seen as clearly as he believed he did when he planned his new race."

Corll clenched his fingers ('To hold tools for your

children,' Hargen had said so long ago) and sprang upright. 'A stupid servant is a useless servant'—Hargen had said that too, and Corll's forehead bulged with a brain to equal that of the man he had carried. But in Corll's eyes bled a rage that was the heritage of the wolf and had not been totally expunged from the most pampered of lap dogs.

But the man on the floor whispered, "Go, my friend."

And as the first of the giants smashed into the room, Corll whirled and leaped for the tunnel door and darkness.

*Ever wonder where all the really good short fiction is being published nowadays?*

*Don't you miss thought-provoking, clearly written articles about science, technology and society?*

*Catch up with the best in*

## EDITED BY
## JIM BAEN

\_\_\_\_ NEW DESTINIES, Vol. 2: Stories by Charles Sheffield, Harry Turtledove, Steven Gould. Also, Gregory Benford on scientists and Charles Sheffield on the theme of conservation of resources.
$2.95          65346-6

\_\_\_\_ NEW DESTINIES, Vol. 3: Stories by Larry Niven, Dean Ing, Charles Sheffield. Also, Jim Baen with "Let's Kill Nasa Today!" and Charles Sheffield on the future of the space program.
$3.50          65385-7

\_\_\_\_ NEW DESTINIES, Vol. 4: Stories by F. Paul Wilson, Poul Anderson, Timothy Zahn. S.M. Stirling on the "woman warrior," Martin Caidin on tele-kInesis, and Charles Sheffield on the myth of nuclear winter.
$3.50          65408-X

\_\_\_\_ NEW DESTINIES, Vol. 5: Robert A. Heinlein Memorial Issue. Appreciations by Jerry Pournelle, Spider Robinson, Charles Sheffield and Yoji Kondo. Two never-before-published poems by Heinlein himself.
$3.50          69796-X

---

# WHAT OUR READERS SAY ABOUT

## LOIS McMASTER BUJOLD

"I read [THE WARRIOR'S APPRENTICE] very carefully with an eye on making criticisms based on my experiences as a former military officer, but each time I found something, you repaired it. . . . I could find nothing to fault in the story. It was well done and well written."
—Kevin D. Randle, Cedar Rapids, Iowa

"I am reading Lois Bujold's THE WARRIOR'S APPRENTICE for the third time. . . . The girl [sic!] plots intricately. I love her writing, and will buy anything she writes."
—R.C. Crenshaw, Eugene, Oregon

"You may be off on a new Space Patrol with the Dendarii Mercenaries. It will strain my purse, but I should cut my eating anyhow!"
—John P. Conlon, Newark, Ohio

"I have been recommending [SHARDS OF HONOR] to my friends, telling them that the book is about personal honor, love, duty, and the conflict between honor, love and duty. I am looking forward to your next novel."
—Radcliffe Cutshaw, Boca Raton, Florida

# AND HERE'S WHAT THE CRITICS SAY:

## SHARDS OF HONOR

"Bujold has written what may be the best first science fiction novel of the year."

*—Chicago Sun-Times*

"A strong debut, and Bujold is a writer to look for in the future." *—Locus*

"An unusually good book."

*—Voice of Youth Advocates*

"Splendid . . . This superb first novel integrates a believable romance into a science fiction tale of adventure and war." *—Booklist*

## THE WARRIOR'S APPRENTICE

"Highly recommended for any SF collection."

*—Booklist*

"Bujold continues to delight." *—Locus*

"Bujold's first book, *Shards of Honor,* was called 'possibly the best first SF novel of the year,' by the *Chicago Sun-Times. The Warrior's Apprentice* is better." *—Fantasy Review*

# ETHAN OF ATHOS